Praise for

THE WATCH THAT ENDS THE NIGHT

VOICES FROM THE *TITANIC*

A Claudia Lewis Award Winner

An American Library Association Best Fiction for Young Adults Selection

A *Booklist* Editors' Choice

"Allan Wolf has imagined his way deep into the cold, dark waters of history and has come back carrying a couple of dozen voices that he discovered there, voices whose authenticity is not only convincing but compelling."
—Ted Kooser, former U.S. Poet Laureate and winner of the Pulitzer Prize

"A remarkable accomplishment."
—Helen Frost, author of *Crossing Stones* and *Hidden*

"Gives voice to more than just the human participants."
—*The Wall Street Journal*

★ "Wolf's carefully crafted characters evolve as the voyage slides to its icy conclusion; readers may be surprised by the potency of the final impact."
—*Publishers Weekly* (starred review)

★ "A multi-octave chorus of voices that is alternately—sometimes simultaneously—spirited, angry, frightened, and mournful. . . . Wolf leaves no emotion unplumbed, no area of research uninvestigated, and his voices are so authentic they hurt." —*Booklist* (starred review)

"Cadence and language gives the whole work epic scope."
—*School Library Journal*

★ "Wolf draws on a prodigious amount of research to fully realize each character; they are real people just telling their stories, all the more poignant because readers know their fates and recognize prophetic comments along the way. . . . A lyrical, monumental work of fact and imagination that reads like an oral history revved up by the drama of the event."
—*Kirkus Reviews* (starred review)

THE WATCH THAT ENDS THE NIGHT

VOICES FROM THE *TITANIC*

ALLAN WOLF

CANDLEWICK PRESS

First paperback edition 2013

The Library of Congress has cataloged the hardcover edition as follows:

Wolf, Allan.
The watch that ends the night : voices from the Titanic / Allan Wolf. —1st ed.
p.   cm.
Summary: Re-creates the 1912 sinking of the Titanic as observed by millionaire
John Jacob Astor, a beautiful young Lebanese refugee finding first love, "Unsinkable"
Molly Brown, Captain Smith, and others including the iceberg itself.
Includes bibliographical references.
ISBN 978-0-7636-3703-3 (hardcover)
1. Titanic (Steamship) —Juvenile fiction.   [1. Novels in verse.
2. Titanic (Steamship) —Fiction. 3. Shipwrecks—Fiction.]   I. Title.
PZ7.5.W64Wat 2011
[Fic] —dc22   2010040150

ISBN 978-0-7636-6331-5 (paperback)

12 13 14 15 16 17 BVG 10 9 8 7 6 5 4 3 2 1

Printed in Berryville, VA, U.S.A.

This book was typeset in Century Old Style and Copperplate Gothic.

Candlewick Press
99 Dover Street
Somerville, Massachusetts 02144

visit us at www.candlewick.com

For Dale and Evelyn

CONTENTS

PRELUDE

PREPARING TO SAIL

-1-

FIRST WATCH

SETTING OUT

-47-

SECOND WATCH

ONE LAST PORT

-91-

THIRD WATCH

THE OPEN SEA

-125-

FOURTH WATCH

FRIVOLOUS AMUSEMENTS

-169-

FIFTH WATCH

TURNING THE CORNER

-217-

SIXTH WATCH

WHISKERS ON THE LIGHT
-287-

SEVENTH WATCH

THE WATCH THAT ENDS THE NIGHT
-373-

POSTLUDE

MORNING
-407-

NOTES

AUTHOR'S NOTE
-435-

THE MYSTERY SHIP
-436-

CHARACTER NOTES
-436-

MORSE CODE MESSAGES
-450-

MISCELLANY
-452-

BIBLIOGRAPHY
-457-

ACKNOWLEDGMENTS
-467-

THE VOICES

OLAUS ABELSETH
THE IMMIGRANT

THOMAS ANDREWS
THE SHIPBUILDER

JOHN JACOB ASTOR
THE MILLIONAIRE

JOSEPH BOXHALL
THE NAVIGATOR

GEORGE BRERETON
THE GAMBLER

HAROLD BRIDE
THE SPARK

MARGARET BROWN
THE SOCIALITE

HAROLD COTTAM
CARPATHIA'S WIRELESS MAN

EUGENE DALY
THE BAGPIPER

FREDERICK FLEET
THE LOOKOUT

FRANKIE GOLDSMITH
THE DRAGON HUNTER

THOMAS HART
THE STOKER

LOUIS HOFFMAN
THE TAILOR

JOHN "JOCK" HUME
THE SECOND VIOLIN

THE ICEBERG

BRUCE ISMAY
THE BUSINESSMAN

CHARLES JOUGHIN
THE BAKER

LOLO
THE TAILOR'S SON

HAROLD LOWE
THE JUNIOR OFFICER

ISAAC MAYNARD
THE ENTRÉE COOK

JAMILA NICOLA-YARRED
THE REFUGEE

THE SHIP RAT

E.J. SMITH
THE CAPTAIN

JOHN SNOW
THE UNDERTAKER

OSCAR WOODY
THE POSTMAN

April 20, 1912
SATURDAY
Aboard the cable ship *Mackay-Bennett*
ATLANTIC OCEAN
THE GRAND BANKS
600 MILES FROM HALIFAX, NOVA SCOTIA

JOHN SNOW
THE UNDERTAKER

Embalmers don't typically make house calls.
If not buried with a splash from their ship,
most casualties at sea are brought to me
at the family parlor on Argyle Street.

In Halifax the water is unavoidable as death.
And death is unavoidable as the water.
Raised as I was in a Halifax funeral home,
you might guess I'd grow up to accept them both.
But I find the dead preferable to the sea.
The dead are more predictable.

To ease my queasy stomach,
I am lying down atop the empty coffins
stacked neatly across the *Mackay-Bennett*'s decks.
Waves toss our small vessel as if it were a toy.
The journey has been cold and slow,
three days' steaming with half a day to go.

As night falls, Captain Larnder informs me,

"We should be among the wreckage soon —
better sleep now, while you still can, Mr. Snow.
The sun will be up soon enough."

Yes, I think. The sun will always come up.
Even after the entire ship of humanity
has struck its berg and sunk,
the sun will rise.

"Good night, Captain Larnder," I say.

"Good night, sir. Rest well," he replies.

Later that night, in my berth below,
I hear the ship's engines finally quit.
Silence fills the dark, and I know
we have reached the spot where the *Titanic* foundered.
They are out there in the water. The bodies. Among the debris.

My name is John Snow.
You could say that my living is death.
I am the undertaker.
I have come for the bodies.

PREPARING TO SAIL

MONDAY, APRIL 1, TO TUESDAY, APRIL 9, 1912

follow the food

follow the rats

scuttle, scuttle

follow the rats

scuttle, scuttle

follow the food

From all over Europe people are clamoring to buy tickets.
The titled aristocrat and the anonymous clerk.
The well-bred Brit with his old money,
the boorish American with his new money,
and the enthusiastic emigrant with little money at all.

Over dinner not so many years back,
my associate, Lord Pirrie, and I conceived
of a fleet of three immense sister ships
the like of which the world had never seen.
These ships would be larger than any other.
The interior decor would be, in a word, palatial,
thus attracting the most wealthy first-class passengers.
And to attract those with lesser means,
White Star Line's second-class accommodation
would rival the Cunard Line's first class.
Likewise our third class would be much nicer
(and more costly) than the norm.

This last detail is important.
While first class gives a ship prestige,
third class is an ocean liner's bread and butter.
If the lower classes are so hell-bent on leaving the continent,
the White Star Line will be there to welcome them aboard—

for a price.

The millionaire thinks *Titanic* is a ship of pleasure.
The emigrant thinks *Titanic* is a ship of dreams.
But they are both wrong. For *Titanic* is not a ship at all.

Titanic is just good business. *Very* good business.

Whenever two words will do,
Mr. Ismay is certain to use ten.
I'm not necessarily a man of few words,
but to sum up *Titanic* I need just one:

big.

Ismay speaks of *Titanic*'s luxury:
her elegant lines, like a yacht for the gods;
her lush appointments; her state-of-the-art mechanics;
her ingenious safety features. Ismay and White Star
cut no costs to build her, I assure you of that.
But in matters of handling, she is mostly just big.
And my plan is to pilot her as I would any other big ship.
I will go as fast as I can and as straight as I can,
from one point to the next until we see New York Harbor.

It seemed like a dream: the name Thomas Andrews
forever associated with *Titanic*!
Even as a young boy, I loved ships.
Lucky for me, my uncle William,
the great Lord Pirrie, was chairman of Harland and Wolff.
Naturally I visited the shipyard often,
and eventually I found work there.
But not as some high-ranking executive.
Uncle would not have that. No. At sixteen,
I began the five-year apprenticeship that would seal my fate.
It meant spending less time tending my bees,
but with my admittance into this shipbuilders' hive,
everything else was of secondary importance.
No job was too small or menial
that I did not work at it for weeks, or months if necessary:
heater boy, riveter, catcher, holder-upper, and carpenter.
I learned from the joiners and cabinetmakers,
the shipwrights, the painters, the fitters, and smiths.
Belowdecks I watched the workings
of the stoker, the greaser, the trimmer.
Above I watched the workings
of the baker, the waiter, the steward.
My longest training came in the drafting department,
learning machine and freehand drawing, applied mechanics,
and the theories of naval architecture.
I adopted and improved upon my uncle's designs.
And eventually the *Titanic* project was given to me.
I feel as though I built her with my own two hands.
And like her loyal minion, I will tend to her needs,
no matter the cost, whatever the tide.

I am the ice. I see tides ebb and flow.
I've watched civilizations come and go,
give birth, destroy, restore, be gone, begin.
My blink of an eye is humankind's tortoise slow.
Today's now is tomorrow's way back when.
Bright Arctic night gives way to coal-black morn.
Tall masts and canvas sails give way to steam.
One iceberg melts away. Another's born.
I am the sum of all that I have seen.
I am the ice. I know the ebb and flow.
Ten thousand years ago, I fell as snow,
and as I fell, my bulk began to grow,
and as I grew, I watched as worlds arose.
The caveman's spear, the woolly mammoth tusk,
arose and clashed and then returned to dust.
I am the ice. I've seen the ebb and flow.
I watched as Abraham and Moses spoke.
I watched the prophets met with wine or stone.
I watched as Christ was nailed upon the cross.
I watched Muhammad forced to flee his home.
I've watched the holy battle to and fro.
I am the ice. I've seen the ebb and flow.
Conceived by water, temperature, and time,
gestating within Greenland's glacial womb,
I carved out massive valleys as I moved.
At last the frozen river made its way
and calved me with a splash in Baffin Bay.
Since then I've traveled southward many weeks,
for now that my emergence is complete,
there is a certain ship I long to meet.

Miss Marie Stene
Ørskog P.O.
via Ålesund, Norway

 1 April 1912
 Monday

 My dearest Marie,

  I cannot bear the thought of returning to
North Dakota without you. I know that you do not
trust steamships. But will you trust me?

  Yours very truly,
  Olaus

The day my father sold his beloved mill,
I knew we would be leaving Lebanon for good.
I finished packing my suitcase
only to discover I could not lift it.
Father turned to look at me struggling—
his one eye infected, his other just tired.
"Whatever you pack, Jamila, you must carry yourself.
Remember, 'The one who takes the donkey up to the roof
should be the one who brings it down.'"

It was Father's favorite proverb.

I am my father's youngest girl of three.
My two sisters, my older brother, and my mother
had already relocated to a place in America.
A place called Jacksonville, Florida.
That left just Father and me and my little brother, Elias.
Now, finally, it was our turn to flee Hakoor
and the mill that my father had worked all his life.
Our turn to flee the Ottoman Turks, who have ruined everything.

Everyone here is out of work, Muslim and Christian alike.
And rather than helping us, as they should,
the Turkish soldiers make our hard times worse.
They enter any house they like, taking whatever they want.
The livestock, the food, and the grain are not safe.
The women—and the girls—are not safe.

So I packed my suitcase onto the handcart.
And under cover of darkness we slipped away from Hakoor.
Father breathed heavily. Elias hummed a tune.
I walked in silence beside the cart,
trying not to look over my shoulder
as we descended our much-loved mountains.

Imagine, if you will, the richest woman in the world . . .
sitting upon a donkey.
I have the photo to prove it: See here?
That beauty atop the beast is my new wife, Madeleine.
And she's laughing, there upon a humble donkey,
as the ancient Sphinx looks on.
Wouldn't the papers love to get ahold of *this* photo?

We wished to linger longer in the Valley of the Kings,
but it just wasn't meant to be. A private matter had come up.
I sent my manservant to arrange the steamer.
Tickets for myself, my servant, my Madeleine,
my Madeleine's nurse, and, of course, my dog:
he's a rather large Airedale named Kitty.
A little joke there, you see. A dog named Kitty.

(Hem, hem.)

My man procured first-class accommodations for us
on what I was told is the most luxurious, well-appointed liner in the world.
The great *Titanic*! But I *was* a bit skeptical.
I'm something of a hotel man myself. (I own several.)

The name is Astor—John Jacob Astor the Fourth—
Colonel Astor. And they call me the richest man in the world.
That's not all they call me, of course. . . .
They also call me spoiled. They call me idle.
They call me shallow and vain.
Then *lecher* began to appear on the menu.
And *fornicator.* And *cradle robber.*
Adulterer and *blasphemer*—
these latest monikers brought on in consequence
of my divorcing Ava Lowle Willing, that celebrated beauty.

Do not pity her. The feelings were mutual;
Ava Willing was all too *willing* to be done with me.

Well, the divorce caused shock enough in itself.
But when I married Madeleine within the year,
the outcry surprised even me.
You'd think I'd been found out as Jack the Ripper!
The churches cried out sacrilege. The papers cried out scandal.
I divorced a woman who despised me;
I married a woman who adored me.
Society calls that common? I call that common sense.

Somewhere between the Sphinx and the pyramids,
Madeleine discovered she was with child.
So naturally we were determined to return to New York,
and why shouldn't we? I *own* half of it.

(Hem, hem.)

And what is more, New York is our home.
So let them ostracize us from their galas and teas.
I say make the most of your life while you can.
We may all of us be dead tomorrow.

Even the richest man in the world.

Say what you will about John Jacob Astor, the man knows who he is—
even if the whole world thinks he's someone else.
That's how it is when you're rich;
you're fair game for every gossipmonger from Denver to Newport.
And believe me, I would know.
I can't sneeze without reading about it in *Town Topics*.
And if Jack Astor thinks *he's* got it rough,
that's nothing compared to how bad rich *women* have it!
We can't hold a real job: our only employment
is motherhood, social work, and tea parties.
We are judged according to the elegance of our hats,
not the wisdom in the heads upon which the hats sit.

My daughter, Helen, and I were in Cairo with the Astors
when we received the Marconi-gram informing us that
my little grandson, Lawrence Jr., had taken ill in America.
I traveled to Paris at once and booked passage
on the next available steamer back to the States—
they're calling it *Titanic,* the world's largest.
I'm told Captain Smith is in charge of things.
Three months earlier, Smith had brought me east without drowning me.
I imagined he could take me back west the same way.
Helen went on to London to have her fun.
And to tell you the truth,
I was rather glad to have some time alone.

Titanic was due to set sail in two days.
My children were grown. My husband and I rarely spoke.
There were no parties to organize. No rallies to attend.
The entire week lay before me with no one to tend but myself.

The prospect delighted and terrified me.

When I was a boy in Comber, I kept nine hives.
The honeybees were a wonder to me.
How they always knew exactly what to do,
each bee's movements in perfect harmony with the others.
If one queen died, they would make another;
if the hive was threatened, they would swarm,
as if they all shared a solitary mind.

You might call Harland and Wolff a shipyard hive,
with no less than fifteen thousand workers,
and I would not ask any one of those men
to risk a job I would not do myself.
I place myself among the workers as often as I can,
walking the yard, clapping a weary man on the back,
lending a hand to handle a beam, swinging
a heavy hammer here, chalking
a well-driven rivet there. One day a red-hot rivet,
dropped from above, fell fifty feet to splat near my shoe,
missing my head by inches. But that was not my day to die.
You take such events in stride. A shipyard is a deadly place,
and *Titanic* has seen its share of tragedy.

Such is the life of a shipyard hive—
sacrifice is made for the sake of the whole.
I remember well, as a boy, watching my bees going about their work.
Through endless exertion and industry, they built their honeycomb palaces
much as men make a huge, luxurious ship. I watched the collectors
return with their pollen-laden legs; I watched the sentries defend the entrance;
and I watched, of course, the dead worker bees dragged outside,
their bodies piling up on the ground.

From death, a wondrous buzzing city born.

I am the ice. I watched *Titanic*'s birth.
I saw the mighty iron keel laid down.
Beneath the gantry and giant floating cranes
it rose, as the limestone pyramids rose
(to transport the souls of the royal and rich)
amid the din of many bustling men.
First they lay down iron Leviathan ribs,
to which workers riveted overlapped seams,
a patchwork quilt of thick metal skin.
And as she grew, I passed down Davis Strait.
I knew what course the Iceberg had to take:
southward toward the ship, the ice goes forth.
Titanic is my compass needle's North.
For no sooner did this wondrous ship take shape
than it dumbly took its toll of human lives.
I am the ice. I watched the workers die.
The first: Sam Scott, unlucky catch boy
who walks the scaffold high up in the air.
Distracted by some loud, well-meant "Ahoy,"
he steps upon a board that isn't there.
And at *Titanic*'s long-awaited launch:
James Dobbins (last to die), not jumping clear,
while he himself Hail Marys and huzzahs,
is crushed by timbers as the people cheer.
Inside Queen's Island's massive shipyard cradle,
where men midwifed the mighty ship to life,
where those to whom the job did not prove fatal
send up a raucous roaring at the sight,
the dead add mournful moaning to the roar.
Remember it. You'll hear that moan again
before the Iceberg's tale comes to an end.

During *Titanic*'s sea trials in Belfast
it fell to me and Sixth Officer Moody
to test the starboard lifeboats, lowering away
with a bosun and seven able seamen each.
We rowed to the dock and back again.
I was appalled by one of the ABs' lack of skill with an oar,
and I told him so. And I didn't tell it gently.
You see, most sailors are not boatmen.
And most boatmen are not sailors.
I happen to be both — at full ease
with the lowliest rowboat or the grandest ship.

Be aware that on these big passenger vessels,
the "crew" are mostly window washers,
waiters, bellboys, and stewards, and most
don't know a scupper from a teacup. Oh,
they're nice enough to have around
if you need to have your pillows fluffed,
but they aren't of much use in a real crisis.
When it came time to report back to Commander Bartlett,
the White Star Line's marine superintendent,
I said,

> "We have tested and inventoried the lifeboats, sir.
> And we find them stocked and ready."

But I was thinking,

> *God help us if we actually need them,*
> *since half the crew won't know*
> *which end of an oar goes in the water.*

Do not speak to me of lifeboats.
Titanic has twenty lifeboats all told.
Four boats more than regulations require.
The Board of Trade inspectors approved them at once
without so much as a second look.
At least that's what I understand;
I was home in Southampton at the time.
It was Commander Bartlett who actually ran her through her paces.
And I assure you, lifeboats were far from his mind.
A captain's main concern must be with his ship,
the ship herself, and how she maneuvers.

For four hours under Bartlett's hand,
Titanic performed her dance on Belfast Lough.
She executed her massive ballet of S curves and turns.
He rang down Reverse Engines to test her stopping distance:
she took three minutes, fifteen seconds,
and all of eight hundred fifty yards
before she came to a dead stop.
Not so agile as a fish perhaps, but what whale is?
Oh, at forty-six thousand tons, she is a whale, to be sure.
But my *Titanic,* she is a *graceful* whale.

I feel that her trials went exceedingly well.
According to what I'm told.
So do not speak to me of lifeboats.
A stable ship like *Titanic* is lifeboat enough.
Of course I am not so foolish as to call her unsinkable.
But I will say this: it would take a fool to sink her.

I may be many things, but I am no fool.

For years someone or other in Parliament has attempted
to increase the number of lifeboats required on a ship.
Of course safety comes before all else,
and we've got more boats aboard than the present laws require.

So don't speak to me of lifeboats.
The shipbuilders refer to the uppermost deck as the boat deck.
But I prefer its alternate name: the sun deck.
Let us not forget that our first-class passengers
use this deck as a promenade so they might take in the sun.
Imagine their disappointment when they arrive up top
hoping to experience a spectacular sunrise at sea,
only to find their view blocked by a bunch of boats?

Lifeboats?

Why clutter a ship's boat deck with lifeboats?

First-class passengers would rather see the sunrise.

We reached Beirut at sunrise. Father sold his cart
to add to the cash he had. Then he had to bribe
an inspection official who "failed to notice" his sick eye.
The ship's whistle blasted, and finally we got under way.

During the entire boat ride to Marseilles, I worried
that the Turks would be waiting when we arrived.
I worried that I'd be taken from my father.
Though I was frightened, I tried my best not to show it.
But Elias's knees were not weak, like mine.
My brother is not smart enough to be scared.
He was everywhere at once, exploring our small ship.
He tried to drag me with him.
"You act like an old woman," he said.
I tried to be polite and patient like Mama would be,
but I wanted to hit him with my shoe!
"Yalla! Yalla! Yalla!" he yells.
Hurry! Hurry! Hurry! His mouth is never shut.

Once we were in France, a man who said he was a travel agent
approached us and offered us lodging at a boardinghouse,
a place to stay while we waited for the next ship bound for America.
Father suspected the hotel man was charging us more than was fair.
Since none of us spoke much French, it was difficult to know.
So we waited. And we waited. Elias ran up and down
the dirty halls of the boardinghouse. *"Yalla! Yalla! Yalla!"*
In my heart, I thought,

> *Perhaps the hotel man charges high rates*
> *because Elias is so loud.*

Mr. Theobald says we'll take a train to London.
Daddy says we're going to America on a big ship.
Alfred says that nine-year-olds shouldn't believe in dragons.
Mummy just cries.

I turned nine last year, on the 19th of December.
My parents gave me a cap pistol and a book about dragons.
It was the best birthday ever.

I used to like that my birthday was right before Christmas.
The holiday feeling would go on and on and never stop.
Then last year, just after my birthday, my baby brother, Bertie, died.
Now no one is looking forward to my Christmas-birthday,
and it's really not fair, since *I* didn't give Bertie the diphtheria—

it was God who did that. Isn't that right?

Sometimes Mum will hug me so hard I can barely breathe—
then she'll cry and I'll ask her if I did something wrong.
But she'll say, "No. You're perfect, Frankie."
And she looks at me, but I can tell she doesn't see me.
Dad says to give 'er time. Dad is a Frank, just like me.
And even though he's the best tool-and-die man in Strood,
he says, "They's some things can't be fixed."

Dad said we all need a fresh start,
so we're moving to a city called Detroit in America.
Dad's friend Mr. Theobald is going with us.
So is Alfred Rush, an older boy who lives nearby.
I asked Daddy if we couldn't rather take a lad my own age,
but Dad said, "No. Alfred's the only other lad we've got."

.... .- .-. --- .-.. -.. / -... .-. .. -.. .

That's my name, *Harold Bride,* in Morse code.

I'm the kind of fellow who wants to be heard!

And I'll bet they heard me shout as far away as Egypt
the day the Marconi office issued my latest assignment:

> ```
> Assistant Telegraphic Operator
> Second to Jack Phillips
> RMS Titanic
> ```

I didn't care so much that *Titanic* was a floating palace
or that it was the largest ship in the world;
what excited me most was that *Titanic* was equipped
with the most powerful wireless system on the sea!
Add to this an opportunity to work with Jack Phillips,
and I just couldn't believe my luck.

So I boarded *Titanic* in Belfast, where Phillips showed me around
the wireless shack: the operating table, where we sit at the apparatus,
the system for logging in messages and calculating sender fees.
And the apparatus itself! What a jewel:
a 5-kW installation with synchronous rotary spark discharger
connected to a huge twin T aerial running mast to mast.
And she's never been used!

I have no idea how *Titanic*'s sea trials went.
Phillips and I were bent over the equipment the whole time.
But that's the way of it: with our earphones and key,
we can converse across a thousand miles
and never leave our seat!

All the way from Belfast to Southampton
we tested the apparatus—sending messages
to the Liverpool and Malin Head wireless stations.
We even reached Port Said, three thousand miles away.
Phillips allowed me to send my own personal message:
I couldn't help but tap out a boast to my friend Harold Cottam,
wireless man on the steamship *Carpathia*.

To H. Cottam, S S *Carpathia*

... .- -.-- / --- -- /
-... .-. . .- -.- / --- ..- - /
-.-. .... .- -- .--. .- --. -. .

Say, Old Man. Break out champagne.
New orders.
Second to Phillips. Sailing *Titanic*.
Bet you wish you had my luck.

Bride

Miss Marie Stene
Ørskog P.O.
via Ålesund, Norway

3 April 1912
Wednesday

My dearest Marie,

I have secured my return to America on the maiden voyage
of the largest and the grandest ship on the sea.

They call her *Titanic*.

I beg you to join me.

Once a fellow has made his fortune, he can even try for
president. Perhaps you might one day be a president's wife.

Most humbly,
Olaus

scuttle scuttle

sniff sniff . . . rats?

scuttle scuttle

sniff sniff . . . food?

scuttle scuttle

sniff sniff . . . food

scuttle scuttle scuttle

scuttlescuttlescuttle

follow the food

follow the food

follow the food

Do you want to know who runs things?
Do you want to know who is in charge of *Titanic*?
The president? No.
The prime minister? No.
Captain Smith? Wrong again!
Bruce Ismay or Thomas Andrews?
Wrong and wrong!

To find out who's really in charge,
just look to whoever is making the food.
It is food that makes everything run,
be it a country or a steamship,
an army of soldiers or a convent of nuns.
And I should know. I'm chief baker.
I boarded *Titanic* in Belfast for the delivery trip
to shake down the ovens and kitchen appliances.

As *Titanic* sailed away from Belfast Lough,
we fed what little crew there was.
As *Titanic* navigated the Irish Sea,
I took an inventory of my riches in the flour room.
As *Titanic* turned up the English Channel,
I was standing at the ovens, watching the bread.

Remove the pans too soon, the center undercooks.
Leave them in too long, the crusts are tough.
Miscalculate the heat, you get black-encrusted mush.

As I stood there, watching the loaves turn to gold,
Isaac Maynard (a third-class entrée cook) stopped in
on his way to the service lift. He brayed like a jackass.

"Cheers, Charlie. I see you're nursemaiding the muffins again.
Well done, old chum. I'd love to stay and chat
while you stand guard, but I've got *real* work to do."

With wooden spoon, I banged upon a metal mixing bowl—
my attempt to scare him from the room like the rat he was.
Clang! Clang! Clang! Then, in a flurry, Maynard was gone.
Maynard was all flash and speed. Maynard was all sizzle and flip.
Him and his showy ways. Him and his dapper waxed mustache.

But where was I . . . ?

Oh, yes. I was watching the bread.

You cannot rush the bread.

Yalla! Yalla! Yalla! Hurry! Hurry! Hurry!
I had begun to feel the same as my brother.
I wanted to join him in singing his *yalla* song.
It seemed we would never leave Marseilles,
cooped up like chickens in our dirty little room.
I kept my brother out of trouble by reading to him.
I can read a little French, much better than I speak—
enough so I understood the newspaper advertisement:

> **RMS *TITANIC***
> **The Queen of the Ocean**
> **46,000-Ton Triple-Screw Steamer**
> **The largest ship in the world, she has no equal**
> **Setting sail from Cherbourg, France**
> **Bound for New York City, U.S.A.**
> **Wednesday, April 10**
> **Third-class berths available**
> **OFFICES OF THE WHITE STAR LINE**

The advertisement showed pictures of grand dining rooms,
clean, elegant cabins, and spacious decks—
and all for third class! Imagine what first class must be like.
Then Father came in, shouting. He was not happy.
His infected eye had gotten worse. It itched
and it leaked so that he wiped it constantly.
"We have been cheated!" he shouted.
"Our ship set sail yesterday. Yesterday!
It does not set out again for another two weeks!"

I had never seen Father so angry.
We packed our things quickly and left that boardinghouse for good.
On the way out, my father swore loudly in Arabic.
Elias giggled to hear such talk.

The travel agent at the boardinghouse laughed
and cursed back at my father in French.
Neither man understood the other,
yet the hatred needed no translation.

"Come!" Father said once we reached the street.
"There must be other ships. Other lines."
Immediately I thought of *Titanic* and the White Star Line,
but it was not my place to tell my father what to do.
Then I found my courage and opened my mouth to speak.
But before I could form the words, Elias sweetly says,

"Father, forgive me, but what about *Titanic*?"
Father looked at Elias suspiciously through his good eye.
Elias, who clutched the paper I had been reading,
held out the *Titanic* advertisement for Father to see.

"I was just reading this to Jamila," Elias lied.

"Well done, Elias," Father said. "Well done."
I felt my face flush with heat. Elias grinned at me.

And as Elias and Father turned to go, I found myself unable to move.
Anger had spilled out of my heart and into my feet.
Father turned and snapped, "Jamila, do not lag!"

I caught up and took my place,
walking behind my younger brother.
We walked in silence, bags in hand,
in search of the local office of the White Star Line.

Miss Marie Stene
Ørskog P.O.
via Ålesund, Norway

5 April 1912
Friday

My dearest M—

It seems that I am a very good salesman. It seems
I will not return to America alone after all.

My brother-in-law, Sigurd, Inga's husband, has
decided he will come. My cousin Peter also. And Karen,
a girl from the neighboring farm, just sixteen years
old and under my protection. Another neighbor, Adolf
Humblen, has chosen to go as well. He'll be looking after
the Salkjelsviks' youngest daughter, Anna.

Oh, Marie! How I wish you would join us. I am
certain that this journey will change our lives forever.

Forever I will always be your
Olaus

We brought *Titanic* into Southampton
late last night on the midnight tide.
Warped her in tight at White Star dock
for loadin' and coalin' and last-minute touches.
By mornin' the whole city was buzzing with the news of our arrival.
The union halls was full o' men hopin' for a berth.
Me, I'll be lookout.
Sure as *Titanic* sets sail, you'll find me in my usual spot,
fifty feet up the foremast in the lookout's cage.

Simply put, a lookout's job is to watch and to watch
and to say what he sees. Some nights it's mighty cold
but the pay's an extra five guineas each month
on top o' me five-pound AB's wage.

Meanwhile me duties was done, leastways until sail day came.
So me and me mate Reggie Lee kept watch round Southampton.
And they was plenty to watch: the *Echo* boys hawkin' their papers,
the trains, the horse buggies, the automobiles.
We stayed out of the pubs on account o' Lee's troubles with drink.
Instead we watched the Saints play football.

And Lee even had a go at ice-skatin' down at Royal Pier.
I seen 'im slip 'n fall maybe a hundred times!
But not me. Don't care much for the ice meself.
I don't give a fig if it *is* all the rage.
I'm more than a bit awkward on blades,
but I'm happy to watch. Always happy to keep watch.
Some folks is just born watchers, I guess.
Leastways, I am.

I watched my father attempt to speak:

> "My name is Niqula Yarid.
> I want *Titanic*. Three tickets.
> Please. Class of third."

My father's awkward French flopped from his mouth
and lurched before the White Star agent like a struggling fish.
It made me wince to see my father so helpless
in front of a man not much older than myself.
But the White Star agent was kind and polite.
He treated us with respect,
and Father did not object
even when the young man reached to inspect
the weeping, infected eye.

The agent's face darkened.
He shook his head and spoke softly to Father.
One word: "trachoma."

Father sat in silence for a long while.

> "I cannot board the ship," he said, "because of my sick eye.
> If I cross the ocean, the Americans will turn me away.
> I must stay here in France until I am well.
> But both of you will go—"

"Without you? Alone?" I blurted out.

> "Yes, Jamila, without me. But not alone.
> You will have each other. I will not discuss this.
> Other Lebanese families will be aboard with you.

Tomorrow you will take the train to Cherbourg.
The next day you will take this *Titanic* ship to America.
Your brother Isaac will meet you in New York."

Brother Isaac? New York? Without Father?

Elias grinned and shouted, *"Na'am. Na'am. Na'am!"*
Yes. Yes. Yes!
Then Father added, "Jamila, you are older.
You must look after your brother."
Elias's grin vanished as suddenly as it had appeared.
"La'a. La'a. La'a!" he shouted.

No. No. No!

non non non, momon.
don't eat my chocolate easter egg.
she is mine. make him stop, papa!

mama gave me a chicken
and it lays chocolate eggs

but papa has taken us away.
and we didn't bring the chicken.

but papa has bought
us chocolate eggs.
chocolate for me and momon.

my name is lolo.
my little brother is momon.
momon is just a baby,
but he can walk.

papa has taken us.

papa makes clothes to wear.
papa is very good at sewing pockets.

"Lolo! Share the chocolates with your little brother."

Lolo, Momon, and I: we are family.
Like the pieces of a jacket, we are stitched together.
All true families are stitched carefully *(with love)*.
Some families are fake.
Fake toy chickens laying candy eggs.
But from now on we are a real family again.
Perhaps not whole. But real.
                    (Louis Hoffman is a fake.)
My real name is Michel Navratil.
But I must live this lie for just a while.
          (I am taking the boys from their mother.)
They will be better off away from Marcelle,
better off away from Marcelle's demanding mother.
None of this is my fault, you know.
I am no John Jacob Astor!
She knew I was a simple tailor when she married me.
I did what I could for the shop,
for our marriage, our home.
I gave everything. Broke my back.
Endured her mother's taunts.

My boys were with me over Easter
and I couldn't bear to take them back.
My friend Louis Hoffman
helped me work out the details.
I'm using his name to board *Titanic*.
I have everything we need for the trip.
Clothing for Lolo and Momon. Biscuits. *(A revolver.)*
Second-class tickets. *(Bullets.)*
I will not have my family torn. Torn beyond repair.

While *Titanic* was loaded with the coal that would be her fuel,
she was also loaded with the food that would fuel her crew.
All nonperishable items were stacked to the ceilings
of specially constructed shacks on the dock.
All of this so customs officials could make their checks.
As well, the inspectors boarded *Titanic* to rummage her stem to stern,
carefully checking the perishables in the ship's refrigerated rooms.

Every can, cut, sack, bottle, and barrel
had to be checked before the ship could sail.
Sweetbreads and sausages, sugar, dried beans,
a mountain of eggs, tomatoes by the ton,
thousands of pounds of poultry and game,
thousands of gallons of cream and milk,
crate after crate of grapefruit and oranges,
asparagus, bacon, ham, fish (fresh and dried),
beer, stout, wine, spirits, coffee, and strong tea,
nearly two thousand quarts of ice cream.

And of course there was the flour—every baker's staple.
Two hundred wonderful barrels of the magical stuff,
each one identified with its own special number.

As I stood dockside, between barrels twenty and twenty-one,
Cook Maynard happened by, a cigar beneath his preposterous mustache,
and he bleated, "Better check for rats, Charlie, old chum.
        Wouldn't want one ending up in a pie!"
Maynard blew a smoke ring and chuckled.

Just as I was reflecting on
how deeply I despised him,
I saw a dark blur scurry past my feet.

scuttle, scuttle

sniff sniff . . . food

The *Titanic* was due to depart from Cherbourg,
a very long train ride all the way across France.
Father entrusted me with one hundred pounds to keep!
"For emergencies only," Father said.
"And to show any customs inspectors along the way."
I had never seen so much money all at once.
"You cannot enter America penniless," Father said.
"They will not allow it. So whatever you do . . .
do not lose this money, Jamila."
In a separate room I placed the treasure
in a linen bag that I tied around my waist, beneath my skirt.

Father hugged me stiffly and shook Elias's hand.
I threw my arms around my father and held tight.
He pried me off. Even Father's healthy eye glistened.
"Go, now, you two. I will join you soon."

Hours later, the rhythmic rocking click of the rails
finally silenced my brother's chatter, and he slept.
Elias's head rested on my shoulder. I could not close my eyes.
My thoughts raced as fast as the miraculous train
that was taking us north to face our future:
Will Jacksonville look anything like Hakoor?
Will a girl like me, from a small mountain village, fit in?
Will I have the proper clothes?
Will my mother have chosen a husband for me?

I put my hand to my waist, checking on the belt.
I looked out the window at the vast world blurring by
and folded my shaking hands in my lap
to keep them from giving me away.

Well, we finally left Strood!
Dad packed his tools into a wooden crate
along with Mum's fancy Singer sewing machine.
(I slipped in my cap gun when no one was looking.)
Then Mr. Theobald, Alfred Rush, Mum, Dad, and me,
we all of us took the train from Kent to London!
What a grand city of black air and dirt,
street vendors, candy shops,
hotels with a loo in every room,
open-topped omnibuses with spiral stairs,
white-coated street sweepers, hansom cabs,
"women of questionable morals," and motorcars.
It was all so exciting I thought I might burst,
though Mum held my hand too tight
and wouldn't allow for any fun at all.
She said we had to get our rest
since the train for *Titanic* was due
to leave very early from Waterloo Station.
Alfred said he was too old to be sent to bed.
Mum said otherwise — so off to bed he went.
Alfred was asleep even before me! Ha. Some man.
I stayed awake all night (or at least a good half hour)
wondering how dirty Detroit might be. And wondering
about baseball. Isn't it just like cricket?
And *Titanic* . . . will there be other boys?
And America. Will there be dragons there?
And our new house. A bedroom to myself?
And our new life. Will Bertie's ghost know where we live?

Maybe there will be dragons in the sea.

I'll see you five pounds.
And raise you . . . ten.

The fellow across from me is the mark.
Actually, I prefer the term client.
Client *sounds more civilized.*
My client is the one with the most to lose.
The other players I could care less about.

I'll take one card, please.

I've had my eye on him for days:
rich kid, on Easter holiday from university,
who fancies himself a cardsharp,
especially when he's betting his daddy's money.
I've been acting the part of the dumb American.
Letting him win a few hands and a few healthy pots.

I think I'm getting the hang of this game.

But the kid stopped winning about thirty minutes ago.
His money is nearly gone. But wait. . . .
He takes two cards and grins. Amateur.

I'll see you ten . . .
and I'll raise you . . . fifty.

Every other player folds.
The rich kid stops grinning, but he's still in.
He knows he's got a good hand.
He puts in his fifty pounds and adds another fifty.
He wants to win Daddy's money back.

Ooh. Another fifty?
That's an awful lot of money.
OK, then. I'll see you fifty and call.

The papers were calling Titanic *the Millionaires' Special,*
and I was looking for transportation anyway
to my sister's in Los Angeles. Of course, I consider
each Atlantic crossing to be a working vacation.
The kid puts down a flush. All hearts.

A flush? Ooh, that *is* a good hand.

I can almost hear him thinking up ways to spend the money.
As I lay down my own hand, I try to stay in character.

Full house. My dumb luck. I believe I've won it all.

Now I can almost hear him thinking up some lie
to explain to Daddy where all the money went.

Good night, gentlemen. I must cash it in.
I've a ship to catch in the morning.

University-Loser-Kid has turned silent and a little green.
I think he might get sick. He looks at me with
bloodshot eyes and says, "Who are you?"

Who, me? My name is George . . . George Winner.

Then I leave. Who am I? indeed.
My name is George Brereton:
cardsharp, trickster, and confidence man.
And I love my work.

I loved my work.
But could I really call it love?
Love seems too weak a word.
Beelike, I was born and existed for my ship.
I lived and breathed the industry of the hive.

I boarded *Titanic* every day as we readied to sail.
We pored over every inch of her,
me and my own expert crew from Belfast.
And as usual whatever details were overlooked
I tended to myself: I installed coatracks, tables,
chairs, berth ladders, and electric fans.
I gave a hundred tours of the ship to a hundred
officials, managers, agents, and contractors.
I made a hundred pages of notes on a hundred
distinct items, from the color of the wicker furniture
to the number of screws in the stateroom hat hooks.

In my hotel room I packed and readied my things.
>   *No detail has escaped my notice,* I wrote my wife that night.
>   *The* Titanic *is now about complete*
>   *and will, I think, do the old firm credit*
>   *tomorrow when we sail.*

In the darkness, my head hummed like a bee's wing.
I do love my wife.
But that final night, I must confess,
I dreamed of a different lady altogether.

HAROLD LOWE ∞ THE JUNIOR OFFICER

We were due to set sail the next day.
I stood on the bridge, awaiting the bells
that would end my midnight watch.
I was aboard now with all the other officers,
and we were to stay on *Titanic* overnight—
all except Captain Smith, of course,
who would wake up to milk and crumpets, I guess,
and skip down to the docks at his leisure.
I'm a ship hopper—that is to say, my only home
is wherever I happen to be berthed.
No house with a white picket fence for me.
I sleep better on water than I do on land.

There were eight of us officers in all,
four senior and four junior,
each with his own private cabin.
I hadn't learned all the names just yet.
Captain Smith was top man, of course,
followed by Chief Officer Wilde.
Then the first and second officers in turn.
It's us junior officers, the third through sixth,
who do most of the grunt work.
I was fifth officer, second from bottom in rank,
though I was competent as any of the others.
Among the *Titanic* officers, I was odd man out.
They mostly knew one another from other ships,
and I was the only Welshman among them.
That was all fine with me.
I pull my weight. I do my duty.

I wasn't there to make friends.

Phillips and I quickly struck up a friendship
during the days leading up to *Titanic*'s maiden voyage.
We shared sleeping quarters
adjacent to the operating room—nothing fancy.
Not even a porthole, but a wonderful skylight
that could be opened from below with a crank.

Late Tuesday evening, I lay awake in bed,
listening to Phillips in the next room cracking at the key

- --- -- --- .-. .-. --- .-- / .-- . /
... . - / ... .- .. .-..

dash-dash dash-dash-dit dash-dit dash-dash

Looking upward, I imagined the invisible words filling the room.
I watched them swirl about, then fly up and out
through the skylight, past the masts and rigging,
on their way to heaven, I guess—

a kitten's small mewl swallowed up by cold, empty space.

I am the ice. I have no need of sleep.
Why do the humans crave it as they do?
While they and I've a secret tryst to keep,
I will not rest. There is no time to lose.
Onshore a young boy dreams himself a man.
Another youngster dreams a future home.
A toddler dreams of chocolate eggs to eat.
A restless girl dreams soldiers in pursuit.
A gambler dreams a trick of all one suit.
On board the lookouts rest their weary eyes,
for sleep is precious rare when out at sea.
The uniformed fifth officer, awake,
awaits the bells that end the midnight watch.
At White Star dock, Southampton's crowning jewel,
Titanic, finally settles down to sleep:
the pantries stocked, the coal bins full of fuel,
the crew recruitment list at last complete.
Come sunrise they'll arrive from near and far.
Come sunrise they'll arrive from every port,
by railway, horse-drawn cab, or motorcar.
Come sunrise they will rush to climb aboard.
For now, her engines dumb, *Titanic* waits.
She waits dim-witted, slow, colossal brute,
to carry on her back her human freight.
I am the ice; I am of water made.
That's why it's now of water that I speak:
Watch how the water licks *Titanic*'s hull.
Hear how the water makes her rivets creak.
See how, before her trip even begins,
the water is obsessed with getting in.

April 21, 1912
SUNDAY
Aboard the cable ship *Mackay-Bennett*
ATLANTIC OCEAN
THE GRAND BANKS
650 MILES FROM HALIFAX, NOVA SCOTIA

JOHN SNOW
THE UNDERTAKER

Sunday arrives, our first day of harvesting corpses,
and I determine to make the best
of the challenging task at hand. Happily,
on this fourth day out, I have found my sea legs
and I keep my breakfast down.
Over coffee, the lads from the late-night dog watch
tell me they spotted bodies floating in the darkness,
rising and falling with the swells,
occasionally bumping the ship's hull.

One of the firemen, Arminias Wiseman, swears,
"It's as if they wanted to clamor aboard!
I didn't sleep a wink all night. I'm undone!"
But I am the undertaker, and I am an old hand at death.
Men who walk among the dead as I do
must cultivate a certain emotional remove.
Indifference. An indifference to death.
Indifference. An indifference to the dead.

I finish my cup and climb to the sun deck.
I inhale the Atlantic's cold April air, ready
for whatever the coming day might bring.
A half mile off the *Mackay-Bennett*'s bow
a flock of seagulls floats on the swells.

Seagulls? So many miles from land?

"Lower away," Captain Larnder commands.
Ropes creak through the pulleys as the first small boat
descends in its davits, carrying a crew of five.

As the small cutter reaches the water, I see a half dozen bodies.
They look strange, as if standing in the shallows of a pond,
heads and shoulders above the surface, buoyed ingeniously
by their bulky life vests of bright white canvas and cork.
The corpses spin slowly, almost gracefully.
Mouth agape, each earnest face turns upward, staring at nothing,
as if the dead were alive, but blind—heads cocked slightly
to better hear what rowdy living men intrude
upon this silent, solemn interlude.

Captain Larnder whispers respectfully, "And so we begin."

I turn again to the far-off flock of gulls—
smudges of white floating on the green waves—
and I admit to myself what I knew at the first sight of them:

Those are no seagulls at all. Those are bodies.

More bodies. Each one waiting in a bright white vest.
My God. My God. My God.
Bodies scattered for miles, in every direction.
Bodies as far as my indifferent eyes can see.

FIRST WATCH

SETTING OUT

SOUTHAMPTON, ENGLAND, TO CHERBOURG, FRANCE

WEDNESDAY, APRIL 10, 1912

Mornin', sir.
Tommy Hart, at yer service.
Reportin' for duty an' all such truck.
What's that?
Me papers?
Well, of course I've got me papers!
I've got me discharge book right here.
You see there,
"Issued by the Board of Trade.
Thomas Hart, Southampton."
Why, what else *would* it say?
Plain as day: "Thomas Hart,"
but me mates all calls me Tommy
and you can, too, sir, if you like.

Say. I wonder, sir, if you might remind a fellow
where, precisely, the other firemen is berthed?
She's a big ship, *Titanic* is, and I wouldn't want ter get lost.
That would be disgraceful inefficient.
And I do detest inefficiency. So if—

Whazzat?

"Down the spiral stair to F deck, at the bow"?
Yes, sir. Right you are. I remember it now.
I'll just be off to stow me kit.
Then we'll get this lady's boilers up!
I want ter get at it. And that coal won't jump
into the furnace on its own, eh?

I'm goin', sir. I'm goin'. I'm on me way.
Name's Tommy Hart. You have a nice day.

Before setting out across the Atlantic
Titanic was to visit two ports of call:
In Cherbourg, France, we would collect
the other first-class passengers,
wealthy adventurers returning to America
from their Mediterranean winter-overs.
We'd also bring aboard more third-class souls,
wretched continentals going to America
to escape their impoverished lives.
In Queenstown, Ireland, yet more emigrants
to swell the lucrative third-class ranks,
all of them eager to spend a bit of their
meager life savings to gamble on a better future.

But these were not the only passengers
to board in these various ports. . . .
There was another class of passenger altogether,
a passenger who could be lifted aboard in a sack
and who did not give a fig for lavish appointments.

I am talking about the envelopes, postcards, and packages
that came aboard bound for letter boxes
more than three thousand miles away.
After all, the "RMS" of RMS *Titanic*
stands for Royal *Mail* Steamer.
The White Star Line had negotiated a contract
with the British government: so long
as we delivered the mails on time,
we would be paid handsomely for it.
The sea post was a brilliant bit of business:
the letters were like thousands of paying passengers
who asked for nothing and never complained!

Sort. Shuffle-shuffle. Slot. Shuffle-shuffle.
Sort. Sort. Shuffle-shuffle. Slot. Shuffle-shuffle.

Nothing ever happens in the postal room.

Sort. Shuffle-shuffle. Slot. Shuffle-shuffle.

Anyways, nothing of the heroic sort.

Sort. Shuffle-shuffle. Slot. Shuffle-shuffle.
Sort. Sort. Shuffle-shuffle. Slot. Shuffle-shuffle.

We sort the sacks. We sort the sacks.
We slot the envelopes. We stack the stacks.
We resack the sorted. We fill the racks.
We fill the racks with stacks of sacks.

Sort. Sort. Shuffle-shuffle. Slot. Shuffle-shuffle.

These envelopes will not sort themselves.

Sort. Slot. Shuffle-shuffle. Slot. Shuffle-shuffle.

The new man, Mr. March, reports for duty.
"I'm Mr. March, the new man," he says.
"We're all of us new to *Titanic,*" says I.

Sort. Slot. Shuffle —

I stop to shake Mr. March's hand.
He's arrived with rubber fingertips in place.
The perfect picture of a sea-post man.

How about a picture and a comment for the paper, Mr. Astor?

"*Colonel* Astor," I corrected the reporter, and sighed.
Before I could answer, the flashes began popping.
It was almost enough to make me curse the man
who invented the camera. Almost.
Walking among the Egyptian ruins,
I had half expected a mummy to spring
from its sarcophagus to Kodak me—
just as I had put my finger up my nose.

We were now back in Paris, boarding the boat train.
And I was already missing the anonymity of Giza,
where everything had been ancient and dead.
Madeleine and I fled New York to escape all this fuss:
the puny scrutiny of the masses,
the mean-minded prurience of the lower classes,
the hypocritical judgment of the upper crust.

And of course the newsmen took their shots
as I bundled my Madeleine onto the train.
Then one of them asked me the question
(they've *all* asked it a thousand times before):
What's it like, sir? To be the richest man in the world?

And I answered him back as I buttoned my fur-collared coat:
"Cold, sir. It is very cold."

And as usual
        as the boat train began its lurch toward Cherbourg,
        where *Titanic* awaited me like a tomb,
the reporter did not even write the answer down.

Early in the morning, we caught another train
that took us, *clickety-clack,* all the way
from London to a city called Southampton.
That made two big cities in as many days—
I was already a world traveler,
searching out dragons to the ends of the earth.
The train pulled up right next to the dock
as if we were royalty. Alfred acted like the Prince of Wales,
walking with his nose in the air.
Then he tripped over Mr. Theobald's bag
and fell onto the platform all in a pile!

Just a few steps away, we were all squeezed into a room
where a man checked us up and down,
putting his fingers into my hair,
looking at my eyes under a bright lamp.
He asked us all our ages:
Alfred said, "Sixteen."
I said, "Not yet, you're not."
Alfred said, "Shut up, you."
The inspector man pinned a tag to my lapel, and off we went
across a long gangway onto the ship—
a canvas overhang, a sturdy metal rail—
there wasn't even the tiniest bit of danger involved.
I was somewhat disappointed.
But once we got aboard, I was so excited
I nearly jumped out of my knee pants.
Mum kept a hand on my shoulder
like she always does when she's nervous.
        She does that—makes a big deal of protectin' me
        when really she wants protectin' herself.

Well, she protected me all the way to our cabin
till my shoulder was black and blue.
I claimed top bunk. Mum took bottom.
Dad said he'd sleep on the sofa couch.
Alfred Rush and Mr. Theobald found their room
at the other end of the ship,
"With the other single men," Alfred said.

Mum wanted to protect me some more,
but I finally made my escape
when she lay down with a cool cloth on her head.
Just as I was sneaking out, Dad caught my arm.
He whispered, "Go on, now, Frankie.
Watch the signs—make sure you stay in third class.
Stick with Alfred, and don't get into trouble."
I whispered back, "Daddy, it's just a big ship.
What trouble could I possibly get into?"
Daddy laughed. "Oh, you'll think of something."

Did I forget to tell ya
that I've got the best dad
who ever sailed the seven seas?

THUMP. THUMP. THUMPTHUMPTHUMP. THUMP.

Sort. Shuffle-shuffle. Slot. Shuffle-shuffle.

"Did you hear that?" says March.
"Did I hear what?" says I.

"That thumping sort of noise," says March.
And there it is, between the shuffles.

Sort. Shuffle-shuffle. THUMP. Shuffle-shuffle.
Sort. Shuffle-shuffle. THUMPTHUMP. Shuffle-shuffle.

"Not to worry, Mr. March," says I. "That's the racquet court next door.
Mr. Wright, the racquets instructor, is warming up, no doubt."

Sort. THUMP. *Shuffle-shuffle.* THUMP. *Shuffle-shuffle.*

"Well, Mr. Wright is making a racket for sure.
The thumps are throwing off my rhythm," says March.
"You'll grow used to it, Mr. March," says I.
"You'll find the occasional thumps break up the monotony."

Sort. Shuffle-shuffle. Slot. Shuffle-shuffle.

Says March, "What monotony?"

Sort. Shuffle-shuffle. Slot. Shuffle-shuffle.
Sort. Shuffle-shuffle. Slot. Shuffle-shuffle.

Oh, he *is* good, that Mr. March. *Sort. Slot.*
Mr. March is a true sea-post man, I say.

"Yes, that's right, Colonel Gracie. We *do* have a racquet court on board."

It is White Star policy that off-duty officers stand at the first-class entrance
to greet the well-heeled cabin passengers.

> "No. I have not read your book, but—
> Yes. Yes, I *would* like a signed copy, thank you."

I make my small talk. I shake their hands.

> "Yes, Mrs. Straus. . . . Yes, ma'am. . . . No, ma'am. . . .
> Oh, no, ma'am. Definitely not. The ship will not sink."

Mr. and Mrs. Straus are a wonderful couple;
they own Macy's department store in New York.

Major Arthur Peuchen, the Canadian lumberman,
informed me that he is "an avid yachtsman" himself
and please feel free to call upon him if I find myself shorthanded.

Mr. Billy Carter slapped me on the back
and said he hoped my "boat" was watertight
as he had a brand-new motorcar stowed in the holds.
I smiled and assured Mr. Carter that *Titanic* did not leak.

Americans.
Smile, E.J. Keep on smiling.

I would be lying to say *Titanic* has no leaks.
Every ship leaks to some extent, certainly.
That is what the pumps are for.
The *large* leaks, of course, are the primary concern,
but they are rare. So long as the rivets are strong
(and I assure you *Titanic*'s rivets are strong—
three million of them, mostly driven by hydraulic machines,
checked and double-checked by trained inspectors),
so long as those three million rivets are strong
the overlapped seams between the plating will hold.

I've considered a possible collision
with some other craft, a dock, coastal rocks in the fog—
there are countless ways to wreck a ship.
But as sure as winter follows summer,
I am sure that *Titanic* will stay afloat.

You see, *Titanic,* like a beehive, is constructed of cells,
sixteen partitioned segments in all. Each cell separated
by bulkhead walls equipped with watertight doors
that can be closed all at once from the bridge.
This way, if one cell was to flood, the water could be contained
in that compartment alone. And the remaining cells
would easily keep the ship afloat. In fact, four cells
could be flooded all at once and still *Titanic* would not founder.

The odds of a breach in five compartments at once . . .
the odds of five breaches that were large enough to allow
the requisite volume of water to enter the hull . . .
Well, I'm not a gambling man, especially when lives are the stake,
but if I *did* make the bet, I daresay I'd be set for life.

The name? Oh, yes, the name is . . . Brayton.
Andrew Brayton, if you please. First class.
Here's five quid if you leave the name off the passenger list.

No sense in giving the purser my real name, of course.

I'd like a stateroom suite with adjacent parlor, please.

A private place to play at cards, away from suspicious stewards.

And I'll be needing to rent a deck chair, too.
A chair next to Mr. and Mrs. Straus will do.
I'm a longtime friend of the family, you see.

Actually, I've never met them in my life,
but I am a longtime friend of their money.

And I have several steamer trunks I'll want sent to my room.

Of course they are mostly packed with stones.
A lone man crossing the Atlantic with no baggage
is a sure sign of a confidence trickster.
In case of a hasty retreat in New York,
I will leave behind only trunks filled with nothing.

Am I traveling for business or for pleasure?

For once I can give up an honest answer.

Pleasure, my good man. Purely pleasure.

ha, ha! momon, listen—
papa is playing a game

oui, momon,
papa is playing a game.
he is playing a name game.

he says his name is louis hoffman
but his name is really michel navratil.
everyone knows their own name.

shhhhh, momon,
it is a secret game.

shhhhh

shhhhh

shhhhh

"My name is Louis Hoffman.
I have second-class accommodation."

(My name is Louis Hoffman.)

"Yes, these are my children. My boys. We are a family."

(My name is Michel Navratil.)

"Their mother . . . my wife . . . she is dead.
But I haven't told the boys yet. They speak no English."

(My name is Louis Hoffman.)

"Yes, we are going to America . . .
to live with relatives."

(My name is Michel Navratil.)

"*Merci,* but my children are tired.
Please, just show us to our room.
We need privacy, please. I want my boys to sleep."

(My name is Louis Hoffman.)

I ran past crowds of people with bundles, bags, and babies,
and I followed the stairs at the back of the ship
up to the deck, where I could look down at the dock below.
I didn't think I had ever been up so high as that.
My knees shook a little as I leaned against the rail.
The big stacks breathed out black dragon smoke.
I felt scared, but it was an "I'm excited" scared.

I ran up to Alfred Rush, who was talking to two other boys.
Alfred says, "What do you want, Frankie?"
I say, "We're supposed to stick together, remember?"
Alfred rolled his eyes, like I'm just some little kid.
But the older boy of the two said, "Hello."
And then he shook my hand! Like a grown-up.
No kid's ever shook my hand before.
"Name's Rossmore," he said. "This is my brother, Eugene."
Eugene said, "Jesus loves you," and *he* shook my hand as well.
Rossmore said, "Eugene's a soldier in the Salvation Army."
I said, "Oh." And just then a bugle sounded.
And a man shouted, "All ashore 'at's goin' ashore."
Titanic's big whistles boomed out, like I figure a dragon would sound.
You could feel that whistle all through your insides,
and Alfred just about jumped out of his skin!

I could hardly believe I got to stay.
No "goin' ashore" for me and my crew.
Titanic is my ship. And I'm her captain.
Traveling the seas in search of dragons.
Rossmore can be first mate. Eugene can be ship's chaplain.
Alfred can be cabin boy and swab the decks.
We can stay on this ship forever if we want.
"Hard astarboard, Mr. Rossmore!" I yelled out.

And "Say us a prayer, Father Eugene!"
Then "Grab a mop, Alfred. We're off in search of dragons!"

Alfred groaned and slumped his head onto the rail,
but Rossmore and Eugene both laughed.
I felt a hand against my back, and it was Daddy,
come up from below. And Mum was there, too.
Then Daddy lifted me up onto his shoulders,
and the whole crowd cheered as the *Titanic* started to move.

BOOM. BOOM.

Sort. Shuffle-shuffle. Slot. Shuffle-shuffle.

"Did you hear that?" says Mr. March.
"Did I hear what?" says I.

Sort. Shuffle-shuffle. Slot. Shuffle-shuffle.

"Sounded like 'boom, boom,'" says Mr. March.
"'Boom, boom'?" says I. "We haven't even left port
and you've already gone loony."

But then I hear the noise myself.
BOOM. Like a cannon.

Sort. Shuffle-shuffle. BOOM. Shuffle-shuffle.

"Do you suppose," says Mr. March, "that we're under attack?"
"I'm sure it's nothing of the sort," says I.
"Shall I go topside to have a look?" says March.

Sort. Shuffle-shuffle. Slot. Shuffle-shuffle.

"You'll do nothing of the sort," says I.
"We're on the lowest deck as it is.
If she starts leaking, we'll be the first to know."

Sort. Shuffle-shuffle. Slot. Shuffle-shuffle.

"Well said, Mr. Woody," says Mr. March.

Sort shuffle-shuffle. "Well said."

Even us officers thought we were hearing cannon fire.

But the reality of the situation was nearly as bad.

It was a nearby ship, the *New York,* tied fast to the dock.

As *Titanic* sailed by, her displacement

drew the smaller ship into the channel.

And as the *New York* pulled away from the dock,

the steel hawsers that tied her down began to strain.

The *New York* was like a stubborn dog pulling at its leash.

The lines stretched out; they gave a sickening creak,

and in an instant they gave way with cannonlike snaps

in rapid succession from stern to bow.

Boom, Boom. Boom, Boom. Boom.

The broken hawsers flung backward

onto the crowded dock like monstrous whips.

It was a wonder that no one was killed outright.

But the worst of the incident was yet to come.

Once broken free, the *New York* came toward us.

Titanic's huge mass draws in the helpless ship.

One hundred feet to go.

The tugs began to race to the *New York*'s side.

Fifty feet to go.

Sailors aboard the *New York*

frantically tossed out catch lines.

Twenty feet.

The steerage

gathered along the rail

began to yell out.

Ten feet now.

Shouting in a hundred

tangled tongues!

"Full astern, Mr. Boxhall, please."

"Full astern, Captain!"

I do not panic.

In forty years at sea, I have never panicked.

Nor would I begin to panic now.

"Ready starboard anchor, Mr. Boxhall."

"Ready starboard anchor, Captain!"

Titanic is the largest ship in the world.

To captain her is a study in trial and error.

A ship this large has an equally large propeller.

In fact this old girl has three.

But I needed only one to give a few quick rotations

to wash away the advancing *New York*.

A bull shrugging off a fly.

One sudden burst from the port propeller.

Just enough time for the tugs to take control of the ropes

and tie off the wayward hulk.

The line of command is straight:

I gave the order to Fourth Officer Boxhall,

who sent it via telegraph to the engine room.

I had the men ready the anchor just in case.

All told, this little incident would cost us just one extra hour.

No problem.

"Weigh anchor, Mr. Boxhall."

"Weighing anchor!"

No panic.

"Let's head on to Cherbourg."

"Aye aye, Captain!"

Straight line.

While boarding the train in Paris,
I met a fascinating lady: Helen Churchill Candee.
The six-hour train ride to Cherbourg
flew by as we got to know each other.
We are both ladies of society,
both of us are mothers with two grown children
(a boy and girl, no less),
and we are both living lives separate from our husbands.
I confessed that I write, and she said she writes, too.
But she listed off a number of published works.
I shared that my grandson in the States had a fever.
She broke down and said she was also going home,
to be with her son, who had been in a flying accident.

When the train came to a stop, we agreed to meet
again sometime along the voyage.
I saw her, later, stepping out onto the train platform
wearing an exquisite pink gown spangled all over
with a soft veil of pale-blue gauze draped over the shoulders,
as if she had just entered a ballroom instead of a railway station.

I discovered along with the other passengers
that *Titanic*'s tenders would be delayed an hour,
something about a near collision with another ship.
A bad omen, said many of the first-class ladies.

But it gave me a chance to stretch my legs along the Grande Jetée
and walk among the lower-class passengers—
a young couple walking arm in arm—newlyweds, I could tell—
a family of five speaking German,
a woman and child speaking Italian,
a boy yelling excitedly in some other tongue—

I know my languages—it was Arabic certainly.
He yells at a girl I take to be his sister.
She catches me looking and turns away,
but not before I notice that she is beautiful.
She is beautiful and she is frightened
and she is waiting . . . just like me.
Waiting for something real to sail into her life.

"I do not care what Father said, Jamila.
While he is away, *I* am the man of this family.
And the man should carry the money!"

Elias was talking too loudly.
Elias was talking too much.
Drawing attention to us.
He talks and talks and talks about nothing.

"*Lalalalalalalalalala,* Jamila!"

That rich man. He is looking at me.
Sketching my face into his notepad.

That rich woman over there.
She is looking at me.
The same way the man with the sketch pad stares.

Finally. Finally. The four glorious funnels
of *Titanic* came into view!
Finally. Finally. Her great whistles blew.

Soon as we neared the Cherbourg breakers,
I did my skidoo to the gangway doors
to do my part haulin' aboard the mails.

I've been to the Cherbourg shore plenty times before.
But this 'ere lady, *Titanic,* was too big to fit.
No Frenchman's dock could handle her,
so she dropped anchor in the roadstead,
starboard side facing France.
Then we waited for the tenders
to bring the passengers and luggage to us.

At the sound of one bell, marking six thirty,
the fancy tender with the fancy folk
pulled up forward with their endless fancy trunks.
The poor classes shared a second tender with the mails
and pulled up along their own entrance aft.
Now, now, we wouldn't want the classes to mix!

Old Johnny Coffey (he's me mate)
was particular anxious to help with the mails.
(I'll tell you here and now: something is not right
with that fellow, else my name's not Tommy Hart!)
Haw! Haw! Haw! Haw!

The ride out to the *Titanic*'s side was a nightmare.
The water was rough, making my stomach flip.
I pulled my headscarf tight against the cold wind.
I wondered how I could survive a week on the Atlantic
if I had this much trouble just riding in a small tender.
All the while, *Titanic* got bigger and bigger
until it looked like an entire city rising from the water.

The ship doctor, an old man, boarded us.
He reached out to inspect me
as if I were one of the mail sacks
that filled every empty space of the deck.
He spoke to me in English, so I didn't understand.
He pulled back my lids with a tiny clamp
and looked into my eyes.
Looking for the sickness that Father had.
He pointed me forward and I walked.

"La. Lalalalalala." I could hear Elias following me.

I stepped onto the gangway that led
from the small boat to the big ship's door.
This was my bridge to America.
The walkway swayed up and down as ten men on each side
attempted to hold it steady. One step forward.

"La la. La la la lalala. Lalala!"

Two steps. And another. I was going.
I was walking across the bridge to America.
The sea lifted the bridge under my feet. Rolled it slightly.
I looked down at the laces of my boots.
My knees buckled. Then I fell like a drunkard.
And I fainted dead away.

HAROLD LOWE ∽ THE JUNIOR OFFICER

This Cherbourg Harbor stop was doubtless
the most chaotic one yet. The steerage who came out
on the mail tender were a motley assortment.
They none of them spoke English. It was all just gibberish.
Italians and other Latin races. Low-class continentals all.
When I saw the girl look down at her boots,
I knew she was about to pass out.
The boy she was with—I guessed he was her brother—
tried to catch her, but they both took a tumble.

I'll bet the girl had never been outside her village.
To someone who has likely never seen a machine
more advanced than a horse plow, I imagine
Titanic was a most impressive sight.
Two stokers helped the girl on board,
and I called for the ship's interpreter.
He was going to have his hands full
with this lot, to be sure.
If these people are so keen to live in America,
why can't they learn the language first?
Even just a few words would be helpful.

I did my junior officer's duties,
and in just under ninety minutes,
we brought one hundred babbling passengers aboard.
Forward of us, the upper-class tender off-loaded
nearly one hundred seventy cabin passengers.
And of course, Captain Smith
was stationed in the first-class foyer
to welcome the rich, famous, and cultured.
While I was down here with the riffraff,
catching fainthearted foreigners.

Smile, E.J. Keep on smiling.

> "Ah, Mrs. Brown. Alone this time? That will not do.
> I'm sure some dashing passenger will soon offer his protection."

Margaret Brown does not need any man's protection.
She is better off without Mr. Brown to slow her down.

Now here comes—oh, no. It's the Harpers. How I dread—

> "Mr. and Mrs. Harper! How was your trip to the pyramids?"

Mr. Harper introduces me to his Egyptian companion,
a dragoman who served as the Harpers' guide.
On a lark they had offered to pay his way onto *Titanic*
    so as to interpret any hieroglyphs and runes
    we might find in the smoking lounge.
Mr. Harper laughs a great belly laugh.

> "Yes, that is most funny, Mr. Harper."

Mrs. Harper informs me that the little Pekingese dog
she holds is named Sun Yat-sen and that "Sunny"
is very excited to be sailing on such a very big "boat."
God in heaven. Please save me from these Americans.

Oh, now *here* comes the terribly rich
Mr. Benjamin Guggenheim, his mistress on his arm.
Thank God Eleanor and I were both born poor
so the concept of fidelity was allowed to take root in us.
Marriage without struggle is like an unfired clay pot.
It is easily made, but it will not stand the test of time.

THOMAS ANDREWS ∽ THE SHIPBUILDER

I can't decide if *Titanic* is my mistress or my wife.

As my career as a shipbuilder became a reality,
my private life went through changes as well.
I moved into my own domestic hive in Belfast
with the beautiful Helen Barbour as queen bee.
And two years later, with the birth of our daughter, Elizabeth,
I became worker bee to two rival hives: business and home.

So *Titanic* has to share my heart with two other ladies.
Helen rarely complains, but I know my heavy workload worries her.
And, indeed, I had planned, these next two weeks,
to spend time with both baby and bees while Uncle William
sailed on *Titanic*'s maiden voyage. But Uncle William took ill,
so the task fell to me. And rightly so.
I know Helen was disappointed, but I was overjoyed!
(Does that make me a cad?)

Of course work must come first. And besides—two weeks apart
will not break our world in two. Helen is a shipbuilder's wife;
she understands the sacrifices . . . and the dangers.

Perhaps I should design a metaphor to encompass both my loves:
I love my wife; she is my flower. I love *Titanic;* she is my hive.
My wife and child are the flowers where I gather sustenance,

but I must always, eventually, return to the hive.

I've got a girl back in Dumfries, soon to be my wife.
Yet here I am sailing on *Titanic* in the company
of not just one mistress but two.
And their names are Eberle and Guadagnini!
They're beautiful Italian *signorina*s—yes, they are:
both are smooth and satiny to the touch,
they've got all the usual curves,
they're narrow and wide in all the right places,
and both of them are over one hundred and fifty years old!
Ha, ha. So what if they *are* violins instead of real ladies?
They're all the company a fellow needs on a long voyage.

You see, I'm trying both instruments out,
runnin' each through her trials if you like,
in order to decide which of the two will be
Jock Hume's "life instrument." The choice is much the same
as choosing a wife—maybe even more difficult.
Choosing a wife was easy enough for me.
Mary Costin will soon be the mother of my child.
So Mary will be the lady of my house,
but my violin, she will become the voice of my soul.

Almost there, E.J.

Finally the last of the first-class passengers.

John Jacob Astor and his entourage are next in line.
And on his arm a mistress of his own, so young.

> "Mr. Astor. Welcome aboar—
> er, yes, *Colonel* Astor. Of course. Of course.
> And hello to you, Miss . . .
> oh, excuse me, of course, *Mrs.* As—"

Oh, my God. The girl is his *wife*?
This is the wife that has caused such talk?
She's not much older than my own daughter, Mel!
She must be less than half Astor's age!
And she looks to be far along in the belly.
I see Colonel Jack has wasted no time.

> "*Mrs.* Astor. The pleasure is all mine.
> I wish you both all the good luck in the world."

Better Astor had taken a mistress and left this poor girl alone.

Captain Smith is slightly better than most
at masking his contempt—but not by much.
When you are as rich as I am, you are forever
surrounded by contrived smiles and false flattery.
From behind his kindly white whiskers, Smith judges me.

Keep Madeleine as your mistress!
That's how he would have it.

But Madeleine would not stand for that.
And Madeleine's father would not stand for that.
And neither would I stand for that.
My Maddie deserves better:
Madeleine is young, but she sees me as I truly am.
Oh, I *am* rich. And perhaps I *am* vain.
But I am not idle, nor am I shallow.
I am a businessman. A writer. An inventor.
A yachtsman. A philosopher. A devoted father as well.
The point is, my Madeleine sees all this.

I am accused of mocking the sanctity of marriage
when in fact I feel just the opposite sensation:
Isn't a loveless marriage, void of respect and affection,
a marriage based on a lie? And isn't a marriage
based on a lie the epitome of sacrilege?

And why should I *not* marry a woman half my age?
Is it so incredible to think that I may actually *love* her?
Are they all too jaded and callous to see . . .

that Maddie has utterly stolen my heart?

While Phillips was at the key,
I was logging in the messages.
Double-checking word counts.
Verifying charges. Helping Jack tackle
the rush of messages arriving
in the pneumatic tube from the purser's desk.

-... .. .-.. .-.. -.--

Have set sail. Billy

... --- -.

She's a big ship. Your son

... .-- .. - .... . .- .-. -

Arrive New York Wednesday. Your sweetheart

"Hey, Phillips," I say, "you got a sweetheart?"
"None of ycr bloody business, Bride," Jack growls.

dash-dit-dash dit-dit dash dash dash-dit-dash-dash

dash-dit-dit-dit dit dash-dit-dit-dash

"Her name is Kitty Bex," Jack says. "And she's a peach."

dit-dit-dit dit-dit-dit-dit dit / dit-dit dit-dit-dit / dit-dash

dit-dash-dash-dit dit dit-dash dash-dit-dash-dit dit-dit-dit-dit

I woke up to the sound of the ship's whistle
and discovered I was lying lengthwise on a bench.
Someone had draped a steamer rug over me.
Then I remembered the doctor examining my eyes,
the gangway rocking, my brother "*lalala*-ing,"
and everything turning to darkness and little white stars.

I sat up, surrounded by total strangers.
My skirt was covered with black smudges.
Elias was suddenly next to me.
He told me two men had carried me to this bench.
I rubbed my eyes, and then I noticed . . . the boy.

He stood atop the base of a cargo crane, not moving a muscle.
All the boys around him were speaking a mile a minute
tearing all about, just like Elias, only in English.
But this boy just stood there.
He stood there in brown woolen knee pants
and a neat pressed jacket, and he held his head as if he were a prince.
He looked as if he was about my age, and . . .

he was looking at me. This boy was looking at me, and I was looking back.
And suddenly I felt a squeezing in my stomach.
My face grew warm. I couldn't breathe.

"Jamila, what are you looking at?" Elias punched me.
And I wondered how the word *boy* could possibly apply
to both my vile annoying brother and the pretty thing before me,
standing on the crane. Pretty . . . boy . . .
in brown knee pants standing on the white crane.

FRANKIE

Well, why don't you go over
and kiss her, Alfred? Ha, ha!

ALFRED

Shut up, Frankie.

FRANKIE

You were looking all gooey
at that girl on the bench.

ALFRED

So what?

ROSSMORE

She's pretty.

EUGENE

Her soul is beautiful.

FRANKIE

Eeeeuw. Yuck.
Go and kiss 'er, then.

ALFRED

Don't be obnoxious.

FRANKIE

What's *obnoxious* mean?

ROSSMORE

Ask Eugene.
He was *born* obnoxious.

EUGENE

I was not *born* obnoxious.

ROSSMORE

Well, you were
a quick study, then.

EUGENE

God loves you, Rossmore.
Even if no one else does.

FRANKIE

What's *obnoxious* mean?

ALFRED

Obnoxious means
acting like a kid.

FRANKIE

So what?
I *like* acting like a kid.

ALFRED

But when you're a grown-up,
you get to do grown-up things.

EUGENE

He's right.

FRANKIE

What kind of grown-up things?

ALFRED

You get to wear
long pants for a start.

ROSSMORE
And smoke cigars.

EUGENE
And stay out late.

ROSSMORE
Drink liquor.

EUGENE
And hot toddies!

FRANKIE
Alfred just wants
to kiss girls.

ALFRED
I'll kiss 'em if I want.
Ain't you never seen
your mum and dad kiss?

FRANKIE
Not since Bertie died.

ROSSMORE
Where do you think
Bertie came from in the first place?

EUGENE
Rossmore!

ROSSMORE
Well, it's true!

FRANKIE

You mean my little brother,
Bertie, came from kissing?

ROSSMORE

Ha, ha, ha ha ha. Ha. Ha.

EUGENE

Ha. Ha, ha, ha, ha. Ha.

ALFRED

Shut up, you two.

FRANKIE

What's so funny?

ALFRED

Frankie, my lad,
I see you are in need of a tutorial
on the ins and outs of procreation.

FRANKIE

The ins and outs of *what*?

ALFRED

Mouth shut, Frankie.
Ears open.
Listen and learn, my son.
Listen and learn.

Sort. Shuffle-shuffle. Slot. Shuffle-shuffle.
Sort. Sort. Shuffle-shuffle. Slot. Shuffle-shuffle.

I notice Mr. March has a ring on his finger.
A ring on the finger of his right hand.

Sort. Shuffle-shuffle. Slot. Shuffle-shuffle.

It catches the light in a pleasing way as he sorts.

Sort. Shuffle-shuffle. Slot. Shuffle-shuffle.
Sort. Sort. Shuffle-shuffle. Slot. Shuffle-shuffle.

"I see you've a ring on your finger, Mr. March.
It catches the light in a pleasing way as you sort."

Sort. Shuffle-shuffle. Slot. Shuffle-shuffle.

"That it does, Mr. Woody. That it does.
A bit of glamour and flash for the postal room." He laughs.

Sort. Shuffle-shuffle. Slot. Shuffle-shuffle.
Sort. Sort. Shuffle-shuffle. Slot. Shuffle-shuffle.

"I see the ring is engraved with letter *M*," I say.

Sort. Shuffle-shuffle. Slot. Shuffle-shuffle.

"Indeed you are correct, Mr. Woody," says March.
"The *M* stands for *March,* of course, you see?
It was a gift from Mrs. March long ago."

Sort. Shuffle-shuffle. Slot. Shuffle-shuffle.

"So," I say, "there is a Mrs. March?"

Sort. Shuffle —

"I'm afraid not," March says, and stops a moment.
"She died just last year. During surgery, you see."

I've put my foot in my mouth this time.
I think of my own Mrs. Woody back home.

"I'm sorry, old man," I say.
"It was not my place to pry," I say.

Sort. Shuffle-shuffle. Slot. Shuffle-shuffle.
Sort. Sort. Shuffle-shuffle. Slot. Shuffle-shuffle.

"It's OK, Mr. Woody. Not to worry."

Sort. Shuffle-shuffle. Slot. Shuffle-shuffle.

"Mrs. March and I will be reunited soon enough.
She left me her forwarding address.
And we both have the same destination label."

Sort. Shuffle-shuffle. Slot. Shuffle-shuffle.
Sort. Shuffle-shuffle. Slot. Shuffle-shuffle.

Sack.

Aside from the ever-present sacks of mail
and a few cross-Channel passengers,
the tenders were now mostly empty.
At last the canopied gangplanks were withdrawn.
With resonant clangs, *Titanic*'s crewmen
slammed the big ship's outer doors shut
and swung the inside gates down with a clatter.
On the forecastle deck, the windlass gears hummed
as *Titanic*'s heavy anchor rose up out of the water.
The machinery slowly hoisted the anchor chains,
link by massive link. The sounds of leaving.
I heard the *ka-ching* of the brass telegraph dials
sending my commands many decks down to the engine room.
Slowly, carefully, the big ship executed a tight reverse turn.
Her bow pointed north as she turned her back on France.
And with a decisive burst of steam-driven power,
this great floating city set out with its cargo of human hearts.
She was the largest moving thing on the planet ever made by man.
Every porthole was ablaze with yellow light
as the sun gave way to dusk and then darkness.

THE SHIP RAT ~

listen . . . silence

follow the rats

      follow the food

         follow the rats
             over the sacks
               across the ropes
                  up the planks

                        follow the food

THE ICEBERG ∽

I am the ice. I see a girl and boy
upon *Titanic*'s deck, their hearts in sync.
The heart, the heart—that little living lump.
A stubborn bird, it never leaves its nest
behind the ribs within its human chest.
One hundred thousand times a day it thumps.
And therein lies the mystery to me:
What magic makes it start? I need to know.
And what sustains it once it starts to go?
The first burst when the egg becomes the child,
a heartbeat starts the human ebb and flow.
Hearts, slow and steady, never fall asleep.
They keep the beat. The meter. Steady rocks.
Like clocks: they tick and tock to track the time.
And when two human lovers meet—they chime.
Within my frozen mass I cannot find
an equal to the heart of humankind.
I'll have my heart when ship and ice align.
Perhaps I'll pick the man they say deceives.
Perhaps the man in love? The girl so rich?
Or better yet the child that she conceives!
Or else the mother needling a stitch
to mend the painful memory of her son?
The tailor who would steal his sons away?
Perhaps the son himself, his heart so young?
I'll have my heart. I have my part to play.
The ice will have his pick of human hearts
as soon as fair *Titanic* plays her part.

April 21, 1912
SUNDAY
Aboard the cable ship *Mackay-Bennett*
ATLANTIC OCEAN
THE GRAND BANKS
685 MILES FROM HALIFAX, NOVA SCOTIA

JOHN SNOW
THE UNDERTAKER

Most of the corpses have gathered in clumps,
each buoyant body a craft crewed by one,
all queuing up as if to start a dead man's sad regatta.

Occasional errant corpses float solo here and there:
a lone woman (unchaperoned) lists to her side;
her right ear dips into each wave as if listening
for the water to speak her name. She wears
an intricate silk nightgown—robin's-egg blue—
that billows at the surface with each sudden southerly gust.
The gown makes the sound of flapping wings,
but here there are no birds. No angels.

Another woman clutches a large shaggy dog.
Was she attempting to rescue a loyal pet?
Was the animal attempting to rescue its mistress?

A dozen men locked arm in arm altogether in a ring.
The soot-faced stokers, the serge-suited bankers,
the bedroom stewards, and the elevator boys.
Did they cry out in unison, or did they sing?
And how long did it take to watch each member
of their choir lose voice and slump to sleep?

No less startling than the numbers of dead,
the countless amount of floating debris:
balusters, banisters, and balustrades,
ornately carved door panels, molding, and trim,
thick splintered planking and delicate deck chairs,
wooden bowls and serving spoons,
multiple bottles of whiskey and beer
and (what is *this*?) a red-and-white-striped barber's pole.
Every item peppered with floating bits of cork.

This cork, so Captain Larnder asserts,
is the insulation from between *Titanic's* adjoining bulkheads.
"This was no simple sinking," says the captain.
And the crew are mostly of the same mind:

      "No simple sinking would have left such a mess."

  "The ship's hull must've ruptured to spill out
  the contents from so deep inside her belly."

     "It had to a been the boilers. Blew 'er to bits, I'd bet."

  "I'll wager she broke up."

And so the conversations go as we go about our work.
All day we keep two boats in the water,
four men at the oars with a fifth at the tiller.
They approach the bodies as gently as the sea allows.
Then the living and the dead begin their awkward dance.
Two grunting sailors lean over the gunwales
to wrestle in each speechless rag doll
while the living men on the opposite side
lean out and away as far as possible,
so as not to capsize and make more dead.

SECOND WATCH

One Last Port

QUEENSTOWN, IRELAND

THURSDAY, APRIL 11, 1912

Feel that wind? Feel the sting of it?

Up here in the crow's nest
there ain't no avoidin' it.
And most fellows wouldn't like it.
But me, I don't think I'd rather be anywhere else.
To me the wind is a mother's kiss.

I don't know who me parents were.
I have been an orphan all me life.
Me mother left when I was a baby.
I'm told she went to a place called Springfield, Mass.
I was brought up in one of those homes,
Dr. Barnardo's, till I was twelve,
and then went to a training school
till I earned my AB's license.

It'd be no exaggeratin' to say
that I've been raised mostly here at sea.
The officers have been me uncles.
Me shipmates are me brothers:
Lee, Hogg, Evans, Jewell, and the rest.
The ship's crew is as close to family as I've got.

You might say the crow's nest
is me own special room. Ha.
Although there's no place t' sit.
And I've got to share it real cozy
with another bloke. That bloke is mostly
me watch mate, Reggie Lee.
He was standing right beside o' me
when we first seen the sun peek up

over the horizon. I'm not good with words,
but I've got to say that the sun
came up red-orange-yellow and lovely.
And if that cold wind was me mother's kiss,
then that big round sun was her face.

I yelled out, "Haaallooooo, Mother!
Thank you for the kiss!"
Reggie, he looks at me an' he says,
"Oww, Gawd! There 'e goes again!"

THE ICEBERG ✍

I am the ice. I've seen the sun arise
for centuries, a hundred thousand dawns.
The sun rose up before the humans came.
The sun will rise long after they are gone.
A man has brains; I envy that about it.
Somehow the lumpy porridge in its skull
forms thoughts that rise like bubbles through the mire
and burst forth from its mouth as a desire:
a wheel, a wing, a gun, a metal hull.
Man would have perished long ago without it.
But can a brain deflect the ice? I doubt it.
Man's fatal flaw is misplaced optimism:
through hubris, it refuses to understand
that chaos is the ruling law of Nature
while order's just a futile dream of man.
I am the ice. I've watched man's primal pride
evolve from gills and fins to take up war,
rise up on sea-foam feet and step ashore,
then sail away on crimson-tinted tides
to spill the blood of kin on distant shores.
You clever ape, adorned in vanity,
survival hinges on one vital goal:
to gather motley quilt squares of humanity
and from the sundry pieces form a whole.
Unite and you might dodge the coming doom
else ape and ice will be united soon.

Of course I am not the man who is actually at the wheel.
That job goes to one of two quartermasters always on the bridge.
Each QM takes a two-hour turn at the helm
while the other tends to the ship's bell,
marking each half hour with a series of clear loud gongs.
If I must ever leave the sea, it may be the bell that I miss the most.
My whole life at sea has been measured out by bells.
This bridge contains a sea captain's mind and soul.
Everything needed to steer a straight course is contained within this room:
Just in front of the wheel is the ship's compass in its binnacle;
the man at the wheel needs look at nothing else.
Telephones allow communication to key points of the ship.
Three polished brass telegraph dials stand waist high,
handles waiting for instructions. I need only rotate
the annunciator dials to relay my commands,
to the engine room, to the docking bridge, to anywhere I wish.

To test the ship's compass, I command that she run lazy S turns.
Imagine if you will being in charge of a ship
the size of a village and feeling her respond to your voice
like a loyal English wolfhound. *Titanic* leaves a telltale
trail of white water in her zigzagging wake,
so large that even the mighty sea
has trouble erasing the memory of her passing.

I will say this with the certainty my thirty years at sea allow:
any absolute disaster involving the passengers is inconceivable.
Whatever happens, there will be time enough
before the vessel sinks to save the life of every person on board.
I will go a bit further: I will say that I cannot imagine
any condition that would cause the vessel to founder.
Modern shipbuilding has gone beyond that.

As we neared Queenstown, Captain Smith
ran the big ship through her paces.
Finally I began to see why this old fellow
with a snow-white beard and a quiet smile
was so revered by those who sail the Atlantic run.
He's a quiet man, to be sure, but he's got the pipes,
and a boiler chest of steam when needed.
I saw him shout one seaman nearly out of his jersey
for failing to secure a hatch fast enough to suit.
But when the task was done to his satisfaction,
Smith gave the startled sailor a knowing nod of gratitude.
I guess that's why so many aboard *Titanic* today
from victualling crew to deck crew to first-class passengers
have followed Smith from ship to ship.

Smith ordered us to adjust the ship's compasses.
He tested her rudder, cutting in wavy lines.
We ran an emergency drill to test the response
of the watertight doors that sealed off the bulkheads
in case there were a breach in the hull.
With the push of a button, bells rang out and red lights flashed
as, belowdecks, the heavy doors automatically shut.

The voice phoned up from the boiler rooms:
"All is working perfectly!"

Then the captain gave orders to prepare lifeboat number two.
The boats were numbered one through sixteen
with odd numbers to starboard, even numbers to port.
We were to swing out boat number two at the ready
just in case some unlucky passenger happened
to take an accidental dive while boarding *Titanic* from the tenders.

As I've said, I'm both boatman and sailor.
I was all too familiar with the lifeboats, and I knew what to do.
I ordered my crew in place to crank out the davits
as I reached across the boat to unhook the canvas cover.

But just as we stowed the canvas, one of the deckhands gasped,
looking down into the boat with wide eyes, and said,
"Sir, I think we've got some stowaways.
Charlie, hand over that davit wrench."
And he swings the wrench down into the boat with a bang.

And even *I* gasped at what happened next,
so taken by surprise was I.
A group of rats came rushing by!
They fell from the lifeboat's drain hole to the deck
and scuttled off to starboard, along the officers' quarters.
I saw maybe a dozen of them.
But to hear the other sailors talk, it was more like fifty.

Happy birthday, Phillips.

> Say, old man, many happy returns.

Best wishes, Jackie boy.

> To long life and a pretty wife.

Cheers, old man!

During my six-hour morning shift on Thursday,
birthday salutations came in from all over the Atlantic.
Phillips said that the *Titanic*'s five-kilowatt wireless
was the best birthday present he could hope for.
Still, it needed constant tweaking and adjusting.
And birthday boy Phillips was a master at this.
He acted quite literally like a boy with a new toy,
and before we had even arrived in Queenstown,
I had learned more from him than I had learned
in all my months at the Marconi Training School.

Phillips's enthusiasm was understandable,
for Marconi's invention was indeed amazing.
Still as a statue, there in the operating room
on the big ship's uppermost deck,
I could speak to the world with a simple finger flick,
as if tapping out an absentminded rhythm.
It was no effort at all really — and yet
the final effect was explosive:

Once depressed, the key would complete
a circuit, which would travel through one thick wire
and connect to four even thicker wires,

which snaked together through a single conduit,
reaching upward through the roof of the wireless shack.
After feeding through a hollow perpendicular post,
these four wires separated and each reached up
nearly two hundred feet into the air, stretching even
higher than the *Titanic*'s four great smokestacks.
Each wire then connected to the ship's massive antennae:
four long spans of heavy bronze cables
that stretched an incredible six hundred feet from mast to mast.
And spread as they were into four perfectly parallel lines,
the whole works looked like the clothesline of some giantess,
wanting only an enormous pair of socks from the wash!

That joke about the socks on the giant clothesline
was Phillips's of course. He was always cracking wise.
His enthusiasm was contagious, and while we celebrated
the birth of Mr. Jack Phillips, we celebrated the birth
of *Titanic* as well. He and she were a good match.

I heard the great ship's engines slow down,
so I sent a wire to Queenstown to announce our arrival.
I began the message as I began them all,
tapping out the official call letters for the RMS *Titanic:*

        M --
        G --.
        Y -.--

each insignificant twitch of my hand
exploded into the ether for a hundred miles in every direction.

It was difficult not to feel like a god.
Difficult not to feel like Zeus,
lightning bolts flying from my fingertips.

Miss Marie Stene
Ørskog P.O.
via Ålesund, Norway

11 April 1912
Thursday

My dear Marie,

This is my last chance to tell you how I feel before I
cross the Atlantic for good.
A door is closing on my old life.
I will write you each day of this most amazing voyage
and each day remind you

that I am forever
your very sincere
and loving
Olaus

Not all of *Titanic*'s boilers were lit for the overnight jog to Ireland.
Meaning I got duty in the engine room assisting the greasers.
Which was why I occasioned to meet an engineer
who gave me a bit of a scare when he looks at me
and says, "Say, friend. Don't I know you?
My name is Shepherd. I think we've met."
I says, "My name is Tommy Hart, sir.
And I'll bet you're just mistaken."
"No. No. I never forget a face. Never.
Have you worked any other White Star ships?"
"Oh, no. Not me. It's me very first time.
I'm new, I am, to the White Star Line!"
"And you say your name is Hart?" says he.
"Like I said, Mr. Shepherd, I'm sure you're mistaken."
He smiled at me suspicious-like, and he says,
"I'm not. I never forget a face."

Just then the command rang down from above
to slow the engines for our approach into Queenstown.
I threw down my rag and my wrench
and slapped the engineer on his sweaty back.
"Good chattin', Shepherd," I says. "But I'm needed up top."

Now, most folks don't know it,
but of *Titanic*'s four funnels, only three is working.
The fourth is what they call a dummy.
It vents the ovens and whatnot from the galleys is all.
And they's a service ladder what goes up
to the very tip-top, allowin' for maintenance and paint.
But I wasn't there for paintin'. Naw, sir.
I wanted to see Scott's Quay come in sight
and get larger and larger as that grand old lady

brought me to Ireland in style, like the king himself.
And once I popped my head out the top—
well—what can I say, folks?—I saw what
God has reserved for the birds.
I heard the wind whip through the strands
of the big aerial strung just above me head.
Sounded like the angels hummin'.

Titanic was too big for Scott's Quay.
Too big for the shallows of Cork Harbor.
So the passengers had ter be tendered out.
One lady, who was lookin' up, she seen me lookin' down.
I waved my cap just as *Titanic* sounded three toots from the hooters.

Oh, it was wonderful peaceful up there.
The sound o' bagpipes came waftin' up from below.
And I wondered what the real Thomas Hart was doing
at that very moment. Probably still nursing a sore head.
Or maybe he's already started getting drunk again.
Sometimes it's best just to stay deep in your cups.
Especially when some thieving bloke has stolen your papers
and set sail, in your place, on the most luxurious ocean vessel afloat.

I suppose he'll eventually have to go home to the missus.
I wonder what sort of excuses he'll use.
Ahhh, who cares? From where I'm sittin',
I feel as if I can see years into the future.
I feel like God himself.
So let the real Tom Hart nurse his whiskey.
Some folks is meant to make excuses.
Some folks is meant to make history.

On board the *Titanic*
11 April 1912
Thursday

Dear Mother,

It pains me greatly to have to write this letter. By now you may have heard that I have taken the children away. I feel in my heart that they are better off with me. Perhaps one day Marcelle and I will reconcile. But the events of the past few months tell me that I must not go wishing after dreams of fancy.

I felt if I waited to act, my boys would have been lost forever to me. I wish that things were different. I wish my love had been enough. Perhaps one day we will patch up the holes like—

I am a good tailor. But I cannot make a suit to fit this marriage. I am watching Lolo and Momon play outside. They are so happy. There is a young French girl who looks after them so I might write.

Oh, Mother. I watch the children play through the window. And I hear the orchestra playing just outside. I am scared. I am struck with the madness of my plan. And what plan do I have? I cannot think clearly.

Please write to Sister. Ask her if I might send the children to live with her in Hungary. They would be happy and safe there. My hope is that we all might be together one day.

Forgive me. They are sounding the ship's whistles. I must post this letter before *Titanic* sails.

Your loving son,
Michel

Rats
in the lifeboat.

Bagpipes
on the poop deck.

Stokers
frightening passengers
from the smokestacks.

And now
Mr. and Mrs. Harper's pet Pekingese
has escaped again.

At least
none of the steerage passengers
went on a fainting spell today.

The Irish
are much less trouble than the continentals.
At least this lot spoke English.

Yes, it was me that played the pipes on the poop deck.
Not Scottish pipes, o' course, but uilleann pipes.
Oh, there's nothin' sweeter. Made for a sweet send-off.
Ya got to remember that most of the lads and lasses
weren't leavin' Ireland on holiday; they were leavin' her for good!

And, yes, it was "Erin's Lament" that I played.
And the tune is full of lament, to be sure.
Though to say the crowd was full of woe—
well, that would not be true at all.

Oh, some of 'em were sorry, I imagine—
but I'll wager the majority of 'em
were sorry not to have left Ireland sooner!

Long ago, when my older brother
would come home with tales
from his long trips out to sea,
he spoke about mysterious sea monsters
and raging storms that ripped sails to tatters.
He spoke about wrecks upon rocks
and exotic lands. Whales leaping.
The high-pitched whine of the bosun's whistle.

Never once that I can recall
did my brother mention filling out paperwork.

So as I signed *Titanic*'s Certificate of Clearance
among all the other forms and mundane details,
I thought about Joseph
and all the things he never told me.
We compile the numbers. I sign my name.
I sign my name. We do the math.
We make a list. I sign my name.

First and second class: six hundred and six souls.
Third class: seven hundred and ten souls.
Crew: eight hundred and ninety-two souls.
Total: two thousand two hundred and eight souls.

These are not numbers, of course. They are souls.

Here's to all the things
we must find out for ourselves.

United States Department of Immigration
Affidavit of the Master or Commanding Officer

I, <u>E.J. Smith</u>, master of the <u>Royal Mail Steamer
Titanic</u>, do solemnly, sincerely, and truly swear that
I have caused the surgeon of said vessel to make a
physical and oral examination of each and all of the
aliens named in the foregoing manifest sheets and
that no one of said aliens is an idiot, or imbecile,
or a feeble-minded person, or insane person, or a
pauper, or is likely to become a public charge, or is
afflicted with tuberculosis or with a loathsome or
dangerous contagious disease, or has committed
a felony or other crime or misdemeanor involving
moral turpitude, or is a polygamist, or an anarchist,
or a prostitute, or is coming to the United States for
the purpose of prostitution, or for any other immoral
purpose . . .

I'm glad I don't have to sign an affidavit
like this for my first-class passengers.
I'd have to ask more than a few of them to leave the ship!

Sworn by me on this <u>11</u><u>th</u> day of <u>April</u>, 19<u>12</u>

<u>Edward J. Smith, Master</u>

FRANKIE
What's that American flag
doing up there?

ALFRED
It's flappin'.
Just like your mouth.

FRANKIE
I thought *Titanic*
was a British ship is all.

EUGENE
Actually, Frankie,
that flag indicates
our destination.

ALFRED
I knew that.

FRANKIE
No, you didn't, Alfred.

ALFRED
Shut it, Frankie.

FRANKIE
You two have American
accents, don't you?

ALFRED
Don't be rude.

ROSSMORE

No. We *are* Americans.

EUGENE

Mother tried
to make us Brits.
But it didn't stick.

ROSSMORE

We're on our way back home.
We live in Providence, Rhode Island.

EUGENE

Our father is the United States
middle-weight boxing champ.

FRANKIE

Honest?

ALFRED

You're pullin' our leg!

ROSSMORE

No, it's true.
Eugene can't tell a lie.
Even a little one. On accounta
he's a soldier in the Salvation Army.

EUGENE

Praise Jesus.

FRANKIE

Wow.

I slept through dinner and through breakfast, too.
I slept better than I had slept in weeks.
I woke up on Thursday feeling refreshed.
I jumped down from my bunk and dressed,
and thinking again of the boy on the crane,
I stopped to put a yellow ribbon in my hair.
My skirt had black smudges all over it—
a result, I guessed, of my fall on the gangway.
I went up on the open deck at the back of the boat.
And looking out over the ocean, I felt calm.
I thought that maybe things would work out after all.
Anyway, there wasn't anything to be done:
we were on a ship at sea; there were no chores to do.
There were no soldiers to worry over.
There was no more packing.
No laundry. No cooking. No cleaning up.
All I had to do was keep track of the money.
The one hundred pounds that Father had entrusted to me.
The money that was tied safely around my—

I froze. I patted along my skirt, to double-check,
the same way I had double-checked countless times before.
The bulge was gone.
No bulge. No money belt.
I swirled around in place and tried again.
No money belt. I ran back down to my room.
I tore through my bedding. My clothes. My bags.
I tore through my brother's bedding and bags.
No money belt. No money belt. No money belt.

The money was gone!

As *Titanic* finally headed west toward America,
I took a moment in my stateroom to peruse
the First-Class Passenger List and Information Booklet.
It was something of a tradition for me, and most everyone else:
a list was always printed up of everyone traveling first class.
There was quite a bit of prestige at stake in whom you shared the list with.
I'd been playing this game for years by then.

Once Mr. Brown and I had made our riches and moved to Denver,
it didn't take us long to realize that first class was made up
of a whole hierarchy of its own. If you were "new first class,"
you weren't quite as first class as the "old first class."

Now, don't get me wrong.
It's not as though Mr. Brown and I were treated like monkeys.
Everyone was civil and kind, but we all knew who was who
and what was what and how was how and why was why.
And if that leaves you scratching your head,
then you know just how *I* felt about it.

Same thing with immigrants. New immigrants
are considered lower class than old immigrants.
So the more generations you are removed from your original
immigrant ancestors, the better off you are.
Now, how does that make sense? In a country
where *every*one is an immigrant!

My father, a good man, was an Irish immigrant,
I'm not ashamed to say. And we were poor but happy.
I know that having money has changed me.
And Lord knows I don't want to be poor again.

But every once in a while I catch myself
actually believing all this first-class nonsense,
and I have to give myself a good solid kick in the backside.
I'm speaking metaphorically, of course.

Still. I kept the first-class passenger list for my scrapbook.
They may have been a pompous bunch of so-and-sos,
but a few of them really weren't so bad.

Reading through the booklet, I saw the following,
under the heading of "Passenger Quarters":

> FIRST-CLASS PASSENGERS ARE NOT ALLOWED
> TO ENTER SECOND- OR THIRD-CLASS COMPARTMENTS
> OR VICE VERSA, AS COMPLICATIONS MIGHT ARISE
> UNDER THE QUARANTINE REGULATIONS.

Now, isn't that a stitch?
Not long ago
I wasn't allowed into first class,
and now that I was in it,
they wouldn't let me out!

First-Class Passenger List
and Information Booklet
RMS *Titanic,* White Star Line

SPECIAL NOTICE

THE ATTENTION OF THE MANAGERS HAS BEEN CALLED
TO THE FACT THAT CERTAIN PERSONS, BELIEVED TO
BE **PROFESSIONAL GAMBLERS,** ARE IN THE HABIT OF
TRAVELING TO AND FRO IN ATLANTIC STEAMSHIPS.

IN BRINGING THIS TO THE KNOWLEDGE OF TRAVELERS,
THE MANAGERS, WHILE NOT WISHING IN THE SLIGHTEST
DEGREE TO INTERFERE WITH THE FREEDOM OF ACTION
OF PATRONS OF THE WHITE STAR LINE, DESIRE TO
INVITE THEIR ASSISTANCE IN DISCOURAGING GAMES
OF CHANCE, AS BEING LIKELY TO AFFORD THESE
INDIVIDUALS SPECIAL OPPORTUNITIES FOR TAKING
UNFAIR ADVANTAGE OF OTHERS.

While all the ladies dressed for dinner,
and the gentlemen smoked their cigars,
I was hard at work preparing my extra sitting room,
placing my empty trunks all around, rearranging the furniture,
just so, setting the scene for a private card game or two.

The plan is simple, tried and true, and very old:
First I befriend Mr. and Mrs. Straus along the promenade.
We become table companions at dinner, where I spend
a good bit on very fine wine—my treat, of course.
Eventually after dinner, Mrs. Straus will adjourn to the reading room,
and Mr. Straus and myself will adjourn to the smoking lounge.
Eventually we will engage in a friendly game of cards,
whatever game he chooses, and with whomever he wishes
playing in as a third or fourth. It doesn't matter.
Because no matter what, I will lose. And I will lose.
And I will lose some more. I may lose for days in a row.
But eventually the voyage will be coming to a close.
Eventually we will play just one more hand—a very large hand.
Perhaps even an impromptu game on the boat train heading home.
And at that point he will lose and I will walk away with his money.

I have an entire week to let it play out. All I have to do
is eat my food. Walk the promenade. Listen to the orchestra play.
And keep placing myself in the proper way, here and there.
Placing myself in the way of the money.

"OK, gentlemen," said Wallace Hartley.
"Let us finish up with Number Sixty-eight,
and, Mr. Hume, let's try to play the piece as it is written.
If you feel that you can improve on Offenbach,
you are welcome to do so on your own time."

Playing second violin in the ship's orchestra
is not great money. But it's steady money.
When Wally offered me the job, I jumped.
I was still in debt for both *Signorina*s Eberle and Guadagnini,
no matter which of the ladies I finally chose.
I was not what you might call rolling in the dough,
and the tips on a luxury ship like *Titanic* can be healthy.
I'm a fairly talented busker as they come—
those rare moments when we might wander
from table to table playing whatever's requested of us.
If you can hum two notes, I can play two minutes.
That's what you call playing by heart, my friends.

And of course I can read the music, too.
I wouldn't have gotten the job otherwise.
I was taught by one of the best, my own dad.
Growing up as I did, the son of a violin mender,
there was no way I wouldn't eventually pick up a bow.

But I don't play "a number"; I play Jacques Offenbach's
beautiful "Barcarolle," the Boatman's Song, from *The Tales of Hoffmann*.
And the passengers listen, not with their ears, but with their hearts.

The Tales of Hoffmann.
Les Contes d'Hoffmann.
Marcelle and I, we saw it in Paris before we married.
I may be a simple tailor, but I know the story.
              (It is my story.)
Hoffmann wears magic glasses
that trick him into thinking a mechanical girl
is actually a woman of flesh and blood.
But I have lost my magic glasses.
(But I have found a gun and bullets.)
No. I'm just trying to protect my boys.
I feel sometimes as if I am a mechanical man.
I feel as if I am no more a man than this ship is a man.
I have a hissing engine where my heart should be.
From my place on the second-class deck,
I can watch the first-class passengers promenading by.
All of them are wearing magic glasses.
They think they are human, but they're really machines.
They think the decks they walk upon are solid.
They think they are in a fancy New York hotel.
They think when they sit in their artificial Palm Court
that they are sitting outside a Parisian café.

I took the name Hoffman from my friend.
(I am not Louis Hoffman. I am Michel Navratil.)
But I am not Hoffman. And I am not a poet.

I have taken the magic glasses off.

Tonight I seen John Coffey for what 'e is!
He's a rat. A rat. A rat, I say!
Well, Johnny the rat can kiss my arse!

I should have known it.
He was just too bleedin' happy.

I should have known it.
Such a gentleman
as we helped that fainting girl
up into the ship.
Such a white knight
when her money belt fell onto the deck.
The money practically jumped into me 'ands!
"Oh, no," he says. "We can't take what isn't ours to take."

I should have known it.
John Coffey.
Such a happy lad
this afternoon as he danced
the sacks of mails onto the tenders.

I should have known it.
John Coffey was lying from the very start.
And he was a better liar than me!

I should have known it.
I should have known it.
I should have known it.

John Coffey's bunk is empty tonight!

.... . .-.

It is only human, I guess, to feel a bit apprehensive
as the *Titanic* steams farther and farther from land.
The passengers can see only water in every direction.
And then the sun goes down, and there is only darkness.
But us wireless men are different.
We look out on the landless vastness
and see the invisible waves of electricity flying
over the horizon in every direction.
The air is full of good wishes. Announcements.
Death notices. Arrival times. And hellos.

--- -. .-.. -.--

In a way, Phillips and I have a kind of second sight.
We can harvest the humanity from the air.
We transform it into words on paper.
We work in six-hour shifts.
Or whatever it takes.
Six hours on and six hours off.
To keep the kcy cracking blue light.
For the next six days, we will be *Titanic*'s only ears.

...- --- .. -.-. .

Titanic's only voice.

The passengers are all aboard. The papers are all signed.
Everyone has found his berth. The sun is going down.
The hard part is over. The rest is all about sailing a straight line.

In the end it is all that basic. Let me explain myself.
Place a dot wherever you are (let's say Southampton).
Now place a dot where you would like to be (let's say New York).
Now, with fountain pen held firmly, connect the two dots
using the straightest possible line. That is all.
That is all a merchant shipping line is—it is a line.
It is a line from Liverpool to Boston.
A line from Cherbourg to South Africa.
A line from Queenstown to New York.

My line has stretched on for years with little diversion from course.
But the last slow miles of my long steady life
will belong to my wife and my daughter and my home.
Barring any disaster, my line will soon end,
with my loving wife and daughter,
at the Southampton Smith house on Winn Road.

So let the Blue Riband Cunarders be the speedy hares of the sea;
I am content to be the tortoise.
This is why my career is so successful, because at the heart of the matter,
my career has been rather uneventful. I am content
to run the straightest line between the two coordinates.
I cannot imagine my career, uneventful as it is,
ever inspiring poets to turn their attention to E. J. Smith.
What would they say?
"Captain Smith, *Titanic* Tortoise! Admiral of the Straight Line!"

It would not make for very good reading.

THE ICEBERG ∽

And so *Titanic* leaves the land behind
beyond the welcome safety of the bay.
Past Roche's Point, from which well-wishers wave
and gulls, like angels, escort her away.
The Viking, Spaniard, Frenchman, German, Brit;
the rich, poor, blessed, cursed, brilliant, daft, or dim;
for centuries they've dared attempt the trip,
drinking wine from crystal, or ale from tin.
Some of them make it, and some of them do not.
Indifferent to all that, the Iceberg floats.
The sun moves low to the west of my mass.
A shadow, cast by my prodigious bulk,
becomes a phantom finger stretching out
to mark the route *Titanic*'s bow needs trace
across the sea's gray-rippled endless face.
The pinnacle of these humans' ingenuity
means nothing to the Iceberg's cold enormity;
the largest moving thing man can devise
is but a trifling dust caught in my eyes.
As if she did not know what lay in store
she innocently leaves her cradle's shore —
as if she'll ever reach the other side.
As if she were a dream, she fades away.
As if she were no larger than a pea,
she shrinks into the vastness of the sea.

April 21, 1912
SUNDAY
Aboard the cable ship *Mackay-Bennett*
ATLANTIC OCEAN
THE GRAND BANKS
685 MILES FROM HALIFAX, NOVA SCOTIA

JOHN SNOW
THE UNDERTAKER

By midday we have found our rhythm, so to speak.
The lookouts shout down directions from the crow's nest
and use flags to signal instructions to the crews in the cutters.
If the water is choppy, they bring in five at a time.
If the water is calm, each boat might risk nine.
I watch them, these hardened men of the sea, variously laugh and weep,
as they go about their chore. To consort with the dead —
to be in such intimate proximity to a body void of life —
makes us who are not dead feel keenly the gift of living.
And so you laugh and you weep and you go about your work.

We on board the ship keep as busy as those in the water.

Each body must be numbered and fitted with a tag.
Each body's effects must be placed into a bag.
Each bag must be numbered with a stencil and paint.
The body stripped of clothing. Examined for marks.
Tattoos. Moles. Scars. Old wounds. Anything
that might provide a clue to the deceased's identity.
With each numbered entry, I attempt some sort of guess.
I must draw my conclusions from the little that is left.
I write the information carefully into a logbook.

I have embalming supplies for seventy at the most.
One hundred and twenty-five coffins for the first class.
And one hundred tons of ice in the holds.
Still, we're not equipped for this many dead.
We've not enough canvas from which to fashion body bags.
Not enough scrap iron to make them all sink.

By sundown of our first day, we have brought fifty-one bodies on board.
And try as he might, Reverend Hind cannot pray fast enough.

THIRD WATCH

THE OPEN SEA

300 MILES OUT

FRIDAY, APRIL 12, 1912

follow the food

follow the food

follow the food

sniff sniff . . . food
food food food—

SNAP!
PAIN PAIN PAIN PAIN
tail pain tail pain

escape scurry escape scurry

painpainpainpainpain

scurryscurryscurry

Snap!

I heard the distinct sound of a rat trap.
My curiosity piqued, I entered the officers' mess
and found that the tables had not been cleared.
All was still, except for a solitary china saucer,
set to spinning by some invisible force.
It made a lazy whirring sound at first,
then gradually became more harried and urgent as the saucer
spun faster and faster and finally stopped.

A large rat trap was lying upside down, empty of any prey.
The trap had been sprung, no longer a thing to be feared.
I considered the empty trap and deduced
that this must be a rat of some experience.
I picked up a steward's silver serving dish
that had somehow fallen to the floor. And suddenly,
reflected in the polished surface of the dish,
I swear I saw the rat flash by, so I turned,
only to find nothing. It had been moving too quickly.
Or perhaps it had not been there at all. But I swear it was.
And I swear it was the very rat I had spotted on the wharf.
But there was a crook in the rat's tail this time.
A crook that somehow reminded me
of Cook Maynard's ridiculous handlebar mustache.

I decided then and there that for the remainder of the voyage
I would refer to the rat with the crooked tail as . . . Maynard.
I would call the rat Maynard . . .

at least until I killed it.

Two hours on and four hours off. I watch. I stomp me feet.
Breathe out clouds into the cold like a bloody London fog.
Wait for Hogg and Evans to spell me and Lee, me mate.
Reggie Lee and me, nesting like two old married pelicans.
Two hours on and four hours off.
If I was more of a thinkin' man,
this lookout business might drive me batty.

Try it yerself. Just *try* to "look out" at nothing for two hours nonstop.
I'll tell you straight: it takes a special talent.

And as a lookout, I've got top-notch vision.
I'm not bragging when I say my vision is keen.
It's a requirement, and we lookouts gets checked regular.
I can look down at the boat deck and count the flowers
that sit on top of the first-class ladies' fancy hats.
Not too many souls on the top deck yet this mornin'—
a few easy promenaders and one speedy lady walker.
You can watch 'em all circle round the decks
and from where me 'n Reggie Lee stand,
it looks something like the planets I studied at school.

I guess that would make me the sun, eh?
I tell Reggie Lee about how the circling passengers
are like the planets orbitin' round the sun.
And us lookouts in the nest are the sun,
and the passengers are the planets.
"Well, if that's true," Lee says with a laugh,
"I'll bet I'm the coldest bloody sun in the universe."

I was up early on Friday, as I am every day.
I like to saunter about the promenade deck as much as any,
but before I do, I prefer a brisk, no-nonsense walk—
a vigorous jaunt to bring the color to my face.
I do like to be rich, but there is a price to pay:
it is difficult to stay in trim when one is not required to lift a finger.
Mark my words: too much money can be a bad thing.

After six laps round the sun deck,
I ducked into the gymnasium, where I was greeted
with a robust, "Halllooo, Mrs. Brown.
Have you stopped in to take a turn at the punching bag?"
This was the vivacious and animated Mr. McCawley,
the ship's gymnasium expert, dressed in his neat white flannels.

My shipboard routine involved a session at the punch bag,
a pastime fast becoming popular among the fairer sex.
"I've come to punch a bit, yes, Mr. McCawley," I answered.
"And when I'm done, I'll have a turn on the wheel if you care to race."
"The wheel" was a stationary bicycle, two of them actually,
side by side, each with a large dial mounted before it on the wall.
The dials showed the cyclists' speed and distance,
which allowed for merry competitions.

I had finished my boxing workout
and had just climbed atop one of the bicycles
when Mrs. Helen Churchill Candee walked in on the arm
of a man I took to be more than ten years her junior.
"Maggie," she said with a winning smile,
"I would like for you to meet Mr. Hugh Woolner.
He is a terribly important investor from London.
Mr. Woolner, may I present Mrs. Margaret Brown,
socialite, philanthropist, and the fastest walker on the promenade."

Our introduction was cut short by Mr. McCawley,
who dragged the handsome Mr. Woolner over to the rowing machines.
Mrs. Candee sat at the bicycle next to mine,
and we watched Mr. McCawley demonstrate
his best Cambridge stroke. Then Mr. Woolner tried his hand.

"How is your room, Mrs. Candee?" I asked. "To your liking?"
"Yes, of course. It is in Louis the Fourteenth style," she said.
"The furniture is designed to look antique, but of course it isn't.
I've written several books on the subject, and I know the difference.
And you, Mrs. Brown, are you satisfied with your berth?"
I told her my room was in the Modern Dutch style,
but I didn't mention I read this on a plaque inside my door.

As we left the stationary bicycles, handsome Mr. Woolner
leaped up to help Mrs. Candee onto the mechanical horse.
Fair damsel safe in the saddle, chivalric knight returned to his oars.
I stood alongside Mrs. Candee as she talked
and set her artificial steed to an easy trot.

"*Titanic* is marvelous," said Mrs. Candee, "but you must admit:
this ship is like anything else that is new and shiny.
It has no heart. I much prefer the antique to the modern."
I whispered, "Your friend, Mr. Woolner, is no antique, Helen."
Mrs. Candee laughed out loud. Then she murmured, "Maggie,
you are bad. Very bad. I assure you, you'll find no scandals here."

"Oh, no?" I joked.

"No, Mrs. Brown. I am much too discreet for that."

Then this grand lady, who was not a day younger than fifty,
flashed me a sly grin and turned her mechanical horse to a gallop.

At breakfast I met a few boys close to my own age.
I knew that they would make good mates
because they could spin in their chairs almost as good as me.
Titanic's big dining hall is called the saloon.
It has long tables with fancy white tablecloths.
But the chairs are the best because they swivel,
and they're bolted down in case some kid (like me)
might swivel just a bit too much and fall over.
I fell off my chair, but the chair didn't fall,
'cause it was bolted down, you see. Mum and Dad
both scolded me, and snooty Alfred rolled his eyes,
but two boys laughed and hooted and they began to spin, too.

One boy's name was Willie and another was Harold.
Harold was on board with five brothers and sisters.
I told Harold that I had just the one brother, Bertie,
but he was dead, so I guessed that didn't count.
Harold said, "I wish that *I* had only one brother,
but I guess I'd rather he not be dead."
Willie had a little brother named Neville, who was just three,
and it made me a little bit low that I wasn't a big
brother to anyone anymore. I told Willie and Harold,
"Being an only kid doesn't really make anything better."

After breakfast we climbed along the edge of a crane.
We ran a race down the wide corridor outside the dining saloon.
We were just drawing out some chalk marks on the outside deck
when a group of officers came walking up.
"It's King Edward," says Willie. "See the white whiskers?"
"No, it ain't," says Harold. "King Edward's dead."
"That there's Cap'n Smith," I said.

And it was Captain Smith, all right. White beard and a long coat
with medals on his chest. All the other officers followed behind him.

"And what do we have here?" said the captain.

"We're chalkin' lines for shuffleboard, sir," I said.

I thought we might be in trouble, but the captain grinned.

"Very well, then, men. Carry on, and keep an eye out for pirates."

"Pirates?" said Willie, but I knew Captain Smith was joshing.

"That's right, son. These Atlantic waters are infested with 'em."

Then the thought entered my brain and flew out of my mouth
before I had a chance to stop it: "Sir," I said, "are there dragons?"

"Dragons?" said Captain Smith. All the officers smiled at that.

"I mean, for real," I added. "You know. Dragons in the sea?"

Then a round-faced man holding a stack of papers says to the captain,

"Sir, we *are* carrying dragon's blood in the hold below."

"It's true," said another officer. "I helped load it myself."

"Ah, yes. Thank you, Mr. Lowe. I had nearly forgotten.

I shouldn't worry about meeting any dragons on this trip.

It isn't the proper season for them, you see.

But we *are* carrying dragon's *blood* below.

The Americans use it to clean bridges and the like.

It's terribly expensive, you see, since dragons are so rare."

"A real dragon? The blood of a real dragon?" I said.

"Dragons are real?" said Willie. "No!" said Harold.

"Oh, it is true, lads," said the round-faced man with the papers.

"Just look." He thumbs through his papers awhile
and says, "Ah, here it is." We couldn't believe it.

He showed us a list of all the things stored below,
all the things *Titanic* is delivering to America.

And there on the list, clear as a sunny day, is written:

DRAGON'S BLOOD, 76 CASES

"It's true," said Willie. "Seventy-six cases," I said. "That's a lot."

"Is that the blood of just one dragon?" said Harold.

"Or do they mix a few dragons all together, like apple cider?"
Captain Smith smiles and says, "Oh, that's just the one dragon.
They're big as a house, as you well know. But you dare not
mix the blood of two dragons. It would burst into flames!"

"True enough," said the man called Mr. Lowe.
"As it is, the blood has to be stored in special cases
lined with steel thicker than the plates of *Titanic*'s hull.
Otherwise the blood would just burn a hole through
the ship's bottom, just like the strongest acid.
Dragon's blood is dangerous stuff."
Captain Smith patted each of us boys on the head,
and he walked on, with the rest of his crew rushing to catch up.

Later, when I told Alfred and the older boys
about the dragon's blood below, they laughed.
"They were just pullin' your leg, Frankie," said Alfred.
"There is no such thing as dragons," said Rossmore.
"Dragons are only in books," said Eugene.

But I know better. I saw it plain as day on the cargo list.
I figured that Alfred, Rossmore, and Eugene were just too old.
I knew in my heart that dragons do exist.
I didn't care what the older boys said. Or how they laughed.
Maybe as boys grow up, they lose their ability to see.

Every morning my off-duty officers and I gather on the bridge,
and from there we set out to inspect the ship, top to bottom.
Purser McElroy usually joins us, as well as the ship's carpenter,
the chief engineer, and my old friend Doc O'Laughlin.
The morning inspection allows me to see the ship firsthand,
and it gives me a chance to get a bit of exercise.
When I saw the group of ragamuffin boys in third class,
I couldn't resist engaging them.

I was not much older than these wide-eyed boys
when my brother, Joseph, would come home with his tales from the sea.
The boys asked if I could use a cutlass, and I had to admit that I could.
It was a skill I learned in officer's training
in the Royal Naval Reserve. Not that it would be of much use
against today's cannon shells and bullets.
They asked about dragons, and I bent the truth a bit.
McElroy and young Officer Lowe joined in the ruse.
The truth is not as intriguing as these young lads might wish.
Oh, I *have* carried my share of exotic and fascinating cargo:
Elephants, camels, racehorses, gold bullion; kings and queens,
dukes and duchesses, boxers, dancers, singers, writers;
Orville Wright, John Philip Sousa, even Guglielmo Marconi.
The list goes on and on. But mostly, a ship's passengers are unknown.
They are poor and by all accounts average.
And the cargo I've hauled over my illustrious career
has been mostly cotton bales and cattle on the way out,
bird guano on the way back. Not so exotic, eh? Bird guano?
And as for danger, from dragons or any other monsters,
I cannot speak of it, for I haven't encountered any.
I've seen my share of rough waters and near misses,
but I've never been in any predicament
that threatened to end in disaster of any sort.

The **MARCONI INTERNATIONAL**
MARINE COMMUNICATION COMPANY, Ltd.

Marconi-gram

From: Capt., *Empress of Britain*
To: *Titanic*
Date: 12 April 1912
Time: 11:00 A.M.

Greetings. Passed through immense ice field in vicinity of 43°28'N, 49°36'W on 9 April. Field ice, growlers, and bergs. Wishing you safe voyage.

The most pressing disaster on a ship like *Titanic*
is a cup of cocoa spilled on a gentle lady's fur coat.
That's what happened as we followed Captain Smith
on the last leg of Friday-morning inspections.
We walked as a fast-moving knot, all business,
and happened to pass a lady reclining in her deck chair.
She had been lost in some dreamy reverie
and was so startled by our sudden arrival
that she flung her mug of cocoa with ruinous effect.

The first-class passengers in particular are quick to forget
that, even as they doze on deck all cozy beneath a steamer rug,
they are actually moving at approximately twenty-two knots;
and that there is a small army of officers, sailors, engineers,
and machines all working belowdecks to make the ship move.
But the ship's officers are not passengers.
It is our job to never forget we are on a ship.

After our tour was complete, all off-duty officers
met at the wheelhouse on the bridge wing
so that we might take sextant readings.
We call this "shooting the sun," for we all point our instruments
at the fiery orb in order to determine our longitude
and thus learn how many miles we've traveled
since performing the same operation at noon the day before.

Friday's reading indicated that we had traveled
three hundred and eighty-six miles in the past twenty-four hours.
As usual, the noon-to-noon run was posted outside the smoking room
so that our pampered passengers might keep progress
or lay down their money to make their bets.

I make it a habit on every Atlantic crossing
to take my chances on the daily mileage pool.
Usually a first-class steward is good enough
to hold the money and keep everyone honest.
In my line of work, of course, it would not be wise to win
in such a public way. And so I always bet wild.
Too high. Or too low. There is a talent to losing well.

On Friday just after noon, I didn't win the pool at all.
But I must say that I got very lucky indeed,
because one of the pool winners for the day
was a charmingly dull fellow named—

Well, it went like this:

Me: Good show, old man.

He: Yes, today's my lucky day. Though it's not all luck, of course.
I make only educated guesses
based on calculations and common sense.

Me: Still, you seem to be the lucky sort.

He: I am at that, sir. I am at that.
I'm not a man who's afraid to take a chance.

Me: I'm just the opposite. I haven't any luck at all.

He: Oh, you must think positively. And remember it's all a game.

Me: Oh, don't get me wrong. I love to play the game.
I just never win. But since I can afford to lose,
I always have my fun. Ha, ha.

He: My name is Stengel. [*Here he offers his hand.*]
        Charles Stengel of the New Jersey Stengels.
        I'm in the leather industry.

Me: Oh, how charming.
        [*I'm using my best upper-crust English accent.*]
        I am Andrew, Lord Brayton. I'm in the, um, leisure industry.
        Ha, ha.
        I do dabble in property and horse breeding—racehorses.
        I'm traveling abroad, quite alone, without servants or staff.
        Nom de guerre. Low profile, don't you know.
        Otherwise the American press can be such a bother.

He: How marvelous. Well, I promise not to give you up.

Me: Allow me to hand you my card. . . .
        Oh, I seem to have given out my last one.
        Not to worry. I shan't bother you another second.

He: Nonsense, Lord Brayton. In fact I insist that you join
        Mrs. Stengel and myself for dinner.

Me: Oh, I couldn't impose. [*This was almost too easy.*]

He: Nonsense. As of right now, your luck has changed.
        We'll have the table set for a third tonight.
        I won't take no for an answer! I'm very persuasive.

Me: Well, then, Mr. Stengel. You have got me.
        I shall see you and Mrs. Stengel when the bugler summons.

After we said our good-byes, I went with all speed
to the purser's office and offered a straitlaced clerk
some incentive money to change my deck-chair location.
My plans had been altered by fate.

Mr. and Mrs. Straus would *not* be meeting me after all.

My new accidental friend would be Mr. Charles Stengel.
Perhaps, I thought, *this voyage
won't end in disaster after all.*

Leastways, not for me.

After the noon-to-noon run was posted,
a rumor began that *Titanic* was attempting
to set an Atlantic speed record.
But anyone willing to bet money on it would have been disappointed.
For the fact is, *Titanic*'s engines are too slow.
I did not—*we* did not—design her for speed.
Oh, she's no tortoise, either. She makes better time than most.
I hope she'll at least match the *Olympic*'s best run.

That Friday afternoon, I was not concerning myself with such matters.
I was double-checking the new sponge holders in the private baths.
The updated number plates on the promenade deck chairs.
The carpet in the captain's sitting room.
My job as head of the Harland and Wolff guarantee group
was to see to the improvements that we had made over the *Olympic,*
Titanic's nearly identical sister ship. I also meant to be sure
every detail of *Titanic* was working the way it should.
To improve upon the *Olympic*'s design, I had consulted the crew.
From the third-class cook to the captain himself,
I let stoker and stewardess alike have their say.
For who knows the ship better than those who work her every day?
When attempting to build a thriving hive, a wise keeper
must listen to the wisdom of the bees themselves.

Because I could not be everywhere at once,
I was in charge of a crew of eight. For myself
I had chosen a cabin on A deck on the port side,
near the aft first-class staircase. From this strategically
chosen berth, I had easy access to every part of the ship.
The interior of my stateroom was simple yet elegant,
with a three-foot oak dado along the lower wall
transitioning into white paneling along the upper.

My room was furnished with a mahogany cot bed
and a handsome mahogany-framed settee.
I also had a small dressing table,
a cane chair, a wardrobe, and a veined marble-top washbasin.
I noted with satisfaction that the electric Prometheus radiator
was performing well. The ceiling lights were sufficiently bright.
And the silver-plated gimbal lamp allowed for reading in bed.

But the luxury of my room was wasted on me.
I was rarely there, so busy was I with the work to be done.
I entered my room only to dress or to sleep
or to consult the ship's deck plans, which I kept there
spread out across the velvet settee—
the settee meant for lounging, relaxation, and long naps.
Naps I never took.

THE SHIP RAT ∾

sleep

safe

hide

tail . . . pain

pain . . . trap

trap . . . danger

sleep

survive

I am not a sailor.
I don't know nothin' about latitude and longitude.
All I know is what I'm about down below.

Titanic, she's got six different boiler rooms,
twenty-nine boilers, and one hundred fifty-nine furnaces.
The forward-most boiler room, number six,
where I work—it's probably three hundred feet
from the engine room, and nine decks below
the bridge, where the captain stands.

Captain Smith may get it into his head
that he wants to stop. So he yells a command
to some other officer, who rings the engine room dial to STOP.
The engineers, they sends the signal to the boiler room,
so us stokers and trimmers will stop makin' steam.

Now, ain't that just the way of the world?
Up on the sun deck, the upper-class ladies and gents
think the captain makes the big ship move
just by clapping his white-gloved hands.

But it's the Black Gang below
that does the dirty work.

Inhale the richness of the air.
Luxurious furs are de rigueur.
Parisian skirt hems. Feet well shod.
It's time to walk the promenade.

Some walk so they might see the sea.
Some walk to see and to be seen.
Six times around, they've gone a mile.
Outfitted in the latest style.

The skirt hems swish. The shoes step-step.
The well-heeled ladies stroll the deck.
They cling to their protectors' arms
and exercise patrician charms.

And at their sides, the gentlemen
(self-made or trust fund) keep in trim.
They're chivalrous. They're masculine.
They tip their black-felt bowler brims.

They walk so they might see the sea.
They walk to see and to be seen.
Ahem. Good day. Good show! Guffaw!
Titanic's first-class promenade.

The scene reminded me of a school of hungry minnows
contemplating the taste of a well-baited hook.
Walking along the promenade, I saw Mrs. Candee, surrounded
by five men, all simultaneously offering their "protection."
When she saw me, she rose from her deck chair,
commanded the men to stay and wait,
then joined me, her arm in mine, for an easy lap round A deck.

Since my trip to Egypt, my mind had been swirling
with the mysticism and magic of ancient civilizations.
I told Mrs. Candee that I was transporting many ancient
figures out of the Egyptian digs en route to a Denver museum.
She in turn talked of her love of ancient tapestries,
a passion she had been pursuing in Spain in preparation for her next book.

Mrs. Candee is progressive in so many ways:
she fights for women's suffrage, she is divorced and happily so,
she supports herself as a writer, and, when no one is watching,
she even enjoys a cigarette. But she is also very old-fashioned.
"I am suspicious of anything modern," she said. "A chair that is
a copy of an antique will not do, for the copy has no heart.
No history. No magic and romance.
I'm only happy with a chair if it has a story to tell."

I said, "I'm happy with a chair that will hold me up."

As we finished our lap around A deck, Mrs. Candee said,
"Mark my words, Maggie—the best is in the past."

That's funny, I thought as I walked on alone.
I was rather hoping that the best was yet to come.

What I most loved about the ancient ruins of Egypt
was the way in which they made me feel more modern.
Not long ago, I wrote a novel set far into the future.
It is the year 2000, and the United States and England
rule most of the world. English is the language of choice.
By embracing science with almost religious zeal,
man has conquered all disease and unpleasantness.
God has given man a brain so that he might create
his own paradise here on earth. With this in mind,
a firm called the Terrestrial Axis Straightening Company
has set out to straighten the tilt of the earth's axis
so that temperatures will be uniform all year long.
One might live in perpetual spring if he chooses,
or else travel to various latitudes to experience
whatever season he fancies, at the slightest whim.

In my vision of the year 2000, mankind has discovered
a new type of energy, called apergy, which uses
the concept of repellent magnetic forces to overcome
the force of gravity. Steam engines are relics.
Moving-picture images and sounds can travel
through the air with the ease of a wireless telegraph.
Man can even fly to other planets: Saturn turns out
to be the final resting place for the souls of the dead.

It may sound far-fetched, but just think
how only a few years ago *Titanic* was a mad dream.

Just think what the year 2000 might bring. What will the world be?
If it were simply a place that would allow me to love Maddie,
it would be enough.

Do not misunderstand me.
It's not that I have a mistrust of the future.
I'm happy ships evolved from canvas sails to steam.
I'm happy my ship has a hull of riveted steel.

But I worry that we have begun to place too much faith in progress.
I don't think that science and technology are the only answer.
What makes a man special is not just his mind, but his heart.
I worry that we will allow machines to override our own instincts.
The Marconi apparatus is truly miraculous,
but it is certainly not essential to navigate an ocean liner.
In the end, a sextant, a compass, and his own keen eyes,
are all a skipper needs to safely cross the Atlantic.

I remember just a year ago, while sailing away from New York,
eastbound on *Olympic*'s maiden voyage,
Tommy Sopwith, the famous aviator, flew his airplane
just over the ship's big wireless antennae in order
to deliver a pair of replacement spectacles
to a first-class passenger who had lost his.
Everyone had gathered on deck to watch the wondrous feat.
Sure enough, the air machine sputtered into view.
And when the pilot tossed out a small brown package,
hundreds of hopeful spectators followed the spectacles
as the package fell in a graceful arc from the sky . . .
and splashed unceremoniously into the water.
With a groan, all onlookers left the rails and went in to dinner.
We sailed on to Liverpool, where I presume
the farsighted passenger purchased a new pair of specs.

As for the airplane in general, I don't really see much future in it.
I can't imagine any mode of transportation
ever replacing the efficiency of steam.

Sort. Shuffle-shuffle. Slot. Shuffle-shuffle.

We sea-post men share a mess
with the young Marconi chaps.

Sort. Shuffle-shuffle. Slot. Shuffle-shuffle.

It's a smallish room up on C deck.
Mind you, I'm not complaining.
The food is quite good.

Sort the sacks. Sort the sacks.
Slot the envelopes. Fill the racks.

I much prefer the regular post
to this new-fashioned telegram fad.
And I said so to the Marconi boys' faces.

Resack the sorted. Refill the racks.
Fill the racks with stacks of sacks.

It didn't take long before the argument commenced.

Sort. Sort. Shuffle-shuffle. Slot. Shuffle-shuffle.

"You showed the young pup, Mr. W.," says Mr. M.
"Thank you, Mr. M.," says I.

"My blood was up, Mr. M.," says I.
"Oh, I saw it," says Mr. M.

Sort. Slot. Shuffle —

OSCAR WOODY ∽ THE POSTMAN
HAROLD BRIDE ∽ THE SPARK

THE POSTMAN *THE SPARK*

Sort. Shuffle-shuffle. Slot.
The post, you must admit, is better.

       dash-dit-dit-dit dit dash dash dit dit-dash-dit
       Wireless beats old-fashioned letters.

Sort. Shuffle-shuffle. Slot.
Wireless is a passing fad.
Letters offer privacy.

       dash-dit dit dit-dash-dash
       Letters are passé.
       Wireless goes out instantly.

Sort. Sort.
A telegram's expensive.

       dit-dit-dash-dit dit-dash dit-dit-dit dash
       A letter is too slow.

Shuffle-shuffle.
A telegram's too brief.

       dit-dit-dit dit-dit-dit-dit dash-dash-dash dit-dash-dit dash
       A letter won't come due to snow,
       or hurricane, or thief.

Slot. Slot.
Wireless is a fad
with no future in it.

dit-dit-dash-dit dit-dit-dash dash-dit
Wireless *is* the future. Remember Jack Binns,
the spark who saved every soul aboard *Republic*
when she sank back in '09? Jack Binns
sent a telegram, not a letter. Speed, old man.
Communication is all about speed.

Shuffle. Sort. Shuffle.
No, young fellow, you are wrong.
Communication is about smell.

dash-dit-dit-dit dit—?
Smell?

Sort, sort, sort.
Here is a letter on its way to America.
It smells of perfume, delicate, yet intoxicating.
And the envelope is sealed; its intimacy is meant
for one man, and one man only. *That* is the future.

dit . . . dit
Uh. It does smell good.

Slot, slot, slot. Shuffle.
Can your blue sparks and hasty memo notes
deliver the scent of a lady in love?

dit
Sometimes, I'll admit, the old ways are best.

Sort. Shuffle-shuffle. Slot.
It's best not to mess with a sea-post man.

dit
Give us another sniff, old man.

When I discovered that my money belt was gone,
I searched every inch of our tiny cabin.
Why was this happening?
If I lost this money, Father would lose respect for me.
He had trusted me, and now I had failed him.
Even worse, though, was the thought of arriving in America.
Without money, the officials would not let us in.

When Elias walked into our room, I nearly slapped his face.
"What have you done with the money, Elias?"
"I've done nothing with the money," he said. "What do you mean?"
"The money belt. It's gone. And you have taken it!"
He said, "I did *not* take it." He was telling the truth.

"Then who? Who? Who has taken it?
How could this happen? Who has been in our cabin?" I said.
"Maybe the old ladies took it," said Elias.
"One of the ladies who helped us get you to the cabin."
The thought of some elderly Lebanese woman stealing the money
was ludicrous. But still, they *were* with me as I dressed for bed.

"That can't be it, Elias. Think. Yesterday is a blur to me.
You must remember something. Someone. Think."

My little brother does not think much about the past or the future,
but he looked up at the ceiling and tried to recall. He said,
"There was a man in uniform there, an officer, when you passed out.
And there were two men, with blackened hands and faces—
I think they were firemen. They helped you onto the ship."

Two firemen. Two firemen? The black smudges on my skirt.
Those smudges were not dirt from the gangway, as I had thought.
Those smudges were not dirt at all. They were coal dust.

When I woke up from my nap,
only to find the men from the purser's office
as well as *Titanic*'s sergeant at arms,
standing beside my bunk, I was shocked.
Shocked and somewhat indignant that they
would for a second think me capable of theft.
I told them, "John Coffey took the girl's money."

"He was acting suspiciously, that fellow was," I said.
I suppose that's the reason he deserted in Queenstown.
I knew from the first, there was something wrong with that one."

Oh, I laid it on thick, I did.
The pursers checked out Johnny's berth
and of course they discovered he had jumped ship.
They set off to the Marconi shack
to wire the authorities in Queenstown.
And good luck to 'em.

By then it was time for another four-hour shift,
so I got up and took me dunnage bag into the latrine.
I was after a fresh pair of socks stowed there,
but first, I stopped to linger in the privacy of me stall,
to fish out the money belt bulging with bills.
Just to make sure it was all still there.
And it was—one hundred pounds, by my count.

Well, what was I to do? I ask ye.
The girl must've tied the belt too loosely.
It fell out of her skirts all by itself, it did.
Titanic is aptly named the Millionaire's Special;
a poor stoker is paid handsomely for his labor.
And even the third class throw sacks of money about.

Stomp. Swish. Pitter-patter. Shrieks and shouts.
The steerage take their walkabouts.
A traveling circus on parade.
Behold the third-class promenade.

Children clamor. Infants wail.
Nappies dry on poop-deck rails.
"Give us a song!" "Come, now, let's dance!"
A chat. A smoke. A game of chance.

They speak, in many varied tongues,
of where they're going, where they're from.
Six months of hard-earned wages paid
to join the third-class promenade.

They walk so they might see the sea.
They walk to see and to be seen.
Their pants well patched. Their skirts homemade.
A poor folks' fashion promenade.

Stomp. Swish. Pitter-patter. Shrieks and shouts.
The steerage take their walkabouts
and talk about the plans they've made.
Titanic's third-class promenade.

FRANKIE
Well, my dad's
the best tool-and-die man
in all of Strood.

ROSSMORE
You don't say?

FRANKIE
He's going to Detroit
to build automobiles.

ALFRED
I'm going to Detroit
to work for my brother.

EUGENE
I hope to do work for
the Salvation Army.

ROSSMORE
Our mom's a seamstress.

FRANKIE
My mum is, too!
I guess all mums are.

ROSSMORE
I'll be seeing my friends
from Oxford Street
Grammar School,
home of
tomorrow's leaders.

EUGENE
home of
tomorrow's leaders!

ROSSMORE

This is the Anthony medal
they gave me when I left.

EUGENE

Not the medal again.

ALFRED

Nice one.

FRANKIE

Wow! Gold!

EUGENE

It's just gold-plated.

ROSSMORE

What if it is, Eugene?
It's still gold.

EUGENE

I'm just saying.

ROSSMORE

My brother
can't tell a lie.

FRANKIE   ALFRED

Salvation Army?   Salvation Army?

ROSSMORE

That's right.

EUGENE

Praise Jesus.

I was frantic with the loss of Father's money.
How could I have been so careless?
Elias kept saying, "You see? Father should have
entrusted the money to me! I'm the man!"

Perhaps he was right. Perhaps I wasn't cut out for this.
In my secret heart, I felt shame at having failed.
I felt anger at Father for placing me in charge.
I felt guilt for feeling angry with my father.

A kind Lebanese man named Fahim Leeni
offered to help. Mr. Leeni was from Tula;
he was on his way to Cincinnati and spoke English very well.
He explained how one of the ship's stokers
had taken the money and snuck away at Queenstown.
Mr. Leeni helped to calm me down a bit.
This poor man had his own problems.
"I was forced to leave my wife, Elsie, in France," he said,
"just as you were forced to leave your father.
But don't worry—you will be together again."

The thought of being reunited with my father
was both comforting and terrifying.
How could I tell him I lost all the money?

That evening I skipped dinner. I stayed inside my cabin.
What will happen once we reach America penniless?
I found a tiny empty space in my secret heart
and wished the *Titanic* would just sink,
and take me with it, to the bottom of the Atlantic.

Miss Marie Stene,
Ørskog P.O.
via Ålesund, Norway

12 April 1912
Friday

My dearest M—

Today, we saw nothing but the open sea. Anna
and Karen did not leave their cabin. Their stomachs are
unsettled, and it makes me thankful that the seas are so
calm. If the waters were at all choppy, these delicate girls
would truly be in trouble.

For exercise I walk with Peter, Sigurd, and Adolf,
exploring the miles of corridors and decks. We walk until
we come to a sign that reads "First-Class Passengers Only."
We walk another way until we come to a sign that reads
"Second-Class Passengers Only." We walk yet another way
and it is "No Third-Class Beyond This Point."

I saw a man standing at the top of a set of steep metal
stairs that join the third-class deck to the second-class
above. There is a little gate there about waist high. And this
man is holding hands across the gate with a lady on the
other side. They say nothing at all. They just hold hands,
ignore the commotion below, and look out over the ocean.

I thought about us, Marie. I thought about the ocean
that now separates us and how that separation grows wider
every minute.

A thousand miles away, I am still your one and only
Ole

Late at night is the best time for baking.
It isn't so hot, and there are no passengers to tend to.
That Friday night, my staff was cleaning up from dinner
and baking the big loaves for the morning.
My cabin on E deck was very near the bakery.
Just one deck down for a quick swig of whiskey.
I had been worshipping at the shrine of Bacchus
almost since I first set to sea as a cabin boy on the SS *Melbourne,*
but I never took a drink before the sun was over the yardarm.
That evening, I had a quick nip in my cabin,
then returned to the bakery, where I spent most of my time at sea.

Like the boiler men belowdecks, we bakers endured the heat of the ovens.
Only instead of being blackened by coal dust, we were whitened by flour.
You might call us bakers the White Gang. Ha, ha.
We were just a small part of *Titanic*'s massive victualling crew,
whose job it was to feed every soul on board:
first class, second class, third class, officers, engineers, Marconi boys,
sea-post men, firemen, sailors, servants, and every variety of steward.
On the few occasions when the bakery was not in use,
I would lock the thick metal doors with the heavy keys
that always jangled at my belt. These keys also unlocked
my secret sanctuary: the flour room.

The flour room was on G deck with the other food stores.
This is where I would sometimes go to be alone
and just stand amid the neatly numbered barrels
the way a wealthy man might stand in his countinghouse.
But that night there was no time. The loaves were cooling on the racks.
The cooks were passing by, carrying sacks of potatoes.
Cook Maynard stepped into the bakery to heckle me for fun.
But now, whenever his handlebar mustache waggled,
I would think of his rodent namesake and secretly smile.

scuttle

scuttle

sniff sniff . . . ?

sniff sniff . . . bread?

sniff sniff . . . bread

scuttlescuttlescuttle

bread

bread

BREAD!

papa is asleep in a chair.
he sits and watches me sleep.
but now i am watching him.

today papa told a lady
that mama was dead.
he thought i wasn't listening
but i was.

in london
we saw dead birds in the gutters.
momon picked one up.
papa slapped momon's hand
and momon cried.

papa said they were orphan birds.
papa said the birds
came from far away.
they came from far away
and they died.

we are going far away too.
papa, me, and momon.
we are orphan birds too.

I am the ice, an Arctic emigrant.
I've seen both life and death along my way,
pushed on by winds and currents turbulent
past inlets, capes, peninsulas, and bays,
each named for brave explorers who got lost.
Another life, another toll to pay.
The ice fox with its fur of winter white,
the ptarmigan with feathers just the same—
against the snow they disappear from sight.
The winter dance of predator and prey.
A polar bear keeps watch upon a hole
in hopes a seal may try to steal a breath.
I've watched the gentle bowheads meet their death
beneath the greedy whalers' barbed harpoons—
the blubber bound to fill Great Britain's lamps,
the whalebone bound for bodices in France.
The snow geese, murres, and buntings fill the air.
The kittiwakes harass the Arctic hare.
Inuits cooking dovekies in a stew;
with teeth worn smooth, an elder woman chews
to make a sealskin soft enough to wear.
I am the ice. I have ten thousand brothers,
all born of Greenland's ancient glacial mother.
A colony of emigrating ice
set sail to reach the heart of paradise.
Soon after our migration had begun,
a million dovekies blotted out the sun;
swept eastward by the Arctic winds they went.
They flew until both wind and wings were spent,
their journey come to this: exhausted flutters
of dying wings in distant London gutters.
I am the ice. I have no need of wings.
I only need the hearts *Titanic* brings.

Friday, our third day out.
Our first full day away from land.
This was the time when the wireless man
feels most at home—*dit-dit-dit-dit dash-dash-dash dash-dash dit.*

From all points of the compass, messages flooded in,
from stations on land or from other passing ships,
and I translated the dits and dashes into language.

`Best of luck on your maiden voyage`

`God Speed RMS `*`Titanic`*`.`

`All good wishes to the White Star Line.`

I even received a relayed message from my mate Cottam,
headed toward the Mediterranean aboard the *Carpathia*.

And *Titanic*'s passengers sent their replies
to New York, to London, to Paris, Toronto,
wherever they wished. It seemed there was no corner
on earth that could not hear *Titanic*'s voice.
During my morning shift, I had fallen behind.
But Phillips, the ten-year veteran, had caught us up
(thirty words per minute!) before his shift was half over.

Messages addressed directly to Captain Smith's attention
were to be delivered by hand to an officer,
and with Phillips at the key, that task fell to me.
"Here's one for the boys on the bridge," Phillips said.

It was from the French liner *La Touraine*.
As I walked with it along the corridor, past the officers' quarters,

I tried not to pry, but one particular phrase
seemed to float upward from the notice . . .

`saw another ice-field and two icebergs.`

It stuck in my mind, for earlier that morning
the *Empress of Britain* had mentioned ice as well.
But that message had not been addressed to the captain.
Had Phillips not stopped me, I would have run it to the bridge,
but now I know to take such notices in stride.
"Nothing to be alarmed about, Bride," said Phillips.
"On the North Atlantic run, we get ice reports
quite often this time of year. But just remember:
they are reports, not warnings,
and unless they begin with **MSG**"—that's Master Service Gram—
"you can take them to the bridge at your leisure.
Paying customers first, Bride. Paying customers first.
Remember: 'Business before brass; customers for cash.'"

A lesson well learned.

The MARCONI INTERNATIONAL
MARINE COMMUNICATION COMPANY, Ltd.

Marconi-gram

From: Capt. Caussin, *La Touraine*
To: Capt. Smith, *Titanic*
Date: 12 April 1912
Time: 7:10 P.M.

MSG. To Captain, *Titanic.* My position 7 P.M. GMT lat.
49°28'N, long. 26°28'W. Dense fog since this night.
Crossed thick ice-field lat. 44°58', long. 50°40'. Saw
another ice-field and two icebergs lat. 45°20', long.
45°09'. Saw a derelict lat. 40°56', long. 68°38'. Please
give me your position. Best regards and bon voyage.

Caussin

The **MARCONI INTERNATIONAL**
MARINE COMMUNICATION COMPANY, Ltd.

Marconi-gram

From: Capt. Smith, *Titanic*
To: Capt. Caussin, *La Touraine*
Date: 12 April 1912
Time: 7:45 P.M.

MSG. Thanks for your message and information. My
position, 7 P.M. GMT, lat. 49°45'N, long. 23°38'W. Had
fine weather. Compliments.

Smith

April 22, 1912
MONDAY
Aboard the cable ship *Mackay-Bennett*
ATLANTIC OCEAN
THE GRAND BANKS
700 MILES FROM HALIFAX, NOVA SCOTIA

JOHN SNOW
THE UNDERTAKER

My search for the names of the dead has begun.

Number the corpse. Fill out the card. Tag the body.
Look for clues. Document the clothing. Disrobe the corpse.
Count the coin, the cash, the checks, the stocks.
Describe the socks. They do not lie. Neither do the shoes.
Listen to the dead men's whispered clues.
Guess the deceased's identity. Determine any damage.
Embalm the upper class if I can. Place the lower classes on ice.
Bag the badly damaged for burial at sea.

"For as much as it hath pleased . . ."

Splash. Splash. Splash.

". . . we therefore commit this body to the deep."

Body after body, I write each entry in my little log,
my Record of Bodies and Effects. *Do not become upset, John Snow.*
So many phrases. Clipped. Succinct. And descriptive.
I must say so much in so little space. I sum up the dead
in an undertaker's grave macabre verse:

SNOW & COMPANY, LTD.

John R. Snow, Jr., Undertaker

Record of Bodies and Effects

NO. 1: MALE. ESTIMATED AGE: 10–12.
HAIR: LIGHT.

CLOTHING: Overcoat, grey; one grey coat;
one blue coat; grey woolen jersey; white shirt;
grey knickers; black stockings; black boots

EFFECTS: Purse containing few Danish coins
and ring; two handkerchiefs Marked "A".

PROBABLY THIRD CLASS

FOURTH WATCH

FRIVOLOUS AMUSEMENTS

---

850 MILES OUT

SATURDAY, APRIL 13, 1912

BRUCE ISMAY ∽ THE BUSINESSMAN

Saturday. Three days since we left Southampton.
Time for the passengers to find their stride.
By now the worries of the world have melted away—
too far from departure to worry about the past,
too far from arrival to worry about the future.
This is when the White Star Line is at its best.
This is the time for frivolous amusements.
Let the Cunard Line race its speeding greyhounds.
Let them arrive in New York on Tuesday if they like.
Titanic is a Wednesday ship. *Titanic* takes her time.
For on board *Titanic,* time stands still and illusion walks the decks.

Outside, the passengers promenade
as if strolling the seaside in the Hamptons.
Indoors, passengers travel the world,
relaxing in the Turkish bath, sweating in the electric bath,
pretending that they're becoming more trim
with before-and-after sessions in the weighing chair.
The Palm Court simulates tea in a Jacobean manor,
with live ivy climbing up the trellised walls.
Descending the grand staircase into the reception room,
the lady imagines herself arriving at the palace ball.
Even the second class are given the illusion that they're in first class.
And the third class imagine that they are in second.
If the day is overcast, the sun still shines
via electric lights behind opaque glass.

This is the time for frivolous amusements.

Yes. I designed *Titanic,* in part, to make guests forget
that they are on a ship at sea: the elaborate trappings
after the fashion of the palace of Versailles.
Rooms in the style of Louis the Fifteenth or Sixteenth,
Italian Renaissance or Modern Dutch,
Regency, Georgian, or even Queen Anne!
Those with the means may choose their illusion.

But there is no escaping the telltale thrum,
that not-so-subtle murmur of propellers and pistons.
It begins in the noisy inferno of the engine rooms
and casts its vibrations to every extremity of the ship
from the chamber pots in the third-class barracks
to the china teacups in the ladies' first-class reading room.

Whenever I feel the slightest self-doubt,
whenever I feel I'm not up to the task,
I need only stop and listen for the thrum
as it rises up through *Titanic*'s rivets and girders
into the very marrow of my bones.

It is the distant drumming of industry and of life.
The calming vibration of the earth turning on its axis.
The certainty of life in my sleeping daughter's breath.
The hum that I hear when I place my ear to a hive.

They told me that the fire had been going since Belfast.
No doubt they coaled up by improperly wetting it down.
The coal wants to burn so badly that it starts on its own.
Now, how about that? More a smolder than a flame,
but that's how it goes. And by that Saturday, the fire was gone.
Though it had taken about a dozen men working round the clock.
Finally the bunker was empty, and I climbed down into it myself
to examine the damage. It took me breath away, it did.
You could easily see where the extreme heat had deformed the metal walls.
It was as if the Devil himself had been trapped inside.

And all the while the fancified folk up top kept on as normal,
for when you're at the top, you're always the last to see the flames.
And if you've got enough servants and working men,
you'll likely never even smell the smoke;
you won't even know you was in danger at all.
There's a dragon on the loose belowdecks:
the coal bunkers are smolderin', the boilers are about to blow,
the ship's dropped a propeller, the stokers and crew are on strike—
that's right, the stokers and the deck crew and the bootblack stewards,
and the cooks and cleaners and the elevator boys.

Ha!

The *Titanic* would come to a dead stop in the water
and she'd likely ride the Gulf Stream halfway to Bermuda
before the toffs in first class started wondering
why no one was putting their dinner on the table.

We shovels the coal
and we puts on the steam.
Like rats, we're the Black Gang
and seldom we're seen.
On deck they forgets
that this ship wouldn't go
without the Black Gang
at the boilers below.

The boilers are dragons,
each furnace a maw.
The Devil's lead fireman.
He lays down the law.
But the Devil forgets
that this ship wouldn't go
without the Black Gang
at the boilers below.

We've fire in our bellies.
We've fire in our 'arts.
We've fire in our britches.
We've fire in our arse!
So never forget
that this ship wouldn't go
without the Black Gang
at the boilers below.

No, never forget
that this ship wouldn't go
without the Black Gang
at the boilers below.

THE FIRST-CLASS PROMENADE ✑

Like figures on a carousel,
around the upper-crust rondelle,
they swagger, sway, sashay, glissade:
Titanic's first-class promenade.

They walk so they might see the sea.
They walk to see and to be seen.
Six times around, they've gone a mile.
A witty joke. A winning smile.

In vogue and cosmopolitan
they clutch their Pomeranians
and walk among the millionaires
or watch from swayback steamer chairs.

Behold the posh aristocrat.
Can you believe he's wearing *that*?
Brown shoes and boater? Now, *that's* odd!
So goes the first-class promenade.

Old money trumps the nouveau riche,
for even first-class has a niche
with which to further classify
each promenader passing by.

They walk so they might see the sea.
They walk to see and to be seen.
They walk in blissful harmony.
They wear their very best facade.
Titanic's first-class promenade.

Today I tried my hand at quoits.
You toss the little ring of rope
in an attempt to lodge it round a peg.

I was at it a good portion of the morning.
And I felt as though I had become quite good.
The quoits landing nearest the little peg win a point.
A "leaner" is good for an extra point; a "ringer" is good for three.
But a ringer that happens to land upside down
is called a "lady" and doesn't count!

"That sounds a lot like politics,"
I said to my playing partner, Mrs. Candee,
who was surrounded, as usual, by her coterie.
"Even if a lady is mentally capable of voting,
her vote doesn't count on Election Day!

"You know," said Mrs. Candee,
"I'm a suffragette as much as you, Maggie.
I've put in my hours at meetings and rallies.
But remember: a woman can legislate in other ways.
For when beauty assails, reason has no part."

Her gaggle of men murmured their approval.

"That's easy for you to say," I replied.
"For you are more beautiful than I."
And in answer Mrs. Candee took my face in her delicate hands,
and she said, "Margaret Brown, you have beauty enough.
All women have beauty enough."

Her gaggle murmured again,
and Mrs. Candee began to hold court
there among the quoits boards.

She said, "If you fling demands at tired men
who hold favors, you don't get them.
If you 'ask pretty,' tactfully choosing
the time that suits the man
and never mind yourself,
only then are you more likely to win.
And this condition will prevail
so long as men are strong
and women are charming."

To punctuate her little speech, she sent a quoit sailing
and it landed upside down and a good three feet
from the pin. It was a "lady," and yet Mrs. Candee had certainly won!
Mrs. Candee could win more points by losing
than I could win by winning.

I am not terribly close to Mrs. Brown,
and yet I know her well enough to know what's wrong.
She is feeling dissatisfied with her money,
because she thought money would help her to like herself.
I don't have that problem because I am "old money."
Old Money figured out long ago that the rich
are just as miserable as the poor—sometimes more so.

From the public and press, I endure
ludicrous extremes of adulation and ridicule.
I am the closest thing to royalty the Americans have got,
but when I raise and outfit my own artillery regiment
and donate my yacht to the cause,
I'm accused of preciousness and playing at soldier.
Yet was I not there, in the thick of it (or at least nearby),
when Colonel Roosevelt stormed up San Juan Hill?
My horse even caught a bit of shrapnel in the fray.
(He pulled through just fine. A wonderful beast.)

I admit there is a certain intensity that my life
may lack because I will never be poor,
because I feel no danger of ever going hungry.
I have never wondered whence my next meal would come.
Indeed I am rich enough to eat a hundred meals
each day for a hundred years and never wash a dish.
Yet what fault is it of mine that I am who I am?
I, and no one else, was born to be the richest man in the world.
It's all a matter of where you happen to be standing
when the bolt of lightning strikes.
I was next in line for the Astor fortune.
I did not position myself in the line on purpose.
These riches and power were given me unasked.
If you were me, you'd feel like a god as well.

I had nearly forgotten, in that moment, who I was.

"Mr. Hoffman? Mr. Hoffman? You're next in the chair, sir."
The barber must have thought I was just a bit strange.

(You are a stranger. You are not who you say you are.)

I have come to the barber shop to shave my mustache
in the hopes that I'll be less recognizable.
(I see you. I know who you are.)
I have no way of knowing if Marcelle may wire ahead.
Of course, this is my right. They are my children.
(Do with them as you please.)

Now Lolo is crying.
He does not want me to shave my mustache off.
Lolo is crying, *"Non, Papa. Non, Papa."*
And perhaps he is right. *(The boy is right.)*
And why should I try to hide my true face?
(You cannot hide from me. For I am you.)

I have done nothing wrong.
(We have done nothing wrong.)

(Stop it! I've changed my mind, you fool!)
"Stop it! Please," I tell the barber, "I've changed my mind.
I have done nothing wrong," I say.

"Of course not, sir," the barber says. "Nothing wrong at all."
"Come back if you like. You know where I am."

(I know where you are.) I do not need to hide.
(We can do no wrong.) I have done nothing wrong.

titanic is the big ship.
titanic is the hot meals.
the edge of the world
outside the big windows.

the barber shop is toys.
the barber shop is dolls
hanging up high.
the barber shop is a razor.
the barber
he wants to shave at papa's mustache.
so i cry.

too many things are gone.

papa is a mustache.
and papa is pockets.
with biscuits. with bullets.
and a pistol. bang. bang.

papa buys me a doll.
my face is wet.
papa kisses my wet face.
momon sleeps and sleeps.

sleeeeeeep
flour egg marmalade
sleeeeeeep
flour egg marma—TUG

sleeeep

tug—

sleeee—TUG
tug—tug—

tug . . . tail

wake . . . ?
   danger . . . ?

        scurry—tug. scurry—tug.
           scurry—tug. TRAPPED.

              scurry—tug. circle—tug.
              pull—stop. push—stop.
            claw—squeal—bite—stop.
            fur-teeth-claw-tail-rats
            fur-teeth-claw-tail-rats
        tails attached. tails attached.
          flour. egg. marmalade.
          tails attached. attached.
        trapped. ratsratsratsratsrats

          rats rats rats rats

           tails attached

As the tale of our stolen money spread,
I began to realize just how many Syrians and Lebanese
were with us on board *Titanic*. Many knew of Hakoor,
and some of them even knew Father and Mother.
All Saturday morning, Arabic-speaking passengers
offered me their sympathies and extended offers of help.
After breakfast in the third-class common room,
I heard a man named Fraza singing at the piano.
He was quite a good singer and very charming,
but of course he was old, nearly twice my years.
A girl my own age named Selini stared at him.
"Is he not handsome?" she said in a dreamy voice.
"He is handsome," I said, "for an old man."
Selini laughed, and as we listened to Fraza sing,
we sat and talked about the lives we had left behind.
It was good to speak with a girl my own age.
I noticed her fingernails, painted dark red.
In my country this was tradition for new brides.
"You are married?" I said.
"Yes," said Selini. "To that 'old man' singing at the piano."
"Oh, I am so sorry, Selini. I did not know."
"No, no." She laughed. "My Fraza is not so old."
She talked with excitement about her new life.
And about the wedding ceremony, which had lasted three days.
She confided how nervous she had felt.
"But Fraza was just as nervous as I was," she said.
"It is a good match. My parents arranged it."
I told her that I would turn fourteen in two days.
I tried to describe how I felt about the brown-knee-pants boy.
"Do not worry, Jamila," she said. "Your parents
will find you a husband soon. After you reach America."
I wasn't sure what to say. Fraza was not so bad-looking.
But Fraza was *not* the boy in the brown knee pants.

-- .- .-. .-. -.-- / -- .

That's "Marry me" in Morse code.

Both Phillips and I had to agree with the sea-post men:
a wireless message is not as romantic as a letter.
And yet a telegram is not without a certain kind of poetry.
Like a poet, a wireless man can say a lot in a few words.
- -.- ... is TKS, for Thanks. --- -- is OM, for Old Man.

> RD means Received.
>
> MSG means Master Service Gram.
>
> GTH means Go to Hell.
>
> The letter for Marconi, simply M.
>
> STDBI means Stand By.
>
> Shorthand for *Titanic* is MGY.
>
> CQ means Everybody Stop Transmission and Listen Up.
>
> D means Danger or Distress.
>
> Q could mean Quiet (but it really means Shut Up).
>
> The newest call is SOS.

> By combining them a little, you can say quite a lot.
>
> CQD: All stations listen. Distress!
>
> TR OM TKS: Transmission received, old man, thanks.
>
> GTHOMQ: Go to hell, old man. Shut up.

Many poems that Saturday shared a common chorus—
from the *Californian,* from the *Montrose,*
the *East Point,* the *Corsican,* the *President Lincoln*:

> Field ice, growlers, some bergs—
> along latitude 41°50' North.

There was no shorter way to say it.

The Marconi boys stand up when I enter the room.
The deckhands do, too, as I go about the Saturday inspection.
But I'm not so unlike these young men.
Even the most grand of men can come from lowly circumstances.
I still slip up from time to time when I speak,
saying "theer" in place of "there," or "weer" in place of "where."
My mother, God bless her soul, could barely read and write,
yet she made sure that her sons all went to school.
It's been a long, long voyage from that little house
in the Potteries to where I stand today.
At over one hundred pounds per month,
I'm one of the best paid sailors on the sea.
With a nice Southampton home away from the docks,
a maid and a cook, spring flowers in the yard.
And when I'm at home, I hang up my captain's cap,
and I sit in my favorite chair by the hearth
with a good-size wolfhound curled up at my feet.
I take this toothpick from my mouth and replace it with a fine cigar.
Because what I like more than anything else
is a good cigar and silence as I smoke it.

But for now I must inspect the decks and go about my duties.
I've earned my position through my own hard work,
not through friends handing me favors.
And if I am paid very well, then at least I earn it honestly.
And at the end of every year, in keeping with White Star policy,
I'm paid a bonus of two hundred pounds
as long as I return my ships in good order.
This year perhaps I will spend my bonus on Mel,
or perhaps her mother, Eleanor, who has sacrificed so much.
Our relocation to Southampton was not popular with her.
But without the sea, there would be no house
no cook, no maid, no Mel, no me.

Us Black Gang are like rats:
if you see one or two out in the open,
you can be certain there's a hundred more hidden away.
But generally we like it that way, shy lot that we are.
We sleep and eat on the middle decks in the ship's bow.
And, by way of a pair of spiral stairs, we descend
to the very lowest deck, then through the firemen's tunnel
to reach our stations at the bins and boilers.
If I wanted to, I might come aboard
and never see the sun for a week,
but o' course that isn't what *I* want.

I like to stretch me legs a bit, and sometimes
me legs takes me places I'm not supposed to go.
Sometimes me legs may takes me toward the luggage holds
to rummage through the trunks and bags.
Sometimes me legs takes me toward a money belt fastened
too loose around the waist of a pretty girl in distress.
But on *this* fine Saturday mornin', me legs
were only in a middlin' mischievous mood,
and they simply took me up top to the aft well deck
to mingle a bit among the steerage folk.
And with me, since Johnny Coffey had jumped ship,
was a new acquaintance, one Mr. Samuel Collins, Esquire,
who was a fireman like meself and a good one at that.

It wasn't long before me legs walked me over to a group of lads
discussing the truth and the blarney about sea dragons.
When it comes to matters of fabricating lies,
I was born to it, else me name ain't Tommy Hart.
And good old Sam Collins, he joined in like Shakespeare.

Hart: Oh, so ya want to hear the real honest truth about dragons?
Well, gather round, boys, 'cause we're only gonna say it once . . .

Collins: For sometimes just the mere talk of sea dragons is enough
to curse a man to a life of warts and gradual old age, it is.

Hart: You'll want to be on the lookout for the "dragon's breath."

Collins: Spot on, Tommy! If you see the dragon's breath,
it's too late. You're as good as dead.

Hart: Now, educated men of science will tell you a lie:
they'll say the thick sudden mist is caused by
the mingling of the warm Gulf Stream waters from the south
and the bitter cold Labrador Current from the north.

Collins: But that's all just cack, that is.
I'm telling you the truth right now: the mist
is called the dragon's breath because that's just what it is. . . .

Collins and Hart: The breath of a dragon.

Hart: For in these North Atlantic waters resides
the most fearsome dragon of them all—
the uh, uh, uh . . .

Collins: The Arctic ice dragon.

Hart: That's right. The Arctic ice dragon.
He lives in ancient caves of ice
dug deep, deep into the glaciers of Greenland.
But every so often, when the winter's been severe

Collins: (as you well know the past winter was)

Hart: and the spring is more than middlin' mild

Collins: (as you know this spring certainly is)

Hart: then the ice from the glaciers breaks off in great chunks.
And some of them chunks float to sea in the form of bergs.
And some of them bergs might have a ice dragon
along for the ride, hibernatin' inside its cave
tryin' to sleep off the summer

Collins: (because as you well know,
ice dragons hibernate in reverse, which is why
you'll rarely see an ice dragon about in the hot months).

Hart: Me 'n Collins had us an ice dragon encounter ourselves.
We was both firemen on the . . . uh . . .

Collins: The *Birkenhead,* it was.

Hart: Of course, yes, the old *Birkenhead.*
Well, everything was fine and well until that iceberg
happens to float far enough south and it starts to melt
and the temperatures start to rise and that's why
the ice dragon wakes up in a terrible, rotten mood.
Well, one day the *Birkenhead* drifts too close,
much too close to the ice dragon's lair.
The beast belches out one vast frigid breath
and suddenly everything stops . . .

Collins: Even the clocks. For time itself was frozen solid.

Hart: The steam in every boiler froze, o' course.

Collins: The burning coals in the furnaces turned to ice chips.

Hart: Even the flames froze solid in midair and shattered like glass.
And every living soul aboard was frozen stiff as a plank.

Collins: Dead in an instant.

Hart: Every passenger. All the crew.

Collins: Every saint and every sinner.

Hart: Frozen like statues,
in the middle of playin' cards, or shovelboard, or dominoes.
The last words they had spoke fell to the decks with a thud.

Collins: Thud. Thud. Thud. Thud. Just like that.

Hart: So if Captain Smith is a smart sailor, and I grant you lads he is—

Collins: Yes, he is—

Hart: He'll keep a sharp eye out for that telltale ribbon of mist.
And he'll watch for the twinkle of "whiskers on the light"
when the very air begins to freeze, because that's the warning sign
that an ice dragon's near, waitin' in 'is cave o' ice.

Collins : So if the boys in the crow's nest don't keep good watch,
we're, all of us, as good as dead.

Hart: And *that's* the truth . . .

Collins and Hart: about ice dragons.

Mum had washed some clothes in our cabin's little sink
and sent Alfred and me out to dry them on the ship rail.
Alfred held out a pair of long trousers that Mum
had made for him from an old pair of Dad's.
A kid from another country came over,
to hang out some laundry to dry as well.
He was the brother of the girl that Alfred fancied.
He spoke only a few words of English,
but that sure didn't keep him from talking!
He told Alfred his name was "Eee-lee-us," from Lebanon.
Alfred said his name and they both shook hands.
Alfred was much nicer to other boys than he was to me.
Alfred and Elias were hanging laundry on the rail
when two stokers came right up to us.
I don't know why they picked us to talk to
from all the other grown-ups and children on the deck,
but, boy, am I glad I got to learn all that they knew—
about dragons. Ice dragons in particular.

I could see Alfred and the boy from Lebanon roll their eyes.
But I didn't care. Here were two real sailors—
well, almost sailors—who'd actually seen a dragon.
When they finished explaining about the *Birkenhead,*
and how it'd been frozen by an ice dragon,
the stoker named Tommy handed me an odd-shaped lump.
It was something like a rock, but smooth in places
as if it had been melted then frozen like ice.
He said it was all that was left of an ice dragon's heart.
He said he got it from another dragon hunter like me.
He said I could keep it! Then he shook my hand.

"Codswallop," said Alfred. "It looks like a clinker to me."
"It's the heart of an ice dragon, boy," said the stoker named Tommy.

That's when Alfred asked the stokers,
"If every living soul dies from an ice dragon's breath
how is it that you two gents survived to know so much?
Why weren't you both frozen dead as well?"

But before they could answer,
Captain Smith came stomping over on his morning inspection.
He took the two stokers aside,
and though I couldn't understand what he was saying,
I could tell it wasn't good.
After he sent the two stokers away,
Captain Smith turned to me and asked,
"Well, son. Have you spied any dragons, then?"

"No, sir. Not yet," I said.

"Not to worry, son," he said.
"I doubt you'll encounter any on this trip.
As I told you before, they *are* out of season."

"Yes, sir," I said, holding tight
to the dragon's heart in my pocket.

Then Captain Smith turned to walk away,
followed by his men. And I heard him say,

> "Pass on the order to the lead firemen and chief stewards,
> and be quite clear: any member of the crew
> found mingling with the passengers
> will be fined five pounds!"

When I first saw Elias talking to the boy—
the boy, the boy in the brown knee pants—
I was terrified. He's doing this on purpose.
He was trying to stir up trouble.

Leave it to Elias to approach a total stranger.
Within the passing of barely half an hour,
my brother had spoken to a couple firemen
and to *Titanic*'s Captain Smith himself.
All while I sat shyly reading my book.

So I took a deep breath and I walked across the deck
to meet the boy in the brown knee pants.
I approached as if, of course, to speak to Elias.
I was not being forward. I was walking.
Speaking Arabic, Elias introduced me
to Alfred. al-Freed. Al-Frid. Alf. Rid. alf-Rid.
The brown-knee-pants boy was alf-Rid.
He had a name and it was: alf-Rid.
Then Alfred said my name: "Jah Mee-lah."
And all of a sudden I had a name. It seemed
I had never had a name until that morning.
"Guess what, Jamila?" my clever brother said.
"Alfred's birthday is tomorrow,
just one day before your own.
He gets to wear long pants."

Alfred's young friend, whose name was Frankie,
lifted a pair of pants from their laundry basket.
Alfred's face turned red, and he reached out
to take back the britches.

That's when
something caught my eye. Something in the basket
where the trousers had been. My blood ran cold.
My heart stopped beating for a second.
And Elias gasped and yelled, "The money belt!"

For there it was, the missing money belt.
Hidden in the basket of the boy named Alfred.
He had been there on the crane the day
that I fainted. He had taken the money.
All the while, I thought the boy was looking at me.
I thought—but all the while—he—

I reached down to pick up the belt
that held my father's trust.
I counted it out slowly to confirm
my father's trust was all still there.
Then I raised my hand
and slapped brown-knee-pants boy across his face.

I thought, *What have you done?*

I said I was sorry.
I burst into tears.
I ran away in shame.

FRANKIE
Wow, Alfred.
Why did that
girl clout you?

ALFRED
I've got no idea.

ROSSMORE
It's that money belt.
She thinks you took it.

EUGENE
Are you OK?
Wow.

FRANKIE
Wow.

ALFRED
I think so. Wow.

ROSSMORE
Wow's right.
She's really pretty.

FRANKIE
Pretty?

ALFRED
Yes, she is.

ROSSMORE

I think she likes you.

ALFRED

Really?

ROSSMORE

Absolutely.

FRANKIE

But the girl
clouted him!

ROSSMORE

Because she likes him.

ALFRED

She seemed mad.

EUGENE

She *was* mad.

FRANKIE

Really mad!

ROSSMORE

It's clear as day to me.
The girl likes him.

FRANKIE

Why didn't you
hit her back?

ALFRED

You don't hit girls.

ROSSMORE

You don't hit girls.

EUGENE

You don't hit girls.

FRANKIE

Even if they
clout you
for no good reason?

EUGENE

Especially then.
You must turn
the other cheek.

ROSSMORE

I'm telling you.
The girl likes him.

ALFRED

She's something.

FRANKIE

I'm glad she doesn't
like *me*. Ouch.

"It is a mystery, Jamila," said Mr. Leeni.
"The English boy says he doesn't know
how your money got into his basket."
Mr. Leeni had come to my cabin to comfort me.
"I believe him," he said. "As does the sergeant at arms.
Elias believes he is not responsible, either.
We all believe he is telling the truth.
Your money belt could have gotten misplaced
among the steamer rugs. What matters is
you've got the money back. You should be glad."

I couldn't explain to Mr. Leeni what really mattered.
I was so relieved to have found the money,
but I had behaved horribly to the boy.
I could never look at him again. It's true.
"I'm sure that God is punishing me somehow,"
I said. Mr. Leeni said nothing, but shuffled his feet.
So I ran from my cabin down the long hall
to the ladies' water closets. The first stall was locked.
Engaged, it read. Even the lock seemed to mock me.
I tried the next: *Engaged.* The next: *Engaged.*
Engaged. Engaged. Then finally the last
door left. And still the lock mocked: *Vacant.*

Thomas Hart ∽ The Stoker

Well, ol' Tommy Hart was goodly rich,
leastways, he *was,* for the better part of a day.
You might ask how a man what strikes it rich
would turn about an' give the riches back.
You might say I had a sudden change o' Hart!
Ha, ha! A change inspired by the Devil himself.
There I was at me boiler down below,
keepin' the coals, not too high, not too low.
But just the touch that only stokers know.
Each furnace gets four shovelfuls, laid on,
a fresh black blanket atop the fiery red.
Once the black coal heated up red hot,
I'd thrust me slice bar along that grate
to raise the worthless hidden clinkers up
and rake them out onto the floor to cool.
Oh, what a fool I was, a fool I was,
when settin' me shovel aside, I used me hands,
with only the protection o' canvas gloves,
to pick those cursed burning clinkers up!
But lo and behold, I felt no lick of pain.
I picked more up, and this time without gloves
and yet the burning heat felt cold as ice,
I tried it thrice a dozen times, I did.
Each time I had the same result: no pain.
I placed me hand again' the furnace door.
I rested me cheek again' the boiler's side.
I opened the door and thrust me whole head in
and rested there with the coals as me pillow!
Like Daniel, the flames consumed me not.
At first I felt immortal-like, I did,
and sort of like a god — the one what makes
the armor and might shoe the horse o' Zeus.

But lookin' down, I saw I'd grown a tail!
And then I felt the horns atop me head!
I was fireman for the pits of bloody hell!
Then I feels the sting of a whip across me back.
And there 'e is—Beelzebub himself.
An' he says to me, "You're mine now, Tommy Hart."
But I says, "Sir, you've made a big mistake,
for I'm not Hart no more than I'm a rat."
Then Satan laughed and said, "I guess you'll do.
You chose to take your wages in advance,
and so you chose to take your chance with me:
four on, four off for all eternity."

I then woke up and found that I'd been dreamin'.
My chat with the Devil had all been in me mind.
So I walked to the head to splash water in me face
and laughed at meself for being so easily spooked.
And that's when I noticed the clinkers in me pocket.
Now maybe I *had* put 'em there me absentminded self,
during the early shift before I took me nap.
Or perhaps it was the Devil what put 'em there.
Either way, the message was clear enough to me.
So when I finally spotted the foreign boy,
I wasted no time cooking up a way
to slip the money belt among his clothes.
My mortal soul no longer on the block,
I stayed awhile to yarn about the dragons.
Then the captain came and ordered us below.
It was a narrow squeak, I'll have you know!

squeak squeak

      screech squeal

            rats rats rats rats

tails . . . attached

   tug—tug—

tails . . . attached

                 scurry—tug. circle—tug.
         pull—stop. push—stop.
                   claw—squeal—bite—stop.
fur-teeth-claw-tail-rats
fur-teeth-claw-tail-rats
tails attached. tails attached.

flour. egg. marmalade.

trapped in the flour barrel
scratch scratch scratch

               scurry—tug. scurry—tug.

                         scurry—tug. TRAPPED.

Miss Marie Stene
Ørskog P.O.
via Ålesund, Norway

13 April 1912
Saturday

My darling M—

Today is a lazy day. Wrote a letter to my sister, Inga.
Again this morning the young couple I've been
watching had a rendezvous at the gate at the top of the
stairs between third and second class, open decks. I
saw the man at dinner and found out he's a Swede! His
name is Nils. And like me, he has established himself in
America. He is now returning to the U.S. after a visit to his
homeland! Sound familiar, eh?
And guess what? The woman he has been meeting
with all this time is his fiancée! The girl's name is Olga.
She so hated the thought of traveling on the sea that Nils
bought her a second-class cabin ticket so that she might
have a better accommodation. Ha.
Should I have done the same for you, my love?
No. I think we both know what your answer would
have been.

Yours,
Olaus

Imagine a game of four players in which
three are working together (albeit secretly) as a team.
The object is to clean out the outside man (our "client")
and split the winnings three ways once the voyage is over.
It's difficult for a client to put the finger
on any one man when no one man came out a clear winner.

But on this trip I unfortunately had to work alone,
which forced me to be more cautious and more creative.
I had an idea. A really big idea. And if it worked,
I stood to make thousands. And Mr. Charles Stengel
of the New Jersey Stengels would help me do it.
It would require many days of relentless deception on my part.
In fact I figured the main payoff might not come until long after
Titanic had arrived in New York. Until then
I needed to proceed slowly. I had all the time in the world.

I would begin by ensuring that Mr. Stengel knew
beyond a shadow of a doubt
that I was *not* a con man out to steal his money.
And so, after lunch in the smoking room,
we were simply two passing acquaintances,
one a wealthy American leather man,
the other a titled English horse breeder,
playing at a casual game of cards. The game went on
for an hour or so, with Stengel mostly winning.

Then, as the dinner hour approached,
Mr. Stengel looked at his watch in a slightly worried way.
I knew from experience that Stengel might be anxious
to return to Mrs. Stengel, who had a dim view of gambling.
(Oh, how I love it when the wife doesn't know.)

Me job as lookout allowed me to watch
all kinds of people: poor, well off, and bloody rich.
The ladies and gents who's got money
can be just as unhappy as thems that go without.

Take me nest mate, Lee. All the money in England
couldn't bring back all he had lost on accounta his drinkin'.
Oh, he finally did stop, but by then it was too late.
A life is a lot like a steamer that way:
you can cut the engines, but the big ship
will take her own sweet time 'fore she'll come to a stop.
And by then you've most likely hit the rocks.

I can see, even without binoculars,
how *Titanic*'s crew ain't so different from the passengers.
And how the first-class passengers ain't so different
from the second-class or the third. They all use the loo.
They all go in to dinner. They all laugh and cry.
They all have a future. They all have a plan.
They all hold hands with their little ones.

I'm a professional watcher, you see.
I'm not always so good with words.
But I can tell a lot about people
just by watching them going about their day.
And from where I sits in the crow's nest,
a rich man and a poor man looks equally small.

"Let us drink to the mighty *Titanic*."

So said the good doctor O'Laughlin
over dinner in the first-class saloon.
He joined me for dinner frequently,
as did Captain Smith and Mr. Andrews.
Tonight I had the lamb (with mint sauce) and a good cabernet.
Andrews had a glass, too. The doctor had a few.
The good captain had nothing to drink at all
and toasted *Titanic* with simple water.

"Let us drink to the mighty *Titanic*."

It seemed a simple gesture, yet in my eyes, it meant the world.
For I couldn't help but feel that they were raising their glasses to me.
I had been opposed at first to the forced merger
of White Star with J. P. Morgan's shipping conglomerate.
But I looked ahead and saw the danger awaiting us if we were to refuse.
White Star was not prepared to survive
the inevitable price war that would follow.
So rather than endure the defeat of handing over
my father's family business to the Americans,
ten years later I was aboard the largest, most celebrated
ship in the world. Not a Cunard ship. But a White Star ship.
A ship that I envisioned and built.
So perhaps you will excuse me if I toasted with too much zeal.
We had sailed through turbulent and unpredictable waters,
and before us it looked like smooth sailing at last.
It seemed the danger had finally passed.

"Hear, hear. To the mighty *Titanic*!"

The Saturday evening orchestral concert had come to a close.
Passengers clapped politely and began to drift off.
After a long day of playing for both first and second classes,
I was still no closer to choosing between my two violins.
The Eberle was easy to play, with a rich, full tone in general.
And it had an E string that shone out like a star.
The Guadagnini's string response was immediate and clear,
from whispering pianissimo to robust fortissimo.
Neither instrument produced nasty wolf tones.
Both were as finely constructed as the *Titanic* herself:
with inlaid purfle along the edges to discourage cracks.
A crack that opens up in a violin can kill the tone
just as a crack in a ship's hull can kill everyone aboard.

All day I did my best to allow each instrument to speak.
Swept up as I was in my passion to hear each violin's voice,
I *may* have embellished a "number" or two, or maybe more.
Needless to say, the celebrated White Star orchestra leader
was not pleased with my "excessive musical tangents."
Mr. Wallace Hartley, as you know, never fails to cross his *t*.

"Mr. Hume, believe me," Wally said as we packed up to leave
the first-class reception room.
"I know the importance of choosing a life instrument.
But while aboard *Titanic,* I want you to consider *this* instrument as well."
With that he produced a pair of scissors from his pocket.
"A scissors?" I said.
"Next time you are tempted to add notes
to the company numbers, remember my scissors.
If you fail to cut out the extra notes,
I promise you, I will cut out a portion of your paycheck."

It *was* a bit dramatic, yet I must admit it got my attention.
Money is a constant worry, and I need it
to pay for whichever violin I choose. Plus, of course,
my father relies on me sendin' my bit to Dumfries to help out.
Soon I'll have Mary and a little one to feed.
And no, I can't afford to just keep both instruments.
All told, I was in debt nearly four hundred pounds.
I would have to sail across the Atlantic a hundred times to make it up!
And of course I will have to sell the loser to help pay for the winner.

With Wally at every turn threatening to use his scissors,
I needed some other way of testing the two violins.
I needed to experience the full range of what these ladies could play.
I promised Wally that I'd behave myself,
at least during official White Star orchestra time.
But I never said anything about behaving myself on my *own* time.
So I decided I'd take the *Signorina*s Eberle and Guadagnini
on a little outing to an entirely different musical testing ground

called steerage!

Our game of cards had resumed after dinner,
poker just for two in my private sitting room.
"Better make this the final hand, Lord Brayton," Stengel said.
"Mrs. Stengel will be worried if I disappear for too long."

"Cheers, old man," I said. "Of course I didn't notice the time.
We'll make this the last hand. As you wish."

I laid down two pair: two queens and two kings.
"I think I've finally got you now, Stengel," I said.
Then he smiled and laid down a nice full house
and won the entire pot, about five hundred dollars.

Stengel seemed pleased and began to gather his winnings.
I stood to say my gracious good-bye, but then,
as if the idea had just come into my head, I said,
"How about double the pot on a single card?"

"How's that?" Stengel asked. His interest was piqued.
"We each turn over one card. The low card wins.
Double the entire pot." I tried to sound merry and impulsive.

Stengel hesitated.

"Of course you don't want to risk it. I was being foolish," I said.
I pretended to be embarrassed.
"No. Of course not, Lord Brayton," Stengel stammered.
"I just don't have that sort of cash. I'd have to write a check."
"Of course, Mr. Stengel. I must apologize. A rude idea on my part."

"Low card wins," Stengel said with new resolve.
"Double the pot. Let's give it a go!"
I even allowed him to shuffle the deck.

As I stepped into the wheelhouse, reporting for duty,
the quartermaster at the wheel said,
"The Storm King didn't earn his name
sailing in waters as still as this."
Because of Captain Smith's history of navigating
through some of the worst possible weather,
the newspapers had dubbed him the Storm King.
"No," I said. "Crossing this calm isn't bound to make the papers."

The quartermaster, named Hichens, was a talker.
"I'm telling you," he said, "something's not right.
The weather is too quiet for this time of year.
It gives me the willies, it does." He sounded ominous.
"Not to worry, Hichens," I said. "Just enjoy the easy ride
while you've got it." But in truth, I was spooked as well.

Although this was my first Atlantic crossing,
every sailor knew that April was a time for strong winds
and relentless rain squalls in these waters.
But as bitter and harsh as the winter had been,
it seemed that the spring was going to be just
as uncharacteristically warm and mild.
It was enough to give any sailor "the willies."
I, for one, am most at home when the sea makes its presence known.
The rocking of a boat is like a lullaby to me.
I find it impossible to sleep in a dead calm.
So, as the sunlight slipped away, my only comfort
was the wind created by *Titanic* herself.
If not for this (and the vibrations of distant engines
speaking to me through the soles of my shoes),
I would have wondered if I was really on a ship at all,
or if I was just an apprentice,
in a safe and tidy little shop back in Wales.

Our evening of gentlemanly wagers had come to this:
two cards would determine the winner.
Lowest card of the two earns double the pot.
Stengel is actually licking his lips. This is too good.
I turned over the first card: the king of hearts.
Stengel's eyes lit up. I let out a convincing sigh.
Stengel turned over his own card next: the ace of spades.
This particular card had appeared many times
in Stengel's hands within the past hour.
Now, however, the ace of spades did not evoke
Stengel's usual whoop and sheepish grin.
"Tough break, old man," I said. "And just at the very last."
He tried his best to look nonchalant
as he opened his draft book, made out the check,
and signed his name: one thousand American dollars.
I noted the color, *pretty pale-blue paper,*
and I placed the check in my left jacket pocket.
"No hard feelings, then?" I said.
Stengel stammered, "Oh. Well. Of course . . .
no hard feelings. It's all just part of the game, of course."
But Stengel could not hide his drooping shoulders and heavy feet.
I had seen this sort of sorrow before. It stews for two hours,
maybe two days, and then it turns to anger. But by *that* time
I have usually made my exit—at least when I'm on land.

That's why, at just the last minute, I cleared my throat,
and I said, "I'll tell you what, Stengel. Hold on just a moment."
And without further fanfare, I removed the pale-blue check
from my jacket and ripped it up as Stengel watched in surprise.
Then in a dramatic improvisation that impressed even me,
I stepped into my private bathroom and flushed the shreds down the toilet.

Mr. Stengel and I were both laughing now.

My client had watched me tear up his check and flush it.

I said, "I don't want you to think that I care about the money.

Our new friendship is worth much more to me."

Our friendship will be worth much, much more, indeed.

Stengel shook my hand. He thanked me.

"Of course," I said, "I don't mean to imply that you need my charity."

"Of course not," Stengel said. "But thank you all the same.

You've made a kind and magnanimous gesture."

And just to assure ourselves that the money did not matter,

we divided the final pot of cash into two equal portions.

Then "Good night, Lord Brayton," said my client.

"Oh, please do call me by my Christian name: Andrew."

"Very well, then, Andrew. See you tomorrow at dinner, I hope."

Mr. Stengel left my cabin, whistling. I began to undress for bed.

I reached into my left jacket pocket and pulled out Stengel's check.

His penmanship was firm. The script of a man in control.

Of course the check I had torn up and flushed had been a blank.

I always kept the blank light-blue checks in my left jacket pocket.

Had Stengel filled out a check on brown paper,

I would have placed it in my right jacket pocket, folded just so.

A gray check would have gone into the pocket of my vest.

In fact I had blank checks of every imaginable color and size

placed in every pocket, as well as a cigarette case, a change purse, and a diary.

In this way I could appear to rip up nearly any check I was offered.

A client who saw me tear up what he thought was his check

wouldn't think it necessary, once we reached port, to block payment.

In most cases I could leave my client's bank with cash in hand

before the client had even gathered his luggage to leave the ship.

Saturday night and my shift finally ended.
I got up and stretched as Phillips put on the phones.
I had barely kept pace with the deluge
of outgoing messages from first-class passengers
with money to spend on a whim.

Eileen. Have cut short our romp in Egypt. Helen
gone on to London. Tell Lawrence Jr. Grandmother
Margaret on the way. Mother.

-. . .-- ...

Enjoying rest. Love Adolphe.

-. . .-- ...

Meet Waldorf-Astoria Wednesday night. My treat.
W.E. Carter.

-. . .-- ...

Dearest. Sea calm. Food delicious. Very busy
here. Kiss for Miss Elizabeth. Tommy.

-. . .-- ...

Vincent. New York by Wednesday, 17. Honeymoon
splendid. Pyramids still standing. Madeleine
sends love. Good news to relate. Kitty accepted
into *Titanic*'s Canine Society. Ha. Father.

I changed into pajamas and fell into a deep exhausted sleep,
only to be awoken by Phillips's loud cursing.
Half dazed, I stumbled out of bed to find him bent over the apparatus.
"What is it?" I asked.
"I think it's the damned condensers," Phillips said.
"The whole bloody system is down."
To remove and examine the condensers was no simple task.
The clock read 11:00 P.M.
This promised to be a long night for Phillips.
"At least the passengers are turning in," I said.
"There should be no more urgent messages to send."

"Are you daft, old man?" Phillips laughed.
"What if Mr. and Mrs. Harper need to inform
the papers that their beloved mutt, Sun Yat-sen,
has just taken a midnight pee at sea?"

Phillips kept talking and laughing
as he set about removing the condensers.
"I can see the headlines now:
'*Titanic* Canine Springs a Leak!'"

And I add:
"'Pampered Pekingese Pooch Poops on the Poop Deck!'"

"Ha, ha, ha. Oh, well done, Bride," Phillips said
as he launched into his work. "Well done, old man!"

Sort. Shuffle-shuffle. Slot. Shuffle-shuffle.

"Late night, Mr. March. What say we knock off?"
"Agreed, Mr. Woody. Let's knock off for the night."

Sort. Sort. Shuffle-shuffle. Slot. Shuffle-shuffle.

"I had a brother named John who died sorting mail," says I.
"I'm sorry to hear it, Mr. Woody," says March.
"Of course, he was with the Railway Post," I say.
March says, "I daresay that demands a moment of silence."
"You're right, of course, Mr. March. You are."

Sort. Sort. Shuffle-shuffle. Slot. Shuffle-shuffle.

"Of course, it's safer at sea than on railway," I say.
"I daresay you're right, Mr. Woody," says Mr. M.
"Been sorting at sea almost two years now," I say.
"I'm in my eighth year now myself," says Mr. March.

Sort. Shuffle-shuffle. Slot. Shuffle-shuffle.

"I've been in seven sea disasters," says Mr. March.
"Seven disasters? In seven years?" I say.
"Yes. I'm in my eighth year now," says March.
"No disasters yet?" I say.
"Not yet, Mr. Woody. No, not yet."

Sort. Sort. Shuffle-shuffle. Slot. Shuffle-shuffle.

"Of course, it *is* only April," says Mr. March.
"Plenty of time, Mr. March," I say.

April 23, 1912
TUESDAY
Aboard the cable ship *Mackay-Bennett*
ATLANTIC OCEAN
THE GRAND BANKS
715 MILES FROM HALIFAX, NOVA SCOTIA

JOHN SNOW
THE UNDERTAKER

More wreckage. More debris. More wasted humanity.
One sailor retrieves an empty jar of Lemco Concentrate:
"Serve hot with a biscuit to ward off seasickness."

We run out of canvas, which defers our endless sea burials.
Tomorrow a delivery ship will bring more supplies.
Today's many bodies will have to go on ice.
After coffee I roll up my sleeves and get to work.
While George, my assistant, enters descriptions into the log,
I open my box of instruments and set about embalming.

Body Number Sixteen. This one was a gentleman, first class,
no doubt with a spot prepaid in the family plot.

With George busy, Arminias Wiseman, the young stoker,
agrees to assist me until his shift at the boilers begins.
We arrange a makeshift table from the top of a coffin.
I cover the body with a towel for propriety
and prop up one end of the coffin to raise Number Sixteen's head
(gravity helps the blood to drain).

"Watch carefully, Wiseman. It's all very simple, really.
Be mindful there, fellow. You're standing in blood."

A small incision on the right side near the collarbone
to accommodate the embalming tube.
Another incision nearby to expose the jugular
in order to drain the blood forced out by the fluid.
Due to my rather crude working conditions,
I place forceps on the drainage vein in place of tubes,
allowing for a faster flow, minimizing blockage by clots.
The formaldehyde goes in; the blood drains out.
Now the trick is to regulate the drainage—
too much and you don't allow for adequate saturation;
too little and suddenly Number Sixteen's veins begin to bulge!

"See the bloom return to his cheeks, Wiseman?
I add pink dyes to the fluids I use.
It brings a rosy, lifelike glow to the face."

I see that, while Number Sixteen's face is flushed,
poor Arminias's face has turned as white as paste.
That task complete ("Are you quite all right, Wiseman?")
I turn to the necessary matter of draining the internal organs.
I insert the long metal tube into Number Sixteen's abdomen
("See here, Wiseman. Near the navel's the best entry point.")
so as to draw out the liquid from the stomach.
Shift right. Spleen. Shift. Now the bladder. Shift.
And. Shift. Just a bit more for good measure.

"And now, Wiseman, to fill all the chest and abdominal cavities
takes about two bottles of fluid. No need to dilute.
It should be full-strength. I've added just a bit of scent
to this batch. Mmmm. A nice wintergreen smell, that.
Here, Wiseman, have a whiff—"

THUD. "Wiseman? Wiseman?"
He's fainted dead away.
Collect one hundred twenty-eight bodies today.

SNOW & COMPANY, LTD.

John R. Snow, Jr., Undertaker

Record of Bodies and Effects

NO. 16: MALE. ESTIMATED AGE: 50.

CLOTHING: Dark grey overcoat; black suit; black gloves; underclothing; marked "G. R."

EFFECTS: Gold watch; memo book; bunch of keys; letter of credit; Guaranty Trust Company, New York, No. 9899; notes in pocket book; $430; U. S. A. Bond in memo book; affidavit of personal prop. For Mrs. G. M. Thorne, N. Y.; letter of indication for above.

PROBABLY FIRST CLASS

ADDRESS IN POCKET BOOK

GEO. ROSENSHINE,
57 & 59 East Eleventh St., N. Y.

FIFTH WATCH

TURNING THE CORNER

1,400 MILES OUT

SUNDAY, APRIL 14, 1912

According to Marconi Company regulations,
if a wireless apparatus fails for whatever reason,
operators are encouraged to rely on the backup unit,
which can be powered by an electric battery if need be.
"Nonsense," said Phillips. "That's only if you don't know how to fix it."
"Do you know how?" I asked.
"How will I know until I try?" he said.
I got little sleep all night, Phillips none.
But at about five o'clock Sunday morning, he shouted out,
"Bride, I've been a fool. The reason I can't figure out
what's wrong with the condensers is that there *is* nothing wrong!
Just look at the burn marks on this casing here."
Sure enough, the lead wires coming from the transformer
had become so hot they had burned through the inside casing.

Another lesson well learned.
Phillips had spent six hours trying to repair something that wasn't broken.
We fixed the *real* problem, two bare wires, in about ten minutes
by simply wrapping the exposed leads with insulated rubber tape.

After that we were back in business!
But we had lost valuable long-range broadcast time.
We knew that our Sunday would be spent trying to catch up.

Until *Titanic* was closer to land, we would have to relay
outgoing messages from ship to ship, which took more time.
And as usual the air was filled with incoming messages as well.
That's why at around nine A.M., as I turned in to my bunk
for a quick nap, I heard Phillips at the headset shout out,

"Another ice message. Enough with the bloody ice.
I've got messages to send!"

The **MARCONI INTERNATIONAL**
MARINE COMMUNICATION COMPANY, Ltd.
Marconi-gram

From: Capt. Barr, SS *Caronia*
To: Capt., *Titanic*
Date: 14 April 1912
Time: 9:00 A.M.

Captain, *Titanic*. Westbound steamers report bergs,
growlers, and field ice in 42°N, from 49° to 51°W,
April 12. Compliments, Barr

My Sunday-morning ritual at sea
was different from every other day of the week.
In place of my usual ship inspection from sun deck to tank top,
on the Sabbath I would inspect the passengers' first-class souls.
As ship's captain, it was tradition for me to conduct
the divine service in the first-class dining saloon.
I usually deferred to any willing clergyman among the passengers.
(Unfortunately there were none to be had that day.)
But at only forty-five minutes, the show was fairly painless
and could be entertaining at times. There were no sermons to prepare,
and all my banter was written out in the White Star Line prayer book.
Mostly though we sang hymns, good ol' Church of England fare,
with members of the ship's orchestra on hand
to ensure that my "parishioners'" spiritual transportation
did not hinge upon the passengers' vocal prowess alone. Ha.

It was the hymn singing I most looked forward to,
for divine services gave me a rare opportunity to warble.
And for whatever reason, that Sunday, I was taken back
to my boyhood, at Etruria British School, where we would
raise up our voices, singing "The Hardy Norseman."
It's hardly a tune one would hear in church,
but as young boys enamored of a life at sea,
we infused the music with our own religious zeal.
That Sunday, now full-grown, standing before millionaires,
I must have let my mind wander a bit, because
as we launched into the last hymn of the service,
the mischievous schoolboy I used to be was up to his old tricks.
The little imp inside of me kept trying to insert
the rollicking words of "The Hardy Norseman" into the solemn
words of "O God, Our Help in Ages Past."

FIRST-CLASS PASSENGERS   *THE CAPTAIN*

> *The hardy Norseman's house of yore*
> *Was on the foaming wave,*
> *And there he gathered bright renown,*
> *The bravest of the brave.*

The busy tribes of flesh and blood,
With all their lives and cares,
Are carried downwards by the flood,
And lost in following years.

> *Oh! Ne'er should we forget our sires.*
> *Wherever we may be.*
> *They bravely won a gallant name*
> *And ruled the stormy sea.*

Time, like an ever-rolling stream,
Bears all its sons away;
They fly, forgotten, as a dream
Dies at the opening day.

> *And we their children still maintain*
> *Their old supremacy,*
> *We've bravely won a gallant name*
> *And rule the stormy sea.*

A thousand ages in Thy sight
Are like an evening gone;
Short as the watch that ends the night
Before the rising sun.

> *Short as the watch that ends the night*
> *Before the rising sun.*

Oh, now, *this* is the way to attend church.
Our sanctuary doubles as a four-star restaurant,
and even as we bow our heads to pray,
the wonders of technology are speeding us across the ocean
at nearly twenty-five miles per hour.
And our pastor is not a man of God but a man of Steam.
Titanic has become our "house of wor-SHIP."

(Hem, hem.)

And why not? If God created man in His own image,
shall we not use our imagination and ingenuity to pay Him homage?
Certainly, there is no more sincere way to praise the Lord
than by building an airplane, an automobile, or a steamship.

God does not help poor souls who make no attempt to help themselves.
God's greatest gift to mankind was a brain.
With this divine tool, man has given birth to modern technology and science.

I'm not saying that the coal miner —
the mill worker, the bellboy — should give up
his common labors to attend science lectures;
upper-class thinkers, inventors, and scientists will forever need workers
to help transform technological dreams into reality.
And the lives of the laboring classes will improve
along with the lives of the elite.

The exalted and rich, the lowly and poor —
religion has long been the opiate that sedates us all.
"Turn your eyes *upward* to God," the priests and pontiffs urge.
I say, "Turn your eyes *forward* to science and technology."
Forward is where the future lies.

The MARCONI INTERNATIONAL
MARINE COMMUNICATION COMPANY, Ltd.

Marconi-gram

From: *Noordam, via Caronia*
To: *Titanic*
Date: 14 April 1912
Time: 11:40 A.M.

Ice Report. Bergs and field ice at 42°N, 49° to 51°W.

THE FIRST-CLASS AND THIRD-CLASS PROMENADE ∽

FIRST CLASS   *THIRD CLASS*

First-class above.

                                       Third class below.
We must retain the status quo.   We must retain the status quo.
Our feet well shod.

                                       Our clothes handmade.

We promenade.

                                       We promenade.

We know our place: noblesse oblige.
We have responsibilities.
We're rich, you see. It is our job
to walk the first-class promenade.

                                       We know our place: to help them out.
                                       What *would* the first class do without
                                       the gardener, nanny, cook, and maid
                                       to walk the third-class promenade?

We are elite.

                                       We're rank and file.

Six times around, we've gone a mile.

                                       Six months of hard-earned wages paid.

We promenade.

        We promenade.

Our feet well shod.

        Our clothes handmade.

We travel abroad.

        We travel to stay.

Politely applaud.

        Huzzah! Hooray!

Pshaw.

        Obey.

No work!

        No play!

We walk
the first-class promenade.

        We walk
        the third-class promenade.

From high up on the promenade deck,
I stopped to throw candy down to the steerage children.
Mrs. Candee calls it "slumming from above."
I see other first-class women watching them, too.
The old couples huddling, all smiles, near the steam pipes.
The dirty-faced children, the masters of imagination,
staving off boredom by climbing on the cranes,
hiding behind the ubiquitous vents and fans,
jumping handmade ropes, dressing handmade dolls.
The sturdy women, laughing, dancing, at ease with their station.
The men, their chests puffed with promise, smoking their pipes.
They are on the lower decks, with nowhere but upward to go.
And where does that leave me?

When I was growing up in Hannibal, Missouri,
there were two kinds of kids:
The river rats lived along the Mississippi,
and that's where they played—the water.
The ridge runners, on the other hand,
lived in the high bluffs above the riverbanks.
As a ridge runner, I was literally *born* on the high road.
I always knew I was meant for better things.

Now, from my perch high above, I watched
a group of steerage boys staring out to sea,
wearing the same expression as their parents.
The same expression I see in my own mirror every morning.
Keep busy. Keep busy. Whatever you do, keep busy.
We are all keeping busy to keep ourselves from dwelling on the fear.
These third-class passengers are sailing into the unknown.
But me—I am returning to the all-too-familiar.

The thought of it makes me want to scream.

FRANKIE

Is your dad really
a boxing champ?

ROSSMORE

Middle-weight division.

EUGENE

That's right, Frankie.

FRANKIE

Well, my dad's
the best tool-
and-die man in Strood.

ALFRED

Frankie, shut it.
Your dad's never won
a trophy, has he?

FRANKIE

You shut it, Alfred!

ROSSMORE

No, no. Frankie,
you *should* be proud
of your dad.

EUGENE

Love your earthly father as
you love your father in heaven.

ROSSMORE

Our dad's not around.
So what if he *is* a champion boxer?
At least your dad's around.

FRANKIE

When I get to America,
I'll get a trophy playing cricket
with the Detroit Tigers.

ALFRED

You mean baseball!

ROSSMORE

I may open my own
bootmaking shop.
I'll earn enough money
to replace this worn-out
leather watch fob.
I'll hang my medal from it.
Did I show you my medal?

ALFRED

Yes!

EUGENE

Yes!

FRANKIE

Can *I* see it again?

"Sixteen years old," said Alfred. "Now I'm an official man."

At lunch on Sunday, we all celebrated Alfred Rush's birthday.
Rossmore and Eugene joined in along with their mum, Mrs. Abbott.
A lot of friendly folks, most of them strangers, joined in
when we gave Alfred a big cheer. Then we all of us ate plum pudding.
The foreign boy, the brother of the girl who gave Alfred the smack,
he came over and shook Alfred's hand. (I'll bet he was after our dessert.)
My dad gave a little speech and said, "Master Alfred's last name, Rush,
fits him, since he's always been in a rush to grow up."
I didn't think it was all that funny, but people laughed anyway.

Alfred's face turned red. And everyone laughed even more.
Even Mum was laughing, but suddenly she was crying.
And I knew it was Bertie. She was thinking about Bertie.
No doubt she was thinking how Bertie would never turn sixteen.
And how Bertie used to stir the plum pudding for Christmas.
Now Bertie won't ever stir the Christmas pudding. But I will.
Bertie would never wear long trousers. But I will.
I'm not dead. I'll still stir the pudding. I'll wear trousers.
I'll turn sixteen. Someday.

Why isn't that enough to stop her tears?

Sundays aboard the *Titanic* were just as busy as any other.
Because my duties were so full, I figured on waiting
to visit the third class until later that evening.
Besides, there was a special dinner planned for Captain Smith,
and it would be a chance to make a little tip money.
I kept my evening plans to myself since White Star frowns upon us
"jumping the gate" into any class but our own.

Meanwhile, all us musicians took a leisurely lunch
as we always did, there in the second-class dining saloon.
Reverend Carter, aboard *Titanic* as a passenger, came through,
telling everyone about an impromptu hymn sing he was organizing,
to be held right there in the saloon. All second class were welcome.
There'd be a short sermon of course, but mostly music.

I think the good minister was hoping that some of us musicians
might volunteer, but if so, he was disappointed.
We all of us graciously declined, but the minister's invitation
sparked a conversation about hymns, music, religion, and death.

Then George Krins, one of the trio stationed in the café,
posed the question that would keep us all talking the whole day:
"If you were on a sinking ship, what would be your final tune?"

"Leave it to a viola player to devise such a morbid lunchtime topic,"
said Fred Clarke, who played an excellent double bass.
"No, seriously," said Krins. "What would it be?
Would you play a robust laughing rag that denies death?
Or a brave, somber, quiet hymn that welcomes it?"

"I'd play the 'White Star March,'" said Ted Brailey,
"then I'd smash up my piano to make a quick raft."

"I'd play 'Nearer, My God, to Thee,'" said Wally.
"I used to sing it in choir. It's a favorite of my father's."

"I'd play something frantic and wild," I said,
"to make death hold his ears! Then, while death was distracted,
I'd play Offenbach's 'Barcarolle.'"

"Number Sixty-eight," said Wally without thinking.

"No," I corrected myself. "'The Boatman's Song.' I would play
'The Boatman's Song' and use it as a lifeboat and row away
with my Eberle and my Guadagnini positioned in the oarlocks."

Now, of course, none of us figured we'd ever put Krins's question to the test.
And unlike the superstitious deckhands and crew,
we didn't think we'd be conjuring any curses by talking
as glibly as we did, about music, and death, and ships going down.
Many of us had been aboard *Olympic* when she collided with the *Hawke*.
The *Hawke* was a naval vessel, fitted with a battering ram no less.
And even with a huge gaping hole in her side,
Olympic still didn't sink. She barely developed a list.

No.
That Sunday afternoon as we talked about death,
we felt as safe as if we were playing a minuet
in a simple easy key
for the London Ladies' Garden Club
charity concert tea.

.. / .- -- / - .... . / .. -.-. .

Another one.

"Now, *here's* one needs to go to the bridge.
This one's addressed directly to the captain," said Phillips.

This one was from another White Star ship: the *Baltic*.
I handed it to Captain Smith myself.

More congratulations. More good wishes.

More ice.

.. / .- -- / - .... . / .. -.-. .

The **MARCONI INTERNATIONAL**
MARINE COMMUNICATION COMPANY, Ltd.

Marconi-gram

From: RMS *Baltic*
To: *Capt. Smith, Titanic*
Date: 14 April 1912
Time: 1:42 P.M.

Captain Smith, *Titanic*. Have had moderate,
variable winds and clear, fine weather since
leaving. Greek steamer *Athenai* reports passing
icebergs and large quantities of field ice today
in lat. 41°51'N, long. 49°52'W. Last night we
spoke German oiltank steamer *Deutschland*,
Stettin to Philadelphia, not under control,
short of coal lat. 40°42'N, long. 55°11'W.
Wishes to be reported to *New York* and other
steamers. Wish you and *Titanic* all success.
Commander

E.J. SMITH ∽ THE CAPTAIN
BRUCE ISMAY ∽ THE BUSINESSMAN

THE CAPTAIN

I used to be the commander
of the *Baltic* myself.

THE BUSINESSMAN

The *Baltic* is one of my ships.

I lent the telegram to Ismay.

Smith gave the telegram to me.

I wanted to show him that
we were traveling
into the vicinity of ice.

He wanted to let me know
the *Baltic* wished us
a successful voyage.

Oh, and the part about
Baltic's wishes for success.

Oh, and the part about
icebergs and field ice.

I wanted to warn him

I hope this doesn't mean

that we may
be forced
to slow down.

that we may
be forced
to slow down.

The MARCONI INTERNATIONAL
MARINE COMMUNICATION COMPANY, Ltd.

Marconi-gram

From: Knuth, *Amerika*
To: Steamer *Titanic*. MSG. via Cape Race to the
United States Hydrographic Office, Washington
Date: 14 April 1912
Time: 1:45 P.M.

DS *Amerika* passed two large icebergs in 41°27'N,
50°8'W on April 14.
Signed, Knuth

Did I say that I was captain of the straight line?
Actually, the business of navigation
(much like the business of life) is not so simple.
The earth, as you know, is not flat—but spherical.
If you were to sail a straight course, you would begin to spiral
up or down along the globe until you eventually reached one of the poles.
Since our guests would rather not disembark in Antarctica,
we have to adjust the direction a little bit here and there as we go.
In sailor talk, we call this the Great Circle track,
the route we took the minute we left Ireland behind.

Around dinnertime, *Titanic* finally arrived at the corner,
a specified coordinate in the middle of the ocean.
Every pilot on the North Atlantic run knows it.
During the spring, when ice is a potential threat,
the corner is set pretty far south, at 42° North, 47° West.
Once we reached the corner, we "turned it"
by changing our southwesterly course to due west.

But that particular Sunday evening, it seemed as if *Titanic*
wasn't the only thing turning the corner.
I knew that my sailing days were coming to a close.
Already I'd passed the age of mandatory retirement.
Maybe it was just the melancholy nature of an old man,
or maybe it was the saltwater pumping through my heart,
but it seemed to me that every move *Titanic* made—
when I put on more boilers, when I adjusted the course,
when I blew the whistles, rang down to the engines,
or simply watched forward across the big ship's bow—
I felt as if I *was* the ship and the ship was me.
So that when *Titanic* turned the corner at 42°N, 47°W,
Captain Edward John Smith, the old man, turned the corner, too.

Even though *Titanic* had turned the corner, as they call it,
it still looked to me and everyone else on board
as if we were just simply in the middle of nowhere,
swallowed up by water and sky. The mighty *Titanic,*
as large as a city block and ten stories high,
may as well have been a single tiny honeybee.
And I was a tiny speck of pollen on the honeybee's thigh.

As my duties aboard *Titanic* became less harried,
I found myself missing my family more and more.
It was as if the farther I traveled away from Helen and Elizabeth,
the more clear in my mind their faces became. Funny—
I am such a stickler for details, why is it that I can notice
that a coat hook has one screw too many,
but I can't see the fine details of my wife's cheekbones,
or the miracle of my daughter's tiny fingernails—
at least not until now, when I'm a thousand miles away?

In everything aboard *Titanic,* I had begun to see my family—
not only in the many passengers but also in the ship herself.
Belowdecks I watched *Titanic*'s two massive
reciprocating engines, four stories tall, fierce iron giants,
their pistons and shafts driving the ship's huge propellers.
To me they looked as if they were mother and father
to the smaller low-pressure turbine engine that drives
the ship's third small center propeller. Just as mother and father
give life to their child, the steam exhausting from the big engines
is diverted into the turbine, steam that would otherwise
be dispersed and lost. The parents give life to their child,
while the child gives meaning to its parents' lives.
It's silly, really, that a machine might instruct a man
in the finer points of the human heart.

As you know, I'm something of an inventor myself.
I've invented a type of bicycle hand brake.
I've invented a useful pneumatic road improver.
A rain inducer. Even a marine turbine engine
like the one *Titanic* uses. How ingenious
to channel the exhaust from the reciprocating engines
into the third turbine engine! The ship's closed loop system
can transform steam into electricity for lights, refrigeration,
food storage, and heat to warm my Madeleine's bathwater.

If only that energy could be recycled indefinitely.
For now, the laws of physics won't allow it.
But just think, once we *do* figure out the secret
(and I have no doubt we will),
we might be able to apply it toward the human body.
Whoever can discover the secret to perpetual motion
could ultimately hold the key to eternal life.

I'm told *Titanic* has turned the corner toward New York.
I hope my unborn child might live to see humanity turn its own corner.
Why, I ask, must everything wind down?
Why must everything come to an end?
It's times such as these,
when I am overwrought with melancholy,
that I remember with delight how terribly rich I am.
If my time on earth is destined to be short,
at least I can live it with my Maddie at my side,

in first class.

(Hem, hem.)

Word came from the bridge down the hall
that *Titanic* had finally turned the corner.
The news meant that the passengers and crew
could breathe easy awhile for the straight stretch home.
But to Phillips and me it meant the opposite.
To us it meant that we were finally within range of Cape Race,
the tip of land off the Grand Banks that was home
to one of the largest wireless receiving stations in the world.
Now we could begin chipping away at
our stack of backed-up messages. We had begun
the day with some two hundred and fifty.
Business before brass; customers for cash.
The money wouldn't come in unless the words went out.

I went up to dinner, leaving Phillips at the key.
I would be sure to mention to the sea-post chaps
that Jack Phillips, first wireless operator aboard
the RMS *Titanic,* was successfully delivering a dozen
messages all over the world without leaving his seat,
all before they had eaten half of their baked haddock.

.-.. --- ...- .

From: MGY, RMS *Titanic*
Sunday, 14 April
6:45 P.M.
Via Cape Race

Hardly wait get back.
Cable made me awfully happy.
Love, Mutzie.

-- ..- - --.. .. .

scurry — tug. circle — tug.
pull — stop. push — stop.
claw — squeal — bite — stop.
fur-teeth-claw-tail-rats
fur-teeth-claw-tail-rats
tails attached. tails attached.

flour. egg. marmalade.

trapped in the flour barrel

      scurry — tug. scurry — tug.

          scurry—tug. *CRACK.*

               free scurry free scurry

             pain . . . tail

         tail . . . free

      leave the Rat King

    leave the flour barrel

sniff sniff . . . food

     follow the food

       feed the Rat King

             follow the food

       follow the food

     escape escape escape

  survive

All day I went without seeing the rat with the crooked tail.
I knew it would have to show itself eventually.
I had dusted flour all around the bakery floor,
hoping to catch a trail of footprints that could tell me
where "Maynard" was hiding. It had to be living somewhere.
Whether or not I discovered any telltale footprints,
I planned on setting traps in the bakery later that night.
But dinnertime had arrived and I knew that no rodent
would come anywhere near the chaos of the cooks and stewards,
clanging, yelling, and stomping about, getting the orders out.
So I put aside my rat-hunting mission (at least for a while)
and set about preparing for the three-ring circus we called dinner.
Like everything else on *Titanic,* it was a circus divided by class.

Ladies and gentlemen, boys and girls,
welcome to the RMS *Titanic*'s three-ring circus
of glamorous gluttony and gustatory good times!

In the center ring:
the first-class eaters fill their plates with hors d'oeuvres—
oysters and consommé Olga—followed by a main course
of salmon in mousseline sauce, roast duck, or filet mignon Lili.
Side dishes of Parmentier and boiled new potatoes, roast squab and cress,
cold asparagus vinaigrette, or pâté de foie gras and celery.
Watch them finish up with Waldorf pudding, French ice cream,
peaches in chartreuse jelly, or (from the bakery) chocolate éclairs.
Everything piled high on plates of fine bone china edged in 22-karat gold.

Over in ring number two:
baked haddock, curried chicken with rice, spring lamb in mint sauce,
roast turkey and roasted potatoes, plum pudding, and ice cream.
Oh, and cheese biscuits straight from the bakery.
All on attractive blue-and-white delftware china
that most second-class travelers could only aspire to at home.

Just two decks down, in ring number three:
watch as the third-class masses eat better aboard *Titanic*
than they ever have before or ever will again.
Ragout of beef, potatoes, pickles, and apricots,
fresh bread and butter, currant buns and tea.
All of it on simple and durable earthenware, with no design,
as plain and blank as their unknown futures.

Now watch all passengers in every ring turn over their menu cards
to place their autographs on the backs
as a record to their loved ones of what they've just eaten.
As if tonight's meal will be their very last.

I could not taste the food.

I had hidden in my cabin all through lunch,
too embarrassed to show my face.

Finally the older women demanded that I come to dinner.
But try as I might, I could not taste the food.
Everything was too foreign.
I longed for the succulent lamb kibbeh back home.
The lentils, chickpeas, tahini, and tabouleh.
The grape leaves stuffed with rice and spiced beef.

The Syrians and Lebanese keep mostly to one section
of the big dining room, so luckily I did not have to face the boy.

"Alf-Frid. Al-Frid. Al-Frid."

I had met the boy.
I had learned the boy's name.
And he had learned mine.
And did I say *marhaba*—hello?
No. I slapped him in his face.
And did I say *as-salam alaykum*—peace be with you?
No. I slapped him in his face.
And did I say *shukran*—thank you, for finding Father's money?
No. I slapped him in his face.

And this was only Sunday evening.
I still had to avoid the boy for three more days.

The dinner was superb.
More talk of the future.
More talk of success.
And, yes, we talked a bit of ice.
On my way to the dining saloon,
Captain Smith had asked for the *Baltic* telegram.
To post it, he said, for the officers to see.

"Will you slow down?" asked Mrs. Ryerson.
"No," I said. "We'll put on more speed
to take us quickly around any danger."

I am no sailor, of course.
My ship was in the best hands possible.
I know nothing of ice.
I'd never seen an iceberg in all my life.
The only ice I knew of
was in the gin and tonic that I lifted
as the good old doctor made yet one more toast.

No matter that he did the same last night;
when dining with Dr. O'Laughlin,
you must expect to lift your glass more than once.
"Let us assign last night's toast to *Titanic*'s stern," he said.
"She's too big a ship to be contained in just one tribute,
so tonight, let us celebrate the bow."

Here, here. Glasses lifted all around.
Ice cubes tinkling like fairy bells.
"Here's to the bow of the mighty *Titanic*!"

"Here's to Captain E.J. Smith, Admiral of the White Star Line!"

The Wideners, George and Eleanor, had arranged it:
a dinner in my honor in the à la carte restaurant.
Just four months earlier in New York, I had attended another,
at the upscale Metropolitan Club, with some of my most prominent
American passengers, including J. P. Morgan himself.
In that toast they called me the "Old Man of the Sea."
These Americans are, if nothing else, zealous in their gratitude.
I must admit I was proud. And I suppose I've earned it.
But, as an "old man of the sea," I know it's unlucky to say so.

On hand that Sunday evening were the Thayers,
John and Marian (of the Pennsylvania Railroad Thayers)
and their boy (a man, now, really) Jack.
Major Archibald Butt, military aide to President Taft.
Even the theatrical director Henry Harris was there
with his wife, Renée, who had broken her elbow.
She said, "I fell and broke it as I was climbing aboard.
But don't worry—I don't blame you! Ha, ha."
It was a merry night. The food was good. The drink flowed.
(Though, of course, I did not partake. Not even a glass of wine.)
One fellow from the orchestra played a lively fiddle.
The company was to my liking. And what's more,
I had the luxury of not one but two good cigars.
Finally, I made my excuses and left the revelers behind.

As I made my way to the bridge along the starboard boat deck,
I placed a toothpick between my teeth and buttoned my collar.
The temperature must have suddenly dropped by ten degrees or more.
Typical spring on the North Atlantic. Nothing to worry over.

The private party was not as merry as I would have liked.
I mean to say the drinking, and the tips, were kept to a minimum.
But what did I expect? First class. Dinner. Mixed company.
All the Americans doing their best to "be British"
in the company of the "Old Man of the Sea."

After Captain Smith took his leave, the party began to disperse.
And as we were packing up the instruments, a young fellow,
who had seemed mostly the odd man out
among the older guests, approached us.

"I wonder if you might play just one more tune," he said
under his breath. "Something rather sprightly and gay.
My father, Mr. Thayer, has been in a bit of a funk, you see.
Perhaps something lively might give him a lift."

"I think we can find a happy number on the list," said Wally.

But while Wally was still thumbing through the booklet,
Signorina Eberle and I started in on a jig—
just a little bouncy something that I made up off the cuff.
And I said, "Join in, lads. I'm in the key of A."

(Wally and John looked at me with their mouths open.)

Speaking through the Eberle, I attempted to conjure up
feelings of my joyful childhood back in Scotland.
Through the music, I ran in green fields. I leaped along sea rocks.
I closed my eyes and imagined the sound of bagpipes,
wafting over the rolling, windswept hills of Dumfries.
The music transported me to my childhood so many years ago,
and the joy I would feel as my father would teach me
those first few scratchy notes. I played and played and played.

I finally opened my eyes only to discover that every guest,
but one, had left the room. Wally and John were still staring in disbelief.
My merry tune slowed, then drooped to nothing
as my bow ran out of steam and stopped.
Mr. Widener, who had just settled his bill with the restaurant manager,
approached me and said, "Your fingers are wonderfully quick.
The music is not my cup of tea, mind you. But I do appreciate your time."

With that he placed sixteen cents in my hand.
"Do have a wonderful night," he said,
and he walked, whistling, from the restaurant.

Wally, John, and I all looked at the sixteen pennies
that lay in the center of my open palm.
Mr. George Widener, banking magnate and board member
of Fidelity Trust Company of Philadelphia,
the very bank that owned the entire White Star Line;
Mr. George Widener, heir to a vast inheritance,
and one of the richest men in the world,
had just given me sixteen American pennies for my music.

Finally Wally grinned and said,
"Well done, Jock. I bet you could buy yourself
a good pair of scissors with that."

The **MARCONI INTERNATIONAL**
MARINE COMMUNICATION COMPANY, Ltd.

Marconi-gram

From: Capt. Lord, *Californian*
To: Captain, *Antillian*, intercepted by *Titanic*
Date: 14 April 1912
Time: 7:30 P.M.

To Captain, *Antillian*. 6:30 pm, apparent ship's time; lat. 42°03'N, long. 49°09'W. Three large bergs five miles to the southward of us. Regards, Lord

My watch was done for the night.
Second Officer Lightoller arrived on the bridge
from his dinner break just before I headed for my bunk.
Captain Smith soon joined us as well,
chewing on his usual toothpick.
The captain said, "I've posted an ice notification:
41° 51' North; 49° 52' West."
There had been talk of ice all evening. Nothing new.
The lookouts had been told to keep an eye out
for bergs and growlers. But good luck to 'em.
The sea was smooth as glass. No wind at all. A flat calm.
We all knew what flat calm meant on a night like this.
There would be no waves to wash against the sides of the ice,
no telltale white water to catch the light.
And with no moon, there was no light anyway.
There were a million stars dotting the sky
but they did little to illuminate the Atlantic blackness.
"There may be a certain amount of reflected light," said Lightoller.
Smith answered, "Yes. Perhaps. Have the lookouts been told?"
"Yes, sir," said Lightoller.
"If there's the slightest haze, we'll have to slow down," said Smith.
"Yes, sir."
"Good man," said Smith. "I'll be in my quarters.
If it becomes at all doubtful,
let me know at once. I shall be just inside."
"Yes, sir."

As Captain Smith walked to his quarters on the starboard side,
I walked to my own room, to port, along the corridor lined with doors.
All officers were housed just behind the bridge and wheelhouse.
The Marconi boys bunked here as well, just down the hall.
In the event of an emergency, we could all be at our posts in seconds.

Lolo and Momon . . .

> *(are sleeping.)*

I had shot the pistol twice, at an empty jar of Lemco.
It was practice. To learn how the gun worked.
My friend Hoffman had placed the jar in the hollow
of a dead tree. Back in France. The jar sat there
nestled in the hollow, and it looked as if the tree
had a heart made of glass. And I shot at it.
I shot two times. And I missed two times.
Ha. You see I'm not a dangerous man. I'm a tailor.
I put things together. A vest. Two sleeves.

> *(Your children are not jars of Lemco.)*

My children are sleeping now. Their hearts
are beating in their chests, like glass in the hollow of a tree.

(Your children. Not hers.
> *Yours to do with as you please.)*

I would sooner hurt myself than my children.
> *(You and your children are one and the same.)*
You. Who are you? In my head? Who are you?
> *(I am you. You are not Louis Hoffman.)*
> I know. I am Michel Navratil.

No, you are not me. Leave my head. Leave my heart.
(OK, then, tailor, make me leave your head.
Use the gun and chase me from your heart. Our heart.)

> I will.

(Well, then. Do not miss.
For if you do, your children are all mine.
Mine alone. And I will not miss.)

You will not hurt my children.

(Then you know what you need to do.
The choice is yours. You are the one with the hands.
I am only your heart. I cannot pull the trigger.)

Do you feel that? The pistol's barrel against our chest?

(Turn the gun on the children while you still can.)

I must turn the gun
on my own heart while I still can.

A knock on the cabin door.
I return the gun to my pocket.
I turn on the light. I turn the knob.

"Hello, Mr. Hoffman?"

Yes?

"Is everything all right?"

(Tell them to go away.)

Yes, I'm fine. I'm just resting.
Won't you come in?

"Well, I'm sorry if we're interrupting your rest.
I'm Reverend Carter. Vicar of Saint Jude's in Whitechapel.
And this is my wife, Mrs. Carter."

Bonjour, madame. How do you do?

"Very well, thank you. Reverend Carter and I
will be conducting a lighthearted hymn sing this evening
in the second-class saloon. We'd very much like it if you could come.
I'd be happy to stay with your children."

(No, not the children. They are mine.)

Oh, yes. Mr. and Mrs. Carter. Of course, forgive me.
I have seen you both at dinner, of course.

"Will you come?"

(No. You must tend to the children. You must finish this.)

Yes. Yes, I will. Thank you. The children will be fine.
They sleep through anything. I'll have Bertha look in on them.
She's a girl on board who's been helping me out with them.
It may do me some good to get out of my cabin for a moment.

> *(Don't go. You have to finish this.)*

It will allow me to clear my head a bit.

"Oh, splendid."

> *(You are going? You are actually going?)*

I am going, of course.

"Oh. Yes. Well, of course. I'm so glad.
Reverend Carter and I were not sure,
with the name Hoffman, if you might be . . .

We were afraid you were of the Hebrew faith, you see."

Me? Jewish? Oh, no. No.
Ha, ha. Far from it.

"One can never really tell, these days.
Names can be so very deceiving."

Oui, madame. I know.
Very deceiving. Indeed.

"FOR THOSE IN PERIL ON THE SEA"

SECOND-CLASS PASSENGERS

Eternal Father, strong to save,
Whose arm hath bound the restless wave,
Who bidd'st the mighty ocean deep
Its own appointed limits keep;
Oh, hear us when we cry to Thee,
For those in peril on the sea!

O Christ! Whose voice the waters heard
And hushed their raging at Thy word,
Who walkedst on the foaming deep,
And calm amidst its rage didst sleep;
Oh, hear us when we cry to Thee,
For those in peril on the sea!

Most Holy Spirit! Who didst brood
Upon the chaos dark and rude,
And bid its angry tumult cease,
And give, for wild confusion, peace;
Oh, hear us when we cry to Thee,
For those in peril on the sea!

I am not a religious man.
I am a simple tailor. And a father.

Ever since my marriage failed,
I felt that my heart was broken.
But now I see that it has been transformed.
My heart has broken open so I might love my sons.

During the hymn singing this evening,
Reverend Carter compared the perils of life
to the perils of the sea. It was as if
he was speaking to me. About my own life.
About my own treacherous seas.

I've been foolish to think that I could
escape the restless waves of my own heart.
I understand now that my problems
will follow me wherever I may try to flee.
Reverend Carter said that God was looking down
on *Titanic,* offering all second-class passengers
a second chance to steer a different course.
As I closed the door to my cabin
and dressed for bed, it struck me how
the confusing voice in my heart was gone.

My mind was as calm as the seas
upon which the *Titanic* now sailed.
I had no idea what the future would bring.
But as Lolo rolled over and slipped his small hand
into my own, I knew somehow that my children
would lead me where I needed to go.

The musicians sleep in a cabin in second class,
E deck, aft, on the port side.
It's a great location, with a separate room
just for the instruments. Best of all, though,
our room is not far down the hall
from an emergency service door that
leads directly to third class and a world of music waiting there.
With Mr. Widener's sixteen cents jangling in my purse,
and with the Guadagnini rosined up and ready for action,
I opened the emergency door only to find
a young lad sitting outside his cabin door in tears.

Turns out he was a Kentish boy named Frankie
traveling with his parents to a new start in America
and though he wouldn't spill the whole story
he seemed to be having trouble with his mum.
He brightened up a bit, though, when we talked about dragons.
Captain Smith himself had shown him a bit of paper,
proving that the *Titanic* was transporting dragon's blood below.

I hated to be the one who told him that dragon's blood
was just the name of a shellac used to finish furniture.
I knew it well, for my father would keep it on hand
to spread over the wood of the violins he would refurbish.
I took the Guadagnini from its case to show him.

"It starts out a deep rich red color, hence the name," I said.
"But still, isn't it made from the blood of a dragon?" Frankie said.
"Sometimes names are a bit deceptive," I said.
"For example, everyone calls me Jock even though I'm really John."

Oh, you should have seen young Frankie's face. So sad.

I tried my best to play my tune backward.

"Of course," I said, "maybe I'm mistaken.

I'm sure that Captain Smith knows what he's talking about."

"Oh, that's OK," said the boy. "I was being silly, I guess."

It was breaking my heart, it was, to see him like that.

And anything I said just made it worse,

so I made up my mind to let *Signorina* Guadagnini speak for me.

She started in with a lively musical rendition of "Frankie and Johnny"

that surprised even me. And the lad from Kent smiled.

That was a good mark in favor of the Guadagnini, if you ask me.

"I've heard that tune," Frankie said. "It's called 'Frankie and Johnny.'"

"That's right, lad," I said. "It's named in honor of us, you see!"

Frankie said, "Mum says that song is about a fallen woman

of bad reputation who goes nutters and murders

her no-good two-timing boyfriend. That's what Mum says."

The old Lebanese women had asked me over and over
to join them in the dining saloon, where many people
were gathered for music and dancing. Finally I agreed.
And, oh, what a noise! The party was well under way.
From the top of the stairs, I saw a group of Lebanese,
one hand frantically waving above the headscarves.
"Jamila! Jamila! Over here." It was Selini
with her new husband, Fraza, who had a silly grin on his face.
When I finally made my way over to our group,
I was surprised to see that Fraza was wearing a nice suit and tie.
"Doesn't Fraza look handsome?" said Selini.
I just blushed, but Fraza laughed.
"It is a special occasion," he said.
"It certainly is a very lively party," I said.
Everyone laughed at that. I was confused.
Are they laughing at me? I wondered.
It seemed as if they were all watching me now.
I had the feeling that they had been talking about me.
No doubt laughing at the fool I had made of myself.
I had just stood to excuse myself and return to my room,
when Mr. Leeni walked up, also dressed in his best suit.
"Oh, you are not going anywhere, young lady.
We would all like a word with you," he said with a stern voice.
My face felt hot. Tears were not far behind.
Then Mr. Leeni's scowl turned to a broad smile.
"OK, Elias," he said. "She's here. You can bring it over."
"Elias?" I said. My annoying little brother
pushed through the crowd, and feigning importance,
he made an elegant bow. Then he held out a plate
spilling over with wonderful chocolate éclairs.
"Happy birthday, Sister!" Elias yelled over the noise of the room.
"A day early, but we thought you needed a lift!"

I had all but forgotten that tomorrow I would turn fourteen!
Everyone around me cheered.
Then everyone grabbed for the éclairs.
"Where in the world did you get these?" I asked Elias.
"After dinner, I asked one of the cooks
if I could have an extra piece of plum pudding.
I told him it was for my sister's birthday. Mr. Leeni translated for me."

Mr. Leeni took up the story from there:
"So the cook twirls his long handlebar mustache.
Then he laughs and says, 'You leave it to me, lad.'
He is gone for just ten minutes and returns with this tray
of pastries, and he says, 'I burgled 'em from the baker. He'll never miss 'em.'"
Everyone laughed as Mr. Leeni imitated the cook,
twirling an imaginary mustache,
and speaking Arabic with an English accent.

"Thank you, Mr. Leeni," I said. "Thank you so much."
"It was all your brother's doing, Jamila. I just translated."
So I turned to Elias, who was grinning from ear to ear
as if to say, Aren't I the best brother in the whole world?
I smiled and said, "Thank you, Brother. That was sweet of you."
And I meant it because Elias *was* the best brother in the world—
at least in that particular moment, he was.

Beautiful! Absolutely beautiful!
I think I am in love!

It was *Signorina* Guadagnini who won my heart
that Sunday evening during the third-class revelry.
I knew that she had a prim and classic side.
But there in the F deck dining saloon, the two of us went wild!
Together we played Irish jigs,
German polkas, and Scottish ballads.
We did a scorching duet with a French hurdy-gurdy.
We even accompanied the Lebanese *dabkeh*!
All night long she followed and never faltered.
Her string crossings were like melted butter.
Her double stops had a pleasurable bite.
She sounded sweet in all registers — high, middle, and low.
Among the third-class passengers, Guadagnini won the show.
My search had finally reached an end.
The Guadagnini passed the final test.
For the finest instrument, like the finest friend,
is the one that allows you to express yourself best.

Mary often says I love music more than her,
but without music I couldn't love at all.

I met a swell grown-up named Jock who plays
in the ship's orchestra for the rich passengers.
He wears a smashing green uniform with brass buttons.
His real name is John, but folks call him Jock anyway—
just like dragon's blood is called dragon's blood
even though it's something that's *not* dragon's blood.

I think Captain Smith and those other officers
were trying to be friendly, but they lied to me.
They think it's all right to lie if you're lying to a kid.
But it's never all right to lie. No matter what.

Jock, the fiddle player, was honest.
He told me the truth about the dragon's blood.
But that doesn't mean there aren't dragons.
I still know they exist. I guess maybe they'll exist
until I have to start wearing long pants like Alfred.

I saw Jock again down in the dining saloon,
where a huge crowd had gathered to play music and dance.
Dad talked Mum into going; she even danced and sang!
She can be very sad and very happy all in the same day.
I never know which Mum she's going to be from minute to minute,
but at least the happy Mum has begun to show up a bit.

Alfred was strutting around in his long trousers
and he was hanging out with the Abbott boys, Ross and Eugene.
Alfred tried to ignore me. But Ross and Eugene were nice.
I stood and watched Jock play music with a few other passengers.
Fiddles, pipes, tin whistles, and drums. Some folks just stomped.
Or they clacked spoons together. Or clapped. Anything noisy.
I couldn't help but tap my feet. A fellow on the bagpipes

kept walking through all the different sections of the saloon,
and the older girls would follow him around, all of 'em dancing.

That girl, the one who slapped Alfred's face and ran off crying,
she was there with a lot of other foreigners.
They were all eating chocolate éclairs in a different part of the room.
And next thing you know, Alfred was over there with 'em!
He was after an éclair, I guess.
Or maybe he was after another slap in the face.

"Happy birthday, Jamila!"
"I hope you will live for a hundred years, Jamila!"
Lebanese passengers kept coming over to me
to bring birthday wishes of luck and long life.
They also came over to eat my birthday éclairs!
The Irish bagpiper strolled by with a tune in my honor.
Selini's husband, Fraza, sang me a song as loud as the bagpipes.
And of course the old women kept saying,
"Soon, Jamila. Soon we shall find you a husband."
Besides Selini, many other Lebanese girls of my age were there.
Many of them I was meeting for the very first time.
I discovered that most of them also had secret hearts,
and their hearts were filled with the same things as mine:
sadness at leaving behind their girlhood homes,
fear that they would not fit in in America,
excitement over the possibilities of the future.
Many of their families were also fleeing from the Turkish soldiers.
Many of their families had endured the same abuse.
Some of their families had endured much worse.
"Jamila," Mr. Leeni said, tapping me on the shoulder,
"there is a young man here who would like to wish you happy birthday."
I swiveled my stool around and just about fell to the floor.
Standing next to Mr. Leeni was the boy in the brown knee pants.
Only he wasn't wearing knee pants, but long trousers.
I felt the heat rush to my face. How could Mr. Leeni do this to me?

The room was filled with music and loud chatter.
To make himself heard the boy leaned over and spoke into my ear:
"Esmé Alfred," he said. My name is Alfred.
And *"Tsharrafna."* It is nice to meet you.

Mr. Leeni said, "Elias taught him how to say it."

"Shukran," I said to Alfred. Thank you. And I looked into his eyes
up close for the first time. He looked back.
I fought the very strong urge to pull my headscarf over my face
to hide my blushing cheeks. To hide my silly grin.
But the boy was grinning, too. And in my secret heart
I admitted that it was not unpleasant standing next to him.

I could feel the narrow, suspicious eyes of the old Lebanese women.
But with Mr. Leeni there to act as chaperone and translator,
we stood together, conversing in the middle of all the chaos.
"My name is Alfred," he said again.
"Yes, I know," I said. "You said that. My name is Jamila."
"Yes, I know," he replied.
"It is my birthday, too," he said. "I am sixteen now."
"I'm sorry!" I blurted out. I had to get the apology off my chest.
"You're sorry that I'm sixteen?"
"No. I'm sorry for striking you."
"It was a misunderstanding. I know."
"But I was foolish. I should have known you didn't take the money."
"I'm glad you have the money back, anyway."
For a moment we ran out of things to say.
Then Alfred said, "Your brother Elias is funny. I like him."
I replied, "I'm not sure I like your taste in friends."
We both laughed.
"But I like *you*. And *you* are my friend," the boy said.
I turned to Mr. Leeni, who was becoming uncomfortable.
"Please ask him, 'If he really *is* my friend,
why has he been staring at me the way he does?'"
Mr. Leeni translated my question and Alfred replied,
but Mr. Leeni would not translate the boy's answer.
Instead he said, "Enough of this talk. The boy must dance!"

Mr. Leeni grabbed Alfred by the hand and led him away
to a circle of people who had already begun to dance the *dabkeh*.

Selini said, "Look, Fraza. It is just like our wedding day!"

The two newlyweds joined in.

"Come on, Sister," said Elias. And he pulled me into the ring

with my brother to one side and Alfred to the other.

We all held hands as the circle moved one way, then the other.

Alfred tripped over his feet. And even though I knew the steps,

I tripped over my feet, too. My brain was focusing on

the warm feel of Alfred's hand in mine.

We all laughed as the music gradually became faster.

And our ring of dancers matched the pace of the music.

"Ah wee ha!" sang out Mr. Leeni.

The old Lebanese women trilled their shrill *zalghouta*.

"Yalla! Yalla!" cried Elias.

Faster and faster we all went around until we were dizzy.

Finally the music stopped and everyone clapped.

Everyone, that is, except for Alfred and myself.

For the two of us were still holding hands.

He looked at me with that same strange look.

And then he leaned toward me.

He placed his lips next to my ear.

And he said something in English I could not understand.

But I could tell it was the same thing that Mr. Leeni would not translate.

And then, without warning, one of the Irish girls screamed.

And then another girl. Another scream.

And a large rat went running across the floor.

A group of boys went chasing after it.

You had never heard such a commotion.

Finally, I saw my brother, Elias, raise the rat in triumph.

He held the disgusting thing by its tail

and ran with it up the saloon stairs and out of sight,

followed by a pack of boys from all different countries,

yelling, cheering, and laughing. My brother's voice
rose above them all: *"Yalla! Yalla! Yalla!"*

I noticed, then, that Alfred was no longer holding my hand,
because Alfred, who used to be my pretty boy
in brown knee pants standing on the white crane;
because Alfred, who was now my pretty man
in brown trousers breathing words into my ear;
because Alfred was running out of the dining room
with the rest of them.

                    "Perhaps," said Mr. Leeni with a wink,
"the boy thought the rat was a better dancer?"

DANGER DANGER

BOOTS BOOTS BOOTS

scuttlescuttlescuttle
weave dodge STOP

scuttlescuttlescuttle
weave dodge scuttle STOP

dodge STOMP STOMP
DANGER BOOTS

scuttlescutt—YANK!

tail . . . caught
lifted . . . caught
high up . . . caught

DANGER DANGER
bite bite scratch claw bite
bitebitebitebitebitebite

tail . . . free

falling . . . turn . . . drop

scuttlescuttescuttle
into the dark
into the walls
escape escape escape

escape

survive

From outside the dining saloon
came the sound of my brother's scream
followed by a chorus of boys' hysterical laughter.
And as quickly as it had stopped, the music and dancing resumed.

Then I felt a tap on my shoulder; it was Selini,
with a wide grin on her face, and she said, "You are beautiful."
"Thank you, Selini," I said, more than a little confused.
"No," she said. "That's what the boy said.
That's what Mr. Leeni refused to translate for you.
But Mr. Leeni told Fraza and Fraza told me.
And now I'm telling you. So now you know.
The English boy said, 'You are beautiful.'"

You are beautiful. You are beautiful.
I placed this comment in various areas of my head,
experimenting with each different feeling,
the way one might place a new chair about the room.
Finally I moved it to the very center of my secret heart.
And I left it there, so that whenever I wanted
I might relive the conversation:

    "Why were you staring at me?" the girl asked.
    The boy replied, "Because you are beautiful."

The MARCONI INTERNATIONAL
MARINE COMMUNICATION COMPANY, Ltd.

Marconi-gram

From: S. H. Adams, *Mesaba*
To: *Titanic* and all eastbound ships
Date: 14 April 1912
Time: 9:40 P.M.

Ice report in lat. 42°N to 41°25'N, long. 49°W to
50°30'W. Saw much heavy pack ice and great number
large icebergs. Also field ice. Weather good, clear.

Miss Marie Stene
Ørskog P.O.
via Ålesund, Norway

14 April 1912
Sunday

My darling Marie,

This has been a long, lonely day. There was a grand to-do
in the third-class dining saloon. A rat ran through. The girls all
yelled. The boys gave chase. Peter, Sigurd, and the girls are still
there. I left early to write you this letter. I could find no joy in the
dancing or the music. I have tried to pray but can find no solace.
Perhaps I am tired, eh? Perhaps I am—

This evening *Titanic* shifted course and turned westward for
New York. The stewards call this turning the corner. And—

Looking out to sea, where there is nothing to see—that
is where I found clarity. We both know the truth of this. Of us. I
think you knew it all along. You were too kind to tell me outright.
And me, the optimistic one, assumed that you would come round.
Assumed that you would "turn the corner" with me.

The temperature outside has dropped. There is a smell of
ice in the air. You are from Norway. You know that smell.

I'm going to bed now. As they say in America, I'm
"turning in."

I have turned the corner. And tomorrow, with the sunrise,
I will throw all these letters in the sea.

Yours very truly,
Olaus

Oh, good show, Stengel. You win again.

The noon-to-noon mileage posting today was 546.
Titanic is going faster and farther each day.

Yes, Stengel, this really is your lucky day.

Now it's just after ten P.M. on Sunday evening.
Gambling's not allowed on Sunday, of course,
but the smoking room stewards have turned a blind eye.
So long as we tip them well, the drinks will keep coming.

Yes, of course. One more drink. And, one more hand.

The stewards are honest men for the most part,
especially if there is easy money to be made,
especially if they feel there will be no victim.

I'll take one card, please.

Stengel, too, is a mostly honest man.
And that's why I think he'll be the perfect client
for what promises to be my biggest scam yet.
I got the idea from Titanic herself, inspired
by the daily mileage pool and watching the Marconi men.

I'll bet thirty.

My plan is to convince an otherwise honest businessman
to invest in a low-risk, yet illegal, con: horse racing.
I convince my client I've got an American cousin
who works for Western Union and who is thus in a position
to postpone the transmission of horse-racing results for just a few minutes,

which would enable me to make bets on the winning horse
before the results have been received.

I'll see your forty and raise you ten.

Because we are not actually changing the race's outcome,
there really is no victim. I'll pretend that I do it all the time.
Never betting any huge sums of money in order to avoid suspicion.
The client, in fact, doesn't need to be anywhere near the track.
My client merely contributes the funds (up front, of course).
It's me and my "American cousin" who face any risk, you see.

I'll see your fifty.

So Stengel contributes a few thousand dollars (cash, of course)
that he figures he can double or triple without lifting a finger.
What has he got to lose, anyway? He knows that he can trust me.
I'm Lord Brayton, after all—breeder of racing Thoroughbreds.
We sailed together on the Titanic, *and I even tore up his check.*
I'll explain to him that it is really me *who is taking a risk on* him
by allowing him in on this foolproof way of getting rich.

Oh, this hand is getting too rich for me, boys.
I guess I'd better fold. I'll not be making a dime tonight.

Then, even before the race is run, I disappear with all the money.
And my client won't tell the authorities
because if he did, he would incriminate himself in the scam.

Good show, Stengel. You win again.

I win. And my American cousin wins.
And since there is, in truth, no American cousin,
I actually win twice.
It's what I call a win-win situation.

listen . . . ?

listen . . . quiet

quiet . . . safe

      sniff sniff . . . chocolate
           chocolate . . . food
             STOP . . . DANGER
                 trap . . . trip
                  trip the trap
                    SNAP!

               take the chocolate

           take the food

               out of the hall

         out of the light

            into the dark

     into the wall

        feed the Rat King food

Except for the night owls in the first-class smoking room,
most of the passengers had been put to bed.
My staff and I, in the bake house as usual,
were busy at work preparing the next day's bread.
I had sailed seas so rough that a roasted chicken
once hopped from its platter into a lady's lap.
But that Sunday night, the sea was calm.
And more flat than I had ever seen it.
I don't believe in spooks and fairies at all.
But I must admit, there was a strange quality to the night.

Down in the flour room, I thought I heard noises, voices.
But the door was locked up tight, it was.
More rats perhaps? Could Maynard possibly have friends?
And speaking of which, earlier this evening I thought I saw,
just out of the corner of my eye, Maynard (the rat),
with his crooked tail. But this time it was just outside my door.
My own private cabin door. Do you suppose the little devil
is following me around? Or am I going nutters?
Then I arrived at the bakery to find the rat trap tripped
and the bait all gone—every crumb. And to top that off,
an entire tray of éclairs left over from the first-class dinner
turned up missing, too. Gone without a trace.
Maybe I had just one drink too many down in my room.
Or maybe I had one drink too few.

I put out more traps around the bakery.
Then I sent off one of my crew to deliver a special cake,
a birthday surprise for one of the sea-post men.
And finally I pulled my chair up to the big warm ovens
to do the thing that I love most: I ended the night
watching the loaves rise up golden brown.

Sort. Shuffle-shuffle. Slot. Shuffle-shuffle.

"The baker has made you a cake, Mr. W."
"A cake," says I. "What on earth for?"
"You know well and good, Mr. Woody,
that tomorrow is your birthday," says March.
"Of course I do. Of course I do," says I.
"But there is no call to make a fuss."
"Of course not, Mr. Woody," says March.
"People are born and die every day."

Sort. Sort. Shuffle-shuffle. Slot. Shuffle-shuffle.

"I should tell you, though, that the other sea-post boys
are hiding in the dining room with the cake.
Waiting to surprise you," says March.
"Then, why tell me in advance, if it's a surprise?" says I.
"Because," says Mr. March, "the surprise cannot be properly
sprung upon you, if you stay in the mail room
tending, as you do, to your late-night sorting."

Sort. Shuffle-shuffle. Slot. Shuffle-shuffle.

"Perhaps just a moment more of sorting
before we go to be surprised," says I.
"Of course," says Mr. March. "The mail
will certainly not sort itself."

Sort. Sort. Shuffle-shuffle. Slot. Shuffle-shuffle.

"Happy birthday to you, Mr. Woody."
"Happy birthday to me, Mr. March."

... ..⁻ .⁻. .⁻. ⁻⁻⁻ ..⁻ ⁻. ⁻.. . ⁻..

Two hundred fifty messages to send.
Phillips was trying to get out as many messages
as possible before his shift ended at midnight.
And I was trying to get as much sleep
as possible before I had to relieve him.

... ..⁻ .⁻. .⁻. ⁻⁻⁻ ..⁻ ⁻. ⁻.. . ⁻..

I could hear Phillips next door,
crackling at the key, talking to himself as he worked.
Late night is good for sending messages:

> Longer distances to be reached.
> Nosey-parker passengers asleep.

... ..⁻ .⁻. .⁻. ⁻⁻⁻ ..⁻ ⁻. ⁻.. . ⁻..

But unfortunately there are a few late-night chin-wags
out there who jam your signal with useless gab.
Two ships cannot send signals at once, you see.
So I knew just what was happening when
I was jolted wide awake by Phillips
shouting out at the top of his lungs,

> "Shut up! Shut up! Shut up!
> I am working Cape Race."

Chin-wag. Jamming. Useless gab.
I fell back to sleep.

... ..⁻ .⁻. .⁻. ⁻⁻⁻ ..⁻ ⁻. ⁻.. . ⁻..
⁻... ⁻.⁻⁻ / .. ⁻.⁻. .

The **MARCONI INTERNATIONAL**
MARINE COMMUNICATION COMPANY, Ltd.

Marconi-gram

From: *Californian*
To: *Titanic*
Date: 14 April 1912
Time: 10:55 P.M.

We are stopped and surrounded by ice—

The MARCONI INTERNATIONAL
MARINE COMMUNICATION COMPANY, Ltd.

Marconi-gram

From: *Titanic*
To: *Californian*
Date: 14 April 1912
Time: 10:55 P.M.

Keep out! Shut up! You're jamming my signal.
I'm working Cape Race.

The binnacle illuminates the bridge.
One human stands attentive at the wheel.
A second stands attentive by the bell
and rings off each half hour to mark the time.
The crow's-nest lookouts stomp their feet and blow
the breath of life to warm their frozen hands.
They watch for nuance in the moonless night.
The lights now out in third-class dining room,
so lively just a scant half hour ago.
Now silent in the second-class saloon,
piano keys await next Sunday's hymn.
The Turkish bath. The swimming pool. The gym.
All quiet but for a knot of first-class men
who play at cards and drink their top-shelf brands.
The gambler deals around one final hand.
The frigid air has cleared the outer decks.
A worn-out steward dims the inside lights.
A bootblack pads his way along the halls
where gentlemen have set their shoes to shine.
And doors pull to with soporific clicks.
And locks slide into place with subtle snicks.
Parents whisper. Sleeping children kissed.
Reverend and wife both kneel to pray.
In boiler rooms, the stokers shovel coal.
The socialite retires to read her book.
The tailor sleeps pressed closely to his son.
The shy girl dreams of romance, new and coy.
The young boy dreams of dragons in the night.
The wireless man attempts to stay awake.
The sea-post men sing round a birthday cake.
The baker watches golden bread loaves bake.
And all the while, in almost every room —
on mantels, walls, in pockets — hands wound tight
tick off the final minutes of the night.

Me 'n Lee bundled up, gettin' ready for our next two-hour shift.
Underclothes. Heavy jumpers. Duffle coats. Gloves.
Wool caps beneath our usual White Star seaman's hats.
And scarves, wrapped tight, to top it all off.
The temperature had dropped by ten degrees
in the past hour. It promised to be a cold watch.
We walked from our berths on E deck up to C deck,
where we stooped through the doorway of the foremast
and climbed the internal ladder all the way up top to the cage.

Archie Jewell and George Symons were there as usual and glad to see us.
"Oi, lads," said Jewell. "Good luck. It's a cold one."
"Orders from the bridge say keep watch
for small ice and growlers," said Jewell.
"But don't go lookin' for the binoculars," said Symons,
"'cause they still ain't there." They'd been missing since Southampton.

You might think that was odd, a crow's nest without binoculars,
but to tell you the truth, binoculars were only of use
when you were attempting to figure out what you was seein'.
They weren't much use helping you see the thing to begin with.
Jewell and Symons wasted no time arguing the issue.
As soon as we arrived, they left, no doubt to crawl into a warm kip.
Then it was just me and Reggie Lee and the cold night air.
We didn't make chitchat. There was no idling about.

I knew Reggie was looking for the same thing I was — a difference.
Any slight variety to the black nothingness.
The "ice blink" of a frozen floe on the horizon perhaps.
"Whiskers on the light," when the air ices up with a shimmer.
A black shape blotting out the bright stars.
I covered my face with my scarf—

chin to cheekbones, forehead to brow—
so that I was looking out through just a slit.
I had to keep blinkin' so my eyes wouldn't dry out.
My breath steamed up against the inside of my wool scarf.

Then . . . a difference. A slight vapor.
Nothing solid. Just a touch of the dragon's breath.

THE ICEBERG ✑

I am the ice. I hear the clock hands tick.
But ice marks time by creak and crack and hiss.
The hiss of air escaping as I melt.
The creak of frozen atoms set to life.
The crack of lines entwining through my mass.
The boom and splash as chunks of me collapse,
mischievous kittens springing all around.
At last my center's shifting. Now it's time.
My next maneuver barely makes a sound.
The frozen dragon's heart within me shifts
and sets my mass to sway as if to dance.
And gravity will partner me, so swift,
that should you dare to blink, you will not see
my underside become the top of me.
Surprise, my little fish. One final trick
before you hear the final second tick.
As you rush through darkness to my side,
the ice has flipped, exposing only black.
Black ice; calm seas; no wind; a moonless sky.
Could Fate provide a better place to hide?
(See now how Fate is on the Iceberg's side?)
Titanic will be, too—if all goes well.
Hear how her engines hum across the swells.
See now her razor bow heave into view,
cleaving the sea's smooth countenance in two.
I see her, too, but she does not see me.
The lookouts on her mast can't make me out.
We've never been so close, my little fish.
Make haste, now. Hurry. Bring their hearts to me.
And do let's get acquainted as you wish.
Shhh. Tick. Tick. Tick. Tick. Tick . . .

April 24, 1912
WEDNESDAY
Aboard the cable ship *Mackay-Bennett*
ATLANTIC OCEAN
THE GRAND BANKS
725 MILES FROM HALIFAX, NOVA SCOTIA

JOHN SNOW
THE UNDERTAKER

I've turned my attention to body number fifteen.
Obviously a handsome gentleman (in his prime).
Yesterday I very nearly buried him from the ship.
But something told me to save this one. He has a story.
George has completed the basic embalming.
Now I begin the finishing touches—
what we call in the business "setting the features."

This is when we make the dead appear asleep.
I like to tilt the head fifteen degrees to the right
so mourners can more easily see the face.
The eyes are next. See how the eyes of Number Fifteen
have sunken in just so? The eyes are always the first to go.
So I slip an eye cap beneath each lid and a touch of glue
to give them shape and to keep them shut.
I straighten Number Fifteen's mustache up.
And I turn my attention to the gaping mouth.
The dead, you see, hold their mouths open
as if trying to pose one final question.

I fix a curved needle with suture string.
Hold back the lips. Thread the needle
through the lower jaw below the gums.

Force the needle through the upper jaw
into the right nostril, through to the left nostril,
and downward back into the mouth, where I tie,
with my own special knot, the two ends of the string.
The knot, of course, must be hidden beneath the lips.
"The embalmers' creed, Son," my father always says to me.
"It only looks like magic if you hide your tracks."

His mouth now forever shut, Number Fifteen
will never speak his name again. But still,
he reveals who he was, to me, in many other ways.
The evidence is here in the bag of effects.
Number Fifteen's pockets were filled with clues.
The receipt from the Charing Cross Hotel, room 126.
The pipe, and the watch, and the second-class ticket.
And in one pocket, a loaded gun. From what
were you running, Number Fifteen? Or what
were you protecting, Number Fifteen? What dangers
has your death undone, Mr. Louis Hoffman?

Arminias, who claims to know his ordnance,
has picked up the revolver to inspect it more closely.
"That's odd," he says. "Two chambers are empty."

And so perhaps Number Fifteen will keep a secret after all.
Where, Mr. Hoffman, did the two bullets go?
Alas, we will never know.

I have sewn shut the dead man's mouth.

SNOW & COMPANY, LTD.

John R. Snow, Jr., Undertaker

Record of Bodies and Effects

NO. 15: MALE: ESTIMATED AGE: 36
HAIR & MOUSTACHE, BLACK

CLOTHING: Grey overcoat with green lining;
brown suit.

EFFECTS: Pocket book; 1 gold watch and chain;
silver sov. purse containing £6; receipt from Thos. Cook
& Co. for notes exchanged; ticket; pipe in case; revolver
(loaded); coins; keys, etc.; bill for Charing Cross Hotel
(Room 126, April 1912).

SECOND CLASS

NAME: LOUIS M. HOFFMAN.

SIXTH WATCH

WHISKERS ON THE LIGHT

ABOUT 1,700 MILES OUT

SUNDAY, APRIL 14,

THROUGH

MONDAY, APRIL 15, 1912

Ding-ding. Ding-ding. Ding-ding. Ding.

"Seven bells," says Reggie Lee
without taking his eyes away from the nothingness.
Thirty more minutes and this miserable day
will be history—gone forever. And I
will be asleep in my warm bed below.
"Seven bells," I says to no one.

I see the strange haze once again.
More like smoke than fog. "Hmm."
Just a subtle wisp of mist.
"Yeah," says Lee. "I sees it, too."
Then the air around the crow's nest
is suddenly alive with tiny shimmers—
like fairies. "Whiskers," says Lee.
"Whiskers on the light," I say.

And still the mist—the dragon's breath
lies low on the water, barely there.
Nothing to be alarmed about.
But the musk. That smell. I ask,
"Remember the skating rink back home?"
Reggie says, "Don't remind me, mate.
Bloody ice. It's the most I've fallen down—
leastways since I stopped drinkin', ha!"

Then a moment of silence
as we both watch ahead through slits
in the scarves wrapped over our faces.
I see, then, a blackness in the blackness.
A certain solid quality to the night
that makes me shake my head.

There amid the sameness, something different.
My palms begin to itch. My heart jumps.
Lee cocks his head. He sees it, too.

Something.

A whale? A rock? A derelict ship?
Still a ways off. Something small.
No. Bigger. Closer. Growing larger
with every passing second.
Lee begins to speak. But my hand is already
on the clapper of the big brass bell.

CLANG! CLANG! CLANG!

And I reach for the crow's-nest phone.
Nothing.
"Are you there?" I say.
Finally a voice from the bridge:
"What do you see?"

As I speak, I keep my eyes fixed
on the monster emerging from the night.
A monster that has already doubled in size.
No mistaking it now.

"Iceberg," I say.

"Iceberg, straight ahead!"

Down at me fires in boiler room six, I was feelin'
all at sixes and sevens from me narrow squeak with the Devil.
I knew, had I not returned that little girl's money belt,
I would've ended up in*side* me furnace instead of feedin' it!
It got me to thinkin' about the path me life was on
and how I might reconsider me evil ways.
When all at once the telegraph dial from the bridge rings
round to the red STOP position. That's right, STOP.
Now Freddie Barrett, the boss of our room crew,
stood gobsmacked for a moment like he couldn't
believe what he was seein'. And who could blame 'im?
Why *would* we be stoppin' in the middle o' the Atlantic?
Then he comes to his senses and yells out, full blast,
"Shut all dampers, boys! An' do it quick.
Somethin's gone wrong." And so we all jumped to it,
slamming the furnace damper doors—*bang, bang, bang,*
bang, bang, bang—like that all the way down the row.
It pained me some to damper a perfectly good rack o' coals.
Then alarm bells started ringing out and the red lights
begun to flash above the automatic watertight door.

"They're closin' the doors, lads!" I yelled. "Break for it!"
I hadn't took but a single step when—*BANG!*—gore blimey.
A noise what sounded like an explosion. And then the hull,
she shook so that I nearly fell. And then I watched the seams
between the hull's big iron plates opening up as a massive
claw of ice ran along the whole length of the wall.
Gawd, it's a bloody ice dragon, I thinks. All that bollocks
about dragons, and now here one was coming to get me!

But quick as it hit, the thing was gone and a jet o' seawater
shot into the room and knocked me to the floor.

The temperature in them boiler rooms reaches near a hundred degrees.
Most of us in the Black Gang wears just short britches
and a thin jumper. I'll have you know, when that water
hit me, I cried out in pain. It felt as if there was a thousand
tiny devils on me, jabbin' their razor-sharp tridents into me flesh.
"Get out! Get out! Everybody out!" someone was shoutin'.
Coal was scattered everywhere. I tried to run but tripped over
an abandoned barrow, and I landed on me back in the water.
It was ice cold. Nearly a foot deep. It took me breath away.
Felt like the Devil 'imself was sittin' on me chest.
And I supposed he really must have been.
And I supposed I hadn't really beat the Devil after all.
And I supposed he was laughing 'is arse off,
'cause when I finally stood up and caught me breath,
I saw that big ol' emergency door shut tight—*clang!*
With little ol' me standin' on the wrong side of it.
And I wondered if Tommy Hart had any idea
just how complicated his life had become.

It felt like the floor had been lifted slightly and tossed to one side.
And there was a minor quivering, a slow, distant scraping
as if God had run His fingernails across a huge blackboard.
I rushed out onto the bridge, where First Officer Murdoch
stood, giving orders to Quartermaster Hichens at the wheel.
Fourth Officer Boxhall was standing by the phones.
"What have we struck?" I asked, even though I knew the answer.
"We've hit an iceberg," Murdoch said. "I put her hard astarboard.
I ran the engines full astern. She was too close. She hit it.
I—I intended to port around it, but she hit before I could finish."
"Close the watertight doors," I said.
"I've closed them already," he said.
"And the bells, to warn the stokers?" I asked.
"It's been done, sir," said Murdoch.

Titanic's decks seemed solid enough.
She was firm as a church and just as quiet.
I walked over to the starboard bridge wing and peered over the side.
Boxhall and Murdoch joined me. This was the very spot
where just twelve hours before we had shot the sun.
"I see nothing," I said, for I saw nothing. "Where's the ice?"
"Sir," said Boxhall, "I think I can just make out
a low-lying growler, there off the starboard quarter."
"We've likely passed it by, by this time, sir," said Murdoch.
Boxhall mumbled something and left the bridge.
I was preoccupied at the moment with what I had just discovered.
From my vantage point on the wing, I saw a large quantity
of broken ice scattered across the starboard well deck,
the open area that served as the third-class promenade.
Aside from the ice, though, everything appeared normal.
"It seems we've had a very narrow shave, Murdoch."

By now the ship had nearly come to a complete stop.
I returned to the bridge and rang the telegraph myself,
setting the dial to "Half Ahead." I had been in ice before.
I had kept a straight line through snow, wind, and waves
and I wasn't about to stop in weather as calm as this.
With Hichens attending the wheel, I spoke to the other QM.
"Mr. Olliver, find the carpenter and have him sound the ship.
Let's see what sort of damage we may have down below."

Then I walked back into the wheelhouse to have a quick look
at the clinometer—the small clocklike instrument
that indicated the ship's trim. "Mr. Hichens," I said,
"can you read that clinometer and confirm what I'm seeing?"
"Oh, yes. I see it, sir," said Hichens. "Five degrees list."

"My God."

The words escaped my mouth before I could stop them.
The clinometer showed a five-degree list to starboard.
The toothpick fell from my mouth to the wheelhouse floor.

Titanic was taking on water.

Slosh, slosh. Lift. Toss.
Slosh, slosh. Toss. Splash.

The mailroom is taking on water, and fast.
My birthday celebration with the sea-post gents
was splendid, but all that is soon forgotten.

Slosh, slosh. Lift. Toss.
Slosh. Toss. Splash.

Mr. March. Mr. Williamson.
Mr. Gwynn. Mr. Smith. And I.
Return to our duties to find two feet of water
in the mail storage room on G deck!

Slosh. Splash. Lift. Toss.

Many bags have already been lost.
Bags of mail so carefully sorted.
Bagged. Stacked. And racked. Now wrecked.
Quickly, we move sacks to the upper deck.

Splash. Lift. Stumble. Lift.

"Your eighth disaster, Mr. March?" I say.
"Yes, Mr. Woody. It appears that's the way."

Another sack, lost. Another sack, spilt.
We are able to save most of the registered letters.
The general mail and prints do not fare so well.
The cold water takes the breath from our lungs.
But that isn't nearly the worst of it,

for with each sack washed away,
ten thousand memories are lost.
"It hurts my heart," says Mr. March,
"to see them all meet this horrible fate."
"Too late to save any more," I say.

Splash. Lift. Stumble. Slosh.

Finally we reach safety. *Stack. Stack.*
On the F deck sorting room. *Lift. Stack.*
Mr. Smith runs up top to inform the bridge.

"I'm knackered," says Williamson.
"I'm wracked," says March.
"I'm soaking," says Gwynn.
"I'm freezing," says I.

From the sorting room, we see the room submerged below.
Letters swirl in circles on the green surface.
"Watch each step of the stairs," says March.
"I see what you mean, Mr. March," says I.
"We have to keep moving the mail," says I.

The water was climbing up tread by tread.

Lift. Tumble. Slosh. Trip. Splash.

The water was not stopping.

-.-. --.- -.. / -- --. -.--

Still in my pajamas, I stood barely awake in the operating room.
I had risen two hours early to relieve Phillips.
"Well, if it isn't Sleeping Beauty," he said. "Did you not feel that tremor?"
"What tremor?" I said.
"About half an hour ago. Felt as if we struck something.
I can't believe you slept through it."
"Very funny," I said as I ducked back into the room to dress.

But a few minutes later, as I sat down to take over the key,
Captain Smith himself walked into the room.
He says, "I've just got word from the carpenter, boys.
We've struck ice. And we're taking on water.
I need you to send out the call for assistance."
Phillips snatched the headphones off my head.
"What call shall I send?" he asked Captain Smith.
"The regulation call for help. Just that," Smith said,
"along with these coordinates. They are only approximate.
But they will do for now." Smith handed Phillips a slip of paper.
"Mr. Andrews will be giving me a status report.
I'll let you know more as I know it myself."
With that, the captain left the room. He seemed calm.
A spot of bad luck was all this was.
An opportunity to watch Phillips work.

dash-dit-dash-dit dash-dash-dit-dash dash-dit-dit
dash-dash dash-dash-dit dash-dit-dash-dash

The sparks begin to fly: CQD. MGY. CQD. MGY.
To every ship within five hundred miles of us.

-.-. --.- -.. / -- --. -.--

From: RMS *Titanic*
To: All Ships at Sea
Date: 15 April 1912
Time: 12:15 A.M.

MGY. CQD. MGY. CQD.
MGY. CQD. MGY. CQD.

I require immediate assistance.
41°44'N, 50°24'W.

After the wonderful party on Sunday night
I dreamed of Alfred Rush.

Alfred was wearing his brown knee pants.
We were back in Hakoor, celebrating my birthday.
And we were laughing and dancing the *dabkeh* in a circle.
And dancing with us were my friends from the village
and my father and mother and the rest of my brothers and sisters,
who I have not seen in so long. All of us holding hands.
But then my family and friends became Turkish soldiers.
They pulled Alfred from me and pushed him to the ground.
They began to slap him as I had slapped him myself
and then surrounded him, dressing him in a soldier's uniform.
Then Alfred stood up with a cold, hard expression
and threw me down with soldiers circling us and dancing.
Alfred then held a large rat by its tail
and he stood over me, dangling the rat in my face.
The rat clawed at the air and screeched in a hideous way,
as if the sound itself was scraping along my spine.

I woke up then and the room was silent except for Elias,
who was snoring loudly with his mouth hanging open.
"Quiet! You sawmill!" I said. And I threw my pillow at him.
He stopped snoring and turned over. The room was silent.
I realized then that *Titanic*'s engines had stopped.

Was I still dreaming? I couldn't tell.
But I knew something was terribly wrong.
I jumped out of bed and put on my coat.

I was already dressed and running,
traveling the crew's passageways so as not to alarm the passengers,
investigating the damage, when I met up with Captain Smith.
"It doesn't look good, Mr. Andrews," he said.
"I'm going up top to send out a wireless distress.
I need you to meet me on the bridge with a full assessment."
As he left me, I felt an invisible hand squeezing my heart.
I could barely breathe. Everywhere I turned, I found water:
the forepeak, which held the ship's anchor chains,
the first three cargo holds, which held the luggage,
the postal rooms, the racquet court, the firemen's quarters,
boiler room six, and on into boiler room five.
I saw water rising in a total of five separate compartments.
And what's worse, in all but one, it was rising fast.
There were breaches in the hull for three hundred feet!
What in God's name could have done such damage?

I ran into Gus the barber, who asked me if we were in any danger.
"My God, it's serious," I said before I could stop myself.
I bounded up the ship's grand staircase, three steps at a time.
Past first-class passengers who were already wondering
what was going on. I dared not stop for fear they would
see the worry on my face. Finally I reached the bridge.
I conferred with Smith and Mr. Bell, the chief engineer.
I calculated the rate of flooding based on the time of the collision
and the reported water levels. Nothing worked out.

In the captain's chart room, I spread out the *Titanic*'s blueprints
and tried to remain calm as I spoke. But I began to stammer
as the horror of the situation emerged from my words:

"W-W-With two compartments f-f-flooded, we could make it to New York.
Three compartments, we'd be dead in the water but still afloat.

But the first four forward compartments—once they fill,
the weight will pull the bow down and water will pour over
the top of the watertight wall between sections four and five.
You see here how this bulkhead only goes up as far as E deck?
Once the fifth compartment floods, the sixth will follow.
And the seventh. And so on until—"

"What about the pumps?" asked Bell. "The pumps
are already clearing the water from boiler room five."

"You may buy some time with pumps,
but once boiler room six fills up, she'll go down fast.
I'm sorry, E.J., but that's the way of it."

"How long do you estimate she'll stay afloat?" he asked me.

"An hour and a half; two hours at most," was my answer.

"Thank you, Mr. Andrews," the captain said. And he turned
to engineer Bell to say, "Shut down any unnecessary systems.
I want to keep these lights on as long as possible."

 "We'll have to blow off the steam," said Bell,
"from the forward boilers, before the water reaches 'em."

"Use the aft boilers if you must; just give me lights.
And put those pumps to work as best you can.
If we gain ten more minutes, we stay dry ten more minutes."

Then placing a toothpick between his teeth, he said,
"Thank you, gentlemen, this meeting is over."
And he walked from the chart room out onto the bridge,
where the other officers awaited his orders.

"UNCOVER THE BOATS!"

What else was I to say?

The sound of the three gongs coming from the crow's nest
had been the warning that my straight line to retirement
was about to meet with an obstacle.

My deck officers knew what to do. They were well trained.
They needed no help swinging out the boats.
"Boxhall," I said, "calculate our accurate position for the CQD.
But before you do, I want you to wake the other officers.
McElroy, pass the order to every steward to serve out the belts.
And McElroy, be sure the passengers actually *put them on*.
Then tell the victualling crew to provision the boats.
And McElroy, once you've done that, I want you to gather the orchestra.
I want music. And, for God's sake, tell them to keep it light."

My God.

I was giving out orders left and right. But I really had no plan.
Two hours? How in hell was I to work with that?
Our only hope was an orderly evacuation and a passing ship,
a ship *very* close to give us time to shuttle the passengers.
We had sixteen lifeboats to work with, and four collapsible rafts.

Of course I knew the precise number of people on board.
I had signed the paperwork myself. My responsibility.
Two thousand two hundred and eight souls.
Twenty boats.
The mathematical disparity stung my brain.
Regardless of how the rest of this story turned out,
I knew it must begin with filling the lifeboats with as many souls as possible.

Then came the deafening roar of the steam escaping
from the relief pipes attached to the big funnels.
The steam was not escaping by accident but by design:
the engineers were letting off the pressure built up in the boilers.
It was nearly as loud as *Titanic*'s whistles.
It was the sound of *Titanic*'s engines shutting down for good.
It was the sound of my long, illustrious career coming to an end.

"Boxhall," he said to me, "calculate our accurate position
so Bride can make corrections to his wireless transmission."

Charting *Titanic*'s location takes very little imagination.
To find out where we are takes mathematical computation.
Since ten minutes till six P.M., the ship
travels a course of South eighty-six, West true.
(Disregard the steering compass course, of course,
of North seventy-one, which deflects two degrees
from the North seventy-three, West standard, compass reading,
for which I have already made compensation.)
I then simply apply this known course information
to the coordinates of my seven-thirty stellar observation,
and the ship's speed of twenty-two knots, estimation.
It's all just dead reckoning from there, don't you see.
And, spit spot, I've got the *Titanic*'s location.

Forty-one degrees, forty-six minutes, north latitude.
Fifty degrees, fourteen minutes, west longitude.

So that Bride can correct the ship's next CQD.

From: RMS *Titanic*
To: All Ships at Sea
Date: 15 April 1912
Time: 12:26 A.M.

CQD. MGY. CQD. MGY.
CQD. MGY. CQD. MGY.

Here corrected position
41°46'N, 50°14'W.
Require immediate assistance.
We have collision with iceberg. Sinking.
Can hear nothing for noise of steam.

Sunday certainly ain't the day of rest
when you're the only operator in the wireless shack.
I'd been at it since seven A.M. and I was undressing for bed.
But I kept the earphones on my head.
If I hadn't o' done that, I wouldn't have heard.
I set my dials to listen in on Cape Race.
I heard a message to *Titanic* go unanswered.
Then another and another. It seemed odd is all.
I knew my chum Harold Bride was second man on *Titanic*.
Though it was past my bedtime, I called *Titanic* on a lark.
Beginning with *Carpathia*'s call letters, of course.

> MPA. I say, old man, do you know
> there is a batch of messages coming
> through for you from Cape Race?

But *Titanic* broke in, stopping my transmission,
and I listened and I wrote. And I watched my hand writing
as if it were commanded by some invisible force.

> MGY. Come at once.
> We have struck a berg.
> It's a CQD, old man.
> Position 41° 46'N, 50° 14'W.

At first I couldn't believe what I was reading.
Were Bride and Phillips playing a trick?

> MPA. Shall I tell my captain?
> Do you require assistance?

> MGY. Yes. Come quick.

That was all I needed to hear. I grabbed my jacket and ran.

When word came down to the bakery to provision the boats,
I was baking the Monday bread.
My staff and I muscled the loaves,
in forty-pound loads, from the racks to the way-goods hoist.
I took a load myself, then reported to my boat station,
where I helped a lady passenger or two into their seats.
The officer was calling for women and children only,
and the boat was already well manned with sailors better qualified than me.
There seemed no reason to linger. So I returned to the warmer world.
And of course, I figured, Why not stop by my room
for a quick, fortifying swig or two from the tumbler?
The stewards all said that the ship was in no danger.
The passengers would likely be back aboard by morning.

Once I had wet my whistle, I returned to check on my staff.
"Hold off, there," I said. "Let's leave a few behind for the morning.
The loaves we pass into the boats are bound to be ruined by breakfast."
I didn't want my entire stock crushed at the bottom of a wet lifeboat.

Just then Maynard (the *human* one) passed by and said,
"There may not be any morning, Charlie. The ship's damaged bad.
If I were you, I'd take it all up top so when *Titanic* sinks,
you'll be prepared. Your loaves still won't be eatable, mind you.
But you could always lash them together to make a sturdy raft! Haw, h—"

SNAP!

As Maynard was braying at me like a jackass,
he stepped on one of the rat traps I'd set in the hall.
So what if we *had* struck an iceberg?
It hadn't turned out to be such a bad night after all.

"Lower away! Lower away! Lower away!" I say.
And they lowered the boat from promenade deck A.
But the windows there were bolted shut, of course.
We had added the windows for the first-class comfort.
On *Olympic,* the ladies had complained of the spray.
A sailor went off in search of a wrench. A wrench?
This ship was going down. A wrench?
"Lower away! Lower away! Lower away!" I say.

I walked across the deck to the starboard side.
And at last, thank God, the cacophony of steam stopped.
In the silence, then, I heard the orchestra tuning up.
The orchestra? No, people. We are not here to dance. Please.
Get into the boats! And then I noted that on that side of the ship,
the officers were allowing a few male passengers in,
because no women on board would answer the call.
"Ladies, please. There are plenty of seats. We must lower away!
Are there any more women before this boat goes?"
They didn't realize the urgency of the situation.
"Are there any more women before this boat goes?"
Already I was losing my voice. So many empty seats.
"Ah, you there. Come along, ladies. Please do jump in."
One answered, "But we are only stewardesses. Members of the crew."
"It doesn't matter that you are a stewardess, miss.
You are all women and I wish you to *get in*.
Perhaps it will serve as an example to the other ladies."

It was all we could do to convince them to don their life vests.
They hung back, huddling, or abandoned the deck altogether.
They loitered about in the gymnasium or the first-class entrance.
They made jokes about their racquet games being canceled.
For even with a slight list, *Titanic* seemed steady and safe.

But I knew the truth of it. After throwing on clothes,
I had arrived on the bridge as Thomas gave E.J. the bad news.

Finally, one lifeboat was lowered away!
Too many empty seats. "Ladies, please!"
Any *one* of these passengers could have simply stepped in.
My God. *I* could have stepped in myself! It pained me to see it.
I was as much a passenger as any one of that indolent lot.
I was no sailor. I had no idea how to prepare and launch a lifeboat.
But I could at least urge the passengers into them.
"Lower away! Lower away! Lower away!"

Not two hours ago, this night had come to such a wonderful end.
Now there I was out of my warm bed, standing on a tilting deck,
wearing coat and trousers over my pajamas, my feet shod in slippers.
"Women and children, please. Please!
Are there any more women to go in this boat?"

"Lower away! Lower away! Lower away!" I say.
The officers were letting the ropes out too slowly.
Only the second boat to go on this side of the ship.
Do they not feel the bow of the doomed ship tip?
"Lower away! Lower away! Lower away!" I say.

All my life I have striven for a strategic position.
How it pained me to see these opportunities missed.
Does this officer not know that this ship will soon founder?
This man, he moves as if he's on holiday.

"LOWER AWAY! LOWER AWAY! LOWER AWAY!"

"Lower away! Lower away! Lower away!"

The dandy in his robe and slippers was becoming hysterical.
He was circling his arms as if trying to fly! Ha.

"Lower away! Lower away! Lower away!"

I slept through the collision. I didn't feel a tremor.
I didn't feel the engines stop. I hadn't felt a thing.
Nor did I hear the roar of the steam. Not a peep.
It was the voices and footsteps down the hall that roused me.
But I didn't need any orders to tell me what to do.
I rose and dressed and loaded my Browning automatic.
(That's right, my revolver, because one never knows.)
I joined Officer Murdoch and the men at boat number seven,
who had already begun to ready it for loading:
unlacing the canvas covers (no rats in this one, I see);
stocking the bread, the water, the blankets;
unbundling the oars; fitting the cranks into the davits;
hauling the falls in their pulleys tight;
coiling the long ends of the ropes onto the deck.

Finding passengers willing to get into the boat
proved more difficult than swinging it out.
Not that I can blame them. Descending in a boat is a dangerous thing,
and the likelihood of *Titanic* actually sinking —
well, the very idea was ridiculous to me at the time.
I admit that the first lifeboat, number seven, was only half full,
but what was I to do, pull out my pistol and force people in?
And besides that, a boat's lowering capacity is typically less
than its floating capacity. With a rope at the bow
and a rope at the stern, a lifeboat is apt to buckle amidships.

"Lower away! Lower away! Lower away!"

Why did Murdoch not tell this damn prat to shut up?
The situation did not improve as Third Officer Pitman and I
next lowered lifeboat number five. That boat could have held
maybe twenty more, but mind you, it was First Officer Murdoch
who determined when to stop the loading. One rather large
gentleman rolled into the boat on top of Mrs. Stengel,
who was knocked unconscious from the looks of it!
You see, to overfill these boats was not so safe.
Nor was it safe to descend too quickly. So when Murdoch
ordered us to lower away boat number five, we did it slowly.

"Lower away. Lower away. Lower away!"

 My God. The plonker sounded like a nervous parrot.
And he *looked* like a nervous parrot, too.
The ropes attached to bow and stern must be released at the same rate
or else you'll dump the people out on the way down —
or someone could be struck by a loose oar, anything.
It takes patience and time to lower a boat safely
down a fifty-foot drop. That's how far it was to the water.
And try as I might to remain coolheaded,
the agitated parrot with mustache and pajamas,
with all of his bouncing about and shouting,
had finally tapped my last drop of patience.

"Lower away! Lower away! Lower away!"

So I turned on him and said,

"IF YOU'LL GET THE HELL OUT FROM UNDER,
I'LL BE ABLE TO DO SOMETHING!
YOU WANT ME TO LOWER AWAY QUICKLY?
YOU'LL HAVE ME DROWN THE WHOLE LOT OF THEM!"

Dear Marie,

I thought that they would tell us what to do. I thought that they would tell us where to go. My cousin Peter and brother-in-law Sigurd spoke no English, of course, so they looked to me. What do we do? What did that officer say? When will we be called to the boats?

Us fellows were all in cabins at the bow on the side where the iceberg struck. It was a terrible noise, I'll tell you. It was a prolonged grinding, like pebbles worked between millstones.

My roommate, Adolf, and I woke instantly. I put on some clothes and walked up the stairs and out onto the open deck at the bow.

I met two stokers there, who told me it was nothing and to go back to bed. But behind the stokers lay a mound of ice. It spread across the front deck there, and that made me suspicious. We who are born of the fjords know what ice is capable of.

As I walked down the stairs to return to my room, I kept missing every other step as if I were drunk. It was hardly noticeable really, but I could tell that the ship was not on level. Adolf had gone back to sleep, so I woke him up. Then I woke Peter and Sigurd, just around the corner. And together we walked to the stern to get the girls.

After the girls dressed, we all went up onto the third-class deck at the stern. A group of men from the lower decks carried luggage and clothing. They said their cabins were knee-deep in water!

But *Titanic* seemed steady. Our little group stood over by a drinking fountain. We waited. What else were we to do?

A moment later, stewards went among us, yelling, "Everyone put on your life belts." Nothing to worry about, they said. Just a precaution. With Peter's help, I went back below and returned with life belts for all six of us.

So we put on our life belts, and we waited some more.

I thought someone would tell us where to go. I thought someone would tell us what to do. I thought so many things. But none of it was true.

From: RMS *Titanic*
To: All Ships at Sea
Date: 15 April 1912
Time: 12:50 A.M.

MGY. CQD. MGY. CQD.
MGY. CQD. MGY. CQD.

We are sinking fast.
Passengers being put into boats.

    MPA. Have put on all boilers.
    Coming toward you at all speed.

It was my mate Harold Cottam on *Carpathia*.
A rescue ship was on the way!
I ran with the news out onto the deck.
I had to muscle my way through crowds
of crew and passengers. Officers were shouting out orders.
A distress rocket rushed up into the sky
and burst with a pop into a million white stars.
When I found Captain Smith and told him the news,
he grabbed me by the elbow and pulled me
all the way back to the Marconi room.
The captain wore a tight, forced smile.
"What are *Carpathia*'s coordinates?" he asked.
Phillips wrote them down on a slip of paper.
"What other ships are you in communication with?"
"A few. The *Frankfurt*. The *Caronia*. The *Olympic*.
Olympic is about five hundred miles from us.
Carpathia is the closest so far. She's on the way."
"What are you sending?" Smith asked.
"CQD," said Phillips. I said, "Why not send out SOS?
It's the new call. And it may be your last chance to send it."
We all laughed. It was, perhaps, a morbid quip,
but it felt good to laugh, anyway.
The captain left the room. I stopped laughing.
Phillips stopped laughing and commenced tapping.

dit-dit-dit   dash-dash-dash   dit-dit-dit

SOS SOS SOS SOS SOS

From: RMS *Titanic*
To: All Ships at Sea
Date: 15 April 1912
Time: 12:55 A.M.

SOS SOS SOS SOS SOS
MGY MGY MGY MGY MGY

Placing women into boats.
Request immediate assistance.
Struck by iceberg in
41°46'N, 50°14'W.
Ready your boats.
Come at once. Distress.

SOS MGY SOS MGY SOS

SOS SOS SOS SOS SOS

A few minutes before one A.M., we saw rockets shooting up into the sky from the front of the ship. That cannot be good, said Sigurd. And of course he was right. Then we saw a lifeboat full of passengers down in the water. Rowing away from the ship. *That* cannot be good either, said Sigurd.

A few of the male passengers began climbing up the arms of the cargo cranes onto the upper decks. Shall we climb up as well? asked Peter. Again I said no. I knew that when our time came, we would be instructed where to go to find the third-class lifeboats.

There was a steep stairway that led from this deck up to the second-class area. With a low gate shut just at the top. Remember, this was the same place where Nils and Olga, the young newlyweds, would have their trysts. Many passengers were lined up on these stairs, awaiting permission to climb up to the boat decks.

More rockets were fired. More lifeboats floated by. We could all spy a ship's light in the darkness. I could see clearly the lantern of a ship's mast. And word went round that it was a transfer ship that had come to take us all off. More rockets. More boats. Still we waited.

We waited for someone to show us to our boats.

Just wait! There's a light. I'm sure of it.
A ship that I can see off the port bow.
I've ordered Boxhall to hail it with the Morse lamp
between the intervals of his rocket firing.

"Tell him to come at once," I said.
"Tell him that we are sinking."

So far there is no response. How odd.
The damned fool ship is so close.
It cannot be more than ten miles away,
much closer than the *Carpathia,* unfortunately.
From the coordinates the Marconi boys gave me,
I calculate she is fifty-eight long miles away.
Even if she were as fast as *Titanic* (and she is not),
she could not go that distance in under three hours.
So even if *Titanic* stays afloat for two of those hours,
there is the problem, of course, of the third.

I used to excel at mathematics at the Etruria School in my youth.
Now I am captain of the straight-and-narrow White Star Line.
One, two, three. A, B, C. It all should be so simple.

Even if *Carpathia* steams in the straightest possible line
from starting point A, she can never hope to reach point B.
Because by then point B will have vanished
beneath the surface of the sea. Ha. A, B, Sea.
My God. My God. The irony.

And my God! Boxhall, try once again to signal that ship.
Does he not see the lamp? Does he not see the rockets?
Why won't the damn fool give us some sort of sign?

I guess the Devil didn't want me, after all.
At least not just yet, 'e didn't.
Else maybe I gots me an angel in heaven lookin' after me.
After the watertight door came down,
I clambered up an emergency ladder
and down the other side to safety.
The Devil had swallowed me up
only to spit me back out again.

Once we'd gathered our wits about us, we got word
that the water wasn't rising as quickly as we'd thought,
which allowed a few of us stokers to return along the ladders
back to boiler room six so that we might draw the fires for good.
For unless we snuffed the fires, the big boilers were liable to blow.
And if even one o' them bigguns were to blow—well—
let's just say that the Devil would have to work a double shift.

We had just finished makin' that row o' boilers safe
when the water rose up high enough to chase us out o' there.
But we were able to keep boiler room five mostly clear
by way of the pumps. With so many workmen
rushing about, things got a bit argy-bargy, and one of the engineers
broke 'is leg steppin' into an open manhole in the tank-top floor.

He wasn't hurt bad, but he couldn't walk at all,
so me and a few others carried the poor sod to the pump room
at the back of the boilers, out of the way of the hubbub.
As I propped the bloke again' the pump-room wall,
I says, "There you are, mate." And he says back,

"Thank you, Sean."

Now, didn't *that* make me heart stop like a spanner in the spokes.

From: RMS *Titanic*
To: All Ships at Sea
Date: 15 April 1912
Time: 1:10 A.M.

MGY MGY MGY SOS CQD
MGY MGY MGY SOS CQD

We are in collision with iceberg.
Sinking head down.
Come as soon as possible.
Get your boats ready. MGY.

The bow of the ship was dipping forward,
which made the deck slant just enough
to make me lose my balance from time to time
as I helped Officer Lightoller load one of the port-side boats.
From the other side of the ship, I heard Captain Smith calling out,
"Women and children first!" through a megaphone.
Next thing I know, the captain is right beside me
and he's advisin' a lady to put on her life vest.
These passengers didn't know what to do without bein' told.
And they wasn't excited about gettin' into the boats at all.

Can't say as I really blame 'em. Not an hour ago,
I was descending from the nest on my way to bed.
Now here I am, still up top workin' like a dawg.
Lee and me didn't feel a thing when we seen *Titanic* bump.
I got the impression it was just a narrow shave is all.
And it wasn't an impressive berg in the least.
It barely came up higher than the forecastle
as we watched it spit ice all across the well deck.
We finished up our watch and came on down as normal.
How such a small chunk o' ice could cause such a commotion,
well, it was beyond me. But I'm just the lookout.
Other 'n that, I just does what I'm told. An' I was told
to stand on deck helpin' the ladies and young ones
into lifeboat number six. Captain Smith was helpin' out, too.
He says, "Come along, madam," and they all comes along.
But *I* says, "Come along, madam," and they takes a step back.

Our boat was full of a good number of women,
though we could have held more, I'd guess.
I stepped into the boat to tend the forward falls.
Lightoller put Quartermaster Hichens in charge,

so he took his place at the stern. And *PLOP!*
PLOP! PLOP! Women were just tossed in from the deck.
I must say, these ladies weren't athletic in the least.
And finally we started dropping toward the water.
The captain called down after us through his megaphone,
"Row straight for those ship's lights over there
with the passengers and return as soon as possible."
I couldn't wait to get my oar in the water.
I figured, the sooner I could reach that other ship,
the sooner I could get back to *Titanic,*
and the sooner I could finally jump into my warm bunk.

I was in bed reading when I felt the impact.
I threw on my robe and slippers
and walked outside to find maybe a dozen men
clad in their pajamas rubbing their hands to stay warm.
The ship's engines had stopped but there seemed no danger,
so I walked back to my room along the corridor
lined with sleepy women standing in their kimonos.
I encountered a steward or two as well. None seemed concerned.
So I climbed back into bed and fell back into my book.

A half hour later, the scene took an extreme turn!
A man who I assume was a steward came along the hall,
waking us all and telling us very firmly to put on our life belts
and make our way to the top deck. So I dressed as warmly
as possible and chose a silk capote for my head.
And perhaps it was the mother in me, but I also gathered up
my extra furs and two extra life belts in case they'd be needed.

Up top I met Mrs. Candee and her coterie.
Mrs. Candee commented that all of us passengers reminded her
of a fancy-dress ball in hell. And I quite agreed.
Everyone wore a hodgepodge combination of sleepwear,
evening wear, and winter wear—all of it layered in disarray.
The orchestra added to the effect when it assembled on deck
and launched into an endless series of ragtime tunes.

Mrs. Candee's young friend, Hugh Woolner, handed her
a sample of the iceberg he had found, but it was so cold
that she dropped it onto the deck. It shattered like glass.
Then he and three other men eased Mrs. Candee into a lifeboat
as if she were a princess made of rare crystal.
I, on the other hand, was snatched up by two strangers
and dropped into the boat like a sack of potatoes.

Around one A.M., an officer came to the top of the steep stairs and he called down for women and children. You should have seen the confusion. Many of the families didn't want to be separated. Many didn't even speak English, and they couldn't make sense of the directions. The ship's interpreter, who spoke only a little bit of Swedish, accepted my offer to help him speak to some of the other Scandinavians.

By this time the whole ship was leaning noticeably in the water. The deck sat at an angle. More rockets. More boats. Adolf became separated from us in the crowd, but we pushed our way through and forced Anna and Karen up the stairs. Karen was very frightened. Sigurd told her, "Just be strong. It will all end well."

There were a few tearful moments when older boys were not allowed past the gate. Two boys argued with their mother, who refused to leave them behind.

After the girls had gone up to the boats, Peter asked once again: "Now, Olaus, shall we climb the crane? Shall we take matters into our own hands?" He was very excited.

"No!" I said. "We wait."

We wait. We wait. We wait.

Now, just you wait.

Since Officer Boxhall has begun to send up the rockets,
I can sense the passengers becoming more agitated.
Suddenly, they are volunteering more readily to enter the boats.
And a few of the more shrewd ones are trying to push their way in.
Oh, nothing is out of hand. At least not yet. But wait.

Wait and see how quickly order can crumble.
Wait and see how badly a straight line can be bent.

I know my third-class passengers have no straight line
to the lifeboats. And I know that the most resourceful of them
will make their way up any way that they can.
But these boats are for the women and children.

    "Women and children, please!" I order
    through my megaphone. "Women and children!"

So far, so good. When the men are refused, they graciously nod.
I see them as they place their wives into the boats,
hoping that they might be offered a seat. So far, so good.

But just you wait.

We'll call for the women and children in steerage soon.
But first, while my passengers are still acting British,
I'll gather my officers below to distribute the guns.
Something small to slip into their pockets. Just in case.

    "Women and children, please! Women and children!"

For if the crowds get out of hand, there will be no time to wait.

At first I thought the voice had returned.
But I fully awoke to realize voices were coming from the hall.
I walked outside to find some third-class passengers
playing at football with a piece of the iceberg
on the deck below my own. When orders were passed along
to put on life vests, I asked a steward if there was any danger.
He replied, "Certainly not, sir. It's just a precaution."
But this same smiling man turned around to another steward,
and, with a grave face, he said there was no hope.
It was certain *Titanic* would not stay afloat.

Up on deck, officers were allowing only
women and children into the lifeboats.
I felt as if God had betrayed me.
Had He finally offered me some clarity of mind,
some hope within my heart,
just to snatch it all away like this?
And what of my children? How could God include
these two young innocents in His cruel, ironic joke?

I felt more alone than I had been in all my life.
I returned to my cabin, where my children slept.
I turned out the light. And I wept.

From: RMS *Titanic*
To: All Ships at Sea
Date: 15 April 1912
Time: 1:25 A.M.

MGY MGY MGY SOS CQD
MGY MGY MGY SOS CQD

We are putting the women
off in small boats.

Just me luck. This gent with the broke leg was Shepherd,
the engineer who suspected me
back when we was stopped at Queenstown.
Everyone in the boiler room was goin' about their business.
I looked about the pump room, and I seen we was alone.

"Do I know you, mate?" I asked.

"You don't know me," he said. "But I know you.
I was a stoker on the *Adriatic* back in '08. Remember that ship?
That was the year that four of the Black Gang were caught
stealing from the passengers' luggage. Two of 'em kept lookout
while the other two did the deed. But there was a fifth man —
the fellow who masterminded the whole thing.
He was a drifter and a troublemaker. But he was smart.
When the police searched the crew's quarters, they found
all the evidence in the four men's dunnage bags and bunks.
But this fifth fellow, his kit was clean as a whistle.
He got off scot-free while the other four dupes went to jail."

"Listen, fella," I said. "That's quite a story, but —"

"No. It's true. Their names were Chalk, Henry, Cavendish, and Kelly.
And they were all friends of mine. I told you, mate,
I never forget a face. Nor a name. And I know your face,
and, as God is my witness, your name's Sean Gould."

"And what if it is? Those four blokes made their own beds.
And they paid the price. I didn't hold no gun to their heads."

"But they were all good men who'd fallen on hard times.
They were honest men with families to feed. Not like you.
For them the job was meant to be a one-off. But you —

it turned out every ship you'd ever worked was burgled."

"That was four years ago, mate. Let it go. It's over."

"Oh, it's over, all right. It's over for *you*," Shepherd said.
"Do you remember who was commander of the *Adriatic*?
His name was Captain E. J. Smith, and I'm sure he'll want to know
his old friend Sean Gould is working the *Titanic* with stolen papers."

Before I had even a moment to contemplate
the situation I was in, one of the lead firemen
puts 'is head into the pump room and says to me,
"Come on, Hart, stir your stumps, man. Everyone's been called
up to their boat stations. Get a move on."

So I turned and walked across the big empty floor o' boiler room five.
What else was I to do? I'd been found out, you might say.
But just as I had one foot on the emergency ladder
to make me way up top, I heard a strange deep rattle
like someone clanging a spanner against the side of the ship.
Only the noise was coming from the wall opposite me—
the wall that held back the water of *Titanic*'s flooded
forward compartments. Two other stokers heard it, too,
and they started scrambling up the ladder behind me.

"Move it, Hart!" said one of the men. "That wall's about to—"

And just like that, the bulkhead gave way with an awful sound
of twisting metal as the water rushed into boiler room five.
The blokes below climbed up over and around me,
stepping on me hands as I clung to the rungs for dear life.
Then after that first rush of water, I was able to get a steady hold.
I took one last look over me shoulder
and I seen the water rushing into the pump room,
where Shepherd was laid up with a broken leg.

Someone called down from the top of the ladder,
"Come on, Hart. Don't be a fool.
There's nothing left to do down there!"

I looks up at the dry deck at the top o' the ladder.
Then I looks down at the rising flood at me feet.
I seen me reflection there in the surface of that water.
An' for just a moment I couldn't remember who I was.
Was I lookin' at Tommy Hart? Or was it Sean Gould?
I don't know which one of 'em done it—Tommy or Sean.
But whichever one it was, 'e took a deep breath an' 'e dove
off that ladder on 'is watery way to the flooded pump room.

SPLASH!

By this time, it was apparent that something was seriously wrong with the *Titanic*. Yet still I waited on the aft deck with the other men. Many, many families were there, too. Women and children who would not or could not be separated from the men. I still had faith that we would be sent for eventually. Our time would surely come.

One man announced that water was rising along a main third-class passageway that they call Scotland Road. This meant that the cabin I shared with Adolf must now be flooded as well. And as for Adolf, by that time he had been missing for nearly an hour. And although I didn't know it at the time, I would never see him again.

We saw no more lifeboats. The strange masthead light we had seen earlier in the distance was no longer there. Another emergency rocket went up.

"Shall we climb up the crane, Olaus? What if no one comes for us, Olaus?"

I told Peter and Sigurd to trust me. So we waited.

After successfully lowering lifeboats seven and five,
I paused a moment to watch the white stars of a
distress rocket explode in the air. I noticed, then,
the parrot man was standing beside me, finally silent.
I worked my way forward, to boat number three.
And forward again to boat number one, where Mr. Stengel,
a large round man who made it rich in leather,
rather rolled himself into it with a good-natured tumble.
"*That* is the funniest thing I've seen all night," I said.
First Officer Murdoch, who was in charge of starboard loading,
was allowing men to enter only after all women had taken a seat.
Leastways, whatever women could be found.

Having loaded and launched all boats at the starboard bow,
I pushed through the crowds headed aft. And as I did,
I noticed the subtle shifting of the ship beneath my feet.
All night she had listed just slightly to starboard, but now
she was doing just the opposite, leaning slightly to port.

"The water is shifting about in her holds," I told Moody,
the tall, thin sixth officer, the only junior under me.
We struggled past the officers' mess and crossed the deck
to the aft-most boats, where two seniors were in charge.
One of them, Second Officer Lightoller, was shouting out,
"Women and children only! Men, stand back. Stand back!"

Well, a dozen men grumbled and stepped back onto the deck
as we put in more and more women. But one young fellow
just sat there like a statue. "Get out of it, son!" I said.
I pulled the young fellow out onto the deck.
And I whispered in his ear, "Be a man, for God's sake. Be a man."
And he shuffled off into the crowd, crying like a baby.

I had to do what I did, and I did it the best I could.
I knew that the last five boats had been lowered without an officer,
and I said so to Moody, who said, "You go in this one.
I'll go down in one later." What's more, it was very clear
that boat number fourteen was in need of protection.
I had gradually realized that the ship was going down fast.
And by that time so had just about everybody else.
Foreign men were hanging out over the rails of the lower decks,
looking up at the boat and talking all their gibberish.
Glaring more or less like wild beasts, ready to spring.
Now, take note that boat fourteen was filled to capacity,
I had no idea how much weight it could stand,
suspended as it was from a rope at each end.
All it would take would be for one bloke too many to jump in
and the hull would buckle in the middle, killing everyone aboard.

Someone had to take the job of fending off jumpers,
so I climbed in myself as she was lowered away.
I pulled my gun and I wasn't very nice about it.
Slowly we dropped past the three open decks
where crowds of crazed Italians stood waiting to pounce.
As the boat went by each deck, I fired a warning shot.
And the shots were effective, I'll have you know.
Did my actions mean the death of one or two foreigners?
I have no doubt. But lest you judge me,
first remember: I had my share of foreign women in my boat.
And I can guarantee you every one of them lived!

From: RMS *Titanic*
To: All Ships at Sea
Date: 15 April 1912
Time: 1:30 A.M.

MGY MGY MGY SOS CQD
-GY MG- MGY S-S CQ-

Women -nd **children**
in smal- boats.
Can-ot last much longer.
MGY.

scuttle scuttle scuttle

carry the food

find the flour barrel

feed the Rat King

into the dark

into the walls

scuttle—

STOP DANGER

jump dodge scuttle escape

into the dark

into the flour barrel

feed the Rat King

SMASH!

listen . . . SMASH!

smash . . . danger

SMASH! . . . DANGER

danger . . . escape

leave the flour barrel

leave the Rat King

into the dark

into the hall

under the bread

hide hunker

escape survive

It was well after one A.M., and by then I knew,
like the rest of the crew, that the ship was doomed.
I was wishing that I had gotten off in my assigned boat.
But there wasn't much to be done about it now.
I'd seen one officer dictate his orders at gunpoint
and roust out about a dozen stokers from their seats.

I saw water along Scotland Road creeping up from the bow.
And I'm not afraid to admit that it unnerved me.
So I stopped into my cabin for another few shots of courage
before returning to the flour room to gather more supplies.
It seemed useless now, not to use the French baguettes I was saving there.

I brought the hoist down from above. And there
on top of my basket of big Viennese loaves—the rat!
It lifted up on its back legs as bold as you please,
holding a large piece of chocolate éclair in its teeth.
I tried to smash the vermin with a baguette, but it was too fast.
It jumped down from the hoist and bolted into the flour room,
but not before I noticed its crooked tail. It was Maynard, all right!

The lights in the flour room had been shut off,
so I had to use an electric torch to see what I was doing.
The refrigerator units had long since ceased their hum.
It was quiet and eerie, like entering a crypt.
I found evidence of a rat nest in one of the empty barrels.
Now, maybe it was the whiskey, or maybe it was the fear,
but I started breaking open the tops of every empty barrel
as quickly as I could, using the butt end of my torch as a club.
In barrel after barrel I found evidence that the rats had been
scavenging food and nesting supplies from all over the ship.
Dining menus, napkins, newspapers, and Marconi-grams,
a list of the first-class passengers' names. An empty jar of Lemco.

They'd been living right under my nose all along!

Then I heard a strange thumping from inside one barrel.
An empty barrel, numbered forty-six. *Thump. Thump. Thump.*
And when I smashed the top of it open, I couldn't believe my eyes.

There, in the bottom, were about a dozen rats—
all of them CONNECTED AT THE TAILS!
Some were dead and in various stages of decay.
Some seemed as if they had been partially eaten.
Some were very much alive but unable to run, joined as they were.
Some were full grown and large, some smaller and young.
And the fur was a variety, from pure white to brindled.
The greater they struggled, the more tightly bound they became.
They twitched and hissed under the brightness of my light.
They clawed and bit at one another in the most ghastly way.

The flour barrel stunk to high heaven
and I could tell they had been this way a long while.
The sight of them set my stomach to turning.
It was all I could do to keep from being sick.

But I noticed something that astonished me even more:
amid the writhing tangle of this many-headed creature
were fragments of a chocolate éclair—
one of *my* chocolate éclairs from the bakery!
Had the rat with the crooked tail been feeding them?
And speaking of which, where had the rodent gone?
Maynard wasn't among the others—that I could tell.

I left the room and shut the door behind me.
Then I made my way up top with my last loaves of bread.
The sight at the bottom of barrel number forty-six
had sobered me up almost completely, and suddenly I felt less
like killing rats and more like saving myself.

I had not even bothered to put on my overcoat.

Mr. Stengel having disappeared for the night,
I stood outside the smoking-room door,
watching all the commotion and having a laugh
with a few other bachelors.
None of us believed the mighty *Titanic* would sink,
least of all me. The largest and most grand ship in the world,
sinking on its first voyage while the whole world watched?
The odds against it were much too high.

As I turned to head back in, I met an unlucky sap,
come up from below. He was wet from head to toe
and shivering with the cold from having jumped
into a flooded pump room to try and save his friend.
He was still a bit delirious and kept telling me that he
was an impostor of some sort. Imagine that.
If he only knew who he was talking to. Ha.
You may know by now that I am no Boy Scout —
but neither am I beyond performing the occasional act of kindness.
I removed my jacket and placed it around his shoulders.
Then I tried to walk him into the smoke room to warm up.
But he refused to go. Instead he grabbed my arm
and leaned toward me, shivering under his breath.
"Mark me words, squire. *Titanic* is sinking fast.
If you know what's good for ye,
you'll go queue up and get a seat while ye can."

The stoker walked off toward the back of the ship,
and I walked toward the boats on the starboard side.
And to further improve my chances, I offered to assist
a baker who was distributing loaves of bread.
"Just hand me the entire basket," I said.

Me lungs were about to burst
when I finally reached Shepherd in the pump room.
But—sorry to say it—I got there too late to save 'im.
His eyes were wide open, staring at me, but not seein'.
And by the time I got back safe to the emergency ladder,
I was nearly a dead man meself.
When Collins and the other stokers pulled me up, they says,
"Hart. You're a dammed fool. Why'd you do it?"

Now, I haven't never explained why I do bad things,
so I don't expect I'll be explaining the good things, neither.
But there's *one* thing I did understand just then:
it wasn't Tommy Hart what jumped in that water;
it was Sean Gould. And that felt good.

Once I caught me breath, I did what I could to help out,
but the water kept movin' from boiler room to boiler room.
So we was all told to beat a retreat to the top deck.
I was just about froze when a first-class gent gave me his jacket.
I didn't figure I'd ever be warm again.

Since there was no room for us stokers in the boats,
I just walked about the deck trying to keep warm.
I happened by a priest at the stern of the ship,
surrounded by a couple hundred passengers and crew,
and he was taking everybody's last confessions, fast as he could.
So I took my turn and says, "My name is Gould, Father.
My name is really Gould. I'm not really Hart."
He looks at me and says, "That's not true, my son.
You are *all* heart. That's all any of us are!"
I tried to tell him that he misunderstood,
but he had already moved on to the next confession.

Then they all prayed out loud to God and Mary.
They prayed and yelled, never lifting a finger to help themselves.
They had lost their own willpower and expected
God to do all the work for them. Now, I'm just a sinner,
and the Devil is mostly who I'm usually rubbing elbows with,
but I *do* know one or two things about God.

God is the Almighty Creator of heaven and earth.
God is all-knowing and all-powerful. True enough.
But God is not so good at the little things,
like turning a doorknob, shoveling coal,
doing up bootlaces, or rowing a boat.
I figure sometimes God means for us to do for ourselves.
What most of us needs is less faith and more imagination.

So rather than pray to God to save my sinful soul,
I walked over to the kennels behind the fourth funnel
and I broke open the lock.

I just sat right down on me frozen arse, and all them pups
gathered around me, wagging their tails, barking hello,
licking at me ice-cold hands, thinking we was on the way for a walk.
Just happy to be out in the cold air under God's bright stars.

There we all was:
Tommy Hart, Sean Gould, and a pack o' dogs,
happy to have escaped from our cages
to walk free and easy on the deck of a sinking ship.

Captain Smith had confided to me early that the ship would sink.
I was a man of science, so I had no misunderstanding
about my chances of survival in water so cold.
For an hour we had waited for the windows on A deck
to be unlocked and opened for loading. Madeleine and I whiled away
some of that time in the gymnasium, where we laughed and chatted
at the absurdity and the promise of the coming months:
there was much to do to prepare for the baby's arrival.
We looked comically frumpy in our bulky life vests.
I showed her how the floatation devices worked
by cutting the canvas to expose one of the cork inserts.
The gymnasium's mechanical camel set us to reminiscing
about Egypt, but it was the future that most concerned us.

Finally our lifeboat was ready for loading.
"I would like to attend to my wife, please," I told the officer in charge.
"She is in a delicate condition," I added discreetly.
"I'm sorry, sir," he replied. "No man is allowed in this boat
until the ladies are safely off." I asked him for the boat's number
and he answered, "Number four." I stepped back.

We were the elite among society's elite:
Astors, Wideners, Carters, Thayers, Ryersons.
And we played by the strictest rules of conduct.
And so as the women began to descend, we men
did our duty and lied to our wives.
And they did their duty and believed what was not true.
"I will see you in New York" were my last words to Maddie.
Then I tossed her my gloves and stepped back into shadow,
knowing I would likely never see her again.
Nor would I ever meet the child now so alive in her womb.

And I would never get to see what the future would be.

Though I did not know it at the time,
it was not my brother's snoring that had woken me.
It was *Titanic* striking an iceberg.

At first Elias would not get out of bed.
"You're not the boss of me," he said.
But then a third-class steward came through:
"Everybody up! Life belts on! Life belts on! Everyone."
Many people did not take the danger seriously,
but I did. My nightmare had surely been a warning, I thought.

We did not even bother to dress, simply put on our coats
and followed the stream of passengers to the rear deck.
Elias was his usual unruly self and played football
with other Lebanese boys, kicking at pieces of ice
they had found at the front of the ship.

And standing there, on the same white crane
where I had first seen him, was the boy in brown pants.
And he looked at me and he waved.
He waited with the English.
I waited with the Lebanese.
We waited there for the longest time.
But I didn't mind because Alfred was there.
We never spoke. We simply watched.

Then a man in uniform called out for women and children,
so Elias and I lined up and waited our turn
before walking up the steep metal steps to the upper decks.
I turned at the last moment to the boy on the crane,

but he was gone.

Eenie-meenie-epatic,
tilia-talia-dominic,
hokey-pokey-tom-in-okey,
ti-tata-touch,
ugily-buggily-boo.
And out goes Y-O-U, you're OUT!

That's how me and my mates do the choosing.
But the *Titanic* man said, "Only women and children.
The rest must stay and wait." Now, tell me: How is that fair?

Mum seems nervous; she's "protecting" me again,
squeezing my hand and holding me close.
She kisses my dad (with everyone watching!),
and Mr. Theobald hands her his wedding ring.
He says, "Give this to my wife . . . if necessary."
Well, that was the silliest thing I've ever heard!

    (I felt in my pockets:
    three gumdrops,
    two seasickness pills,
    one dragon's heart.)

And when Mum tries to get Alfred to follow, he pulls away.
"But we're going to ride in a boat, Alfred! Come on!" I said.
"No, Frankie. You go on. I'm staying with the men."
Then my dad looks down at me and he says,
"So long, Frankie. I'll see you later."
"OK, Dad," I said.
Have I told you my dad's the best
tool-and-die man in all of Strood?
He is. That should be enough right there.
To let him go for a ride in the boat.

From: RMS *Titanic*
To: All Ships at Sea
Date: 15 April 1912
Time: 1:40 A.M.

--D. **SOS**. SO-. **CQD**.
MGY. M--. **MGY**. MG-.

Engine ro-m **ge**-ting flo-ded.

Finally, about two A.M., the gates were swung open, and there came down a call that all third class were now allowed onto the boat deck. I told Peter and Sigurd, "You see. I told you we would be taken care of." Peter leaned over the water fountain to take a sip before heading up to the boats. No water came out, of course. "You'll soon have all the water you want, fella," a passing crewman said with a laugh. "Good luck finding a boat up top. All of 'em's already gone."

We all laughed at that. Imagine it. We were laughing!

Peter, Sigurd, and I walked up the steep metal stairs, while many passengers and crew headed the opposite way. "Keep going," I told them. It was not so easy reaching the boat deck, but when we arrived, we found no boats left! Only ropes and scattered loaves of bread. As far as we could tell, every bracket that had once held a lifeboat was empty!

"Why did you make us wait?" said Peter. "We could have climbed the cranes," he said. "Why did you make us wait?"

Why did I, Marie? Why did I make them wait?

"Yalla, yalla, yalla!" I call out to my brother.
He stops at every window to look in at the ship.
"Look, Jamila. It is the gymnasium.
Bicycles and rowing machines! Let's try them out."
"No, Elias. *Yalla!*" I say. I am cold and tired and scared.
I wish I had my proper clothes. I hear my name.
"Jamila!" It is Selini and Fraza, sitting in a boat.
Selini speaks to me in Arabic.
The sound of my own language calms my nerves.
"Climb in," Selini says. "This is one of the very last boats."
I climb in and take a seat next to her. Elias joins us, too.
"Will the boat sink?" I ask. "I thought she could not sink!"
"Oh, I think she will," says Fraza.
As Fraza says this, one of the officers shouts out something
and he comes over to us. Fraza speaks to him.
I do not understand what they are saying, but the officer is angry.
Fraza stands and argues in English. Then he sits down
with a defiant look on his face. Then a gun!
The officer has a gun and points it at Fraza.
We all gasp and Selini lets out a scream.
She grabs at Fraza as he steps over me, back onto the deck.
Fraza must pry her hands from him.
"I will be all right, Selini, I will find another boat."

I can hear the sound of water rushing over the front of the ship.
Suddenly our boat begins to lower. Selini weeps.
Fraza looks down, his eyes full of tears as well.
And I'm reminded of my father, with his own weeping eye.
And even as I console Selini, who grieves for her husband,
in my secret heart I am rejoicing for my father.

Hey, Mum, look, that's the girl that smacked Alfred.

Why does she get to go? But not Rossmore and Eugene?

Why don't they just do "eenie-meenie-epatic"?

That's what I would do if I was captain.

I mean if I *were* captain. Is it *was* or *were*?

Why are you wearing Mr. Theobald's ring?

Ouch. You're squeezing me, Mum.

I want to sit over there.

Can we sit over in that spot there?

Hello, Rossmore! Hello, Eugene! Get in.

> *(Pssst. Mum. Did you know*
>
> *their dad is a boxing champ? But he's not around.)*

I wonder what sort of boat Dad will get.

Can I help row?

I have two seasick pills if you need one.

And I have two gumdrops.

I had a third one, but I ate it.

> *(Pssst. Mum. I think there's a Chinaman*
>
> *hiding under that bench. Look. See?)*

Whoa! Here we go. We're scraping the side.

This is brilliant!

> *(Hey. Why are those two men allowed?*
>
> *Did you see, Mum? They just stepped right on in.)*

Oh, look—you can see through the porthole.

Those boys are playing tag!

> *(Pssst. Mum. Who are those men?*
>
> *They waited till we was going down*
>
> *and stepped right in.)*

Why do they get to go, but not Dad?

Did they do "eenie-meenie"?

I was in the right place at the right time.
What matter that it happened by accident or design?

As I have said before and I will say again,
I strive in all things to be mindful
and to position myself to the greatest advantage.
That is the dictum I live by.
And yet you'd make me your scapegoat
because I took a descending boat.
Was I to let it pass me by?
There was a space. An empty seat.
What would it serve, then, not to fill it?
Is it *my* moral duty to stay with the ship?

Yes, others had been turned away.
Yes, other men had been denied.
But remember, I took no part in that.
In fact I helped the women in
and then stepped back while the ladies sat.
Decorum dictates you must die;
common sense requires you live.
And if you speak for God, you lie,
so judge me not lest you forgive.
Heaven is not so much a place
as it is an opportunity.
I'll choose the time and place I face
my moral responsibility.
And regardless how it makes you feel,
would you have me die for an ideal?

What matter that it happened by accident or design?
I was in the right place at the right time.

From: RMS *Titanic*
To: All Ships at Sea
Date: 15 April 1912
Time: 2:00 A.M.

MGY MGY MG- S-- CQD
MG- -GY --- -OS CQ-

Engine room full up to boilers—

By now we were walking down the slanted deck, like walking down a gentle hill. *Titanic*'s nose was that far down into the water. We went to the very front of the ship. There we discovered what looked to be the only boat left hanging in a set of launching brackets. A ring of men linked arm in arm were keeping away anyone other than woman or child who dared enter that last precious boat. I saw a man pass two young boys through the ring. He said a few words to the oldest in French. Then he turned and rushed away, weeping.

Yes, my sleepy Lolo.
We are going on an adventure.
We are getting into a small boat.
Yes, Momon, too.
That is right; Momon is sleeping.

They will play pretty music
while you get into the boat.
I hoped we could go together,
but these men will not allow it.

The ladies will take care of you.
Papa will join you later.
Please, remember me to your mama, Lolo.
And give her my best.
My greatest wish
was that we one day
might all be together.

My watch?
Yes, here is my watch.
Just the right fit
for your tiny hand.
But now Papa needs it back,
so he can count the minutes
until he sees you again.

No, you cannot have your doll.
There is no time.
Now, Lolo, you must—
Lolo, I am sorry.
I am so sorry.
For everything.

everything is gone.

papa bought me a doll.

the doll is gone.

papa's gold watch is gone.

papa's pipe is gone.

papa's pistol is gone.

papa's pockets is gone.

papa is gone.

mama. gone.

crackers. gone.

the big ship. gone.

momon. not gone.

i want my doll.

my doll is gone.

By this time the entire forward third-class promenade, where I had stood just two hours earlier, was completely underwater. An officer who was attempting to connect a raft to some launching ropes called out, "Are there any sailors here?"

And although I had many years of experience at sea, I did not volunteer my help because Peter and Sigurd urged me not to. We must stay together, they said. As the bow of the ship plunged forward, we three ran back up the slanted deck. The incline became so steep that we had to stop and cling to one of the brackets.

Surrounded as we were by such terror, it was almost comical to hear the orchestra playing. The sounds of the violins were so beautiful.

For our impromptu lifeboat-filling concert,
Wally combined the quintet and the trio
to create a one-of-a-kind deluxe orchestra.
It was a rare treat for all eight of us to play.
Those of us who had already changed
out of our uniforms, like me, put them back on.
These were snappy-looking get-ups: green,
with gold piping and brass White Star buttons.
Once dressed, we gathered in the entrance
to the first-class saloon, so that Ted and Percy
could take turns at the piano there.
That's when the ragtime numbers ruled.
I had brought along the Guadagnini,
and she was in rare form all through the night.
The more I played her, the more I knew
she would be my main instrument for life.

We moved the whole band out onto the boat deck itself,
where we no longer had the benefit of the piano,
so we played mainly jigs, reels, and marches—
all punctuated by the whistle and pop of emergency rockets
detonated at regular five-minute intervals.
As a rule, the steamship musician is heard and not seen.
It was a treat to come out from behind the potted palms
to really show our stuff. I thought, *If Dad could see me now!*

But the surreal quality of our task became more pronounced
with every launched lifeboat. The more tilted the deck,
the more desperately and passionately we played.
As the ship sank lower, I sank deeper into the music.
I tried to get the angle of my bow just right against the strings,
experimenting with where to play in relation to the bridge,
savoring the alterations that each minute shift would bring.

Anything to avoid the world of danger that surrounded us.
This may help you understand why we continued playing,
as we did, all the way to the evening's climactic coda.
The music became our protective shell, keeping death at bay.

As *Titanic*'s forecastle disappeared underwater,
one or two musicians wandered aft to tend to other matters.
Wally called out, "Number One Hundred Fourteen, boys."
Then he looked at me and added,
"That'd be 'Songe d'Automne,' of course."
And we played it soulfully and slow as lower and lower
the ship's bow dipped. With a clunk a cello was laid on the deck,
followed by steps. Another clunk, a viola this time. More steps.
A clunk, a double bass, laid down. But Wally stood firm
and segued into the strains of "Nearer, My God, to Thee,"
just as he said he would. And to pay him homage, I played along
and I played it sweetly—and by the book—note for note,
until I noticed, here and there from Wally, a variation on a phrase,
a seventh added in for flavor, a trill to thrill, a run for fun,
and then a lilt, a leap, a thunderous screech!
Wally had launched into a masterly improvisation that transformed
the hymn into a bird, a dog, a windblown tree, the snow,
and he finished with a quiet, weeping tremolo.

"Bravo, my friend," I said. "Bravo."
I reached in my pocket. Unfastened my purse.
And I emptied its contents onto Wally's open palm.
When he saw it was Widener's sixteen cents, he laughed.
We laughed a duet. Fell silent. Shook hands.
Then the bubble was burst.

And we prepared for the worst.

Speaking in Norwegian, I asked my brother-in-law if he could swim and he said no. I asked my cousin if he could swim, and he said no. I showed them how to move their arms and legs. The life vests would keep their heads above the surface. Then the bow of the ship suddenly went down fast, and there was a kind of explosion. The deck raised up so steep that the people around us could not stand on their feet. So they fell down and slid into the water right on the ship.

Women and children. Crashing into the vents and railings as they fell. It was a terrible sight. And there was nothing I could do but hold on tight.

After I let the dogs out for their run,
Titanic's stern rose up so steep the poor animals
slipped and lost their footing just like the people.
I clung to the deckhouse's wooden handrail
and climbed the incline till I could round the corner
into the first-class smoke room, where I saw
but just one man left in the whole place.
He was standing in his pajamas at the fireplace mantel
staring at the picture what hung there.
He weren't wearing his life preserver at all.
He had it draped on a chair there, all lonesome like.
And it occurred to me, with the man so preoccupied,
I might be able to snatch it away without his even knowin'.
I could just take it like I took Tommy Hart's discharge book
or like I took that foreign girl's money belt.
Or like I took all them knickknacks and doodads
while me mates kept watch on the *Adriatic*.

You see, Sean Gould truly had turned over a new leaf,
but I figured it was all just a waste if he was dead.
So why not have my first act of goodness be
to help save the skin of a sinner-turned-saint?

I was somewhat startled when I turned to see
the stoker standing there, soaking wet and shivering
in just short pants and dinner jacket. Startled?
As if anything could startle me now. After this.
"That's a right lovely picture, that is," he said.
"It's an original by Norman Wilkinson," I said.
I pointed to my life vest, draped over a chair.
"If you value your life, you'll put that on."
"No, sir," he said. "I can't do that. It's yours.
Much as I want it. I shouldn't take it from you."
I asked, "What's your name?"
"Name's Hart," he said after a moment's hesitation.
I placed the vest on the stoker myself.
"Well, then. We must certainly protect the heart of the hive.
My name is Andrews. I designed this ship.
This is *Titanic*'s only real working fireplace. The rest are all fake.
This mantel is sculpted from veined marble. I watched them install it.
Do you have any children, Hart?"
"No, sir," he said. "Least none that I knows of. Ha."
"Ha. Yes, well, I have one child. A lovely little girl."
The floor lifted. Shifted under my feet.
Everything that had once been square was turning askew.
The hive was in trouble. The bees had begun to stir.
"Let's make a go of it, sir," the stoker urged.
"You haven't no chance if you stay inside."
"No, Hart," I said. "Other little girls are still on this ship.
And that is why I must stay."
"But, sir. You surely cannot save them all!"
"Exactly so, Hart. Exactly so. And that is why I cannot go."
The stoker ran across the room, but stopped and turned to say,
"I'm sorry, sir. She was a grand ship, she was."

"I'm sorry, too," I said. And the stoker was gone.

What I love about shipbuilding is the hivelike efficiency,
flurry of workers, attention to detail, ingenuity of design.
I was bred, born, and raised to build ships
just as the queen bee is nurtured in its cell.
When a hive becomes crowded, the bees will swarm

and fly as a mass to some high branch.
And there it will wait an hour, a day, or two,
while its scouts seek out another home.
But there is nowhere for this swarm to go.
There is nowhere. Nowhere left to go.
No time for the scouts to . . .
   There is no time.
      I am not ready.
   Too many details.
      Too many   little matters   left to fix.
         Helen!   Elizabeth!
            The tilt of the floor.
   Must fix.   The broken glass.
      I'll call the   staff.
   The passengers
            are   not   comfortable.
   The leather chairs
         are tipping.

               Fix it.

               Fix it.

            Everything

                  is falling.

            The bees have
                  nowhere
               to go.

From: RMS *Titanic*
To: All Ships at Sea
Date: 15 April 1912
Time: 2:17 A.M.

MGY MGY SOS CQD
MGY MGY SOS CQD

MGY MGY SOS CQD

MGY MGY SOS CQD

MGY MG- -OS CQD

MGY -G- -OS C-D

M-Y -G- -OS --D

M-Y -G- -O- --D

M-Y -G- -O- --D

M-Y -G- -O- --D

M-Y -G- -O- --D

M-Y -G- -O- --D

M-Y -G- -O- --D

M-Y -G- -O- --D

M-Y -G- -O- --D

V V V V V

I stand still.
Not out of cowardice
but out of compassion.
I know full well
what we are about to lose.
I am not an arrogant man.
Every soul aboard means
as much to me as my own daughter.
My Mel. My little gillie.
Thank God. Thank God
she cannot see her hero now.

The bow plunges. Lurches.
Then settles a moment.
I watch from the bridge
as the water glows green.
Green like . . . like what?
Dragon's blood?
No. Just the lights
from the lower decks
still shining through.
And now I bow and I am in it.

Ahhhhh! The cold burns.
I cannot breathe.
Breathe in. My gillie. My dogs.
Exhale. The blue smoke of a bold Punch Robusto.
On my front porch on Winn Road.
Taste the pensive sting of cigar smoke.
Inhale the taste. Hold. Ponder. No one speaks.
All things cease.
                    The captain exhales.

I watched Captain Smith
dive forward. His long blue coat.
His neat white beard. He bowed,
took a header, and disappeared.

Not five minutes earlier
the captain had released us.

"You've done your full duty.
You can do no more.
Abandon your cabin.
Look after yourselves.
I release you. I release you."

But Phillips kept at it.
His head tilted. His eyes closed.
MGY. CQD. MGY. CQD.
Fifteen words per minute.
He tapped at half speed.

But the signal became weaker and weaker
as the boilers were shut down row after row.
Then finally we go.
And once on deck, we go our separate ways.
Phillips goes aft. But I go forward to help
Officer Lightoller atop the officers' quarters.
We push a collapsible raft from roof to deck,
but it lands upside down. I jump down myself,
and as I grasp an oarlock, I go sailing on a wave.
I am submerged. Gulping saltwater. Holding on.
And the cold is stabbing me, over and over.

The water was washing up the deck, closer and closer.

Sigurd wanted to jump, but I wanted to stay with the ship as long as possible. The deck tilted even more. We heard the loud snap of breaking cables as one of the ship's huge funnels fell forward with a tremendous splash. When the water was just five feet away from us, we joined hands and jumped. But my feet became tangled in ropes, and I had to let go to free myself. It all happened so fast. There was so much water. So much splashing and crashing. And it was so dark. I had to let go. I had no choice.

After that I could not see Peter or Sigurd. I called their names. I called and called. I could not find them.

Lift. Toss. Lift. Toss.

"Just one sack left, Mr. Woody," says March.
"Just one sack left, Mr. March," says I.

Lift. Toss. Lift. Toss.

I say, "Somewhat soggy, but just so."
He says, "I will not let it go."
I say, "I know it, March. I know."

Lift. Toss. Lift. Toss.

He holds one end. And I the other.
Mr. March with his handsome ring marked *M*.
"Mr. March, we have become like brothers."
"I agree, Mr. Woody. And in such a short time."

Lift. Toss. Lift. Toss.

"I'm afraid we've run out of deck," says he.
"You're right, of course, Mr. March," says I.
"Let's jump it," says I. "My count. On three."
"We'll count together, friend," says he.
"Good-bye, Mr. Woody." "Good-bye, Mr. March."
"One.
Two."

Lift. Jump.

"Three."

I tossed about fifty deck chairs overboard to port.
Someone, I thought, might make a raft of them.
The ship began to plunge. I struggled aft
up the incline to the poop deck, crossing to starboard.
And there at the very stern of the ship, I held on tight
just before she twisted to port with a shrug
that sent a hundred fifty or more on a long fall.
Titanic's tail lifted up nearly perpendicular,
then she dropped back down to horizontal,
then back up again like a giant metal duck looking for fish.
I flung my leg over the rail and knelt on the outside,
and I stuck to the hull like a barnacle.
Then for a moment she lingered, and it seemed
perhaps she may just float after all.

But then she began her slow descent.
Down I went at about the speed of the first-class elevators.
And in the same way I wait for the perfect instant
before pulling the bread from the ovens,
I waited for just the right moment
to step off into the water. Like bread,
to rush it would be to ruin it. To wait too long
would make it extra tough. Down she went.
Four. Three. Two. One. And I simply stepped off
into the water and began to dog-paddle along,
as if I had eased into the *Titanic*'s swimming pool.
And though the water was painfully cold
I didn't soak my head. I barely got my hair wet.

And the ship was gone. Without so much as a burp.

From: *Carpathia*
To: RMS *Titanic*
Date: 15 April 1912
Time: 2:21 A.M.

MPA.
Our boats are ready.
We are coming to you
as fast as possible.
Have doubled watch
in engine room.
Prepare your boats.

THE ICEBERG ∽

I've played my part; now water rushes in.
Alive, but blind, it feels its way inside.
It fills the coal bins, climbs the bulkhead walls.
It flows along the first-class promenade.
The water has its way. It does not knock.
It pushes open ornate stateroom doors.
Over third-class tables set for morning meals.
Along long Scotland Road the water feels
its way down stairwell, bathtub drain, and loo.
The kitchen galleys. Pantries spilling food.
It strokes piano key and fiddle string.
Caresses velvet wall. Shakes chandelier.
And fills *Titanic*'s holds with ice-cold tears.
The hull cannot withstand the water's weight.
She stands upon her nose. She lingers there.
And just like mankind's fleeting mayfly life,
the lights go out. Flick on, then off again.
And at long last, she slips into the deep.
And where the great *Titanic* used to be,
behold the souls left floating on the sea.
The dying flail their arms and gasp for breath.
The living row their boats safely away.
The dying from the darkness call for help.
The living sit upon their oars and wait.
And safe within their boats, they circle round
and listen as the circle's center dies,
as grief and fear are transformed into sound—
a roar they will remember all their lives.
The price they pay for daring to survive.
Indifferent to their pain, I turn toward home
while fifteen hundred anguished voices moan.

Stomp. *Swish. Pitter-patter.* Shrieks and shouts.
The steerage take their walkabouts
and talk about the plans they've made.
Titanic's third-class promenade.

help

come back

god help us   so cold

let go of me   freddo   cannot swim

our father who art in heaven

daddy   over here children   come back

They walk so they might see the sea.
They walk to see and to be seen.
Ahem. Good day. Good show! Guffaw!
Titanic's first-class promenade.

kälte   where's my child   here mummy

save us   someone   please   so cold

cannot breathe   why are we here   get away

sigurd   peter   tsumetai   where are you

don't cry my sweet   we're here   hey you in the boats

cold   hurts to breathe   help us   help me

love you my darling   hold my hand   krýo   come back

god help us   let go of me   cannot swim

daddy   bring back the boats   hold on to me dear

They walk so they might see the sea.
They walk to see and to be seen.
Their pants well patched. Their skirts homemade.
A poor folks' fashion promenade.

let go   you'll kill us all   we'll stay together

up on this door   keep moving your arms

come back   over here children   no no

swim for that driftwood   rossmore   eugene

zimno   we're over here

And at their sides, the gentlemen
(self-made or trust fund) keep in trim.
They're chivalrous. They're masculine.
They tip their black-felt bowler brims.

where's my child   here

bring back the boats

heaven   my god

we're here

heaven

They speak, in many varied tongues,
of where they're going, where they're from.
Six months of hard-earned wages paid
to join the third-class promenade.

Inhale the richness of the air.
Luxurious furs are de rigueur.
Parisian skirt hems. Feet well shod.
It's time to walk the promenade.

help

come back

* follow my voice   we'll stay together*

* why is this happening   cold   cannot breathe*

help us   are they coming back

Stomp. Swish. Pitter-patter. Shrieks and shouts.
The steerage take their walkabouts.
A traveling circus on parade.
Behold the third-class promenade.

*   take my hand   froid   I see a boat*

someone   please   lost my shoes

* follow me   can't stop shaking   frío*

* ruined my best hat   help us   stay together*

* my god   come back   we're here*

hello   we shan't be on time now   save us

*   aaaaaah   daddy will protect you   so cold*

*   someone   please   good luck*

stay calm now   why are we here   let go

Some walk so they might see the sea.
Some walk to see and to be seen.
Six times around, they've gone a mile.
Outfitted in the latest style.

*   you'll drown me   holodnyi   am I dying*

* god bless boys   stay warm   hold my hand*

help me   come back   where are you

*   are you there   kaldt   hurts to breathe*

* over here   keep moving   cannot swim*

Children clamor. Infants wail.
Nappies dry on poop-deck rails.
"Give us a song!" "Come, now, let's dance!"
A chat. A smoke. A game of chance.

hallooooo   can't breathe   let go of me

* we're over here   come back*

* bring back the boats*

heaven   my god

we're here

heaven

The skirt hems swish. The shoes step-step.
The well-heeled ladies stroll the deck.
They cling to their protectors' arms
and exercise patrician charms.

April 25, 1912
THURSDAY
Aboard the cable ship *Mackay-Bennett*
ATLANTIC OCEAN
THE GRAND BANKS
750 MILES FROM HALIFAX, NOVA SCOTIA

JOHN SNOW
THE UNDERTAKER

This morning a wireless telegram instructs us to cease
all sea burials at once. "Thank God," sobs Reverend Hind.
In the past four days we have sent over the side
one hundred and sixteen neatly bound bodies.
They are below this very moment, some two miles down.
Scattered about the seafloor like canvas cocoons.
Waiting for Nature to make her next move.
I've seen bodies, sunk for days in cold freshwater ponds,
fill with gases and eventually float to the surface,
their features perfectly preserved in thick grave wax.
But the ocean is another matter altogether;
she rarely gives up her dead. And of course,
below the waves, there are many mouths to feed.

My assistant, George, and I are running low on embalming fluid
and other supplies. We work at a furious pace,
cutting corners where we can. We forgo
setting any more features until we return to Halifax.
I fear that by the time we get these bodies to shore,
many will be decayed beyond any possible embalmment.
And all the while new bodies keep arriving on board.
Each one tagged. And bagged. Investigated. And recorded.
The numbers so much easier than the names.

Every night around six, the chief steward comes forward
with a pail of English rum. Each man fills his mug
with a double ration. And none of them hoards his tot
for a later drunken binge. They must put the spirits down
to keep their spirits up. The smell of death is everywhere.
It permeates our clothing. It seasons every bite of food.
Corpses cover every inch of the deck.
Corpses lie piled in the passageways.

By sundown we add eighty-seven bodies to our load.
I climb below and stumble to my berth.
I lie down and I dream that I am dead.
Then I wake up and assure myself that I am yet alive.
But I realize I'm sewn into a canvas bag.
I try to speak. "No, wait. I'm alive."
But my mouth is sewn shut with my own special knot.
Reverend Hind drones, "We commit him to the deep."
And I'm tossed. And falling. And.

Splash.

Then I wake and sit up in my bunk with a gasp.
If the living can dream they are dead, I think,
perhaps it can happen the other way round.
Could I be just a corpse that refuses to die?
Do I wake? Or sleep? Do I wake? Or sleep?
Am I alive or dead?
I flip the questions all night long
like a coin inside my head.

I hear them outside.
A moaning. A roar.
The sound
of the hundreds of them dying in the water.

SEVENTH WATCH

THE WATCH THAT ENDS THE NIGHT

ABOUT 1,700 MILES OUT

MONDAY, APRIL 15, 1912

There we were, in a large half-empty lifeboat,
twenty or so women, and only two men to crew us.
Then from out of the sky drops Major Peuchen,
the Canadian businessman, wearing as many clothes as myself,
under his life vest. He's shinning down a rope,
and he drops into the boat like a badly dressed pirate.

Captain Smith is shouting down to us to make for the light
of a ship in the distance, but Major Peuchen is scrambling
to place a plug into a hole in the bottom of our boat.
"I can't find it!" he keeps shouting and splashing.
The man at the helm (the same crewman, I'm told, who had been
steering the big ship when she hit the ice) was deranged.
"Hurry it up!" he snarled. "This ship is going to founder!"

Major Peuchen suggested to this awful man
(I later learned his name was Quartermaster Hichens)
that he might row and allow one of the ladies to steer,
but the sailor would not have it.
"Captain Smith placed *me* in charge of this boat," he said,
"so I'll do the steering and you'll do as you are told."

Hichens was screeching out orders and shaking like an aspen,
partly from the cold but mostly from intense fear—
which his domineering arrogance did little to mask.
He asked for a drink from Mrs. Baxter's silver brandy flask
but she refused him, offering him a steamer blanket instead.
In turn, I offered him one of my furs, and thus
bundled up as he was, it looked as if a trained bear
was in control of our boat's rudder.
And that wasn't far from the truth.

Mrs. Candee and I took up oars to row with Major Peuchen.
And across from Peuchen a shy lookout named Fleet

worked dumbly at his own oar and studied his feet.

Meanwhile, Hichens stood up at the helm, ranting,

"Quickly. Row faster. We must get away.

She's going to founder. Don't knock that plug out.

You, place your oar at more of an angle.

Now, row! Unless you want to die like all the rest of 'em.

I was on the bridge. I know how damaged she is.

Row faster. We have got to get farther away.

We're going to be pulled in by the suction!"

Hichens had been raving this way for nearly an hour

when I remembered attending the World's Fair in Chicago,

where a man lost his nerve at the top of the big Ferris wheel.

The woman he was with simply placed her skirt over his head.

This maneuver had the same calming effect as hooding a falcon,

and the man soon calmed down. Now, as I considered Hichens,

I cringed to think what he might do if the other ladies

and myself all removed our skirts and flung them over his head.

For the moment, though, I kept my skirt on.

I kept my mouth shut. And I rowed.

That's when someone shouted, "My God, what's happening?

See there! What's happening to the ship?"

Even though we were nearly a mile away by then,

we could still make out *Titanic*'s brightly lit outline

as the stern rose up and the lights blinked out.

Then it was just a dark silhouette where stars should have been.

And then it was gone altogether.

Then the moans. There was no one voice that stood out.

From that distance it was just a horrific roar.

"OK, men. For starters, you can just leave any tobacco
in your pockets," I said. "It will only make you thirsty."

The mighty *Titanic* was gone.
She had lifted her stern into the air
to what sounded like explosions, as her boilers no doubt
came loose from their beds and crashed down through
every metal bulkhead along the way toward the bow.
Then she paused as if taking a long breath to prepare,
and she slid out of sight. No suction. No turmoil.

My main concern, now, was for those boats left floating.
I tried to ease the alarm among the women in my boat
by recommending that a good song to sing at a moment like this
would be "Throw Out the Lifeline." My quip was not well received,
but at least I tried. I wasn't there, anyway, to comfort the women.
I had more urgent matters to attend to, and I wasted no time.
Blowing my whistle, I called a small flotilla of boats together.
I said, "I want all these boats tied up by their painters,
head and tail, so as to make a more conspicuous mark."
I figured we were more apt to be seen by a rescue ship
if we were all together. And what's more, I could hear
(as well as anyone) the terrible cries of those dying in the water;
I wanted to be sure that none of these lifeboats attempted
an ill-considered rescue that would result in more deaths.

The women were becoming hysterical.
Some women demanded we go back.
Some demanded that we not risk it.
"I would rather die than do nothing," one said.
"It's not *your* life I'm worried about," another replied.
"I think we're fools if we go back," one snipped.

"I think it is our moral duty," another snipped back.
I yelled out at the top of my voice, *"I think*
the best thing for you women to do is to take a nap!"

Honestly, I was trying to be kind.
Perhaps it came out more harshly than I planned it.
Given the circumstance, I hope I might not be judged for it.
I wanted to be clear that we were not rushing in to the rescue.
My boat was already dangerously overcrowded
and it would take just one swimmer,
swinging a leg up onto the side, to capsize us all.
Yes, many of our boats had empty spaces,
but what good are fifty seats when there are
fifteen hundred fighting each other to fill them?
Let me be quite firm when I say this:
had any of us rowed a boat into that swarming mass,
which was alive with thrashing limbs and clawing hands,
we all of us would have wound up dead.
To have done so would have been suicide.

And even if it were remotely possible to do so,
who would you choose to come aboard and live?
Who would you choose to stay behind and die?

Eenie-meenie-epatic,
tilia-talia-dominic,
hokey-pokey-tom-in-okey.

Mum tried to protect me
when the *Titanic* was about to sink.
She held one of my ears against her heart
and covered my other ear with her hand.
With her free hand she covered my eyes.

I couldn't see what was going on.
And I couldn't hear the sounds very good.
But since Mum was holding me so close,
I heard the whole thing from inside her chest.
There was thumping like a bass drum at the circus.
Clanks and clinks like Dad's metal shop in Strood.
Snapping sounds like my cap gun.
Ripping sounds like Mum pulling out a seam.
Rumbling sounds like Mum's Singer sewing machine.
Between her heartbeats: Clangs. Bangs. Tearing.
Pulley wheels creaking . . . Beat. Beat. . . .
as Bertie's coffin is lowered. Beat. Beat. Beat.
Then sobbing. Wailing. A dragon's call.
The roar-up of a football stadium. Beat. Beat.
I close my eyes tighter and hear:

> Bertie smiling with birthday cake on his face.
> Dad clapping me on the back. Tousling my hair.
> So long, Frankie. I'll see you later.
> Photographs ripped from a scrapbook.
> Ti-tata-touch,
> ugily-buggily-boo.
> And out goes Y-O-U.

I was then in the water with hundreds and hundreds of others. One man clung to me. He yelled, "Help me, please. I cannot swim." But he was holding my head down under the water. I had to beat him away.

And just as I got free from him, another man latched on to me. I had to beat him away as well. I called out for Sigurd. I called out for Peter. If they answered, I could not hear. Everyone was yelling.

More hands held on to my head. To my life jacket. Pulling me down. I yelled out, "Get back. Get back. I am only one man! I cannot save you all." So I fought them off and I swam away.

I saw a shape in the dark. I thought at first it was a small iceberg, but it turned out to be a group of men standing in a life raft. It was a boat with collapsible canvas sides, only the sides were not up. And the boat was completely swamped.

I tried to climb aboard, but I was kicked back into the water.

What else was I to do? I hung around there and swam to the other side, where I was allowed to climb aboard. No one extended a hand. Only one man spoke. He said, "Don't tip us over."

I climbed up into it. And I stood. You could not sit down. To do so would be to sit submerged. So we all stood up. In water nearly up to our knees.

No one spoke.

It seemed we would sink at any moment.

I am sinking.

Even with the life vest, I am being pulled under.
Pulled downward against a grate with the rushing of water.
A wave rolls up like timpani. The big funnel falls
with the crash of bass drum and cymbals.
I am turned over in the water like a trill.
I come to the surface to gasp for air
but the cold won't allow me to breathe.
Another wave. Another grating. More rushing water.
And I'm shot upward with a sudden gust.
The stars are above me. Above the surface of the water.
And I am below the surface. Looking up. Watching stars.
Watching the Guadagnini as she floats from my hand.
Then music pours from her into the water.
I feel its warmth. Like summer. I'm surrounded by her music.
I am "Frankie and Johnny." I am "Nearer, My God, to Thee."
I am Joyce's "Songe d'Automne," Offenbach's "Tales of Hoffmann."
I am "Sérénade Mélancolique" by Tchaikovsky.
The future coo of the child in Mary's womb.
I am every beautiful sound I ever sent forth into the world.
And I follow the notes backward to their beginning.
To a warm, sunny room in Dumfries.
My hands are tiny. My violin half-size.
My father stands beside me. He places
my small fingers on the instrument's neck.
String by string by string.
"Now, play beautiful music," my father says.
And I do.

"The one who takes the donkey up to the roof
should be the one who brings it down."

As I listened to the terrible sound of those dying in the water,
I wondered, Who is responsible for *this* donkey?

"This is God's donkey," Father might say.
Elias was clutching my arm. Listening.
Around our boat, I looked at the faces in the darkness:
nearly all of us there were from the third class.
I saw and heard many Lebanese and Syrians.
Mostly women, children, and babies.
Four Chinese men had crawled out from under a seat.
I did not blame them for hiding at all,
after seeing Fraza forced out at gunpoint.
Two well-to-do gentleman sat quietly at the back.
They had stepped in at the last minute while the boat was being lowered.
And had it been that simple? Had Fraza only needed to linger awhile?
What about Mr. Leeni? What about Alfred?

Alfred's young friend Frankie sat nearby.
His mother clutched the boy tightly, covering his ears.
None of us wanted to hear it. But we could not help it.
I imagined I could hear Alfred whispering through the din.
"You are beautiful," he would say.
But I could not hear his lovely voice
without hearing the awful moans of those in the water.

When I finally surfaced,
it took a moment to realize that the collapsible boat
was still overturned and that I was *underneath* it.
I lingered a moment in the large pocket of air
before swimming out from under and away.
Realizing there was nowhere to go,
I gradually made my way back to the collapsible.
And by that time there must have been twenty men,
most of them standing, on the boat's upturned keel.
As I pulled myself up, I was warned to be careful.
I scrambled to the stern. A fellow sat down on my feet.
I hadn't the strength to push him off.
I called out for Phillips but got no answer.

The calm water was beginning to roll
and with each slight swell a burp of air
would escape from beneath the boat
and we would sink just a slight bit more.
I heard an officer's voice, taking charge.
Second Officer Lightoller. "Lights" we called him.
He was organizing those who could stand,
keeping them as close to the keel as possible,
instructing them to go left or right as needed.
Lightoller recognized me from the Marconi shack
and asked if we'd been in contact with any ships.
"The *C-C-Carpathia*," I stammered. "She's on her way full speed."
"You hear that, boys?" said Lightoller. "A ship's on her way.
Every man who is able needs to stand up and dance.
To the left, now. Slightly right. That's it. Steady now."

I had dog-paddled through the splashing mass.
At the center of the struggling crowd, chaos
had overtaken common sense as people lashed out,
splashed, and flailed like a tangle of rats.
As I swam outward, the circle began to thin out
and calm down. This is where most passengers
were floating, easily buoyed by their life vests.
The water was unearthly cold. It almost burned.
Like red-hot needles driven into the skin.
And within seconds a throbbing ache had penetrated
my bones and joints. I kept on swimming.
A sleepy calm began to spread through the crowd.
I swam on outward through the dying.
In my mind I could not erase the sight of the tangled rats
I had seen at the bottom of flour barrel number forty-six.

Finally the dead and dying thinned out to nearly nothing
and I spotted what turned out to be a group of men
standing atop one of the ship's Engelhardt collapsibles.
The boat was upside down, and the men were shifting
to one side, then the other to keep their balance.
Swimming up to it, I saw that it was very full.
I attempted to climb aboard but was kicked back into the water.
"Easy, boys," I said. "God bless."
It is simple math, I know:
a muffin tin that's made for a dozen will not fit thirteen.
Even so, you should never kick a muffin for making the attempt.
I hung about the raft awhile and dog-paddled
around to the other side, where I tried again to grab hold.
And again, a boot kicked at my frozen fingers.

"Leave that one alone, you heartless wretch!" came a familiar voice.
"You may as well be stomping the fingers of a world-class violinist!"
It was Maynard. (The human.) He sat down at the edge.
And he held out a trembling hand. "Grab hold," he said.
And he helped me to hoist myself up.
I stayed there perched, half in, half out. Just to have
that small relief from the intensely cold water seemed a miracle.
And what's more, the feel of Maynard's hand in mine shot hope
to my every extremity faster than the strongest whiskey.

Maynard's mustache was all out of shape, a matted comical mess.

"I shan't let go of you, baker," he said. "I will die before I do.
We'll get out of this, yet. Just you watch."

"I would rather die taking action
then live and do nothing!" I said.
"We have to go back."

"We'll do no such thing," said Hichens.

"Could we not row back, sir?" said Mrs. Candee to Hichens.
She was obviously attempting to "ask pretty," as she called it.
"Are you daft?" he spat back. "It's just a lot of stiffs out there now.
It's either us or them. If we go among that lot, they'd swamp us."

"But we can't just sit and do nothing!" I screamed.

"Listen, lady. Even if I was to give over this rudder
(which I will *not* do), do you really think everyone here
wants to risk certain death by rowing out to save them stiffs?"

"There's no talking to that one, Mrs. Brown," said Major Peuchen.
The ship's lookout, the quiet thing named Fleet, only bowed his head.

Perhaps it *was* a foolish idea. Perhaps it *was* suicide.
And even if this oaf at the helm had wanted to return,
I had a sense that the majority of the ladies in our boat
would have talked him out of it.
I was stunned into silence.
We pulled in our oars.

And we listened as the moaning
gradually,
ever so slowly,

began to die.

I helped a stoker who was wearing just a thin shirt and short pants to climb aboard. He also had a fancy gentleman's dinner jacket on under his life vest. I forced the man to stand and gave him a slap to wake him up. "Do not go to sleep," I said. "If you go to sleep, you go to sleep for good."

Some of the other men told me to stop helping people aboard the raft. "We were here first, friend. Don't ruin a good thing by inviting more to board than we've room for."

So I stopped.

I watched one swimmer kicked away. And then another. I began to cry out, but I stifled my protests. I could see it was true. Even one more might tip us all into the sea.

If Sigurd or Peter had found the raft, we would not have been able to take them in. Our raft was like a crowded country, and each swimmer was an immigrant seeking refuge. Refuge that we refused to give.

As a rule, I prefer to play at cards over dice.
When holding cards, you can conceal your hand.
You can therefore bluff, connive, and ambush.
(Not to mention cheat.)
Dice, on the other hand, require no skill. You simply toss them out
and you rely on luck. And I am not one to rely on luck.
Yet if luck comes knocking, I'll answer.

The stoker who informed me about *Titanic*'s true condition,
the stoker who informed me where to find my boat—
that fellow was my unanticipated ace—certainly worth
the price of a good tailor-made dinner jacket.
I volunteered to distribute the baker's bread,
figuring that it would gain me easier access.
When no women answered the call to board,
I stepped into the first boat I saw, taking the bread with me.
Once I had secured my seat, I tossed the basket into the stern.
So what if the other boats went without bread?
There was no butter or marmalade to spread on it, anyway.

On the way down, our boat scraped slightly against the ship.
Then the bow dipped down. Then the stern dipped down.
It was a rocky ride. But that was not the worst of it.
We finally made it safely down, only to encounter
a tremendous torrent of water pouring from the ship's side.
It nearly swamped us and pushed our boat backward.
The sailors were having a difficult time releasing the ropes
attached to either end of our boat, which was a bad thing
because unbeknownst to *Titanic*'s crew above,
we had drifted backward into the path of another boat,
which was descending directly on top of us!
It creaked closer and closer until our screaming and shouting

stopped the descent, leaving the boat hanging
precariously over our heads, so close you could touch it.

Finally our crew cut the ropes and pushed us out from under.
As we rowed away, I felt like I'd been duped.
Not thirty minutes earlier I had been having a smoke
and a whiskey in the midst of a lucrative game of red dog.
Now I was wet, cold, and wedged tightly among
a group of hysterical women and crying children,
floating in a boat on a moonless night in the middle of the Atlantic.
And when I heard one of the crew
say that our lifeboat was number thirteen—
well, I just had to laugh out loud at that! Lucky thirteen.

Our lifeboat became silent as we watched
the mighty *Titanic* vanish from our sight. And I thought,
Maybe number thirteen is not so unlucky after all.

Then the moaning reached out across the water.
If Stengel is dead, I thought, *at least I've got his bank draft.*
I'll have to cash it before the bank knows he's gone.
I won't have any luggage to slow me down,
and I've got the check right here in my—

dinner . . . jacket . . . pocket.

The stoker!

I'm tired.
I just want to sit down.
Why does this man
not let me sit down?
I'm so, so tired.

"Who are you?" I ask.
"Leave me be," I say.
"Who are you?"

"I am Abelseth," he says.

"Who am I?" I try to ask.
But no words will come.
I am too cold to speak.

I just want to sit down.
I just want to go to sleep.

Why won't this man
let me sleep? Let me sleep.

Tommy Hart
needs his sleep.

Oh, God.
The absurdity of souls residing on Saturn.
The absurdity has just struck me for the first time.
Maybe Jupiter. Maybe Mars. I am so cold.
Where shall I go now? When I leave this body,
where shall I go? I am so terribly cold.
Considering my present luck, I'll find myself stuck
in some damp, moldy, ancient English castle,
with cousin Willy and my ex-wife, Ava,
forced to endure an eternal game of mah-jongg!

(Hem, hem.)

I am growing sleepy. I know what that means.
My consciousness begins to blink on, off, on, off, on.
Like the stutter of the telegrapher adjusting his set,
I hear intermittent static as I move from one frequency to the next.
I have left 1912. I have left my Madeleine behind.

I move my dial a century into the future: the year 2012.
Armies are still at war. The poor are still poor. The rich still rich.
Glaciers continue to shed mountains of ice into the oceans.
The world still tilts at twenty-three and one half degrees.
The entire human race stands idly by as the great ship lists.
I see it so clearly, how we are all of us on the *Titanic*'s deck,
steaming happily toward destruction or stopped dead in the water—
content that human ingenuity will keep us afloat forever
or at least till we are rescued by some passing steamer.
But from where I watch, I can see the truth of it:

we are alone.

We are the only ship in the vastness of a cosmic sea,
sinking lower every second. No lifeboats left to launch.

Finally, I've reached my destination.
No light.
Just calm.
Quiet.
Peaceful.
Until suddenly
the darkness is shattered by an explosion of magnesium powder.
"Welcome to Saturn, Mr. Astor!" the photographer says.
"*Colonel* Astor," I correct him, with spots in my vision.
And even in the afterlife, they ask the same thing:

"What was it like, sir? To be the richest man in the world?"

And I answer them back,
still shivering from my travels,
dripping wet with knowing,
as I remove my life vest for good:

"Cold, sir. It is very cold."

I am.   so cold.

Cold beyond description.

But I am.   alive.

Life gives no guarantees.
I know this.
We are each
just a child's balloon
floating amid the cutlery.

But I am alive.

I stay alive
because I am a man.   of the sea.

I stay alive.
Because I know no earthly hell.
Can last.   forever.

I stay alive
because.   someone must be there.
When the loaves are done.

I stay alive.
Because Maynard.
Refuses.   to let go.

Paddle. Float. Gasp. Shiver.
Shiver. Paddle. Gasp.

"Must hold on, Mr. Woody," says Mr. March.
"We must deliver this final sack," I say.

Paddle. Float. Gasp. Shiver.
Shiver. Paddle. Gasp.

I hold tight to the sack of registered mail.
Mr. March holds tight to the sack as well.
He's growing weaker. I can tell.
His fingers are loose against the canvas.
The gold ring with the letter *M*.
Only, from where I am, it's upside down.
"I see your ring is upside down," I say.
"From where I am, the *M* is a *W*," I say.
"Ha. Ha," says Mr. March. He shuts his eyes.
"A *W* for *Woody*," says he. "For *Woody*."

Float. Float. Gasp. Shiver.
Shiver. Float. Gasp.

He drops the sack. I drop the sack.
"There goes the sack of mail," I say.
But Mr. March has gone away.
He looks my way, but he doesn't see.

"Let's just float, Mr. M.," says I.

Float. Turn. Float.
Turn. Float. Float. Away.

"We've been floating here long enough," I said.
"I need a few volunteers. We have to go back."

The sound of the dying had lasted so long.
But now it was becoming too silent, too quickly.
From boat to boat I moved my passengers out
so I might replace them with a makeshift rescue crew.
But these people had no sense of urgency.
One lady moved as if she were attending a picnic.
"Jump, God damn you! Jump!" I said.

Finally I was able to transfer about fifty passengers
to give us extra room for more. And we rowed
as quickly as possible toward the mass of people.
But by then it was silent as a grave. And a grave was what it was.
"Slow up, boys," I said. "We're coming in among them now."

I called out into the gloom of the barely breaking dawn.
I scanned the grisly scene. Checking each upturned face for life.
One blank stare after another. Oddly enough I saw no women.
But hundreds of men, bobbing upright in their life vests.
I detailed a man at the bow of our boat to push the bodies away —
the water was so thick with the dead, we could barely row.

The first passenger we found alive was an enormous man
that took my entire crew of seven to pull in. He was soaked well through
and bleeding from the mouth and nose. We propped him up
at the stern of the boat. Took off his collar and loosened his shirt
so he might better breathe. But he was too far gone already.
Next we found a Jap who had tied himself to a door.
The water was washing over him
"What's the use?" I said. "He's dead, likely."

I was about to turn the boat away when I noticed the knots.
He had tied himself to the wreckage
using a bowline loop knot with a half hitch.
"Hold on, boys," I said. "I've changed my mind.
Let's pull the Jap aboard. Why not?" And so we did.
One of the crew rubbed his chest.
Others rubbed his hands and feet.
And within not half a minute, the little fellow
jumped up and stretched his arms over his head.
Then he stomped his feet. He said something in his own
strange language. He placed an oar in an oarlock,
and he stayed at it all night. I'd never seen a better sailor.
I'd trade any thirteen of *Titanic*'s crew for just that one Jap.

He was a boatman. Just like me. He knew his knots.

After that we pulled in two more, bringing the total to four—
three living and one dead. And by then dawn was fully breaking
so that we took in the full horror of the mass of floating dead.
A slight dragon's breath of mist clung just at the surface.
For a moment of fancy, I felt as though I were a boatman in hell.

Then a wind picked up and blew the mist away.
And we saw it, plain as day: a ship. In the distance.
Coming our way. "Let's step that mast, boys," I ordered my crew.
"That's a steamer as sure as I have saltwater in my veins.
But let's waste no time waiting for her to find us.
We're going to be sure she doesn't bungle the rescue.

Now, hoist that sail!"

"Look there," I said. "At that light on the horizon. It's a ship. Come to rescue us."

The stoker in the dinner jacket slumped in my arms. "Do not go to sleep *now*." I chafed his coal-blackened hands as I spoke. "Not when salvation is so close!"

The stoker just stared at nothing and said, "Who are you?" It may sound odd, but I think he was asking the question not of me but of someone else. He acted as if he were conversing with a number of different imaginary people. First a man named Heart. Then a man named Gold. Then finally the Devil. He tried to shrug me away and said, "Leave me be. Just leave me alone." Then the stoker died in my arms.

The rescue ship was in plain sight!

Then out of the mist, we see another lifeboat rush up to ours under a billowed sail.

"You look as if you need a lift," said the officer at the helm. On board he had a Jap or a Filipino at one oar. A very large man propped at the stern looked to be dead. It was an odd sight to behold, but beautiful.

"We can't last another minute," someone answered. And it was true.

We jumped to the safety of what I found out later was lifeboat number fourteen, and the officer's name was Lowe.

There were maybe a dozen of us left alive. Many had fallen off during the night. That stoker wearing the dinner jacket—the man who died in my arms? He was one of three dead bodies left in the raft.

Then we turned toward the ship, tacking on under full sail.

Who are you?

I had emptied every bin of fuel.
I was a derelict ship set adrift.
Rudderless. Me boilers cold.
From bin to bin I searched me soul,
and finally in one corner
I seen a tiny lump of coal.
But when I picked it up,
it crumbled to nothin'
between me frozen fingers.

Leave me alone.

I was no longer alone.
Sharing the empty bin with me
was Tommy Hart, Sean Gould, and the Devil.
They spoke together as if they were a single voice:
"The rescue ship has arrived!" they said.
"But first," said the Devil, "we'll need
your official certificate of discharge, please."

I searched me jacket pockets and found
only a worthless bank draft, ruined by water.
"Someone's done burgled me discharge book," I said.
And all of them—Tommy, Sean, and the Devil—
laughed out loud in three-part harmony.
So I quickly turned to take my leave,
only to discover
there weren't no door.

Then the Devil tips his captain's cap
and laughs. "Welcome aboard."

When I woke up,
I was looking through
a little metal circle
in our lifeboat's canvas side.

I had to close one eye
to watch the world
that way. So small.

When I raised my head
from Mum's lap,
the world became so big
I couldn't see it all at once.

The sun was up
and we were surrounded by icebergs
like frozen floating mountains.
I wondered which one held
the ice dragon's crystal cave.

I had woken up when I heard the cheers.
Another steamer ship was near.
Likely my father had arranged it.
The adults were afraid
that we wouldn't be seen,
so they set my mother's hat on fire,
and lifted it up on the end of an oar!
Imagine that. Mum's good straw Sunday hat!
It was brilliant.

Then the men started rowing like mad.
"Dad's sure to see *that* signal torch," I said to Mum.
"There's no way he could miss *that*!"

When I heard a rescue ship was near,
firing its rockets over the horizon,
I knew it had to be the *Carpathia*.
My only concern was whether we could last
long enough for the ship to reach us.
One man, the chief baker, had been dangling
half in the water all night long. It seemed a miracle
that he was still alive.

Then Officer Lightoller saw another lifeboat in the distance,
and he blew on his whistle and waved.
And lucky for us, what turned out to be lifeboat twelve
waved back, turned around, and was by our side in no time.

The baker said, "Let go, Maynard." And he swam
with a funny dog-paddle over to meet boat twelve.
They pulled him in. Then one by one we each transferred.
Lightoller was last man off and he took command.
Lifeboat twelve had been launched half empty,
so there was plenty of room for us. I searched the faces
for Phillips, but he was nowhere to be seen.

As we rowed our way toward the waiting *Carpathia,*
I took in my surroundings for the first time.
In the daylight, about twenty icebergs were visible
all around us, some of them over a hundred feet high.
They were a variety of colors, sizes, and shapes.

.. -.-. . -... . .-. --.

Last night no one could believe we'd struck an iceberg at all.
Now I could only wonder how we didn't strike one sooner.

My experience in lifeboat number six
had grown more bizarre with each passing minute.
Without warning, a man emerged from under a bench
and scared the life out of many of the ladies.
He spoke to us in what I took to be Arabic
and tried to work an oar with his clearly broken arm.
Another stowaway showed itself when Mrs. Rothschild's
overcoat began to bark. And eventually she unbuttoned
to reveal a small Pomeranian hidden against her bosom.

Then a wind picked up.
Speaking as sweetly as I could, I asked Hichens,
"Why not set the mast and sail to take advantage of this breeze?"
He scoffed, "Because we tossed them out, of course,
to make room for more passengers."
"But the boat is half empty," I pointed out.
"Is that my doing?" he said.
Major Peuchen, leaning over his oar,
reminded us all again that he was "something of a yachtsman."
"Does this look like a bloody regatta to you?" said Hichens.

It occurred to me that lifeboat number six
was under the protection of two of the men
who had wrecked the *Titanic* in the first place.
The man now raving at the tiller had been at *Titanic*'s wheel
when he failed to turn away in time.
The quiet submissive thing at the oars
was the official lookout, who had failed to see
a chunk of ice the size of a mountain.

When we ladies noticed a light on the horizon,
Hichens said, "It's just a falling star. An omen of death."

When the light proved to be a steamer on the horizon,
Hichens said, "They won't see us from that distance."
When the steamer did not pass us by but stopped a few miles off,
Hichens said, "They're just here to pick up the bodies."
"Should we not row toward the ship and save ourselves?"
suggested Mrs. Candee, attempting to plant the idea in Hichens's head.
"Nobody touches an oar," he said. "Let them come to us."

I stood up.

"Ladies," I said, "anyone who is able, take an oar.
If we work in shifts, we can make it to the safety of that ship.
And the exercise will help to keep us warm."

Hichens stepped toward me, saying, "I'm in charge of this boat!"

"You take one more step toward me, fella," I said,
"and I swear to God, I'll throw you off this boat myself!"
My delivery must have been convincing,
since Hichens shrank back and whined, "You stay away from me
and stop rockin' the bloody boat."
Then for the first time all night, the wilting lookout spoke up,
saying, "Watch your language, Hichens.
Don't you see you're talkin' to a lady?"

"I am in charge of this boat," Hichens mumbled.

"Then you take charge of your little end," said Mrs. Candee.
"And we shall take charge of the rest."
"Well spoken, Candee," I said.
"Thank you, Brown," she said.
And we put our frail, helpless backs into it.
And we didn't let up until we placed our dainty feet
upon the solid decks of the RMS *Carpathia*.

THE ICEBERG ∽

They knew. They knew what damage ice can do.
And yet they kept advancing, all the same.
Titanic's wound proved mortal. Now she's gone.
But metal, coal, and engines weren't my aim.
My prize was left there floating on the sea.
The humans left alive upon their boats;
some selfishly looked only to themselves.
But mostly they assisted those in need.
Surprisingly few were fueled by greed.
Surprisingly most were fueled by hope,
a hopefulness that, even through despair,
illuminates the dark and morbid night.
An officer sends up his final flare.
The rescue ship comes steaming into sight.
Then sunlight reinstates some normalcy.
Each little boat approaches with what's left.
A bosun's chair lifts females to the deck.
The infants ride in canvas postal sacks.
The baker makes his way up on his own.
His feet in pain from frostbite's knife-sharp sting,
he climbs a Jacob's ladder on his knees.
The wireless man is forced to do the same.
The lookout, immigrant, and tailor's sons,
the gambler, refugee, and socialite,
the boy who hunts for dragons: all ascend.
Ascend to end the watch that ends the night.
And as they do, the ice leaves with the tide,
a dozen souls all clinging to my side.

April 26, 1912
FRIDAY
Aboard the cable ship *Mackay-Bennett*
ATLANTIC OCEAN
THE GRAND BANKS
760 MILES FROM HALIFAX, NOVA SCOTIA

JOHN SNOW
THE UNDERTAKER

Most folks would rather not know this fact,
but here's the honest truth of the thing:
as living creatures we are each of us
already in the first stage of decay.
The bacteria in our guts is kept at bay
while we are alive. But once we die,
our own bodies consume us from the inside out.

Embrace this fact and learn to love it.

Every living thing decays.
Be it a worm, a fish, or an alley cat.
Be it an elephant, a horse, a rat, or a man.
Both rich man and poor man. Both sinner and saint.
The earth is forever trying to reclaim
the clay from which the flesh is made.

In the first twenty-four hours,
the surface of the abdomen turns a bluish green.
The eyes film over. Blood, no longer circulating,
settles and pools due to the effect of gravity.
Rigor mortis sets in to stiffen the limbs
but soon recedes in the ebb and flow of moldering.

Blowflies and houseflies lay their eggs.
Putrefaction begins. Gases bloat loose skin.
The young maggots hatch and do their dance.
New odors attract the beetles and mites.
The creamy flesh turns black, slips off,
as the fluids seep forth and the body flattens.
New smells exude to call more insects
for the final macabre buffet of mold, fermentation,
and dry decay. Then the moths flutter in
for the hair and the skin. So you see

why my skills are in such high demand.
A good embalmer can stop death's watch for a while,
enough time for loved ones to curse or to sigh,
to wail, to weep, and say their good-byes.

Today the ship *Minia* finally arrives
with many much needed embalming supplies.
And so after taking aboard fourteen more bodies,
Captain Larnder sets our course southwest toward Halifax.
In all we've found three hundred and six bodies.
One hundred and sixteen we returned to the sea.
That leaves one hundred and ninety aboard.
The first-class dead in the privacy of their coffins.
The steerage laid out upon the windswept decks
under loosely draped tarpaulins that rise and fall.
For all the world it looks as if the corpses can breathe
as our cargo ship of sorrow picks up speed.

POSTLUDE

MORNING

ABOARD THE RMS *CARPATHIA*

MONDAY, APRIL 15,

THROUGH

THURSDAY, APRIL 18, 1912

Once I was safely aboard the *Carpathia,* I watched as each lifeboat came in. I watched for Peter and Sigurd. I watched for Adolf. But each time I was disappointed.

Those of us who had been in the water knew the truth of it. No one could live for long submerged in that water. The coldness drew the very life from your bones.

Anna and Karen are both safe, thank God. Anna tells me that Mr. Ismay, the ship's owner, was in the boat with her. People have begun to whisper. They wonder why Mr. Ismay was given a place when so many other men were refused. As for me, I do not wish death upon any man.

My legs are badly frosted. The pain is difficult to bear. It is very difficult even to sit up to write this letter to you, my Marie. But I must say one final thing before I'm done.

As the *Carpathia* steamed away from the wreck site, we were pulled up short when we encountered a floating shelf of ice some twelve feet high. It stretched on as far as the eye could see. Our ship was forced to navigate around it. One hour. Two hours. Three hours. Four hours. The ice floe was more than fifty miles long, with icebergs rising up like mountains from the fjords at home. None of the crew had seen its like before. It seemed as if God had drawn a line along the water that no man would be able to cross.

Now, my dear friend, I must close this letter. In two more days we will reach New York. And now I must write to my uncle and my sister. I must explain to them how God drew a line of ice that Peter and Sigurd could not pass. My tears fall when I think about it, because I saw what I will never forget as long as I live.

Yours,
Olaus

I had to climb up the rope ladder on my knees.
My feet were that badly frostbitten.
Ours was the last lifeboat to reach the *Carpathia,*
which caused no end of anguish to those waiting
to see loved ones. Like forgetting the yeast
and watching a loaf that will never rise.
On board our rescue ship, life was good.
To thaw me out when I first arrived,
they popped me in an oven like one of me own pies!
You should have seen Maynard (the human) laugh at the sight.
And I laughed, too. Because I was alive.
And because I was given all the brandy I wanted.
And just to be sure it kept on flowing,
I convinced the *Carpathia*'s doctor that the brandy
was speeding up my thawing process.

Later I was able to walk on my own
up on the top deck, where many of *Titanic*'s lifeboats
had been brought aboard and stowed.
Maynard (the human) happened by and said,
"It's a miracle that each of those boats
was stocked with your bread and they still stayed afloat!"
I replied, "And a miracle that the weather was so calm
with such a great windbag as you about."
"I see you've been into the brandy, Mr. J.," Maynard went on.
"For purely medicinal purposes, Mr. M.," I said. "Care to join me?"
"Don't mind if I do," said Maynard.
He twirled his ridiculous waxed mustache.
And as we turned to go, I realized how much
medicinal brandy I had already taken,
for I could have sworn I saw (out of the corner of my eye)

a rat with a crooked tail scurry by.

The MARCONI INTERNATIONAL
MARINE COMMUNICATION COMPANY, Ltd.

Marconi-gram

From: Bruce Ismay, RMS *Carpathia*
To: P.A.S. Franklin, US Pres., IMM
Date: 15 April 1912
Time: 11:00 A.M.

Deeply regret advise you *Titanic* sank this
morning after collision with iceberg, resulting in
serious loss of life. Full particulars later.
Bruce Ismay

The night is done. The mourning has begun.
From sea, word fills Southampton's weary streets.
From Northam's cottages beyond the bridge,
wives bring their children out to learn the news,
past the crepe-draped pillars of sad Guildhall,
past townsfolk dressed in black, past Union Jacks
half-mast in dingy private garden paths,
past public house, where mourners raise their pints.
Past all of this the women, infant-hipped,
with toddlers gripping to their mothers' skirts:
the knickered boys and pinafored young girls,
toward Canute, where the White Star Office is.
After three days' wait, the list is going up,
the clerk ticks blue chalk lines against black slate.
A name takes shape, a trimmer: Allen, E.
Or is that Allen, F.? The letters blur.
One brother safe, the other left at sea.
Now Allsop. Anderson. Ashcroft and Ashe.
So many gone before the letter *B*.
Already empty-coffered from the strike,
so happy for the chance to earn their keep.
The blue-chalk names of the living and the lost,
the latter long. It makes the women weep.
The men bite firmly on their manly pipes,
their eyes red-rimmed, their sea-worn faces peaked.
In Northam, where so many firemen lived:
now fatherless, one hundred twenty-five,
the orphans of those crew who don't survive.

.. / .- -- / - .... . / .. -.-. .

R. Abbott; E. Abbott; A. S. Allsop;
J. J. Astor; H. E. Buckley; F. Goldsmith;
Wallace Hartley; Thomas Hart; L. Hoffman . . .

We were sending out the names of the dead.
It was an endless list.

I was laid up in *Carpathia*'s hospital with bandaged feet,
and I had determined never to hear another dit or dash.
But when Captain Rostron and my old friend Harold Cottam
asked if I would assist in the wireless shack, I said yes.
I reasoned that the work would help fill
the hours of sleeplessness that I was enduring.
I could not close my eyes, you see,
for fear that I might not wake up again—
like the other men who had closed their eyes
and slipped off the bottom of our upturned boat.

Mostly I prepared messages while Cottam worked the apparatus.
"Hello," he said on Tuesday evening. "It's a note from the president."
"What?" I asked. "You mean Mr. Marconi?"
"No," said Cottam. "The president of the United States!"

It was, indeed, President Taft, seeking information
about the fate of personal friends of his.
The whole world wanted to know what had happened.
The whole world wanted to know the names of living and dead.

John "Jock" Hume; J. S. March; T. W. McCawley;
J. Phillips; E. J. Smith; O. S. "Oscar" Woody;
J. Phillips; J. Phillips; J. Phillips . . .

The list went on forever.

Late that night, I took my turn at the headset
and intercepted a message stating that *Titanic*'s
passengers and crew had all been rescued
and put off in Halifax! Ha. Imagine that.
Perhaps it had all been just a nightmare.
But then why were my feet wrapped in bandages?
Why was I in such pain? And where the devil was Phillips?
My eyes burned from lack of sleep.
The high-pitched crackle of the wireless became one
indistinguishable blur of nonsense.
I readjusted the set's frequency and discovered
a strange signal coming through the discordant noise.
It was weak at first, but grew stronger
with each small turn of the dial.
Then I could hear it plainly. The signal was faint
but the words were clear enough.

```
CQD. MGY. SOS. MGY.

To: H. Bride
Urgently request assistance.
Very cold. Please come at once.
41°43'57"N, 49°56'49"W.
It's a CQD, old man.

J. Phillips
```

THE ICEBERG 〰

I am the ice. Ten thousand years
I've waited for a chance to feel.
I've gathered bodies all around.
No sound. No sense of loss.
The sun beats down.
My mighty mass shows less and less.
Perhaps the Iceberg's heart will out.
And shout forth from some hidden cave
that melts within me.
The living humans sail away.
They cry. They laugh. They hurt.
I've gathered bodies all around.
They huddle to me. But for what?
Where is the sound? Where is the sound?
The Iceberg shrinks. I'm swept
by currents brisk and warm.
While all about me heartless humans swarm.
In life devour. In death devout.
Their lifeless bodies, ice throughout.
A hundred fickle fires gone out.

Once we were on board *Carpathia,*
I had all the hot chocolate I could drink.
Dad didn't show up before we had to go away,
but Mum says he'll likely meet us in New York.
"So long, Frankie. I'll see you later." That's what he said.
My dad didn't get to be the best tool-and-die man in Strood
by saying things he didn't really mean.
Mum kept busy sewing clothes from blankets
and whispering to Mrs. Abbott.
    (Don't tell Mrs. Abbott, but we're pretty sure
    that Eugene and Rossmore didn't make it.
    Alfred was with Dad, so he's probably all right.)
Sam Collins, the friend of Tommy Hart who knows about dragons,
was a real pal and showed me around *Carpathia*'s boiler room.
The floor was scattered with a thousand dragon hearts!
It was brilliant.
The stokers declared me an official member of the Black Gang,
and all I had to do was drink a glass of water and vinegar
with a raw egg floating on top.
It's what us stokers call a Bombay oyster,
and I drank it in one gulp! Everybody cheered!
"That'll make a man of ye!" someone said.
I said, "No, thanks, bloke. Grown-ups got no imaginations!"
They all laughed at that.
I was sad when Sam told me Tommy didn't make it.
"Now, *there* was a grown-up with imagination," I said.
"He was a great chum, all right," said Sam,
"but he sure as bollocks wasn't Thomas Hart!"

THE ICEBERG ∽

I am the ice.
I've gathered bodies all around.
The sun beats down.
The sun beats down.
I'm less and less.
My heart will out.
Shout from some hidden cave.
More bodies join me
on my way.
I am the ice.

Do not misunderstand me.
I was thankful to God that He left me alive.
But could He not have let me live
with just a tiny bit of cash in my pockets?

What luck when I spotted none other than Mr. Stengel,
with his wife, all safe and sound aboard *Carpathia*.
When I explained to him that my funds were now
at the bottom of the Atlantic, Stengel had no idea
that some of those funds were actually his own.

I must have acted well the part of the sad English aristocrat—
    stoic hero who had saved many lives, without proper clothing,
        far from home, a stranger in town, embarrassed for funds—
for Stengel insisted that I be his guest once we reach New York.

"Excellent," I said. "I would be delighted.
And while I'm getting all my affairs in order,
perhaps we could discuss a little idea I have.
An idea that might prove profitable
for a betting man such as yourself."

"Oh, really?" said Stengel.

"Oh, yes," I answered, "but you'll need to keep it under your hat.
We mustn't let the secret out. It has to do with horse racing."

Stengel said, "Oh, Lord Brayton, I haven't any luck with horses at all."

I whispered, "Mr. Stengel—Charles—I happen to have enough luck
for the both of us. Now, trust me when I tell you,
this is a win-win proposition. I'd bet my entire London estate on it."

Quartermaster Hichens had warned me not to rock the boat.
But since I boarded *Carpathia,* that's all I have done.
I beseeched the first-class ladies to donate
whatever hand-me-down clothes they could spare.
I mingled among the steerage class, making sure
that everyone had a place to go once we reached New York.
I did my best to get word to loved ones,
covering the cost of many telegrams.
I took up a subscription for funds to help the destitute.
And I formed a committee to thank *Carpathia*'s crew
with extra pay and a loving cup for Captain Rostron.

Mrs. Candee showed up on deck perfectly coifed and powdered,
dressed in black velvet and ermine. Flaunting a perfect size-five shoe.
"Perhaps I am vain," she said. "I *am* the victim of a disaster,
but that doesn't mean I must dress like the matron of an asylum."
Mrs. Candee's approach works for her,
but as for me, I'm better off meeting an obstacle head-on.
It's how I've always done it. That's who I am.
I may have made it safely to the *Carpathia,*
but I still don't feel safe. No woman is safe, truly.
So long as we are denied equal say. Equal votes.
Equal representation. Equal opportunities. Equal wages.
So let Mrs. Candee wear the latest fashion.
I'll do the same. (I don't want to *be* a man!)
But I'll keep my ugly life vest on
over top of my beaded Parisian gown.
And I'll wear it as a reminder
that we are not yet standing on solid ground.
And as I rock whatever boat I choose, I will ask for justice.
And I will *not* "ask pretty."

Elias was sleeping down below
when the *Carpathia* finally reached New York Harbor.
It was raining. Foggy. And dark.
Small boats full of men shouting and waving followed us.
But it was not they whom I endured the weather to see.
I was there to glimpse the famous Statue of Liberty.
As I watched from the decks, it started to thunder,
and during one brief flash of lightning, I saw her.

"You are beautiful," I said within my secret heart.
Since boarding *Carpathia,* I had found speaking to be very difficult.
What right did I have to talk of my grief?
I had lost only a boy I had just met and barely knew.
What was my sorrow in comparison to those
who had lost husbands, brothers, and even children?
I began, that day, a vow of silence that would last for weeks.

You are beautiful.

He had said it to me that wonderful Sunday night.
Every time he spoke, I had felt his breath in my ear.
It was the most amazing and wonderful sensation.
As if his voice had rushed into my head,
falling, like water, into my chest, past my stomach,
along my legs, crashing into my feet,
returning upward to fill me like a warm mist.

The boy in the long trousers standing on the white crane.
He had given me something more valuable
than the contents of a money belt.
He had given me a memory that would sustain me
A memory that I would hold in my secret heart. Forever.

The Iceberg ∾

I am the ice
I ebb
I flow
warm Gulf Stream
currents sweep
me south
Give birth
Destroy
Restore
I go

It had been exciting aboard the *Carpathia*.
Although it wasn't as fancy as *Titanic,* I had fun
being an official stoker and drinking hot chocolate.
We had passed maybe a hundred icebergs,
but *Carpathia*'s captain knew more than Captain Smith.
Carpathia's captain gave those ice dragons a wide berth.

There was a brilliant thunderstorm that night
when our ship got in at New York Harbor.
They say we passed the Statue of Liberty, but I couldn't see.
Each time the lightning flashed, someone would shout,
"Look! Look! There she is! I see her torch. I see her crown!"
If Dad had been there, he would have lifted me up.
On Dad's shoulders I was taller than grown-ups.
Whenever he held me up like that, he called me his "little bucket."
He said, "Even the deepest well is useless
without a bucket sitting on its shoulder."
Mum says Dad might not be home for a long time,
but I already miss him a lot. When Dad's around,
Mum is a lot happier and she doesn't protect me as much.
If I miss Dad this much just after a few days,
I can imagine how much Mum misses my little brother.
And just because she misses Bertie
doesn't mean she loves *me* any less.
Gosh, I miss my dad like a big hungry stomach,
but that doesn't mean I love *Mum* any less.
Dad will have to get a new set of tools.
Mum will have to get a new Singer sewing machine.
And I guess I'll be needing a new cap pistol, too.
Our family lost a lot when *Titanic* went down.

But we finally made it. We made it.

And as we got near New York City—wow!
I had a strange flipping and flopping in my stomach.
The reporters yelling from the boats all around us
reminded me of the sound of the people left behind in the water.
The sudden flashes from the cameras
reminded me of rescue rockets lighting up the dark.
The faraway sound of the Salvation Army band
reminded me of Jock Hume and his fiddle band
playing as me and Mum got into our lifeboat.
Then I thought about Eugene because he was
a soldier of God in the Salvation Army. And Rossmore.
And Alfred. And they were all out there in the cold, dark ocean.
They were out there with the Singer and my pistol,
and Daddy's tools—Daddy's tools were never coming back.

I don't know what happened to me
(and with all those people watching, too)
but I started to cry.

Just a little bit.
            Then a lot.

Mum held me and just then I didn't mind a little protection.
She looked at me and smiled, and I figured out
how maybe one way I could take care of Mum
would be to let her take care of me.
At least until Dad met up with us in Detroit.
And he will. We just have to be patient. And watch.
I heard him say it clear as day. I heard him say it.

"So long, Frankie. I'll see you later."

THE ICEBERG ∾

I am

```
.--. .... .. .-.. .-.. .. .--. ...
.. ... / -.. . .- -..
```

I hadn't realized that we had arrived . . .

    until the men walked into the wireless room.

I hadn't realized the men had entered the room . . .

    until one man placed his hand upon my shoulder.

I hadn't realized it was Guglielmo Marconi's hand . . .

    until he told me his name.

I hadn't realized that my left foot was badly sprained . . .
that my right foot was still numb with frost . . .
that I was delirious with fatigue . . .

    until I tried to stand.

I hadn't realized I kept tapping out the names of the dead
long after Cottam had turned off the apparatus . . .

    until Mr. Marconi said,
    "That's hardly worth sending now, son."

I hadn't realized that my voice was so weak . . .

    until I tried to speak.

    "Mr. Marconi," I said, "Phillips is dead."

.--. ....-.. .-.. .. .--. ...

I hadn't realized . . .

until I heard myself say it out loud.

.. ... / -.. . .- -..

JOHN SNOW
THE UNDERTAKER

Finally the dead have crossed the Atlantic.
Finally the dead have completed their journey.
Finally the dead are allowed to disembark.
Thirty horse-drawn hearses, lined up at Purdy's Wharf,
patiently wait as the first-class bodies are brought off first.
Then second. Then third. Classified in death as in life.
Only the horses speak their solemn nickers
as they climb the steep ascent from the docks
up North Street to the Mayflower Curling Rink.
This place of joy and laughter and sport
now a makeshift morgue by virtue of its floor of ice.
Countless canvas cubicles holding three coffins each.

A coffin for each body. A space for every coffin.
The Halifax Deputy Registrar of Deaths
takes charge of all the personal effects.
The canvas bags that hold the clues
of what and when and how and who.

Louis Hoffman: Body #15

Gold watch, loaded revolver, pipe in case

John Jacob Astor: Body #124

Gold watch; cuff links, gold with diamond;
diamond ring with three stones; £225 in English notes;
$2440 in notes; £5 in gold; 7s. in silver; 5 ten-franc pieces;
gold pencil; pocketbook

Oscar Woody: Body #167

Watch; fob; chain and clip; 2 fountain pens; knife;
cuff links; 1 gold ring; keys and chain; $10.02; letters

Thomas L. Theobald: Body #176

Silver watch and chain; tobacco pouch; pipe; razor;
memo book; gold pin; comb; gold ring, marked "C. T.";
knife; three studs; 4s. in purse

Rossmore Abbott: Body #190

Watch inscribed "Oxford Street Grammar School";
chain and fob, with gold medal marked "Rossmore Abbott";
pocket book, empty, and two knives

John "Jock" Hume: Body #193

English lever watch; cigarette case;
violin mute; empty purse

Wallace Hartley: Body #224

Nickel watch; gold chain; gold cigar holder;
telegram to Hotley, Bandmaster *Titanic;*
stud; scissors; 16 cents

John March: Body #225

Gold watch and chain; fountain pen;
diamond tie pin; gold ring, letter *M.*

The dead lay waiting. On display.
The rich will come to take their loved ones away.

The poor will wire ahead for the effects.
The unidentified will simply wait.
Such is the case with body number four. A boy.
A child who wasn't even two years old.

Unidentified: Body #4

Grey coat with fur on collar and cuffs;

brown serge frock; petticoat; flannel garment;

pink woolen singlet — brown shoes and stockings

A boy who won't play ball. Or roll a hoop.
Or stoop and learn to tie his laces.
Or learn to tell the time.
Or carry a watch at all.
I had convinced myself that it was better not to feel.
Detachment made me better at my job I thought.
But here is this lonely forgotten boy. The age of my own.
Sleeping upon ice he will never learn to skate.

I have been so long among the dead,
I have become a kind of corpse myself.
Just as I "set the features" of the deceased,
I create my own personal mask as well.
I am the undertaker, keeping emotion at bay:
My grief is a smile. My sobs are laughter.
Easy jokes are my whispered prayers.
Bodies are as driftwood: silent curiosities
to be shaped, polished, and gracefully displayed.

Finally I leave the dead behind till tomorrow.
And I walk to the pub for a pint with the boys.
They listen to the tale of my recent voyage of sorrow.
Then we raise our glasses. We make some noise.
And we drink to the children who will never be full grown.
And we drink to the travelers who never made it home.

THE SHIP RAT ～

hide hunker

wait listen
listen wait

    sniff sniff . . . food?
                   scuttle scuttle scuttle
                          follow the food
   scuttlescuttlescuttle

        follow the food
across the deck

     through the rail

         onto the rope

      follow the rope
        find the food

         onto the dock . . . into the city

   scuttlescuttlescuttle

         follow the future

             follow the food

NOTES

Author's Note

On Wednesday, April 17, 1912, the RMS *Titanic,* the largest and most luxurious ship in the world, was due in New York, carrying 2,207 men, women, and children. It never arrived. Instead, that same day, the cable ship *Mackay-Bennett,* a much smaller and less glamorous vessel, set out from Halifax, Nova Scotia, to collect the bodies of *Titanic*'s passengers and crew left floating in the Atlantic.

So what happened?

Beginning that night of the sinking, April 14 to 15, a sea of information (some reliable, some not) began to accumulate. Now, one hundred years later, it's still pouring in. Learning about the *Titanic* disaster is a lot like learning the banjo. Easy to play, difficult to master. While *The Watch That Ends the Night* is fiction, it is born of painstaking (and sometimes simply painful) research.

The truth is how you tell it. In order to write *The Watch That Ends the Night,* I've allowed fancy to play within the confines of fact. When it comes to historical fiction, history is the birdcage; fiction is the bird. The included biographies will help somewhat to distinguish bird from cage.

Let me apologize in advance to any *Titanic* enthusiasts who might discover historical errors within these pages. Careful readers will note that Captain Smith's final count of souls on board does not match the numbers in the Miscellany that follows. Like many *Titanic* facts, the numbers of lost and saved vary among sources. The same inconsistencies exist in the numbers of passengers in each of the three classes. I've chosen to base my final numbers on Encyclopedia Titanica in general and on Lester Mitcham's research in particular.

But my aim in writing *The Watch That Ends the Night* was not to present history. My aim was to present humanity. The people represented in this book lived and breathed and loved. They were as real as you or me. They could have been any one of us.

And that is why, after a century, the *Titanic* still fascinates.

Writing a historical novel is like making soup. You spend a lot of time gathering ingredients, but eventually you've got to start cooking, even if you are missing one or two spices. I regret that I was unable to read all the forthcoming books due to mark the centennial of the *Titanic* sinking. I also regret not being able to obtain a rare copy of Frank Goldsmith's out-of-print autobiographical book, *Echoes in the Night.* I'm sure I may have gotten a few things wrong; the biographical notes, following, will reveal a couple of them. But if you are a connoisseur of all things *Titanic,* please be kind to the cook. And just enjoy the soup.

THE MYSTERY SHIP

Most *Titanic* historians agree that there was a ship within sight of the sinking ocean liner that night. Many eyewitnesses, both passengers and crew, claimed to have seen a ship's lights. But what ship was it? The American and British inquiries both identified the SS *Californian,* whose ice warning Phillips had abruptly cut off earlier that evening. Crewmen aboard the *Californian* testified that they saw white rockets launched at intervals, yet neither the ship's captain nor the officers on duty made any attempt to communicate via the ship's wireless. Be warned: among Titaniacs, the mystery ship's identity is an incendiary issue. In *The Watch That Ends the Night,* I have chosen not to name any particular ship because its identity is not relevant to my story. The fact is that a ship was there. And for whatever reason, that ship did nothing.

CHARACTER NOTES

OLAUS ABELSETH ♦ THE IMMIGRANT

Olaus Jørgensen Abelseth was born June 10, 1886, on a farm east of Ålesund, a small fishing village in Norway. Eventually he moved to South Dakota and established a farm there before returning to his homeland for a visit. He set out for the return trip with five other Norwegians, including his cousin Peter Søholt and his brother-in-law, Sigurd Moen. As I've depicted in my tale, Abelseth waited with his group and many other third-class passengers on the ship's stern deck. By the time the men were called up onto the boat deck, the boats were all gone. By the time that all three jumped overboard, the ship had begun to plunge. Olaus eventually climbed aboard Collapsible A, the same swamped raft containing Rhoda Abbott, mother of Eugene and Rossmore. Although Abelseth did attempt to help a man who died in his arms, it was *not* the mysterious stoker, Thomas Hart, as I've depicted here. And although Olaus did write a postcard to his girlfriend, Marie, once he was safe in New York, most of his correspondence in this book is fiction. A notable exception is the final sentence of his final letter, which is taken directly from a letter he wrote to his sister, Inga. Olaus testified before the United States Senate's inquiry into the sinking and eventually returned to his farm in South Dakota. He married a Norwegian named Anna Grinde and had four children. Anna died in 1978 at the age of one hundred. Olaus, who had been twenty-five years old the night *Titanic* sank, died in 1980, at ninety-four.

THOMAS ANDREWS ✦ THE SHIPBUILDER

Thomas Andrews Jr., born February 7, 1873, in Northern Ireland, was the nephew of Lord William Pirrie, principal owner of Harland and Wolff shipbuilders. He was reportedly an active, inquisitive, and intelligent fellow who kept bees and excelled at building ships, a career he was thoroughly groomed for. His somewhat gushing biography, by Shan Bullock, depicts Andrews as a man's man, liked by all. He was certainly well known to the ship's crew. Chief baker Charles Joughin even baked Andrews a special loaf of bread. He was reportedly concerned over the massive emigration from Ireland, which leaves one to wonder if he felt conflicted building the very ships that were facilitating that exodus. As *Titanic* was sinking, Andrews went from deck to deck urging passengers and crew to put on their life vests. Bullock records the story of Andrews standing in the smoking lounge with his own life vest on a chair nearby. In reality it was not Thomas Hart but a steward who found Andrews there and tried unsuccessfully to persuade him to save himself. When he went down with the *Titanic,* Thomas Andrews left behind a wife and young daughter. He was thirty-nine years old.

JOHN JACOB ASTOR ✦ THE MILLIONAIRE

John Jacob Astor IV, born July 13, 1864, in Rhinebeck, New York, is often depicted as shallow, whiney, arrogant, and something of a dim bulb. But he invented several devices, including a bicycle brake, a "rain inducer," a pneumatic road-improver, and a process to convert peat into fuel for automobiles. And he wrote a science-fiction novel titled *A Journey in Other Worlds* that shows quite a bit of imagination. He was also a businessman and land developer. In a time before television and movies, the filthy-rich members of upper-crust society were the topic of gossip, headlines, adulation, and judgment. The forty-seven-year-old Astor's divorce and remarriage to the eighteen-year-old Madeleine Force caused something of a scandal. As far as I can tell, stories of Astor being crushed when the foundering *Titanic*'s forward funnel fell are not correct. His body, Number 124, was recovered by the *Mackay-Bennett* on April 22. As I've depicted in this book, his effects included a gold watch and a small fortune in cash and coins. Nineteen-year-old Vincent Astor traveled to the makeshift morgue in Halifax to identify his father's body and arrange for its transportation back to New York. On an unrelated note, J. J. Astor's private yacht, *Nourmahal,* was apparently involved in not just one, but two collisions of its own—one with a ferry, the other with a second yacht, *North Star,* owned by the Vanderbilt family.

GEORGE BRERETON ◆ THE GAMBLER

Cardsharps and con artists were fixtures on board luxury steamships at the turn of the last century. Enter George Andrew Brereton, of Los Angeles, California. He was on the passenger list as George Brayton, although it is unclear if Brayton was an alias or a simple typo. Brereton's shipboard activities are a mystery, as is the exact lifeboat in which he descended. Some suggest that he left the ship in lifeboat nine, rather than thirteen, as I have depicted. What *is* certain, however, is that upon safely arriving in New York, Brereton (with an accomplice) attempted to lure fellow survivor Charles Stengel into a scheme to fix the results of horse races. Stengel wanted no part of it, and a fight ensued. By the time authorities arrived, Brereton had vanished. Years later, in 1933, Brereton was caught and arrested for trying to run a similar scam in San Jose, California. And on July 16, 1942, George Brereton shot and killed himself in the house where his wife had committed suicide twenty years earlier.

HAROLD BRIDE ◆ THE SPARK

Most, though not all, of the wireless transmissions included in this book are real. I have kept the distress signals in the order of transmission, though the actual time may be off by ten minutes or so. In reality *Titanic*'s first distress signal was sent out at 12:27 A.M. (April 15), a bit later than I've depicted it here. The final distress signal was likely sent out just after 2:00 A.M. (a bit earlier than I've depicted). Some suggest that faint signals (including the famous v v v v) heard by the *Virginian* after 2:00 A.M. were from *Titanic,* though this has been called into question. Harold Bride received one thousand dollars from the *New York Times* for his exclusive story. His buddy Harold Cottam got $750. Guglielmo Marconi himself testified at the United States Senate inquiry. After the sinking, the Marconi Company's stock increased in value by four hundred percent. Bride married in 1918 and worked as a radio operator until 1922, when he moved to Prestwick, Scotland, and became a salesman. Like many other passengers and crew, Bride allegedly did not like to discuss the *Titanic*. He died at the age of sixty-six on April 29, 1956.

MARGARET BROWN ◆ THE SOCIALITE

Although Margaret Brown is arguably the most famous of all *Titanic* passengers, this was not the case in 1912. She was far from the backward and boisterous woman depicted in the modern stage musical and the movie based *very* loosely on her life. Known to most as the "Unsinkable Molly Brown," she was never called Molly in her lifetime. And although she came from a humble social and financial situation, she was actually part of what would eventually be termed the middle class. Her husband, J.J. Brown, earned his fortune as a foreman in the mining business through hard work more than luck. And she never hid her fortune in the woodstove! Far from being ostracized, she became a fixture in Denver society, active in philanthropy and politics. She had an interest in drama, and she studied languages, including German, French, and Russian.

Although it seems reasonable to assume that two rich ladies traveling unescorted may have met, the close shipboard friendship that Brown strikes up with the fascinating Helen Churchill Candee is fictional. Many of Candee's remarks regarding fashion, furniture, and gender relations in this book come directly from her own writings.

Their lifeboat officer, QM Robert Hichens, was sent to prison after attempting to murder a man in 1933. During that time he attempted suicide. He was released four years later and eventually died aboard a cargo ship on September 23, 1940.

In July of 1920, Margaret Brown and two of her nieces were passengers aboard the wooden steamer *Quinneseco* when a coal-bunker fire nearly burned through the hull, forcing them to make an emergency landing in Halifax. Mrs. Brown spent three days making floral tributes and placed a wreath on all 150 of Halifax's *Titanic* graves. Margaret Tobin Brown died of a brain tumor on October 26, 1932, at the Barbizon Hotel in New York.

EUGENE DALY • THE BAGPIPER

On January 4, 1913, Daly, who survived the sinking on upturned collapsible B, filed a claim against the White Star Line to cover the loss of five hundred dollars cash, two suits of clothes worth fifty dollars, and a set of bagpipes worth fifty dollars. He was also seeking a further ten thousand dollars for "personal injuries to the lower half of my person, which injuries are of a permanent nature."

Years later, Daly's only daughter claimed that her father had actually recovered completely and remarked that he was a lively step dancer. In his final years, although he used a cane and had both bad hearing and bad eyesight, he would walk to church every day. According to his daughter, Daly would stop oncoming Bronx traffic as he slowly crossed a busy intersection—upright and stately as a king. "If any driver honked at him," his daughter remembered, "he would whack the bonnet of the car with his cane and yell in his loud brogue, 'What's yer hurry? When God made time, he made plenty of it.'" Good advice from a man who survived the *Titanic*. Daly's time finally ran out on October 30, 1965. He was eighty-one.

FREDERICK FLEET ♦ THE LOOKOUT

Not surprisingly, Fred Fleet was thoroughly questioned at both the U.S. and British investigative hearings. Soon after the sinking, Fleet left the White Star Line. For the next twenty-four years, he was employed on Cunard and Union-Castle ships. In 1936 he left the sea for good, taking a job as a shipbuilder with Harland and Wolff, the company that had built *Titanic*. In his twilight years he sold copies of the *Daily Echo* on a street corner in Southampton. He had married Eva LeGros in 1917 and was reportedly very devoted to her. The marriage lasted forty-eight years and produced one daughter, two grandchildren, two great-grandchildren, and two great-great-grandchildren. In 1965, twelve days after his wife, Eva, died, he visited his family one last time. Then Frederick Fleet returned home and hanged himself in his back garden. He was seventy-seven.

FRANKIE GOLDSMITH ♦ THE DRAGON HUNTER

Frankie and his mom, thirty-one-year-old Emily Goldsmith, made their way to Detroit as planned. They found a house near Navin Field, where the Detroit Tigers played baseball. Unfortunately, the roar of the crowd would remind the boy of the sound of the *Titanic* passengers dying in the water. Frankie got a job as a milk-cart driver and later became a professional photographer, a craft he honed as a civilian employee of the U.S. Air Force during World War II. He married in 1926 and had three sons with his wife, Victoria.

Later in life he began to speak publicly about his *Titanic* experience, becoming a frequent guest at meetings of the *Titanic* Historical Society, which eventually published his memoir, *Echoes in the Night*. Frank remembered quickly joining a gang of about eight boys near his own age. Young Willie and Harold could have been part of that gang, though it's just my guess. And even though Rossmore and Eugene Abbott were much older, they almost certainly met Frankie while aboard *Titanic,* since the Abbott boys' mother, Rhoda, and Frankie's mother had become close friends during the journey.

Frank and Victoria Goldsmith relocated to Florida, where he died of heart failure on January 27, 1982, at the age of seventy-nine. A couple of months later, on April 15, the anniversary of the sinking, Frankie Goldsmith's ashes were scattered into the sea, reuniting him at last with his father. I've corresponded with Frankie's grandson Thomas, who remembers his grandfather's *Titanic* tales, including the "Eenie-Meenie-Epatic" counting rhyme. Rossmore and Eugene's mother, Rhoda Abbott, was the only woman who went down with the ship and survived. She never recovered from the grief of losing her two boys.

THOMAS HART ◆ THE STOKER

Titanic lore tells us that an impostor boarded the ship posing as Thomas Hart, of Liverpool, whose papers had been stolen. The impostor allegedly went down with the ship. A wonderful story . . . if only it were true. From the very beginning, the story of Thomas Hart and the mysterious impostor contained more holes than the *Titanic* itself. But sometimes a falsehood is so ironic and compelling that writers are loath to muddle up the details with the truth. I was duped like everyone else. I began writing the story of Sean Gould as a fictional character based on a real person. But as it turns out, Gould is fiction based on fiction.

Titanic researcher and myth debunker Senan Molony reasons convincingly that it was actually stoker James Hart, of Southampton, who was lost. James had signed on as "J. Hart," but an early list of the dead erroneously presented "J. Hart" as "T. Hart." The list eventually reached Liverpool, where another stoker named Thomas Hart lived. Thomas Hart's concerned relatives hired a lawyer to see if this "T. Hart" might actually be their Thomas, but dropped the matter when Thomas showed up very much alive. Thomas, a bachelor with no connection whatsoever to the *Titanic,* was unaware anyone thought he was missing. The White Star Line quickly discovered and corrected the transcription error. But not before the *Liverpool Daily Post* ran a short notice reporting Thomas Hart's discharge book had been stolen and conjecturing (incorrectly) that an impostor had boarded *Titanic* in the stoker's place. The *Cork Examiner* ran the story. The *New York Times* ran the story. The more the falsehood was told, the more it became the truth.

Although my fictional Sean Gould (aka Thomas Hart) did not exist, the story of the theft ring aboard the *Adriatic* (under command of Captain Smith) is a real incident. And Tommy Hart's mate, stoker John Coffey, really did leave the *Titanic* hidden among the mail sacks on a tender at Queenstown. Coffey reportedly wanted to see his mother. The name, Sean Gould, itself I borrowed from one of my neighbors, best known for stoking the coals of his backyard barbecue.

LOUIS HOFFMAN/MICHEL NAVRATIL ◆ THE TAILOR

Michel Navratil was born in 1880 in what is now Slovakia. By 1902 he was living in France and working as a tailor. He and Marcelle Caretto married in May of 1907 and had two sons, young Michel Marcel (Lolo) and Edmond Roger (Momon). But by 1912, the couple had separated. Since he died in the sinking, no one will ever know what Navratil's plan was once he reached America.

His body, Number Fifteen, was collected by the *Mackay-Bennett* and found to have a loaded revolver in the coat pocket. The two missing bullets are my own invention. Ironically, since his alias was a Jewish surname, he was buried in Halifax's Baron de Hirsch Cemetery, which was reserved for *Titanic*'s Jewish victims.

JOCK HUME ◆ THE SECOND VIOLIN

John Law "Jock" Hume, a resident of Dumfries, Scotland, was twenty-one when he died in the sinking. His body, Number 193, was identified and buried at Fairview Lawn Cemetery in Halifax. As I've depicted in this book, Hume's effects included a violin mute and an empty purse. The body of Wallace Hartley, the bandleader, was found with sixteen cents and a pair of scissors. These very real items gave birth to the fictional scenes of my story. Fistfights erupt among Titaniacs when discussing what the band's last song was. "Songe d'Automne"? "Nearer, My God, to Thee"? A ragtime tune? Some witnesses claim the band did *not* go down playing at all. Again, the truth probably lies somewhere in the middle. Just two weeks after the sinking, Hume's father, Andrew, received a bill for the cost of the band uniform that his son had selfishly taken with him to the bottom of the sea. To make matters worse, neither the Eberle nor the Guadagnini had been insured. Neither were they paid for. A sixteen-foot-tall monument to Hume was erected in Dumfries' Dock Park with a brass plaque that reads, "Nearer, My God, to Thee." I have corresponded with Yvonne Hume, the musician's great-niece, who argues that Jock was actually considered first violin while Wallace Hartley was simply orchestra leader. She also alerted me that John Hume had a fiancée, Mary Costin, already pregnant, waiting for him at home. Mary named her little girl Johnann, after the baby's father. Recent scholarship, available to me after this book was completed, suggests that Jock Hume's father may have fabricated the story of the Guadagnini and the Eberle. But lest we judge the elder Hume too harshly, Yvonne Hume wisely reminds us that Andrew Hume was a father, full of grief and anger, whose son had been taken away from him forever.

THE ICEBERG

It is difficult to say with certainty where the iceberg came from. But the best guess is that it was calved from one of the many glaciers on the western coast of Greenland. As many as ten thousand bergs are produced there each year, although relatively few ever make it as far south as the North Atlantic shipping lanes. Once the ice broke off from the land, it probably flowed north to make a large scenic loop around Baffin Bay, then headed south along the coast of Baffin Island and onward to Labrador and the Grand Banks, off Newfoundland. This journey may have taken as long as two years. As it rounded Labrador, where the Labrador Current merges with the warm Gulf Stream, the berg would have begun to melt rapidly. It would have hissed as millions of air bubbles, trapped for centuries, escaped. Cracks would have formed with the sound of cannon shots. Chunks the size of pianos would have fallen away. The berg would have become unstable and flipped over. The newly exposed surface would have appeared perfectly clear—or black, indistinguishable from the night. At the British inquiry into the sinking, Seaman Joseph Scarrott said that the iceberg "resembled the Rock of Gibraltar looking at it from Europa Point. It looked very much the same shape as that, only much smaller." Indeed, the berg was about medium size as icebergs go. Lookout Fred Fleet estimated it to be about fifty feet tall, barely reaching the height of *Titanic*'s forward well deck.

J. BRUCE ISMAY • THE BUSINESSMAN

While many accounts, both fictional and nonfictional, depict Bruce Ismay as a spineless villain, I found no evidence to support this. Most negative attacks upon Ismay's character seem to have originated with newspaper publisher William Randolph Hearst, who allegedly had a grudge against the president of the White Star Line. On the contrary, it seems that Ismay did all he could to expedite the loading of boats up until every boat was gone. Was it cowardice to take a place in the last boat as it was being lowered? Or was it simple common sense? Was he cowardly for not going down with the ship? Or was he heroic for facing a world hungry for answers? Even if he had been solely responsible for the paucity of lifeboats, he was simply following the accepted practices of the time. (The rescue ship, *Carpathia,* didn't have enough lifeboats for everyone aboard, either.) And lest we forget, there wasn't enough time to launch the few boats they had. Equally laughable is the misinformed image of Ismay bullying Captain Smith into recklessly speeding forth into dangerous waters. By most accounts, Ismay was well received in England upon his return. And while the *Titanic* tragedy was certainly not a high point of his career, neither did he become the ostracized recluse of lore. He soon resigned as president of the International Mercantile Marine Company and as chairman of the White Star Line, though he remained an active executive member of the business that he had inherited from his father. Neither was he destitute. When he died on October 17, 1937 (at age seventy-four), he left an estate worth seven hundred thousand pounds, or about three million dollars.

CHARLES JOUGHIN • THE BAKER

Chief baker Charles John Joughin was a valuable witness at the Senate inquiry because he was aboard the ship up until the very moment she disappeared below the surface. Having climbed to the aft-most part of the ship, Joughin clung to the rail of the poop deck and literally rode the ship down as it descended, nose first. While most victims were dead or unconscious within twenty minutes, Joughin estimated that he was in the water for a remarkable two hours. Joughin, and others, claimed that he was saved, at least in part, by the alcohol he had consumed that night. Science and common sense tell us, however, that alcohol consumption actually *accelerates* hypothermia. My theory is that Joughin, no stranger to water, was able to remain calm. Isaac Maynard, the cook, would have been a familiar face, not to mention a warm hand, once Joughin had made it to the side of their overturned life raft. Last, Joughin's testimony at the British inquiry suggests that he was able to hold his upper body out of the water, thus keeping the vital organs much warmer. Joughin claims that he barely got his head wet, which implies he was never completely submerged, which would further prevent heat loss. While Maynard really did reach out his hand to Joughin that night, the prior animosity between them is fictional. Joughin's comment that the *Carpathia* crew "popped me in an oven like one of me own pies" is taken directly from a letter he wrote to historian Walter Lord. On December 9, 1956, Charles Joughin died in a hospital in New Jersey. The cause of death was, ironically, pneumonia.

LOLO • THE TAILOR'S SON

Michel (Lolo) Navratil Jr. and his younger brother, Edmond (Momon), caused quite a sensation in America. When their father had passed them into what was one of the last remaining lifeboats, he did not explain their real identity to anyone. Eventually their mother, Marcelle, put two and two together and figured out that the two mysterious *"Titanic* waifs" were her own missing boys. Little Edmond grew up to become an interior designer, builder, and architect. While fighting in World War II, he was captured and held prisoner, an experience that harmed his health. He died young, at the age of forty-three. Michel Jr. became a university psychology professor and lived near Nice, France. As the last living male *Titanic* survivor, he became a frequent speaker at *Titanic* conventions in Europe and the U.S. In the summer of 1996, Michel paid an emotional visit to his father's grave in Halifax. He died on January 30, 2001, at the age of ninety-two.

HAROLD LOWE • THE JUNIOR OFFICER

By most accounts, Fifth Officer Harold G. Lowe had a very colorful personality. He apparently had an early falling-out with his father and left home for the sea at the age of fourteen. By the time he boarded *Titanic,* he and his father had reconciled, but he didn't settle down until 1913, when he married and moved to Colwyn Bay, in North Wales. Lowe's rough language and abrasive treatment of the ladies in lifeboat fourteen became part of the official testimony at the Senate inquiry. One woman suggested he had been drinking. Lowe informed the Senate that he "doesn't drink anything stronger than water." What's more likely is that Lowe was not a man who suffered fools lightly. Add to that the extreme nature of the unfolding disaster and I think Lowe deserves a little latitude.

When explaining his altercation with the frantic Bruce Ismay to the Senate, Lowe was reticent about repeating his exact language. Ultimately the inquiry leader, Senator William Alden Smith, had Lowe write the offending language on a piece of paper. Senator Smith deemed the language suitable for those listening and Lowe told the story as I've depicted it in this book. The offending word was *hell*. Lowe was also forced to produce a written apology for his repeated use of the term *Italians* to describe any unsavory passenger who tried to force his way into a boat. His apology was only slightly less offensive than his initial remarks.

Lowe did have his supporters among the many passengers whom he saved that night. Mrs. Henry B. Harris, the lady with the broken arm who attended the Sunday evening dinner in Captain Smith's honor, presented her rescuer with a sextant, telescope, and binoculars, all inscribed: "To Harold Godfrey Lowe, 5th Officer RMS *Titanic*. The real hero of the *Titanic*." Love him or hate him, Harold Lowe was in charge of the only lifeboat that returned to pull survivors from the water.

Lowe had two children with his wife, Ellen. And though he remained at sea, he never became captain in the merchant service. He eventually retired to his home in North Wales. Lowe's interests included woodworking and photography. He also sketched and painted watercolors. He died at the age of sixty-one on May 12, 1944.

JAMILA NICOLA-YARRED • THE REFUGEE

Jamila's father really *was* forced to stay behind because of an eye infection, which probably saved his life. But with about sixty-four Lebanese and Syrian passengers aboard *Titanic,* the young teenager and her brother would have been well protected. Most sources say that Jamila (whose name is sometimes spelled *Jamilia*) turned fourteen on the day of the sinking.

Jamila's father really did give her a hundred pounds to take to America, but the theft is fictional. The money sank along with the ship. I also fabricated Jamila's shipboard romance with Alfred. It seems probable, however, that Jamila would have encountered Selini Yazbeck, who was just a year older and newly married to Antoni (Fraza) Yazbeck. If Fraza's body was retrieved, it was not identified. Fahim Leeni, a Syrian-born passenger, may also have been known to Jamila. Evidence suggests that Fahim (aka Philip Zenni) ended up in lifeboat six with Margaret Brown, Fred Fleet, and the abusive quartermaster, Hichens. Jamila eventually made it to Jacksonville, Florida, and Anglicized her name to Amelia Garrett. At age fifteen, she married a nineteen-year-old grocer named Isaac Isaac. Elias became Louis Garrett. Jamila died on March 8, 1970. Elias passed away May 30, 1981.

THE SHIP RAT

There actually were rats aboard the *Titanic*. One third-class passenger mentioned seeing a rat on Sunday evening during a lively gathering in the saloon. Another witness, a stoker, claims to have seen a half dozen rats running through the boiler rooms a couple of days before the sinking. Rats regularly gained passage aboard ships via the mooring lines or hidden in food stores or other cargo. But could these rats actually get their tails tangled together to create the mythical Rat King? Again, it seems that rat kings really do form, though it is extremely rare and must take place under strict conditions. The rats must have hairy prehensile tails (as is the case with the ship rat, also called the roof rat or black rat). The rats must be packed in tightly, as they would be if sharing an underground burrow (or a flour barrel). Add in some sticky substance like blood (or eggs and marmalade). Provide cold temperatures as found in winter (or refrigerated storerooms), and *voilà,* instant Rat King!

E.J. SMITH • THE CAPTAIN

One cannot help but ponder the irony that Bruce Ismay has been demonized over the years, while Captain Smith, the man responsible for navigating the ship, is continually touted as a hero. As is the case with all history, the truth lies somewhere in the middle. Edward John Smith began his life at sea as a thirteen-year-old cabin boy for his older brother, Joseph. Seventeen years later, E.J. as he was called, joined White Star. And by 1912, Smith, who really *did* resemble the late King Edward, had become the de facto admiral of the company and one of the highest-paid officers of any merchant vessel. He and his wife, Eleanor, had only one child, a daughter named Helen Melville—"Mel" for short. (And no, she was *not* named after the author of *Moby-Dick,* much as we all wish it were true.) In his many letters to her, Smith would always allude to any future event by adding "*D.V.*" or *Deo volente,* "God willing." Smith was likely nearing retirement although there is every indication that he would have captained White Star's third sister ship, *Britannic,* on its maiden voyage as well. Harold Bride reported seeing Smith on the bridge as *Titanic* began its plunge. A popular newspaper story at the time depicts Smith rescuing a baby and handing it to entrée cook Isaac Maynard. Then the popular captain allegedly tossed his life vest, waved farewell, and sank beneath the waves. There are so many holes in this story that I won't even begin.

My depiction of Smith was inspired by Gary Cooper's *E.J.: The Story of Edward John Smith, Captain of the Titanic.* This book contains details, from E.J.'s habit of holding a toothpick in his mouth to the fact that Smith was *not* in command of the Belfast sea trials and delivery trip, that I found nowhere else.

JOHN SNOW ◆ THE UNDERTAKER

John R. Snow Jr. was the chief embalmer for Nova Scotia's largest undertaking firm, John Snow & Company. He was one of two embalmers aboard the *Mackay-Bennett,* hired by the White Star Line to retrieve whatever bodies could be found. Sixty-nine-year-old Arminias Wiseman (who was a twenty-two-year-old fireman at the time) recalled how one corpse tumbled from a pile of bodies and seemed to pursue an engineer down a passageway. Captain Larnder and Reverend Hind were actual members of this macabre expedition as well. Alan Ruffman's book *Titanic Remembered* is the most complete source of information about Halifax and the retrieval of bodies. Still, we know very little about the real John Snow. One photograph shows him aboard the *Mackay-Bennett* as he busily sews canvas bags to hold the dead's possessions. He doesn't look seasick at all. Another photo depicts him as a ruggedly handsome man in suit, tie, and overcoat, watch chain hanging from his vest, posing on the wharf in front of towering stacks of coffins. He peers straight at the camera with a grim face and a mysterious smirk.

My fictional version of John Snow is a composite of many *Mackay-Bennett* crew. It was Captain Larnder who actually likened the corpses to a "flock of gulls resting upon the water." And Snow's depiction of the many sea burials comes from the journal of chief electrician Frederic Hamilton, who witnessed seventy-seven in one day.

Born in Roxboro, North Carolina, Oscar Scott Woody was one of five sea-post men aboard *Titanic*. He had spent seventeen years with the railway mail service and had switched to the ocean service only two years earlier. He turned forty-four the night of the sinking; he and his new bride had been married only eighteen months. John Starr March, forty-eight, had lost his wife during a surgery ten months earlier. During March's eight years as a sea-post clerk, his ships had been involved in seven previous emergencies. He assured his two worried daughters that he would never drown at sea. His body, Number 225, was recovered wearing the gold ring with monogrammed *M,* which helped with the identification. Woody's body, Number 167, was also recovered. He was identified and buried at sea.

Fates of other historical persons mentioned in this novel:

Note: This is a list of the real-life *Titanic* passengers and crew mentioned in this book, divided into lost and saved. For those who were lost, I have noted if they were passengers or crew. For those who were saved, I have included the number or letter of the lifeboat in which they were rescued. For the more obscure characters, I have added reminder notes to help reference them. I present it all here as accurately as I am able.

LOST:
Eugene Abbott (passenger), Rossmore Abbott (passenger), Thomas Andrews (designer), John Jacob Astor (passenger), Quigg Baxter (passenger), Joseph Bell (chief engineer), Theodore Brailey (orchestra), Archibald Butt (passenger), Father Thomas Byles / took last confessions (passenger), Father Ernest Carter (passenger), Lilian Carter (passenger), John Frederick Clarke (orchestra), Frank Goldsmith (passenger), Benjamin Guggenheim (passenger), William Gwynn (postman), Henry Harris (passenger), Wallace Hartley (orchestra), Adolf Humblen (passenger), John "Jock" Hume (orchestra), Nils Johansson / Olga's fiancé (passenger), Kitty (dog), Georges Krins (orchestra), John March (postman), Thomas McCawley (gymnasium steward), Hugh McElroy (chief purser), Sigurd Moen (passenger), James Moody (sixth officer), William Murdoch (first officer), Michel Navratil/Louis Hoffman (passenger), William O'Loughlin (surgeon), John "Jack" Phillips (wireless man), George Rosenshine / body number 16 (passenger), Alfred Rush (passenger), Arthur Ryerson (passenger), Jonathan Shepherd (engineer), E. J. Smith (captain), John "Jago"

Smith (postman), Peter Søholt (passenger), Ida Straus (passenger), Isidor Straus (passenger), Percy Taylor (orchestra), John Thayer Sr. (passenger), Thomas Theobald (passenger), George Widener (passenger), Henry Wilde (chief officer), James Williamson (postman), Oscar Woody (postman), Frederick Wright (racquet court attendant), Antoni "Fraza" Yazbeck (passenger)

SAVED:
Rhoda Abbott (A), Karen Abelseth (16), Olaus Abelseth (A), Madeleine Astor (4), Léontine "Ninette" Aubart / Guggenheim's mistress (9?), Frederick Barrett (13), Hélène Baxter (6), Joseph Boxhall (2), George Brereton (9, 13?), Harold Bride (B), Margaret Brown (6), Helen Churchill Candee (6), William "Billy" Carter (C), John Coffey (deserted), Samuel Collins (1), Neville Coutts (2), Willie Coutts (2), Eugene Daly (B), Alfred Evans (15), Frederick Fleet (6), Emily Goldsmith (C), Frankie Goldsmith (C), Archibald Gracie (B), Henry Harper (3), Myra Harper (3), Irene "Rene" Harris (D), Hammad Hassab / the dragoman (3), Robert Hichens (6), George Hogg (7), Bruce Ismay (C), Archibald "Archie" Jewell (7), Charles Joughin (B), Reginald Lee (13), Fahim Leeni (6?), Bertha Lehmann / watched Lolo and Momon (12?), Charles Lightholler (B), Harold Lowe (14), Olga Elida Lundin / Nils's fiancée (10), Isaac Maynard (B), Bertha Mayne / Mme. de Villiers (6), Edmond "Momon" Navratil (D), Michel "Lolo" Navratil (D), Elias Nicola-Yarred (C), Jamila Nicola-Yarred (C), Alfred Olliver (5), Arthur Peuchen (6), Herbert Pitman (5), Elizabeth Rothschild (6), Emily Ryerson (4), Anna Salkjelsvik (C), Annie May Stengel (5), Charles Stengel (1), Sun Yat-sen / dog (3), George Symons (1), John "Jack" Thayer (B), Marian Thayer (4), August "Gus" Weikman / the barber (A), Eleanor Widener (4), Hugh Woolner (D), Selini Yazbeck (C)

Morse Code Messages

Coded messages appear in most of the pieces in the voice of Harold Bride, the Spark. Each message is translated below, or else you can use the following key to decipher them yourself.

A .-	J .---	S ...
B -...	K -.-	T -
C -.-.	L .-..	U ..-
D -..	M --	V ...-
E .	N -.	W .--
F ..-.	O ---	X -..-
G --.	P .--.	Y -.--
H	Q --.-	Z --..
I ..	R .-.	

page 20–21
    Harold Bride
    Say OM break out champagne

page 42
    Tomorrow we set sail
    MGY

page 77
    Billy
    Son
    Sweetheart
    Kitty Bex she is a peach

page 119
    Her only voice

page 150–151
    Better, new, fast, short, fun, be—

page 163
    Home

page 183
> Marry me
> TKS
> OM

page 210
> News, news, news, news

page 233
> I am the ice
> I am the ice

page 240
> Love, Mutzie

page 277
> Surrounded
> Surrounded
> Surrounded
> Surrounded by ice

page 297
> CQD MGY
> CQD MGY
> CQD MGY

page 315
> SOS SOS SOS
> SOS

page 400
> Iceberg

page 413
> I am the ice

page 425–426
> Phillips is dead
> Phillips is dead

RMS *TITANIC* MISCELLANY

The Ship
Gross tons: 46,328
Length: 882 feet, 9 inches
Height: 175 feet (from keel to top of funnels)
Number of decks: 9 (excluding tank top)
Number of propellers: 3
Number of engines: 3
Top speed: 23 knots
Number of funnels: 4
Number of rivets: 3,000,000
Number of boilers: 29
Number of furnaces: 159
Coal capacity: ≈ 6,600 tons
Coal consumed per day: ≈ 650 tons
Potential passenger capacity: 3,547

The People (with survival numbers)
Total number of people on board: 2,207 (712 survived)
Number traveling first class: 324 (201)
Number traveling second class: 277 (118)
Number traveling third class: 708 (181)
Number of crew members: 885 (212)
Number of musicians: 8 (0)
Number of postmen: 5 (0)

The Children (under twelve)
Total number of children on board: 107
Number in first class: 5
Number in second class: 22
Number in third class: 80
Youngest passenger aboard: 9 weeks (Millvina Dean)

The Lifeboats
Number of boats *Titanic* could accommodate: 64
Number of boats *Titanic* actually carried: 20
Number of boats required by law: 16
Total potential capacity: 1,178

Total actually placed in boats: 659
Number of lifeboats successfully launched: 18

The Time
Time required to build *Titanic:* ≈ 3 years
Time required to sink *Titanic:* ≈ 2 hours, 40 minutes
Time required to watch the movie *Titanic:* 3 hours
Time required for *Titanic* to reach the sea floor: ≈ 30 minutes
Time required to fill *Titanic*'s coal bins: ≈ 24 hours
Time required to cross the Atlantic: 6 days
Time *Titanic* sank: 2:20 A.M., April 15
Time in New York: 12:18 A.M.

The Survivors
Total number of people who survived: 712
Number of female and child survivors: 389 (54.6% of total)
Number of male survivors: 323 (45.4% of total)
Number of men who survived after going down with the ship: ≈ 52
Number of women who survived after going down with the ship: 1
Last survivor to pass away: Millvina Dean, May 31, 2009; age ninety-seven

The Lost
Total number of people lost: 1,495
Total number of bodies recovered: 330
Number of autopsies performed: 0
Official cause of death: drowning
Likely cause of death: hypothermia
Last body found: sometime in June, two months after sinking
Number of bodies never found: ≈ 1,165
Number of bodies buried at sea: 119
Number of bodies brought to Halifax: 209
Number of bodies claimed: 59
Number of bodies buried at Halifax: 150
Largest family lost: All 11 members of the Sage family, third class

Titanic vs. the Iceberg
Weight of *Titanic* (with contents): 52,310 tons

Weight of iceberg: ≈ 100,000 tons
Speed of *Titanic* at time of collision: 22½ knots (≈ 26 mph)
Speed of iceberg at time of collision: ≈ 1/3 knot (< 1 mph)
Age of *Titanic:* 3 years
Age of iceberg: ≈ 10,000 years

The Dogs
Number of dogs aboard: ≈ 12
Number that survived: ≈ 3

The Cost
Cost of *Titanic,* fully equipped: $7,500,000 (£1,500,000)
Price of first-class ticket: ≈ £26–£250
Price of second-class ticket: ≈ £10–£25
Price of third-class ticket: ≈ £7–£20
Cost of U.S. inquiry into sinking: $2,385
Cost of British inquiry into sinking: $87,500 (£17,500)
Cost to White Star for contracting the *Mackay-Bennett:* $550 per day
Cost to visit the wreck site today: ≈ $300,000 per day

The Wreck Site
Location: 41 degrees, 44 minutes North; 49 degrees, 57 minutes West
Depth: 12,500 feet, or 2.4 miles (3,810 meters)
Pressure: 6,000 psi
Plant life: none
Amount of light: none

Also of Interest
Number of life jackets: 3,560
Number of third-class passengers called to testify at British inquiry: 0
Number of honeymooning couples: ≈ 13
Number of new grooms lost: 9
Number of married couples: 107
Number of couples who survived together: 22
Number of elevators in first class: 3
Number of elevators in second class: 1
Number of elevators in third class: 0
Number of black passengers: 3 (Joseph Laroche, of Haiti, and his two children)
Number of black crew members: 0

Number of cigars: 8,000
Number of bottles of beer: 20,000
Number of bottles of wine: 1,500

Selected Luxuries
4 restaurants • 1 heated swimming pool • 1 squash court • 2 libraries • 2 dog kennels • 2 barbershops • 1 gymnasium • 2 music ensembles • 1 darkroom • 1 onboard newspaper • 2 physicians • 2 masseuses • 1 Turkish bath

Selected Food
7,500 pounds of bacon and ham • 25,000 pounds of poultry and game • 40,000 fresh eggs • 2,500 pounds of sausage • 40 tons of potatoes • 3,500 pounds of onions • 800 bundles of asparagus • 5,500 pounds of tomatoes • 2,250 pounds of peas • 7,000 heads of lettuce • 2,200 pounds of ground coffee • 800 pounds of tea • 10,000 pounds of rice and dried beans • 10,000 pounds of sugar • 200 barrels of flour • 10,000 pounds of cereal • 36,000 oranges • 16,000 lemons • 1,000 pounds of grapes • 1,120 pounds of jam and marmalade • 1,500 gallons of milk • 6,000 pounds of butter

Selected Cargo
anchovies, auto parts, beans, biscuits, books, boots, butter, calabashes, cameras, candles, cheese, china, cognac, dragon's blood, eggs, elastic cords, feathers, felt, film, flowers, furniture, golf balls, gramophones, grandfather clocks, gum, hairnets, lace, leather, linoleum, melons, mushrooms, opium, orchids, photos, rabbit hair, sardines, shelled walnuts, soap, speedometers, surgical instruments, tea, tennis balls, toothpaste, tweed, vermouth, whiskey, and window frames

Countries of Origin Represented by Passengers and Crew
Argentina, Armenia, Australia, Austria, Belgium, Bosnia, Bulgaria, Canada, China, Croatia, Cuba, Denmark, Egypt, England, Finland, France, Germany, Greece, India, Ireland, Italy, Japan, Lebanon, Lithuania, Mexico, Netherlands, Norway, Peru, Poland, Portugal, Russia, Scotland, Slovenia, South Africa, Spain, Sweden, Switzerland, Syria, Thailand, Turkey, United States, Uruguay, and Wales

On pages 368–369, the word *cold* appears in nine different languages in addition to English:

freddo = Italian
frío = Spanish
froid = French
holodnyi = Russian
kaldt = Norwegian
kälte = German
krýo = Greek
tsumetai = Japanese
zimno = Polish

Sources

Beveridge, Bruce, et al. *Titanic: The Ship Magnificent.*

Eaton, John P., and Charles A. Haas. *Titanic: Triumph and Tragedy.*

Encyclopedia Titanica: www.encyclopedia-titanica.org

Meredith, Lee W. *Titanic Names.*

BIBLIOGRAPHY

Numerous so-called instant books about the *Titanic* surfaced in 1912. They tend to contain half-truths, whole falsehoods, tall tales, and outrageous lies. For example: *Sinking of the Titanic: Most appalling Ocean Horror with graphic descriptions of hundreds swept to eternity beneath the waves; panic stricken multitude facing sure death, and thrilling stories of this most overwhelming catastrophe to which is added vivid accounts of heart-rending scenes, when hundreds were doomed to watery graves, compiled from soul stirring stories told by eye witnesses of this terrible horror of the briny deep.* Whew. What follows below is a partial list of books I consulted in preparing *The Watch That Ends the Night*. Remember that even the best of these books may contain some erroneous information. Keep an open mind, and look to the middle ground. If you want to limit your introduction to just a few titles, you might try those marked with an *. Books that are primarily contemporary voices of the time are marked **. These, along with the U.S. and British inquiry documents, offer written or transcribed accounts directly from those who were there. Finally, if you are a complete *Titanic* nut, you will not be able to live without both volumes of *Titanic: The Ship Magnificent*. These two books weigh a ton and cost a fortune, and they are guaranteed to make you the ruination of any party! Just ask my wife.

Books

Archbold, Rick, and Dana McCauley. *Last Dinner on the Titanic*. New York: Hyperion, 1997.

Astor, John Jacob. *A Journey in Other Worlds: A Romance of the Future.* Charleston: BiblioBazaar, 1990. Originally published in 1894.

Ballard, Dr. Robert D. *The Discovery of the Titanic.* New York: Warner Books, 1987.

**Barratt, Nick. *Lost Voices from the Titanic: The Definitive Oral History.* New York: Palgrave MacMillan, 2010.

**Beesley, Lawrence. *The Loss of the SS Titanic: Its Story and Its Lessons.* New York: Houghton Mifflin, 1912.

Beveridge, Bruce, Scott Andrews, Steve Hall, and Daniel Klistorner. *Titanic: The Ship Magnificent.* Two volumes: *Volume One: Design & Construction; Volume*

Two: Interior Design & Fitting Out. Stroud, Gloucestershire, U.K.: The History Press, 2008.

Biel, Steven. *Down with the Old Canoe: A Cultural History of the Titanic Disaster.* New York: Norton, 1996.

————, ed. *Titanica: The Disaster of the Century in Poetry, Song, and Prose.* New York: Norton, 1998.

Brown, David G. *The Last Log of the Titanic.* Camden, ME: International Marine/ McGraw Hill, 2001.

Brown, Richard. *Voyage of the Iceberg: The Story of the Iceberg That Sank the Titanic.* New York: Beaufort, 1983.

**Bryceson, Dave. *The Titanic Disaster, As Reported in the British National Press, April–July 1912.* New York: Norton, 1997.

Bullock, Shan. *A Titanic Hero: Thomas Andrews, Shipbuilder.* Ludlow, MA: 7 C's Press, 1995. First published 1912.

Cooper, Gary. *E.J.: The Story of Edward John Smith, Captain of the Titanic.* Lulu Print on Demand, ID: 1535715, self-published.

Eaton, John P., and Charles A. Haas, *Titanic, Destination Disaster: The Legends and the Reality.* New York: Norton, 1987.

————. *Titanic: A Journey Through Time.* New York: Norton, 1999.

*————. *Titanic: Triumph and Tragedy*, second edition. New York: Norton, 1994.

Geller, Judith B. *Titanic: Women and Children First.* New York: Norton, 1998.

**Goldsmith, Frank J. *Echoes in the Night.* Indian Orchard, MA: Titanic Historical Society, 1991.

**Gracie, Col. Archibald. *The Truth About the Titanic.* New York: Kennerly, 1913.

Hume, Yvonne. *RMS Titanic: "The First Violin": The Story of the Great Liner's Bandsman, John Law Hume.* Catrine, Ayrshire, Scotland: Stenlake Publishing, 2011.

**Hyslop, Donald, Alastair Forsyth, and Sheila Jemima. *Titanic Voices: Memories from the Fateful Voyage*. New York: St. Martin's Press, 1997.

Iversen, Kristen. *Molly Brown: Unraveling the Myth*. Boulder, CO: Johnson Books, 1999.

**Jessop, Violet. *Titanic Survivor: The Newly Discovered Memoirs of Violet Jessop Who Survived Both the Titanic and Britannic Disasters*. Introduced, edited, and annotated by John Maxtone-Graham. Dobbs Ferry, NY: Sheridan House, 1997.

Kaplan, Justin. *When the Astors Owned New York: Blue Bloods and Grand Hotels in a Gilded Age*. New York: Viking, 2006.

**Kuntz, Tom. *The Titanic Disaster Hearings: The Official Transcripts of the 1912 Senate Investigation*. New York: Pocket Books, 1998.

Lightoller, Charles H. *Titanic*. Ludlow, MA: 7 C's Press for the Titanic Historical Society. Originally published 1935.

Lord, Walter. *The Night Lives On*. New York: William Morrow, 1986.

*———. *A Night to Remember.* New York: Henry Holt, 1955.

*Lynch, Donald, and Ken Marschall. *Titanic: An Illustrated History*. New York: Hyperion, 1992.

Maxtone-Graham, John. *The Only Way to Cross: The Golden Era of the Great Atlantic Express Liners—from the Mauretania to the France and the Queen Elizabeth II*. New York: Macmillan, 1972.

McCarty, Jennifer Hooper, and Tim Foecke. *What Really Sank the Titanic: New Forensic Discoveries*. New York: Citadel, 2008.

Merideth, Lee W. *1912 Facts About Titanic*. Sunnyvale, CA: Rocklin Press, 2003.

———. *Titanic Names: A Complete List of the Passengers and Crew.* Sunnyvale, CA: Rocklin Press, 2002.

*Quinn, Paul J. *Titanic at Two A.M.: Final Events Surrounding the Doomed Liner: An Illustrated Narrative with Survivor Accounts*. Hollis, NH: Fantail, 1997.

**Rostron, Sir Arthur H. *The Loss of the Titanic*. Ludlow, MA: 7 C's Press for the Titanic Historical Society. Originally published 1931.

Ruffman, Alan. *Titanic Remembered: The Unsinkable Ship and Halifax*. Halifax: Formac, 2000.

Sebak, Per Kristian. *Titanic: 31 Norwegian Destinies*. Oslo: Genesis Forlag, 1998.

Spignesi, Stephen J. *The Complete Titanic: From the Ship's Earliest Blueprints to the Epic Film*. Secaucus, NJ: Burch Lane Press/Carol Publishing Group, 1998.

**Thayer, John B. *The Sinking of the S.S. Titanic*. Ludlow, MA: 7 C's Press for the Titanic Historical Society. Originally published 1940.

Wade, Wyn Craig. *The Titanic: End of a Dream*. Revised edition. New York: Penguin Books, 1986.

Walker, J. Bernard. *An Unsinkable Titanic: Every Ship Its Own Lifeboat*. New York: Dodd, Mead, 1912.

**Winocour, Jack, ed. *The Story of the Titanic As Told by Its Survivors*. [The collected accounts of Lawrence Beesley, Charles Lightoller, Archibald Gracie, and Harold Bride.] New York: Dover, 1960.

Articles

**Brown, Mrs. James J. "The Sailing of the Ill Fated Steamship Titanic: Full History of Titanic's Trip." *Newport Herald,* May 28–30, 1912.

**Candee, Helen Churchill. "Sealed Orders." *Collier's,* May 4, 1912.

Harmon, Craig. "A Night to Remember." Unpublished, undated. Galion, OH. http://www.lincoln-highway-museum.org/20Days/012-Index.html

Periodicals

The Titanic Commutator. The official journal of the *Titanic* Historical Society. Indian Orchard, MA.

Voyage. The official journal of the *Titanic* International Society. Midland Park, NJ.

**Government Documents

United Kingdom. Parliament. *The Report of the Inquiry into the Loss of the "Titanic."* Cd. 6352. 1913.

————. *Return of the Expenses Incurred by the Board of Trade and Other Government Departments in Connection with the Loss of the "Titanic."* Cd. 6738. 1913.

United Kingdom. *Wreck Commissioner's Report: Proceedings Before the Right Hon. Lord Mersey, on the Formal Investigation Ordered by the Board of Trade into the Loss of the SS "Titanic."* London: Jas. Truscott and Son.

U.S. Congress. Senate. *Hearings on "Titanic" Disaster to Investigate Collision of White Star Liner with Iceberg and Rescue of Passengers, Officers and Crew by Steamer "Carpathia," April 19–May 25, 1912.* 62nd Cong., 2nd sess. S. Doc. 726.

————. *Loss of the Steamship "Titanic": Report of a Formal Investigation into the Circumstances Attending the Foundering on April 15, 1912, of the British Steamship "Titanic," of Liverpool, After Striking Ice in or near Latitude 41°46' N., Longitude 50°14' W., North Atlantic Ocean, as Conducted by the British Government.* 62nd Cong., 2nd sess. S. Doc. 933.

————. *Report of Investigation into Loss of British White Star Liner "Titanic."* 62nd Cong., 2nd sess. S. Rep. 806

————. *The "Titanic" Disaster: Speech of Hon. William Alden Smith.* May 28, 1912. 62nd Cong., 2nd sess. S. Doc. 850.

White Star Line. *Record of Bodies and Effects (Passengers and Crew S.S. "Titanic") Recovered by Cable Steamer "MacKay Bennett" Including Bodies Buried at Sea and Bodies Delivered at Morgue in Halifax, N.S.* Public Archives of Nova Scotia, Halifax, N.S. Manuscript group 100, vol. 229, no. 3d, accession 1976-191. 1912.

Encyclopedia Titanica Research

Encyclopedia Titanica contains biographies of every character I've written about in *The Watch That Ends the Night*—excluding Sean Gould, of course. I found the following ET research articles particularly helpful. All were accessed at http://www.encyclopedia-titanica.org.

Bigham, Randy Bryan. "Life's Decor: A Biography of Helen Churchill Candee." ET Research, December 23, 2005.

Bracken, Robert. "The Mystery of Rhoda Abbott Revealed." ET Research, June 7, 2004.

Brown, David G. "Chronology—Sinking of S.S. *Titanic.*" ET Research, June 13, 2009.

Candee, Helen Churchill. "Sealed Orders: A *Titanic* Survivor's Classic Tale of Love and Fate." ET Research, December 23, 2005.

Chapman, Earl. "Gunshots on the *Titanic.*" ET Research, July 30, 2001.

Engberg-Klarström, Peter, and Tad Fitch. "Plucked from the Sea?" ET Research, July 11, 1999.

Halpern, Samuel. "Iceberg Right Ahead." ET Research, April 29, 2006.

———. "It's a CQD Old Man: 41.46 North, 50.14 West." ET Research, January 9, 2009.

———. "Rockets, Lifeboats, and Time Changes." ET Research, March 4, 2010.

Herbold, Mike. "George A. Brereton—Mystery Man." ET Research, January 28, 2001.

Jacub, George. "Loading the Rear Boats." ET Research, May 29, 2008.

Klistorner, Daniel. "A Thorough Analysis of the 'Cave List.'" ET Research, April 1, 2004.

Krebes, Richard. "Defending Fleet and Lee." ET Research, January 14, 2009.

———. "Rheims, Lightoller, and the Officer's Suicide Enigma." ET Research, October 14, 2008.

Mitcham, Lester J. "The Statistics of the Disaster." ET Research, February 14, 2001.

Molony, Senan. "The Hart of the Matter." ET Research, October 11, 2010.

———. *"Titanic's* Violinist and a Villainous Murder." ET Research, March 26, 2004.

Nielsen, Jan C. "The Morning After . . . Where Were the Bodies?" ET Research, September 20, 2002.

Owens, Luke. "CSI *Titanic:* Who Died How?" ET Research, June 26, 2007.

Pfeifer, Henning. "The Iceberg—Resurfaced?" ET Research, July 9, 2001.

Ticehurst, Brian J. "Classified in Death: Recovering the *Titanic*'s Dead." ET Research, March 31, 2007.

Internet Resources

ALL AT SEA WITH DAVE GITTINS
Some nice articles here. Gittins's article "Bright 'Sparks'" was particularly useful as I developed Harold Bride's character.
http://www.titanicebook.com

BILL WORMSTEDT'S *TITANIC*
A wealth of articles, by Wormstedt and others, along with useful links to many of the most important *Titanic* Web resources. In particular, Wormstedt's article

on the lifeboat launching sequence, cowritten with Tad Fitch and George Behe, is about as accurate an assessment as possible. A must-have bookmark for any *Titanic* enthusiast.   http://wormstedt.com/titanic/

ENCYCLOPEDIA TITANICA
Hands down the most valuable Web resource for *Titanic* enthusiasts. Includes articles, a discussion board, and biographies of every passenger and crew member.   http://www.encyclopedia-titanica.org

THE FATHER BROWNE PHOTOGRAPHIC COLLECTION
This amazing site contains the last photos taken aboard the *Titanic* by Frank Browne, who was a passenger traveling first-class from Southampton to Queenstown.   http://www.titanicphotographs.com

GEORGE BEHE'S *TITANIC* TIDBITS
An informal site containing very useful "chapters" about various Titanica. http://home.comcast.net/~georgebehe/titanic/

MARCONIGRAPH.COM
A wonderful collection of articles about the *Titanic* and other famous ships. "*Titanic*'s Engine-Order Telegraphs" by Bill Sunder includes up-to-date research on the telegraph wireless and on the ship's pulley telegraph, which went from the bridge to the engine room—how it worked and how it looked. Includes a link to movie stills of a bridge's telegraph in use. Also useful is "Spark's *Titanic* FAQs" by Parks Stephenson.   http://marconigraph.com/titanic

THE NATIONAL POSTAL MUSEUM
The website for the National Postal Museum, a Smithsonian Institution museum. This site includes a wonderful *Titanic* sea-post exhibit. http://www.postalmuseum.si.edu/titanic

NOVA SCOTIA ARCHIVES AND RECORDS MANAGEMENT, HALIFAX
A virtual exhibit and searchable database built around a very rare archival document: the "Disposition of Bodies ex *Titanic* Recovered up to May 13, 1912." http://www.gov.ns.ca/nsarm/cap/titanic

PAUL LEE'S *TITANIC* PAGES
Lee, author of *Titanic and the Indifferent Stranger,* includes many good articles on the *Californian* controversy and other topics of *Titanic* interest (How did

Ismay leave the ship? Were *Titanic* and *Olympic* switched? and more). Also of interest is Lee's transcription of the correspondence included in the "Lord-McQuitty Files," part of Walter Lord's research for his two books on the *Titanic*. http://www.paullee.com/titanic/index.php

TITANIC INQUIRY PROJECT
The complete transcripts of both the U.S. Senate hearings and the British inquiry. An amazing undertaking. Also contains valuable links to some of the best *Titanic* websites.   http://www.titanicinquiry.org

TITANIC RESEARCH AND MODELING ASSOCIATION
If you want to get really specific about the great ship's nuts and bolts, ask a model maker! This site is a "rivet counter's" dream. Many good informative articles as well.   http://titanic-model.com

TITANIC-TITANIC.COM
Like Encyclopedia Titanica, this site offers message boards, articles, biographies, and more.   http://www.titanic-titanic.com

Audio Resources

And the Band Played On: Music Played on the Titanic. I Salonisti. Decca, 1998.

Music Aboard the Titanic. Carol Wolfe, arrangements. Inside Sounds, 1998.

Titanic: Music as Heard on the Fateful Voyage. Ian Whitcomb conducting the White Star Orchestra. Rhino, 1997.

Titanic Serenade: Music from an Age of Elegance. Andy Street. Eclipse Music, 1998.

Titanic Societies

BELFAST *TITANIC* SOCIETY
http://www.belfast-titanic.com

BRITISH *TITANIC* SOCIETY
http://www.britishtitanicsociety.com

CANADIAN *TITANIC* SOCIETY
http://www.canadian-titanic-society.com

IRISH *TITANIC* HISTORICAL SOCIETY
http://www.iths.ie

SCANDINAVIAN *TITANIC* SOCIETY
http://www.scandtitanic.com

SWISS *TITANIC* SOCIETY
http://www.titanicverein.ch

TITANIC HISTORICAL SOCIETY
http://www.titanic1.org *or*
http://www.titanichistoricalsociety.org

TITANIC INTERNATIONAL SOCIETY
http://www.titanicinternationalsociety.org

Acknowledgments

For offering quiet places in which to write, I thank: Jennifer Murphy and Paul Hersey; Abby and Austin Walker; Karen Kotiw and Scott Severtson; Ken and Nadine Delano; and Jared Rutledge at Waking Life Espresso in West Asheville.

For expertise with turn-of-the-century wireless communication and Morse code: Mike Byer (whose dad happens to be my mechanic) and Stephen C. Phillips of Southampton, and his amazing Morse Code Translator. For violin advice: Rachel Elrod.

Thanks to the rats of Falconhurst, living and dead, who contributed so much.

To Candlewick Press, which still believes in the magic and sanctity of books. Sherry Fatla (inspiration for the eponymous Fatla Line-Counting Device) for bringing passion and meaning to the book's design. Hannah Mahoney for her superhuman copyediting. Katie Cunningham for her shrewd eye and contagious enthusiasm. And especially my editor, Elizabeth Bicknell, who exhibited ruthless clarity at every stage of this project. This book is as much hers as it is mine.

For advice, inspiration, conversation, brain picking, and/or early draft-reading: Simon Wolf, Ginger West, Laurie Wolf, Thomas Taggart, Don Silver, Christine Charbonneau, Jay Hardwig, my friends at WINC (Writers and Illustrators of North Carolina), Bob Falls at Poetry Alive!, Tony Morris and my family at Sun Soo Tae Kwon Do, Yvonne Hume, great-niece of John Law "Jock" Hume, and Thomas Goldsmith, grandson of Frankie Goldsmith. Also, all my peeps at Loyd Artists, especially Peggy, John, Bunny, and Susan.

For the many, many, many *Titanic* enthusiasts and historians who bring light to the message boards of Encyclopedia Titanica, including but not limited to: George Behe, Tad Fitch, Philip Hind, Paul Lee, Senan Molony, Inger Sheil, Michael Standart, and Bill Wormstedt.

And per usual, when the ship goes down, these are the folks I want in my lifeboat: Ginger, Simon, Ethan, and Jameson.

A century before the Titanic set sail, a courageous group set off to cross America by its waterways.

New Found Land

LEWIS AND CLARK'S VOYAGE OF DISCOVERY

A novel in verse by ALLAN WOLF

Searching for the fabled Northwest Passage to the Pacific Ocean is a Corps of Discovery led by Captains Lewis and Clark. In a masterful work, Allan Wolf brings their journey to life in the voices of the expedition, from the captains to teenage Sacagawea; from a one-eyed French Indian fiddler to Clark's slave and Louis's dog. Through fights with bears and dangerous waters, these voices will haunt you long after the voyage is done.